GHOST STORIES FROM THE PACIFIC NORTHWEST

Margaret Read MacDonald

GHOST STORIES FROM THE PACIFIC NORTHWEST

Margaret Read MacDonald

With an introduction by W.K. McNeil

This volume is part of
THE AMERICAN FOLKLORE SERIES
W.K. McNeil, General Editor

August House Publishers, Inc.
LITTLE ROCK

Printed in the United States of America

10 9 8 7 6 5 4 3 2 1   HB
10 9 8 7 6 5 4 3 2 1   PB

LIBRARY OF CONGRESS CATALOGUING-IN-PUBLICATION DATA

MacDonald, Margaret Read, 1940-
Ghost stories from the Pacific Northwest/ Margaret Read MacDonald.
p. cm.
Includes bibliographical references.
ISBN 0-87483-436-8 (hb: alk. paper).—ISBN 0-87483-437-6 (pbk. alk. paper)
1. Ghosts—Northwest, Pacific. 2. Ghost stories, American—Northwest, Pacific.
3. Haunted houses—Northwest, Pacific. I. Title.
GR109.5.M33   1995
398.2'09795'05—dc20   95-34554

Executive editor: Liz Parkhurst
Project editor: Rufus Griscom
Design director: Ted Parkhurst
Cover art and design: Byron Taylor

AUGUST HOUSE, INC.   PUBLISHERS   LITTLE ROCK

Contents

Acknowledgments

My thanks go out to the many librarians of the Northwest who responded to my requests for help with research in their areas. In particular I thank Nancy Gale Compau, Northwest Collection, Spokane Public Library; Deborah Brewer, Reference Librarian, Bellingham Public Library; Catherine McKinney, Library Director, Whitman County Library; Cynthia A. Garrick, Reference Coordinator, Yakima Valley Regional Library; Judy McMakin, Reference Librarian, Richland Public Library; Rosemary Nagle of Eugene, Oregon; and Bob Polishuk of Port Townsend, who helped follow up my leads in that area. Sharon Sherman and Bill Goldsmith of the Randall V. Mills Archives at the University of Oregon went out of their way to help with my research there, and I heartily appreciate that help. Former Washington State Folklorist Jens Lund provided countless leads and got me into this project in the first place, for which I thank him. And of course my thanks to Bill McNeil for editing this folklore series, and to my August House editor, Liz Parkhurst ... every author should be blessed with an editor like Liz.

Foreword

This book compiles for the first time information about ghostly happenings in the Pacific Northwest. Several interesting local collections have already been published, but this is the first attempt to pull material from the entire area together. I began the book expecting to discover ghost stories ... the kind one would tell to a pack of Cub Scouts at camp to scare the daylights out of them. The folklore archives at the University of Oregon yielded quite a bit of this sort of material, but when I began to research in British Columbia, at the Vancouver Public Library, I discovered a fascinating clipping file of recent ghost sightings. My research took a turn, and consequently the book you hold is not a collection of tellable stories, but a gathering of puzzling events. To the folklorist these events are intriguing because of their remarkable consistency. To point this up I have included a ghostly index at the book's end.

THE FOLKLORIST LOOKS AT HAUNTINGS

This book was prepared and edited by folklorists—people who study the traditions people pass from one to another. The folklorist isn't particularly interested in proving whether or not the story collected is true. The folklorist is curious about the traditions surrounding the hauntings and about the traditions people have developed for dealing with haunted places.

The folklorist might suggest that the stories people have heard about hauntings affect their interpretation of reality. Having heard that ghosts rap on walls and float around in misty forms, folks who hear creakings in their old houses or see a waft of mist drift by interpret this as a haunting, rather than seeking another explanation. To the folk-lorist the consistency of the haunting information gathered in this book would support this theory. People see and hear what their tradition has led them to expect.

The paranormal investigator, however, might find the remarkable consistency in ghostly behavior to be an indication that these events really are occurring.

ABOUT THE APPENDICES

I have included a number of appendices to help the reader:

The Index of Ghostly Motifs lists various types of paranormal experiences and tells us in which of our stories these occur. Notes for each story also mention which motifs appear in that story, so you can consult the index to see if other similar incidents are mentioned in this book.

If you happen to live or work in a space you believe to be haunted, you will find our index useful. Check for the problems you are encountering in our index. It may be reassuring to find that others have had experiences similar to yours.

The folklorist will not find this index surprising. It is based on the *Stith Thompson Motif-Index of Folk-Literature* and Ernest Baughman's *Type and Motif Index of the Folktales of England and North America*. Some motifs have been expanded but few had to be added for this 1995 index. Most of these ghostly occurrences were being reported in the sources examined by Thompson and Baughman, sources which dated for the most part from the late nineteenth and early twentieth century.

To help you locate ghostlore on a particular theme, a **Subject Index** for the Index of Ghostly Motifs is included. It is quite detailed, so if you are having problems with a bell-ringing ghost or a ghost who snuffs out candles, for example, you can look up similar occurrences by checking the subject index, which will refer you to that motif in the ghostly index.

In case you want to check out the ghostlore of a particular locale, geographical place names are included in the subject index.

For complete citations for sources and for a listing of those motifs indexed from each citing, see the **Notes.** And because one book could not begin to describe all of the ghostly sightings which are recorded in Nortwestern sources, a small section of **Brief Notes on More Northwest Hauntings** is included. These incidents are indexed in the Index of Ghostly Motifs but are given only a one-line description in this book.

THE SOURCES FOR THESE STORIES

The information presented here is taken mainly from two sources: student research projects from the Randall V. Mills Folklore Archives at the University of Oregon and newspaper reporting from regional papers. Both sources present problems. The student projects are mainly third person accounts ... this happened to a friend of the person being interviewed. So the tales show the marks of a series of storytellers. The newspaper accounts give many useful first person quotes, but anyone who has ever been interviewed by a reporter knows that the published account of just what one says often strays a bit from the fact. Other sources include the writings of individuals who have personally experienced hauntings, and interviews with a few persons who have had ghostly occurrences. The veracity of almost all of these reports could be questioned, but the overwhelming consistency in their accounts is interesting.

The Northwest's Ghosts

The ghost stories included here were gathered by searching for the terms "ghost," "apparition," "spirit," and "haunt" in folklore archives, newspaper indexes, and library collections and by asking around for "ghost stories" and "haunted sites." The material collected shows a consistent picture of the phenomena Northwesterners call a "ghost."

The ghost almost always appears alone. It is wispy, non-substantial in form, often gray. The ghost which appears does not speak, though in one case the ghost appeared to make eye contact and gesture. After a few moments it vanishes or exits, sometimes through a wall.

In cases where the ghost is heard, it is not seen. The ghost may moan, cry like a child, or speak a simple phrase or single word. The ghost does not carry on a conversation.

In the Northwest ghosts seem to have developed a musical capability as well. Ghosts sing, play the organ, fiddle, and flute, and select radio stations to suit themselves.

There is usually an effort on the part of the owners of the haunted home to discover some dire event which occurred on this spot to explain the ghost. But not all Northwest ghosts are derived from disasters. Some just like to hang about.

Northwesterners seem inclined to accept their ghosts as part of the family. In archival and newspaper reports there is no mention of a ghost doing physical harm to its hauntees, though ghosts do occasionally poke people in the back or sit on their legs while they are in bed. And one man was bashed in the head with a pillow by an aggravated ghost.

On the other hand, investigations by Northwest psychics turn up unpleasant entities at times. They speak of "friendly" spirits who are easy to live with, and of "unfriendly" spirits. The latter strike terror into those who encounter them. Living alongside these unfriendly spirits can result in mental depression or sickness, and psychics suggest exorcising them or moving out.

One reason for the non-threatening nature of the Northwest ghost may lie in the way we define "ghost." Supernatural encounters which terrify or harm tend to be classed as demonic. Had I searched under such headings as "demon" and "satan" I would likely have turned up tales of unpleasant experiences with the paranormal.

Some spirits manifest themselves as apparitions, other homes find themselves beset solely by poltergeists—a phenomena in which objects move without human assistance. Plates fly through space, pictures fall from walls, doors slam, lights go on and off, and sometimes—horror of horrors—toilets explode! Some theorize that poltergeist activity may be a form of psychic energy emanating from the living in the residence. Teenagers seem often to be at the center of such poltergeist activity, and in some cases the activity has stopped once the teen was removed from the building.

Several other paranormal entities might be classified as ghosts at times. Paranormal entities which offer aid are, in this decade, often considered "angels." In one of our tales a man riding the rails has his life saved by a phantom watchman; in another an apparition warns of a fire. A different book might class these as "angel" interventions.

Our Northwest ghosts cannot be summoned for questioning, though mediums are sometimes called in to try to persuade the lingering spirit to depart. The spirits themselves seldom communicate and are in fact often described as almost holographic, appearing over and over again performing the same action. Communication with dead relatives is performed by mediums and is a paranormal genre usually separate from that of the uninvited household apparition.

Our Northwest ghosts are seldom the ancestors of their hauntees. The recent arrival of many Northwesterners to this area means that ancestors have been laid to rest far away, so ancestral homes replete with ghostly relatives are few. The moment-of-death apparition is common, but this brief spirit visitation, which brings reassurance to a loved one at the time a distant relative dies, is seldom referred to as a "ghost."

Native American, Asian, and Latin American cultures in the Northwest honor and expect the presence of their ancestral dead, but these traditions seem in no way related to the phenomena Northwesterners call a "ghost." The use by our press of terms such as Native American "Ghost Dancing" and the Chinese "Night of the Hungry Ghosts" are misleading.

Here then are a few first person accounts of ghostly encounters in the Pacific Northwest. I limited my research to Oregon, Washington, and British Columbia, though I was sorely tempted by reports of ghost rats and phantom monks over in Idaho. Though several of our tales come from the dry interior, most are set along the beaches and forests of our rainy coasts. So settle back in your arm-chair, envision dark pines shrouded in mists, and let our Northwestern ghosts drift through your open window.

For more folkloric background on these Northwest ghost stories, read the introduction that follows. For the ghost stories themselves, turn to page 27.

Introduction

Ghost stories, or narratives about the return of the dead, have often occupied the attention of American folklorists. Yet, despite the volume of publishing activity on this subject, the study of ghostlore in the United States is still in its infancy. That is particularly true for the Pacific Northwest; this, after all, is the first book by a folklorist devoted to the ghost narratives of this region.[1] Why have folklorists neglected this aspect of Northwest folklore? There are undoubtedly many reasons but one factor likely is an assumption most folklorists make about the requirements for thriving ghostlore.

Although not a folklorist, the early American author Washington Irving offered the following description of a haunted house that encapsulates many of the most popularly held beliefs about where ghosts appear: "It was one of the very few remains of the architecture of the early Dutch settlers ... The house stood remote from the road, in the centre of a large field, ... there were traces also of what had been a kitchen garden; but the fences were broken down, the vegetables had disappeared or had grown wild, and turned to little better than weeds ... Part of the roof of the old house had fallen in, the windows were shattered, the panels of the doors broken, ... The appearance of the whole place was forlorn and desolate at the best of times; but, in unruly weather, the howling of the wind about the crazy old mansion, the screeching of the weather-cocks, and the slamming and banging of a few loose window shutters, had altogether so wild and dreary an effect, that the neighborhood stood perfectly in awe of the place, and pronounced it the rendezvous of hobgoblins."[2] Irving's haunted house fits perfectly the conclusion of Louis C. Jones, the first American folklorist to provide an analytical study of ghostlore. For such traditions to thrive, Jones said, "one needs a section that has been settled for a considerable length of time, where the houses are old, and at least a fair share of the population is permanent."[3]

Although Oregon, Washington and British Columbia are not newly settled, they are relative newcomers when compared to New England and other areas east of the Mississippi. Non-Indian settlement in the region only began in the last decade of the eighteenth century, and extensive settlement did not occur until after the arrival of missionaries in Oregon in the 1830s. Beginning in the 1840s caravans of settlers took the Oregon Trail westward from Independence, Missouri to Fort Vancouver. By the mid-1840s over one thousand people yearly were making this westward trek. At that point in time, of course, many eastern states had permanent non-Indian settlements stretching back well over a century.

If one accepts Jones's dictum about the requirements of ghostlore, then it means that relatively recently settled regions, particularly those with a highly fluid population, can have no ghostlore. It also presents a tantalizing question: Does a region have to be settled for a specific length of time before such traditions arise? Will the older settlements always have a richer ghostlore tradition than those places more recently settled? This book demonstrates that such conventional assumptions are suspect if not invalid. In places where it appears that there is no ghostlore, it may be that no one has sought such materials there, or it may be that ghostlore is more difficult to collect there than it is elsewhere.[4] In any event, it is evident that setting a specific number of years that a community, state, or region has to be settled before ghost traditions appear is a risky endeavor.

In his analysis Jones offers some criteria by which New York ghosts and those from the Pacific Northwest can be compared. These include appearance, purposes, and character, when and where they return, activities, and methods of ridding oneself of ghostly visitations. Jones noted three forms in which returning dead appear: "First, he may appear so lifelike that unless one knows from prior knowledge that the person is dead or unless one sees him vanish, he is mistaken for the living; second, he may reanimate his corpse; or third, he may appear in a spectral form of some sort.[5] All three forms are found in this collection of Northwest lore, but the last seems especially prominent. There are instances where the narrator deals with more inexplicable deeds and noises than with actual ghostly sightings, such as the strange happenings in the haunted house at Chilliwack, British Columbia. A vast majority of these tales, however, have ghosts taking some spectral form, whether as the apparition of a sad little girl, a woman in a rosewood bed, a caring hostess, an elderly woman, or the cloudy, faceless figure in the shape of a human being that appeared in Chilliwack. Those ghosts that do take some recognizable form appear lifelike until they simply fade away. Generally, they seem unchanged in appearance from their living state.

Less common in the present corpus are examples of the living corpse. One notable example is Rufus Porter's experience, but the corpse witnessed by Porter differs from most of those discussed by Jones in that he had long been dead. Those living corpses found in New York ghostlore were recently deceased. In their most common form they sat up in their own coffin and even spoke to mourners attending their wake. The point-of-death apparitions who appear to inform relatives of their deaths are the Northwest ghosts that most closely approximate the living corpses of New York.

In New York the less clearly envisioned revenants are not commonly referred to as ghosts; labels such as "apparition," "presence," "spook," "spectre," and "shrouded spirit" are more common. Most of the same labels are found in the present narratives, but frequently "ghost" is used even for many of the returning dead, such as Oscar, the obedient ghost, where the haunter is only heard. Frequently, though, the Northwest revenants, like those in New York, are characterized by whiteness or by lights.

A sizeable percentage of the New York ghosts died violent or sudden deaths, by murder, áccidents, suicide, or by legal execution. With the exception of the latter causes of death, the same methods of departure are found among the supernatural visitors whose activities are recorded in the present collection. The ghost narratives analyzed by Jones usually include some purpose behind the return, but in several cases the visitation seems motiveless, or at least the story does not provide an explanation. If the present texts are representative, and care has been taken to make them so, then the same situations hold for Pacific Northwest ghostlore. Most of the narratives provide some reason for the ghost's return, nevertheless several narratives give no explanation of why the ghost has chosen to return to the haunting site. Occasionally, though, as in the case of the haunted houses on Lombard Loop Road in Sawyer, Washington, those being haunted offer some speculations about the purpose of the visitations.

What prompts the ghostly returns? Jones offers seven explanations commonly encountered in New York ghostlore. Based on the relatively small sample given here it is evident that at least that many motives are found in Northwest ghostlore. One of the most popular motivations is the return to complete unfinished business. One example is the ghostly cradle rocker of Applegate River, Oregon who returns to finish rocking her little brother's cradle, an activity that in life was interrupted by a mudslide. Especially interesting to theater buffs is the ghost of actor Charles Laughton who, apparently frustrated over not making his final stage appearance, returns to haunt the Shakespearean Festival in Ashland, Oregon. Other Northwest ghosts return to read books they were unable to finish, to continue parties they had enjoyed, to cook for boarders in a boardinghouse, to call attention to the place where their bodies were buried, to help nurses with patients in the hospital where they died, and to complete numerous other unfinished tasks.

Pacific Northwest ghosts also return to warn or inform. Many appear to foretell death, such as the green lady who materialized before members of a Jacksonville, Oregon family for this purpose. Sometimes, as in the case of Kathleen Belanger's son, the ghost appears to tell a family member of his own death. An entire train of supernatural visitors forecast an Alberta engineer's death in a train wreck. Near Mt. St. Helens, Washington, a lady hitchhiker warns those who pick her up of a forthcoming volcano eruption. At other times the ghost returns for less ominous reasons, to remind someone of an operation or to let surviving spouses know that they are still around keeping an eye on them.

Several Northwest ghosts return to protest something. The ghost at a theater in Yakima, Washington seems to hate rock and roll concerts, so much that whenever one is scheduled he hides equipment and causes havoc with the lighting. Some believe that the ghosts at a Seattle theater are upset about the sale of their haunting spot. A Steillacoom, Washington ghost lets it be known that he hates yuppie sauces. Many Northwest ghosts return to express displeasure with those who disturb their graves. While one frequently finds protesting ghosts those punishing spirits commonly encountered in New York are rare. Can it be that Northwest ghosts are a less vindictive lot? Or is this a point that cannot be safely made without more evidence?

Jones finds that many ghosts return to guard and protect, and this book provides evidence that the same is true of Northwest ghosts. Sometimes, as in the case of a British Columbia spirit, the ghost is a husband who still looks out for the welfare of his wife. At other times, as in the case of the Capitol Theater ghost who saved a girl's life, the supernatural savior is not related to the person protected.

Just as in New York, some Northwest ghosts return to re-engage in their lifetime activities. A hotel manager in Prosser, Washington stays on in the hotel he formerly ran. In Oregon a piano player continues to play his instrument at a resort hotel even though he has been dead for many years. Long dead lighthouse keepers return to their old lighthouses and ghostly drivers still run their stagecoaches, and many other restless dead reprise their lifetime occupations.

Also popular in New York and the Northwest are those spirits who return to re-enact their deaths. A man hung by outlaws in Rogue River, Oregon appears annually on the anniversary of his death to relive his final moments as a human. Most dramatic of all death re-enactors are the crews of phantom ships that bring back the scene when they departed this life. The experience of the *Valencia* that haunts the British Columbia coast is the most notable example given here.

Jones finds ghosts that reward the living in small supply in New York and, judging from the present collection, the same motif is rare in Northwestern ghost narratives. Based on a sampling this small this point should not be strongly emphasized.

If there is a universal tradition in ghostlore, it is the reaction of fear upon seeing these supernatural visitors. Ironically, this attitude is usually unjustified because most ghosts are not malevolent. In a majority of the tales given here the ghosts are neither out to do harm or to aid those who see them; in many cases the reasons for the ghostly return are unclear. The spirits, however, often provide reasons for one to wish their departure. Many ghosts that never materialize make nuisances of themselves by doing things like breaking glass, knocking books off bookshelves, pulling the legs of sleeping people, and snoring.

Ghostly returns of two types are recounted in the present book: spirits that return for a brief time and those that constantly manifest themselves to human beings. Sometimes a ghost may appear only once, for example, at the time of his or her death, but usually they are around for a longer stay. This is in marked contrast to what Jones finds in New York, the vast majority of narratives he examines describe a single appearance of a supernatural being. In the Northwest the ghost is sometimes doomed to return for a certain period of time, generally a few years. Frequently, they are bound to the site of their hauntings as long as the place exists. The majority of Northwest ghosts appear indoors, usually in houses, hotels, and restaurants, but also in museums, theaters, college dorms, lighthouses, boiler rooms, firehouses, libraries, and various other public buildings. However, unlike the ghosts Jones finds in New York, the Northwest ghosts seem to have no preference for country over city life, flourishing just as well in urban as in rural settings. Many appear in trains, on ships, along roadways, and even on a golf course. Of course, the restless dead of this region, like those in New York, prefer to wander at night rather than in the daytime.

The range of ghostly activities in the Northwest is very broad, as it is in New York. When Jones writes that "almost the entire range of human action is represented, except the procreative act and childbirth,"[6] he could be speaking about Northwestern ghostlore as well as that of New York—except that one Northwest ghost is said to have engaged in the former! Though the most common ghostly activity appears to be walking, ghosts also frequently open and close doors, ride in automobiles, and speak. Usually when they speak it is to warn the living or to give them information. While ghosts sometimes give directions for the finding of their own corpses they occasionally accomplish this goal by simply appearing near where their earthly remains are buried. They show more imagination in the sounds they make than in their conversation. They groan, cry, moan, cough, whisper, laugh, sing, ring bells, and play the piano.

The vanishing hitchhiker narratives given here differ slightly from those found in other parts of the United States. Commonly she provides an address to which she wants to go; invariably someone at that address admits the ghost was once a member of the family. The absence of this motif from the present collection does not mean that it isn't found in Northwest ghostlore; it may signify nothing more than that MacDonald chose to include versions more uniquely Northwestern.

Various methods for laying a ghost are utilized in the Northwest. In many cases, though, those being visited by ghosts are content to live with them. Sometimes exorcism is attempted. Psychics, rarely religious figures, are brought in to lay the ghost or a seance is arranged for the same purpose. Occasionally, merely ordering the spirit to take what it wants and leave produces the desired result. At other times more drastic measures, such as burning or tearing a house down, are necessary to stop the hauntings. Those who have left behind unfinished business sometimes disappear once the survivors discern the reason for the return. It is unnecessary to lay some ghosts, notably those who return for a brief time, such as for the sole purpose of announcing their own death to a relative These ghosts voluntarily disappear once they have accomplished what they set out to do.

In New York Jones finds two types of animal ghosts: humans who return as animals and spirits of animals who return in their own guise. The former is not found in the present collection but, again, too much should not be made of this fact. It may mean that MacDonald encountered no such narratives rather than that they don't exist in Northwestern folk tradition.

The several texts compiled here provide evidence that many of Jones's conclusions about New York ghostlore apply equally well to that of the Pacific Northwest. The most notable differences are in the places of appearance, the frequency of their return, animal ghosts, and their nature. Clearly, Jones's claim that one needs a long settled region with ancient houses and a relatively non-fluid population is, at least, open to question. Moreover, the present collection shows that Northwestern ghosts thrive as well in urban settings as in rural ones. Whether these are the major differences between Northwest and New York ghostlore will have to be determined after further study. If MacDonald's collection and its accompanying motif index spur such needed work it will have performed a valuable scholarly service.

W.K. McNeil
The Ozark Folk Center
Mountain View, Arkansas

Notes

1. On this topic, for many other genres of folklore, American scholars have generally concentrated on the states east of the Mississippi River, specifically on the southern United States. Exceptions, such as Jan Brunvand's *The Vanishing Hitchhiker: American Urban Legends and their Meanings* (New York and London: W.W. Norton & Company, 1981) are primarily devoted to some other topic, in this instance urban legends, rather than ghost narratives, or as in the case of Hector Lee, *The Three Nephites* (New York: Arno Press, Inc., 1977; reprint of a work originally published in 1949) devoted to the ghostlore of a specific religious group.

2. Washington Irving, *Hearthside Tales*, selected and edited by Patrick F. Allen (Schenectady, New York: Union College Press, 1983), pp. 87-88.

3. Louis C. Jones, "The Ghosts of New York: An Analytical Study," in Louis C. Jones, *Three Eyes on the Past: Exploring New York Folk Life* (Syracuse: Syracuse University Press, 1982), p. 52. This essay originally appeared in *The Journal of American Folklore* (October, 1944).

4. Sometimes the informants are afraid of being laughed at for believing in such things as ghosts. There are, of course, also many other reasons why someone might be unwilling to relate such narratives to collectors.

5. Jones, p. 37.

6. Ibid., p. 53.

SECTION ONE:

AT HOME WITH GHOSTS

A surprising number of Northwesterners find themselves living with ghosts. Since my family lives in a Seattle suburb of new homes and tract cul-de-sacs, I was surprised to learn that neighbors had ghosts in their bedroom. Their home is less than twenty years old, yet two women in old-fashioned garb appear at their bedside and stare at the couple. They just look for a while and then go away and my friends don't seem terribly disturbed by their occasional visits. Until I heard these perfectly rational friends speak of this, I had always assumed that ghosts did not exist. But if these friends say they saw two women standing by their bed… well, I tend to believe they saw just that.

As I researched this book I learned that their experience was a fairly normal encounter. Surprisingly most Northwesterners accept their ghosts without too much fuss. Though a few call in exorcists, more learn to live with the spirits and even seem to enjoy their company.

Here are accounts of haunted homes, haunted apartments, and even haunted neighborhoods. If you too have an uninvited house guest, you may find it encouraging to learn that you are not alone… and that co-existence with an occasional spirit seems to work just fine for many Northwesterners.

A HOUSE LIKE YOURS
—BUT HAUNTED

Every town has at least one dark, decrepit, and deserted old house. We pass and murmur with a shudder, "That looks like a haunted house." It seems, however, that ghosts are just as apt to be hanging out in your own home. And your house need not be aged to inherit a ghost. Some of them seem to hang around sites, ready to move into anything new built on that piece of ground. Hauntings in suburbia are not all that uncommon.

Here are an array of house haunting accounts from British Columbia, Oregon, and Washington.

Portrait of a Ghost

CHILLIWACK, BRITISH COLUMBIA

Artist Mrs. Hetty Frederickson of Chilliwack, British Columbia tried an unusual technique to lay her household ghost. She painted her—or was it his—portrait!

Hetty, her husband, Douglas, and their five children moved into the huge old house on Williams Street in Chilliwack in 1965. The house met the needs of their large family nicely except for one thing: the large upstairs bedroom which Hetty hoped to use as a guest room appeared to be haunted. Footsteps were heard ascending the stairs at night and in the morning drawers were pulled out of the dresser in the guest room and the heavy iron bedstead looked as though it had been shoved around the room. The bed seemed to move around night after night until it at last reached a spot in front of the big front windows where it rested and remained.

Other ghostly manifestations were found throughout the house. The sound of breathing would be heard in an otherwise empty room, and a sudden waft of perfume would assail the occupants' nostrils. In addition, Hetty began to have a recurring nightmare. In her dream she saw a woman lying on the floor of the upstairs hall. "She is sort of mummified and she has a red dress on with yellow flowers, a cheap cotton dress," Hetty told reporters, "and she is terrified."

In an attempt to lay this suffering ghost, Hetty set up her paints in the haunted bedroom and stayed awake for three nights running, in hope of painting the ghost's portrait. On the third night, a vague light did appear by the window, but it was too faint to sketch. "It looked like a cloudy figure. It was the shape of a human being, but no details, no face. I closed my eyes and opened them and it was still there. I didn't dare get up. When it went, it just disappeared. I could definitely smell perfume."

Hetty decided to paint a portrait combining the ghostly shape by the window with the face of the woman in her dream. "It was not easy," Hetty said, "Every time I tried to paint, the face would start out as a man even as I tried to paint a woman. But I really concentrated and at last painted the likeness of the woman."

Hetty's portrait, a large six by four foot canvas, was not entirely completed. She painted only one side of the ghost's face, basing this on the woman in her dreams, the other side she left dark and incomplete, except for a tiny white dot to mark the eye. As the days passed, however, the face on the painting began to complete itself of its own accord. Gradually the dark side of the face lightened. An eyelid, a nostril, and the outline of a cheek appeared. A thin moustache and a darker shadow under the cheek were added to the side she had already painted in. Later the moustache faded and a beard began to appear.

The painting was definitely becoming something other than the woman on the floor in the red dress with the yellow flowers. Hetty resolved to get to the bottom of the haunting and began to research the house's history. "I intend to find out if someone has been living here with this dress on," she told reporters, "because I can describe it absolutely."

As she probed the house's history she heard stories of a man who had committed suicide at this house, and rumors of a woman who had been murdered and bricked up in a chimney. She was able to confirm the reports of the suicide, but the murdered woman eluded her. She and her husband began exploring the house for an old brick chimney. They found none, but on removing paneling in the attic they uncovered a boarded-up door leading to a turret room. This room, Hetty felt, was the scene of her dream, the place where the woman's body had lain on the floor.

In an effort to prove that her ghost or ghosts were real, Hetty invited two reporters from the *Vancouver Sun* to spend the night at her house. On June 1, 1966 the reporters spent a fairly uneventful night in the haunted bedroom, though at one point they did hear a thump in the hall outside.

"In the hall, brightly lit, we found a piece of linoleum, about three by two feet, lying face down on the floor about a yard from the bedroom door. Originally it was on the wall of the bedroom ... Mrs. Frederickson had brought it back into the room to show us where it had been, then took it back out again. At first the friend and I attributed the sound we both heard to the piece of linoleum having been propped up against a wall, and then falling to the ground and sliding. We thought no more of it until Mrs. Frederickson returned and was told of the incident.

" 'But the lino was not against the wall. I put it in the closet,' she said, indicating a small closet opening off the hall. She opened the narrow door to the closet to show where the lino had been, lying at the bottom at a slight angle from the floor. If this was so, the lino could not have got into the middle of the hall by natural means.

"As night turned to early morning, coffee mugs were refilled again and again, cigarette butts rose higher in the ashtrays. There were no other incidents. Mrs. Fredrickson was disappointed. 'I feel I have got to prove what I saw has happened. I hoped to see the bed or the drawers move for myself in the presence of other people so they could see it too,' she said. She had so far only found the furniture in different positions and not witnessed anything actually in motion."

In May of 1966 Hetty invited Professor Geoffrey Riddehough of the University of British Columbia to examine her mysteriously changing painting. Professor Riddehough was a member of Britain's Society for Psychical Research, but he seems to have added nothing to her information about the hauntings.

By this time, the news of the ghostly events had made the house a subject of such community rumor that Hetty decided to hold an open house and let the local children see the site for themselves to stop the gruesome stories they had begun circulating. However her plan backfired. On Sunday, June 5, not just the local children arrived on her doorstep. Hordes of curious adults lined up, over 700! The front steps collapsed under the weight of tightly packed oglers, and the whole house suddenly gained the status of a tourist attraction. From then on the Fredericksons had no peace. Gawkers drove by night and day, and strangers would even enter the yard to peer into their windows. Hetty told reporters that she didn't dare go out onto the porch to sweep for she feared what children would think if they saw a lady with a broom in hand on the porch of the "haunted house." In desperation, the family left Chilliwack and moved to a non-haunted spot on Vancouver Island. The painting was lent to the Pacific National Exhibition, where it was seen by thousands of visitors.

As for the haunted Chilliwack house, it stood empty for a time and was severely vandalized. Then the Fredericksons rented it to a group of twelve musicians, who reported no ghosts during their stay. In 1972 a family with eight children moved into the house, but did not stay long, as they too found other "occupants" living there. Doors banged, the thermostat was continually turned up to 80 degrees, and their dog "Lucky" was terrorized. The children began having nightmares. By 1973 the house was for sale again. Some years later, a fire broke out in the basement and the house was burned to the ground.

(Source: Vancouver Sun *reporter Michael Cobb; unsigned articles in* Vancouver's The Province.*)*

Watch the Hanky-panky, Grandpa's in the Bedroom

ELLENSBURG, WASHINGTON

When Doug Clark, a Spokane columnist, put out a call for true ghost stories he received this one:

Reuben, a security guard who didn't want his real name used for fear of being institutionalized, said he was 16 and living in Ellensburg when his girlfriend canceled their movie date.

"Pam said she had to stay home and do the laundry, so being 16 and amorous, I decided to go over and help her and just maybe enjoy some of the thrills of young love," said Reuben.

He should have stayed at home.

"I kept trying to get her interested in other things beside laundry, but she was busy folding the clothes. She finally told me to go in the kitchen, which I did reluctantly."

Pam's kitchen faced a back bedroom and when Reuben looked into it, he was startled to see an old man dressed in coveralls sitting in a chair and staring back at him.

"I was freaked," said Reuben. "I thought, Oh no, what if this guy heard me coming on to Pam?"

Running back into the laundry room, Reuben angrily told his girlfriend she should have said they weren't alone. Pam was puzzled and asked what he meant. Reuben told her and she burst into tears. "That's my grandfather," she said. "And he's dead."

(Source: Spokesman-Review *columnist Doug Clark.)*

A Ghostly Washerman, A TV Watching Ghost, and Other New Westminster Haunts

NEW WESTMINSTER, BRITISH COLUMBIA

In 1967 Jim and Lou Dodds purchased a run-down old Victorian home in New Westminster and began the long project of restoring the house. Jim is a carpenter by trade and took this on as a long term project; the family moved in and began slowly renovating a room at a time. When reporter Shelley Fralic visited the Dodds on Halloween Eve in 1982, remodeling was still in progress. However, Jim's carpentry skills hadn't been enough to deal with this house; they had to call in a medium as well.

It began in 1969. A family friend who was living with the Dodds at that time awoke one night and saw something startling out of the corner of his eye. A man was standing at the bedroom window looking out. He was dressed in a long coat and wore a hat, seemingly from an earlier era. The man appeared to be middle aged. He stood there for a moment and when the friend turned to get a better look he vanished. Later Rags, the family dog, was found quivering under the bed.

Lou has seen a woman walking down the stairs. "The shadow of a woman. It was the only thing it could have been. She was wearing a long dress." And when Lou does housework late at night sometimes she feels "a whirlwind around me. It's cold and follows me."

The ghost—or at least one of the ghosts—appears to like to watch television too. Lou says she will often be sitting alone watching TV and suddenly sense someone sitting close to her on the couch. She will look at Rags and find him staring at someone who isn't there.

Jim has only encountered the house spirits once. One evening as he turned off the downstairs lights and started up to bed he felt something take his hand. He had just reached for the newel post at the bottom of the staircase when "someone or something grabbed my hand." Whatever it was, it held on as he began to ascend the stairs "as if someone were walking with me and holding my hand." Finally Jim pulled his hand away. "I didn't know what to think. I wasn't scared, but it was very real. I thought maybe there was some circulation problem in my hand or something. I still can't explain it."

And then there is the bathroom light. It is an old switch which has to be pulled hard to turn off and on. But at night when everyone is downstairs the switch will be heard flicking off and on.

Finally the Dodds called in a medium, David Young, who had moved to Vancouver from England a few years earlier. Young had found most of the haunted houses he visited in Vancouver to be merely a result of the inhabitants' overactive imaginations. But at the Dodds' home he did sense spirits. He told Lou that the spirit of her father's sister, who had died of leukemia at the age of twelve, was a regular visitor. And in the Dodds' bedroom he saw a figure he could not explain. An elderly man with a pointed beard was standing over an old fashioned washtub on a tiled floor. The man was scrubbing clothes and grinning.

Jim had a possible explanation for this figure. A man had once visited the house who said he had grown up there as a child in 1914. Questioned about the house's history the man told them about a baby which had died there. He remembered also carving his initials in a wall near the laundry room where an old Chinese man used to come and scrub clothes in a washtub.

Young felt the Chinese washerman was simply an imprint from the past and not the haunting spirit. The other haunts, he said, might just be visitors from the spirit world returning to their home. "When you move away from a place and then go back and visit, where do you go first? You go home. Spirits do that too. Sometimes they just pass through. Everyone at one time has felt something brush up against them, a presence, a tingling. Most people just don't admit it."

(Source: Vancouver Sun *reporter Shelly Fralic.)*

Saved from a Burning House

Port Townsend, Washington

Rose Anne Nowak told reporter Eleanor Nelson about an unusual happening in her home:

Twenty-five years ago ... I experienced this lady who I feel came to warn me about a fire that was happening on the third floor of our home. There is no other explanation for me to have seen her that particular day. She had blonde hair and was wearing a long green skirt and blouse. My first thought was to reassure her that everything was all right. I wanted to give her the message that I was really taking good care of her home. When I reached out to touch her, she disappeared. Then someone knocked at my door to tell me that my house was on fire. Ordinarily I would have been frantic, but I remained calm and remembered what my father had told us during fire drills when we had been little. He said to touch the door and if it was hot not to open it. This was to contain a fire and prevent it from spreading. The fire department told me that it had started as a result of a glass prism in the room that the sun hit and had set a quilt on fire. They credited me with having kept the fire under control by not opening that door. But I credit the spirit, whom I consider an angel, with having saved our home.

(Source: Port Townsend Leader *reporter Eleanor Nelson.)*

The Man in the Cowboy Hat Teaches Math

RICHLAND, WASHINGTON

R ichland mother Barbara Sponholtz awoke from a deep sleep one night to see a man standing beside her bed. He was tall, dressed in Western style clothing. At first she just stared, frozen with terror. The man turned and walked out of the room and down the hall toward her children's rooms. With enormous effort Barbara leapt from bed and ran after him into the hall just in time to see him turn into her daughter's room. But when she snapped on the light and scanned the room she saw no one. Just her four-year-old daughter Heather, sleeping soundly.

This was the beginning of many strange occurrences in their Richland home. "I never believed in ghosts," Sponholtz told reporter Kathleen Knutson. But several months later she and her husband were startled out of their sleep by the loud rattling of their heavy dresser and mirror. There was the man again, only this time he was only visible from his gold belt buckle down. Greg Sponholtz spoke to the ghost. He told him the couple was happy to have him in the house and would not harm him. The man vanished.

Unfortunately this direct confrontation did not calm the spirit. Instead he became more active. The Sponholtzes saw him on most days, catching a glimpse of him out of the corner of their eyes. He took up the habit of annoying Barbara every morning by mimicking a child's voice and calling, "Mommy, mommy."

The Sponholtzes now remembered a strange incident the previous year when their daughter Heather was only three. One morning she had begun doing math problems at the breakfast table. Amazed, the family questioned her about how she had learned this. She said she had learned how to do problems from "the man who comes out of my closet." The family chalked it up to childish imagination. "You know kids," said Barbara. "We didn't think anything of it. And that was months before we saw the ghost."

Their home was only thirty years old, built on the old Hanford bus lot. None of the home's previous owners matched the description of the man. They wonder if he might have been attached to one of the antique furniture pieces in their home. A difficult to open door on her china closet was found open one day ...

But their annoyance with the ghost reached a peak when the toilet bowl exploded, drenching the ceiling and everything in the room. They asked their pastor for advice, and he advised them not to move out unless the spirit became violent.

One fall day, shortly after the exploding toilet bowl incident, Barbara was standing at the kitchen sink when she felt the hair on the back of her neck stand up. Behind her the ghost began his usual taunting: "Mommy ... Mommy ... Mommy ..."

Sponholtz couldn't take it any longer. "My nerves were shot, and I didn't know what the next step would be. I just yelled and burst into tears. I said, 'Take what you want and leave!' "

Apparently the ghost heeded her request. "There was no 'Mommy' in the morning, and I waited for him to show up all day. He never did. And that's fine with me."

(Source: Tri-Cities Herald *Kathleen Knutson.)*

The Glass-Breaking Ghost

SPOKANE, WASHINGTON

In October of 1990, Spokesman-Review columnist Doug Clark put out a call for true-life ghost stories. He drew a remarkable response. Bob Lund, a Spokane landscaper, told of ghostly goings on in his kitchen:

It happened in 1975 at 1824 E. 12th. He was watching TV with his fiancee when they were startled by the sound of breaking glass. "It seemed like it went on for 20 seconds," said Bob.

By the time they reached the kitchen, the noise had stopped. Before them every cupboard stood open and the floor was covered with broken glass. Every breakable item—cups, glasses, bowls, plates—had been shattered. Yet all of the plastic items still sat in cupboards unmoved. Bob checked the windows and back door. Everything was locked. He got out a level and found the shelves to be perfectly straight. No earthquakes had been recorded.

Nothing he could come up with would explain what had happened.

"You could always feel a presence in that house," he said. "But I know one thing. We were the only ones in the house at the time all the glass broke." Lund laughed. "The only ones alive, anyway."

(Source: Spokane's Spokesman-Review *columnist Doug Clark.)*

The Rocking Ghost

SPOKANE, WASHINGTON

Reporter Doug Clark heard from yet another Spokane reader with a ghostly guest:

For years, whenever Irma Breesnee had a party, she set an extra place at her table. It was for Mr. McCloud, whose ghost she believed inhabited her house.

"From the first day I moved in, I had very strong feelings that there was somebody with me all the time," says Breesne, a Grand

Realty employee.

Mr. McCloud, she says, was the deceased former owner of the house on East 20th. At first, the signs that he hadn't checked out were small: The back of an unused chair had repeatedly rocked against her piano, leaving scratches. Piles of laundry became inexplicably stacked and folded. Doors were opened by unseen hands. Then one day, Breesnee's niece arrived from Canada. She scoffed at her aunt's stories of a paranormal houseguest.

"She ran downstairs to get her purse and came back as white as a sheet," says Breesnee. "She said she saw Mr. McCloud sitting in the chair and then described him in great detail." But Breesnee didn't know what Mr. McCloud looked like. So the next day the women drove to the Davenport Hotel. Breesnee had heard that a picture of McCloud, once a successful businessman, was hanging on a wall. They eventually found it. The more they stared, the more they felt icy fingers walk up their spines.

"She had described him to a T," says Breesnee. "Absolutely to a T."

(Source: Spokesman-Review *columnist Doug Clark.)*

A Sad Little Girl

SPOKANE, WASHINGTON

Several years ago Micah Colby, an agent for Grand Realty in Spokane, heard of a haunting during a conversation with a family of Baptists who owned a peculiar looking house on Eighth and Arthur:

It was a dozen years ago when the family decided to remodel their home. They tore into one of the walls and made a chilling discovery. There was an enclosed room on the other side. It wasn't long afterward that an eerie apparition began wandering their hallways. They all say the same thing: a sad little girl dressed in an old-fashioned white nightshirt. She looked lost and afraid.

As time went on, the house was sold. Colby tucked the tale in the back of her mind until one night years later when she drove home via

Arthur. She came to the corner where the Baptists had lived and glanced at the house. "It had become a crisis nursery," says Colby. "And it still gives me goose bumps every time I think about it."

(Source: Spokane Spokesman-Review *columnist Doug Clark.)*

"Come Out and Help Me!"

TACOMA, WASHINGTON

In June of 1970, Tacoma News Tribune *reporter Dwight Jarrell visited the distressed Pacinda family, and wrote this report:*

The home is in a quiet residential neighborhood at 4314 S. 8th Street. It is a low and rambling bungalow with wooden siding and a fieldstone chimney, built sixty years ago. Mrs. Francine Pacinda, who purchased it last October, is convinced it is haunted. And a series of eerie, unexplainable ocurrences in the night make it a modern day ghost story.

Mrs. Pacinda, a forty-one-year-old widow, moved into the spacious two-bedroom home Oct. 24. Living with her is her twenty-one-year-old daughter, Mrs. Linda Maldonado, also a widow, a younger daughter Pamela, age ll, and Mrs. Pacinda's grandson Nicholas, eighteen months. Two weeks after they had moved in, at around 10:30 in the night, the first ominous episode occurred. Pamela, in the bedroom shared with her mother, heard a scurrying sound like mice across the ceiling.

"She called me and I came in and we both listened for three or four minutes." Mrs. Pacinda recalls, "I remember saying, 'That can't be mice,' because workmen had just finished blowing insulation into the attic. Then the noise stopped and we just sort of shrugged it off."

But the incidents which followed were impossible to ignore. The family was in the living room visiting with friends one evening when suddenly from Mrs. Pacinda's bedroom came the violent slamming of a door. "It was as though someone was angrily opening and then slamming the door shut, and it happened three or four times before I could get over the shock and run down the hall to find out what it was," she said. No one was there.

Another night the family returned home at 11 P.M. "There's a light on in your room," Mrs. Pacinda told her older daughter casually, thinking they had forgotten to turn it off. When they walked into the house, the light was out.

On another night, when Mrs. Pacinda had gone to visit friends, her daughter Linda was in the kitchen when she heard her mother's voice saying, "Come out and help me."

"I thought Mom had returned," Linda said. She walked through the dining room into the living room but no one was there. Fifteen minutes later the same voice cried out the same words again. And again, the room was empty when Linda rushed in.

One night at 3 A.M., moans from the dining room filled the house and dishes started rattling in the kitchen cupboards.

On yet another occasion a chandelier started swinging. Mrs. Pacinda reached up and halted it. As she walked away it started its ghostly swaying again.

Another night Mrs. Pacinda and Linda listened from their bedrooms for three or four minutes to footsteps running up and down the length of the house. The runner was invisible.

That was in May, and suddenly there were no more incidents. "We thought it was over," Mrs. Pacinda said. But Wednesday night the family was together in the living room. Suddenly the sound of a doorknob being twisted impatiently came from the kitchen.

"It kept up until we rushed in and then it stopped," Mrs. Pacinda said.

The family would like to leave the mysterious house for good, but are tied there by financial bonds. "Every penny of our savings is in this house," Mrs. Pacinda says, "We just can't leave." She and her family have one hope. "Maybe someone will read this who knows how to get rid of a ghost," she says.

· *(Source:* Tacoma News Tribune *reporter Dwight Jarrell.)*

Pine Panel Voices

TACOMA, WASHINGTON

The pine paneling in one of the bedrooms of a Tacoma rambler hosts something strange, but no one can figure out just what. Owner Pat Stromberg wrote to the *Tacoma News Tribune* in October of 1985, telling of her family's strange experiences.

"There is nothing formidable or eerie about the exterior of our little beige shoebox nestled cozily in an expanse of towering pines, bright petunias and protective hedges. Step inside to a general air of peace and serenity. The oak-trimmed fireplace and handcrafted knotty pine cupboards are two of the many solidly-built features which seemed to conspire to convince us that this fixer-upper was the house of our dreams."

The dream begins to fade at dusk when a chilling shadow seems to worm its way out of the darkened, winding corridor leading to the three family bedrooms. "Ours is a curious hallway. It's almost as if the necessity of a series of bedrooms was an afterthought which led the builder to construct the tunnel-like hallway leading to them." The Strombergs use the end room as their master bedroom; their son sleeps in the middle room. "It is within the pine-paneled gingerbread of my daughter's bedroom that we first became aware of the other 'presence' ... this growling, groaning, and whirring thing within the wall. We call it the Sleeping Ghost."

The Stromberg daughter has better things to do than worry about ghosts in the walls, however. She just turns up the stereo and goes about her business. "With her rock music and ringing phone, my teenage daughter is very adept at ignoring the throaty growl which seems to emanate at odd intervals from the northeast corner of her room above one of the two twin beds. When the cool, dark hush of a breezy Tacoma night begins to sink in, and the branches of a nearby pine gently tickle the window, my daughter begins to deal with the strange, cantankerous snoring sounds in her own direct way. The girl just talks back to the rackety spirit and it seems to mind her."

"I told it to go away again," she told her mom, "And guess what? It did." Usually after she bawls it out, the ghost will leave the family alone for a week or so before it starts up its racket again.

"Unexpectedly, and often on a bright and very sunny afternoon, I will hear the muffled sighing again, then the groan from within, as if something or someone is trapped in a one-dimensional universe behind the solid panel," Stromberg said.

"What could it really be? An outside pump, perhaps? Even some cross-wiring, or a faulty cable hookup? We've checked for a possible explanation, a rational, 'Oh, so that's it!' kind of explanation. There is none, only a pine-paneled wall with a life of its own tucked deep inside, and—who knows?—maybe even a secret or two."

(Source: Tacoma News Tribune *reporter Kathleen Merryman.)*

The Obedient Ghost

VANCOUVER, BRITISH COLUMBIA

In 1978, Anne and Jim Houseman moved into the home of friends on East Second Avenue in Vancouver. The friends had gone off to northern British Columbia to work for several months on a construction project and offered their house to the Housemans rent free. There was only one hitch. They admitted that the house already had another resident. One they couldn't see but were likely to meet.

Before they left, George and Sandy had introduced them to "Oscar." As the two couples sat around talking about the move one December evening, Sandy pointed out, "Oscar is around now. He keeps turning off the red Christmas lights." Anne's chair was right beside the Christmas tree. She reached over and tightened the one loose red light. A few moments later she turned to look at the tree again. Another red light had been loosened and was out.

No one knew just when Oscar had started haunting this small turn-of-the-century house, or just who he was. But he seemed a friendly enough house spirit. The Housemans hadn't been moved in long when one cold January morning they were awakened in the wee hours of the morning by the tea kettle whistling merrily away in the kitchen. It obviously had been turned off when they went to bed hours earlier. "Stop it, Oscar!" Jim called out good-naturedly. The whistling stopped immediately.

After that whenever Oscar got up to his tricks Jim would simply call, "Stop it, Oscar!" and the playful ghost would desist.

One of his favorite activities seemed to be moving things around. From the spare attic bedroom would come the sound of furniture being moved across the floor. And one evening as Anne was vacuuming the living room, she cleaned the hearth around a copper kettle. She kept standing there, then turned off the vacuum and left the room. Behind her she heard a scraping sound as though someone were dragging the kettle along the hearth. Turning, she found the kettle had been moved from one end of the hearth to the other.

Oscar loved also to play with the fireplace poker. He would keep it swinging back and forth for fifteen or twenty minutes at a time.

And Oscar did seem to be a caring ghost. One evening when Jim was away at a convention and Anne was lying in bed alone, she heard muffled footsteps outside her door. She lay quietly listening to see what Oscar was up to now. Then she sensed movement in the room. The quilt she had pulled over her moved, and an unseen hand quietly began tucking her in.

(Source: Ghosts: True Stories from British Columbia by Robert C. Belyk, from an interview with Anne Houseman.)

The Rosewood Bed

VANCOUVER, BRITISH COLUMBIA

Vancouver's West End is a dense mass of apartment buildings today, but for years it was the scene of quiet streets and gracious homes. In the early 1930s a middle-aged couple moved to Vancouver and built a large modern house in the West End. The woman was outgoing and friendly, but the husband was reclusive and did not associate with his neighbors. After about six months the wife died suddenly after a brief illness. The husband informed the doctor that she had suffered from a heart condition and the cause of death was certified as a coronary attack. The husband sold the house and moved away immediately, leaving no forwarding address.

The young married couple who purchased the house soon found that they felt ill at ease in the building. The large room on the main floor, which had served as the master bedroom, made them particularly uncomfortable. After a while they decided to remodel the house and redecorate. In the process they knocked out walls and enlarged the drawing room to include the former master bedroom. When the redecorating was complete the couple held a housewarming party and invited six couples, close family friends. The party was lively until midnight, when a chill suddenly descended on the room. All stared at a spot at the far end of the drawing room where the master bedroom had once been located. There the apparition of a large rosewood four poster bed appeared before their eyes. A woman lay on the massive bed, near death. She stared in horror at a man sitting beside her. The man was smiling a self-satisfied smile.

"That's the man who built the house!" cried one of the guests. "And that's his wife. She died here in the house. But why is she looking at him that way?"

"That's where the master bedroom was," whispered the young wife. "We didn't like the room, so we took out the wall."

The vision faded and the guests departed quietly, vowing to tell no one of this strange thing they had seen. The young couple sold the house and moved elsewhere. They sold the belongings of that room, leaving all trace of the hauntings behind. One of the women who had witnessed the apparition attended the sale of effects. Among the items being sold was the new drawing room carpet, which had just been laid down before the party. She examined it. There were four deep indentations in the rug, set in a rectangle, as if a large, heavy, object had rested on it... an object just the size of a four poster bed.

(Source: The Province *reporter Greg McIntyre;* Some Canadian Ghosts *by Sheila Hervey.)*

A Caring Hostess

VANCOUVER, BRITISH COLUMBIA

In 1972 two young British biologists moved to Vancouver and settled into a two bedroom house in a middle-class neighborhood about a mile north of the Fraser River in the southern part of Vancouver. The house had been built around 1943-45:

"Some weeks after moving into the house in March, my husband and I were sitting around the dining-room table enjoying dinner and chatting merrily. I was seated with my back to the window at the front of the house, facing a door which led into a small, squarish hallway from which opened two more doors ...

"I suddenly stopped talking as I saw a woman walk through the dining-room doorway and stop about two feet away from my husband. My face apparently changed in appearance, as my husband turned to his left to see what I was staring at. The woman had disappeared. He did not see her. He is skeptical when it comes to ghosts, but he is convinced that I did see something.

"The whole incident lasted only a few seconds, but the woman appeared to me with perfect clarity. She was an elderly person, in her late fifties or early sixties, with a pleasant face and dark gray hair seemingly drawn back into a bun or similar hairstyle. She was wearing a high-necked, long-sleeved, light-colored blouse and a skirt of dark, heavy material. I got the impression that the skirt was longish (falling well below her knees) and that she was wearing heavyish stockings and sensible shoes. In other words she was somewhat old-fashioned in dress.

"Over the blouse and skirt was a flowered apron with a bib top and straps over the shoulders. She had one corner of the apron skirt in her hands as if wiping them. Her attitude was one of coming to see that guests were comfortable and satisfied. I could almost hear her say, before she disappeared, 'Is everything all right? Good!'

"The incident was in no way scary. In fact, it was rather the opposite, as though we had been checked on by a caring hostess, and as if she herself was satisfied with what she saw."

The couple checked on the house's history and learned that two middle-aged ladies had lived there. One or both had been school-teachers. And one had committed suicide through carbon monoxide poisoning in her car. Little more was known.

Some time later her husband invited two cohorts to dinner. One of them brought along his girlfriend. The young woman seemed very pale when she arrived and was quiet all evening. At last it emerged that the young woman had been fond of the teacher who once lived here and had often visited her in this home. She had not been to the house since the suicide and had been shocked to discover that this was where her boyfriend was taking her for dinner. Her description of the teacher matched that of the caring hostess ghost who had approached the couple at dinner.

The ghostly hostess was never seen again. The couple assume that she felt satisfied with her home's new owners and had no more need to visit.

(Source: Extraordinary Experiences: Personal Accounts of the Paranormal in Canada *by John Robert Columbo.)*

The Washing Machine Ghost

VICTORIA, BRITISH COLUMBIA

Rick Johnston moved into an old house on Vernon Street in Victoria in 1977. He didn't think anything of it when the departing tenants called over their shoulder as they left, "Take good care of our friend." But he was soon to learn just what they meant.

Not long after Rick had moved into the house, he and a friend were sitting in the living room talking one night when an ashtray suddenly raced from one end of the coffee table to the other and leaped off onto the floor.

Johnston began to notice that his bedroom door, which he closed carefully every night, was open each morning when he awoke.

And the ghost liked a warm house. Johnston would often return from work to find the heat turned up as high as it would go.

Strangest of all, the old ringer washer in the basement would start up by itself. "I'd be sitting there at night and I'd listen and it would be on. I would go down and turn it off and unplug it. But when I got up in the morning it would be on again."

Eventually Rick just moved out. Sometime later the house was torn down and a supermarket built on the spot.

(Source: Ghosts: True Stories from British Columbia *by Robert C. Belyk.)*

Rental Ghosts

Thinking to escape ghosts by living in a modern apartment house? Think again. It seems spirits may remain on certain plots of ground even after their original haunt has been torn down. Buildings are sometimes built over cemeteries, disturbing the residents. And spirits are believed to occasionally enter a home accompanying a favorite antique.

The good thing about a haunted rental unit is that it usually rents very cheaply!

The Burglar-Proof Apartment

Capitol Hill Area, Seattle, Washington

When Leon Thompson moved into the old apartment building in Seattle's Capitol Hill area in 1966, it didn't take him long to figure out that his apartment was haunted. His invisible roommates started carrying on the very first night he was there. The old wooden building had formerly been a rooming house, and Thompson believed most of the guests were loggers. Whoever had stayed behind, they were a pretty active bunch. Kitchen towels flew through the air. The sound of furniture being dragged across the floor came from the next room. Unseen bodies sat on the legs of sleeping guests, pinning them flat so that they could not turn over in bed.

Once a visiting woman was thrown clear across the room from a large chair to the sofa. "As I watched the woman become airborne, I looked in disbelief," said Thompson. "As soon as the woman landed, she picked up her glasses, her hat ... and headed for the door."

Living with in-house ghosts has its advantages though. "One

night while I was gone someone broke into my apartment, but I'll never know what happened, except the woman who had the apartment next door told me that there was a lot of screaming and she opened her apartment door … just in time to see two big guys running for their lives down the hallway." Leon is pretty sure his ghostly friends routed the robbers for him.

And another advantage of living with ghosts: "My apartment was haunted so I got it for half price because no one else would live in it for more than a couple of days."

Thompson lived happily with his ghosts until 1971. "I enjoyed those days living with my invisible roommate and his friends. I never had any problems with the ghosts, but I know they protected me from others."

Thompson's current living roommate, Ray Tweedy, says he has known Thompson for a long time and is convinced these stories are true. And he has even seen some pretty strange goings-on in their apartment in suburban Kent, he says.

(Source: Seattle Times *reporter Leon A. Espinoza.)*

Children's Gravestones Pave the Path
to a Haunted Fourplex

COQUITLAM, BRITISH COLUMBIA

It took the residents of a Coquitlam fourplex a while to discover the cause of their bizarre hauntings. Lights suddenly began to flick on and off, TV sets changed their settings, and footsteps echoed where no human was stepping. The residents named the ghost "Harry" and tried to get along with him. One woman told reporter Walter Melnyk that she could taunt "Harry" into showing his hand.

"One day I told a visitor that he would have proof soon enough (that Harry exists). Then the toaster came on by itself and melted a plastic bread holder. Another time the lights were acting strange and I said, 'Perhaps we ought to invite Harry up for tea.' Just then the heating element where the teapot was sitting came on."

A psychic named Ralph Hurst was summoned. He dangled a chain from the ceiling and taunted "Harry" to come and move it. Harry did ... just a wee bit. "Harry" told Hurst that his real name was Albert Johnstone and that he was a twice-married, somewhat lazy Scot, who enjoyed a good time. He said he had died in the mid-1950s in a logging accident, and had been chasing after a sweet young relative he had been close to, when he arrived at the fifteen-year-old fourplex. Hurst said Albert was a fun spirit who just happened to enjoy the physical plane.

The seance held in the apartment of the tenant Lucille Schneider seemed to settle her qualms for awhile. At times, however, she thought she saw the image of a child out of the corner of her eye. And this gave her cause for alarm because she had learned something about the premises that began to explain the hauntings. In the summer of 1985, the owner had improved the property by putting in a walkway of laid granite stones. The broad flat stones made a handsome enough walkway, a pleasant addition in rainy Coquitlam weather. Shortly after this, the strange occurrences began. One day Mrs. Schneider turned one of the walkway stones over on an impulse. She was shocked to discover that the "paving stone" was really the headstone from a child's grave! Checking, the residents discovered that the 130 granite paving stones were all gravestones ... from the graves of children. It turned out that the stones have been removed from graves at the Woodlands School for the mentally disabled when the school decided to turn its small cemetery into a park. The grave markers had made their way as "paving stones" to this Coquitlam apartment house.

Though the psychic's explanation that the "ghost" was really a good natured man eased Mrs. Schneider's mind, she did still think she saw small ghostly faces peering at her now and then.

If there were indeed indignant child spirits around they obviously had chosen another apartment to haunt. Next door lived the Hutton family, a mother and four children. The children kept seeing faces pressed against the windows of their apartment. The children's beds would begin to shake in the middle of the night. And the children held a morbid fascination with the tombstones lining their walkway.

Local children played at turning the stones over to read the names of the children once buried beneath. Eventually the building's owner had the tombstones removed. But the hauntings did not stop.

In December of 1986, Mrs. Hutton came face to face with a hooded apparition ... and it was not a child. "I was coming out of the kitchen and there was this figure standing there—he had a robe with red scribbling on it, but no face. I never believed in this kind of thing—I'm not crazy." Mrs. Hutton packed her family and moved. "There is no way in God's earth I am staying in this house," she told reporters.

After that the hauntings decreased. Mrs. Schneider and the others stayed on, relieved that the spectre had picked someone else's apartment to haunt.

(Source: Articles by Province *reporter Walter Melnyk; Article by* Sun *reporter Salim Jiwa.)*

A Ghostly Tenant

TACOMA, WASHINGTON

Phyllis Wire bought a large old Tacoma home in 1969 and began fixing it up as a rental. The home had been built in 1899 and required a lot of work. Phyllis, who has a number of rentals, is accustomed to working in them alone and has never had strange encounters before. But in this house there was a feeling of a "presence" following her about. She would feel a tap on the shoulder, think she heard a whisper.

One day she was working in four bedrooms upstairs which are interconnected by their closets. She had her small Pomeranian dog for company and her husband and children were working elsewhere in the house. Since she was spooked by this particular house, she didn't like working in it alone.

"I knew I was safe as long as someone else was in the house with me. My family had to leave and, knowing I wouldn't stay alone, asked me to go with them. 'No,' I replied. 'I'll stay and finish this bedroom.'"

They had barely left when Pepper started barking. I thought someone had come in downstairs, but no one was there. As I started painting again, I could hear someone in the other bedroom. I called out again. No answer. I was getting nervous. Taking my small dog, we checked out the other bedrooms. No one was there. But Pepper was barking, and I could feel someone close to me. With a leap, we ran down the stairs and out on the porch. The family teased me, and checked the house out, but to no avail. My friendly ghost would not make herself known.

"I never gave much thought to her until three years ago when Karen, our renter, called and asked if I believed in poltergeists. Taking a deep breath, I answered that I did. She asked if I knew that there was one in our house. I replied that I did, and expected her to say that she was moving. Instead, she informed me that there are two—a male and a female—that they are friendly and like her children. They hide things like the book you are reading, but she and the children are used to it."

So the renters stayed on and the ghost or ghosts were apparently content with their joint tenants.

(Source: Article in Tacoma News Tribune.*)*

HAUNTED NEIGHBORHOODS

One interesting phenomena in the Northwest is the neighborhood sporting several haunted homes. Perhaps the "haunted cul-de-sac" will become a term of the future. As houses become packed closer and closer together in our suburbias will ghosts drift from home to home?

Here are tales from Wells, British Columbia, a recent gold rush town built during the strike of 1932; Duvall, Washington, a small town in the foothills of the Cascade Mountains; and the Lombard Loop Road area near Sawyer, Washington. It is not clear from these accounts whether the appearance of spirits in several homes is believed to be a coincidence, or whether the same spirits are believed to wander the neighborhood.

Three Haunted Houses on One Dead-end Road

DUVALL, WASHINGTON

Former publisher Gil Hackenbruch lives in a turn-of-the-century home on a heavily wooded road on a hill east of Duvall. Bruett Road dead ends and has not one but three haunted houses.

Gil noticed his ghost a few years ago. He was reading late at night one evening. The clock had just struck one when he noticed something moving out of the corner of his eye. Only his reading lamp was on in the large, antique-filled living room. But in the dark hall he saw movement.

"I stared … at a woman wearing a long flimsy gown. She was staring back at me and pointing down the hall into my wife's bedroom. She had light gray hair that matched her gown. Her face had no emotion in it. She didn't make a sound. And three seconds later, she vanished. Faded into nothing." He ran down the hallway to his wife's room but found her sleeping peacefully. She had seen nothing.

A month later, Hackenbruch was again in his easy chair reading his newspaper late at night. He heard the kitchen door open and heavy footsteps cross the floor and go down the double flight of stairs to the basement. He heard the bedroom door downstairs open and close. Then silence. Hackenbruch assumed this was his son, Eddie, returning from his date and going down to his bedroom. Five minutes later Eddie came in the door. Hackenbruch asked how Eddie had got outside again, and Eddie said he had just got home. The two grabbed a shotgun and flashlight and ran down the stairs to search the basement rooms. Nothing was there.

"I don't know what it means," Hackenbruch says today. "I'd never thought of ghosts before. I've thought of it often since then, I can tell you that."

Hackenbruch's neighbor, Einor Ryan, witnessed a most unusual occurrence at the Hackenbruch home back in 1948. It was the same night the former owner of the home died. Ryan looked out his window that night and saw the unoccupied home across Bruett Road totally lit up. "The whole house lit up," marvels Ryan. "One end to the other. I learned later it was the same time he died."

Ryan's wife used to hold seances in his basement. Ryan says he saw apparitions rise behind her when she called up spirits, reciting incantations from old books she studied.

After her death her books were stored on a bookcase which Ryan had bought at an auction. The bookcase now exhibits a knocking phenomena. Three distinct raps can be heard at times. The new owner of the Ryans' house, Irishman Bob Cronin, is convinced there is a natural explanation for the knocking. He had a carpenter examine the bookcase, but nothing seemed amiss. Cronin moved the bookcase to new locations within the house, but the knocking continued. He finally moved it to the attic.

"It still raps," he says. "Three times. Quite sharply. But I won't get rid of it … it intrigues me."

Cronin's daughter, wife, brother, and a writer friend from Scotland have also heard the rappings. "My Scottish friend roared down the stairs at 3 A.M. one night and said he'd heard footsteps and rapping ... He refused to go back up.

"My brother also slept two nights up there, and came flying down the second night screaming, 'It keeps rapping! It won't stop!' He's never come back either."

A third Bluett Road resident claims she, too, has been visited by the dead. "There's nothing unnatural about it," she says. "They're all around us. You could see them if you wanted to. But most people close their minds. We're all going to be like them by and by."

(Source: Bellevue Journal American *reporter Patricia Wren.)*

Three Haunted Houses on Lombard Loop Road

SAWYER, WASHINGTON

The winding Lombard Loop road east of Sawyer seems to have three haunted homes. The Mahres moved recently into a new brick home set in an orchard just a few yards from their older house. According to Helen Mahre, the old house has a ghost. "I'd close the doors and they'd be opened ... I'd hear noise at night, and rattling and footsteps going up and down the basement stairs. Fred said it was my imagination, but then a hired man moved in and he said it was haunted too. As a matter of fact, six people lived there after us, and they'd all come over and mention the house was haunted."

Mrs. Mahre said an Irish priest told her the house was probably built on an ancient Indian grave and that similar happenings in Ireland were caused by violating graves.

The ghost, says Mrs. Mahre, is "very friendly." It would try to scare people off for a few weeks and then quit.

The Mahres' son, Rick, now lives in the house and says it isn't haunted at all. Mrs. Mahre, however, thinks the ghost just doesn't bother her son because he was raised there. "It's as if the ghost knows him."

Across the loop is a modern one story rambler, remodeled from a cabin. It was haunted until a year ago. When an extra wing was added on to the home the spirits inexplicably left! The couple who live there had heard footsteps crossing the floor at night. Lights had flicked on and off. And worse yet—voices had been heard.

The wife reported, "We would also hear voices—day or night, it didn't matter. You could hear a woman, very clearly saying 'Help.' Very distinctly. It was the only word you could understand. We even thought about bringing in a priest or something who specializes in spooks. But the neighbors told us not to mess around. That if they were bad spooks they'd hurt us. So we just left them alone. I used to be so scared, and I would pray that it would go away. One day I was so scared and mad that I started cursing in my head ... every bad word I could think of ... and it left me alone."

The ghost also seems to have liked music. One night they came home to find the house locked as they'd left it and the stereo going full blast.

But since the remodeling project, the ghosts seem to have been laid to rest. At least that's what this couple hopes. They refused to give their name to the paper, fearing the house might be hard to sell if the ghosts came back.

Another haunted house used to stand just down the road on the loop. Mr. and Mrs. Johnnie Finley lived there for six weeks fourteen years ago. That was long enough. "I would be alone with the kids— my husband went to college nights and after I went to bed at 9:30 or 10 P.M. two copper plates would fall off the living room wall," says Mrs. Finley. "Then I would hear footsteps. I know it sounds corny, and a noise like a chain being dragged across the floor." She couldn't investigate the basement stairwell, where the noise began, because "something just stopped me."

The Finley children had discovered a grave on the hill behind the house on the day they moved in. It was marked with a little white fence and a wooden cross.

Within six weeks the Finleys had had enough of the ghost and moved out. Mrs. Finley watched families come and go from that property for years. She says an average of one family a month moved into and out of that house.

The home's last owners, The James Youngs, did not believe it was haunted. But by 1976 the house had fallen into such disrepair that they decided to burn it and clear the property. "It went up like paper," said Mrs. Young. "It made hardly any smoke."

(Source: Yakima Herald Republic *reporter Patricia Wren.)*

A Neighborhood Rapping Ghost

WELLS, BRITISH COLUMBIA

Wells, British Columbia experienced a gold strike in 1932 and much of the town sprang up at that time. The cul-de-sac on which Ron Candy lived consisted of homes built, like his, mainly during the early 1930s. Candy lived in the house twelve years and told writer Ron Belyk about repeated rappings at night. Usually three definite knocks on the roof or the back wall of his house. A guest staying with Candy once woke him in the middle of the night, mistaking the rapping for the sound of someone trying to break into the house. The other strange phenomena at this home was a strange column of perfume which hung just outside the house, especially in winter. "You'd be walking along and you'd walk into this column of very pungent perfume. You could walk in and out of it ... and you wouldn't smell it anywhere else."

Just across the cul-de-sac stands a log home, recently constructed, but set on the foundation of an old cabin that predated the town of Wells. In this home the ghost of a woman has been seen. And here too loud rapping noises on the roof keep folks up at night.

(Source: Ghosts: True Stories from British Columbia *by Robert C. Belyk.)*

RURAL GHOSTS

The haunted house we see in our imagination is perhaps most often in a rural setting—standing alone and ghostly down a dark lane, surrounded by a few barren trees pointing their stark branches at the moon. Of course, since this book draws its material from actual experiences with ghostly visitors, we present here rural homes which are inhabited by the living as well as the supernatural.

The Old Applegate Place

APPLEGATE RIVER NEAR YONCALLA, OREGON

One of the most famous of Oregon's haunted spots is the old Applegate farm near Yoncalla. The house was built by Oregon pioneer Charles Applegate in 1852 so it has had plenty of years to accumulate lingering family ghosts. The strange goings-on were the topic of local legends for years, but Applegate descendant Shannon Applegate brought them to the attention of a wider audience with her charming account of her family's history, *Skookum: An Oregon Pioneer Family's History and Lore.* While she was writing this book *Eugene Register-Guard* reporter Dean Baker interviewed her about the strange goings-on in her home. Living alone with her small children in the big old house, Shannon was having to deal with a host of restless Applegate forebears. She feared they might disapprove of her writings—which were about them.

Shannon heard voices and thumpings night after night. Then the babysitter heard them too and called a neighbor to sit with her until Shannon got back home. That night the thumpings were more insistent than ever, and the voices of a man and woman arguing could be heard from above.

There came an evening when she could stand it no longer. "One night in my bedroom when the voices were particularly loud and I felt like I was about at the end of my rope, I decided to take the direct approach," Shannon told Baker. She spoke into the darkness, telling the listening ghosts that she was trying to write an accurate history of the family. She reminded them that she had as much right to live in this home as did the dead, and asked for their cooperation in her project. At the time she had been reading by kerosene lamp in an effort to capture the feeling of the house in its pioneer days. "The kerosene lamp dimmed. It was like a shadow passing over it, and sitting upright in bed, I fell into one of the deepest sleeps I have ever had."

Eventually Shannon learned to live with her family spirits. Once she saw an empty chair rocking and smelled pipe smoke and whiskey. "In that case I really did feel that it was great-great-grandfather Charles ... I believe that unequivocally. I even said 'Hello.' "

Shannon has her own interpretation of these events.

"If somebody walks in and out of the same door and slams the screen nine hundred times in a lifetime or sits in a certain place on the porch, something may linger there—some energy. Sometimes I think it's like a change in the wind current when you feel these things. Suddenly, because the wind is coming from another direction, you can hear sounds from away far off. They are maybe always going on—everything existing at once—and what you hear then is echoes.

"I don't think about them as ghosts or spirits. I just think that I am experiencing residues of very old energy. Some of it comes from specific people."

In 1971 Shannon wrote to a friend calmly talking of her house "visitors." She described a cycle of sounds and manifestations: sometimes they were there, sometimes not. When she began plans to fix up the attic as a studio, every time they discussed rearranging things in the attic the Seth Thomas clock in the front room would bong. But that clock hadn't worked for months and could only be made to chime manually.

A humming was heard about the house every evening around 7 P.M. Shannon thought her housemate Susan was doing the humming. Susan thought it was Shannon.

One evening friends arrived. They stood on the porch and listened to fiddle music coming from inside for quite a while before discovering that no one was home.

And one night she and Susan both moved to answer a knock on the front door. And so did someone else. "Well no one is there, Suz," Shannon said, peering out the window. She thought it odd that Susan, standing on her right, had changed her dark blouse for a light one. Then Susan spoke ... from her left. The woman on the right, who Susan also sensed, was wearing a white blouse with long sleeves. "I was left with a kind of after-image of a young woman's face, with hair pulled back," wrote Shannon.

Shannon concluded her letter to her friend, "I am not much disturbed by our 'visitors' who are probably not 'visitors' at all. We abide here together .... I hope this does not cause you to think twice about coming to see us next summer. Think of it as an adventure."

(Source: "Vibrations: Quavering echoes of the dead still live on, some say, in creaky old Applegate House" *by Dean Baker,* Eugene Register-Guard; Skookum: An Oregon Pioneer Family's History and Lore *by Shannon Applegate.)*

The Rocking Cradle:
Preserving a Ghost for History's Sake
Applegate River, Oregon

Jenny Alexander, age nineteen, recounted this story heard from her grandmother:

She told us one which was quite interesting ... she called it her Rocking Cradle story. And this occurred out along the Applegate, the river that runs past town .... There was a family that lived there ... they were called the Stevens, I believe, and my grandparents went to go visit them one day. And they were all sitting in their living room talking and all of a sudden this old cradle that was sitting beside the fireplace began rocking. And it was creaking as it moved and my grandmother of course was amazed, you know. She couldn't figure out why the cradle was moving by itself. There was no one there rocking it. The lady of the house, she went on to explain that the cradle rocks by itself quite often and that the house had been in her family for generations. And after each family had left, they just left the cradle in its place sitting by the fire. It was not moved. And for as long as she could remember the cradle rocked by itself. There was no explanation for this.

She went on to explain to my grandmother that there was an old family legend behind all of this that ... had been passed down to explain why the cradle rocked. She said that many, many years ago when the house was first built ... there had been a fault in one of the walls in the room. And one day the oldest daughter, she was about ten years old, was sitting by the fire and rocking the baby in his cradle. And there had been a lot of rain that year and she started feeling some shaking, and she realized what was happening ... that there was a mudslide. And so she immediately covered ... the baby, just threw herself, you know, over him. And the family said this rocking is caused by the ghost of the girl who comes back to sit by the fire and watch her little brother. And this is the only reason that they could give for this mysterious rocking.

Well my grandmother, not accepting this, you know, this is just too far out for her ... she went outside the house and searched all around ... and inside the house, covered all the areas ... and she couldn't find ... any logical or so-called "scientific" reason for why this would happen. And ... this house is still there. And I don't know, when you hear these stories and go by these places ... it's kinda neat to think about, you know, the stories that you've heard.

*   *   *

Jenny had heard many such stories from her grandmother. She related them to University of Oregon student Leslie Clason when Leslie was collecting stories for her folklore class. Leslie asked Jenny why she thought her grandmother told these stories:

She was very proud of living here. These were roots, you know. This is where she has been raised and she's always really interested in the history of the area .... She wanted us to know this, you know, she felt it was important that we know about our roots, we knew about things, you know, that had happened in the past ... a lot of people in the valley are like that, you know, they're proud ... they want people to know it! They're a special kind of people. ... When telling the stories, you kinda preserve the people that have been around and the people that have helped shape this valley and make it the type of valley ... the unique type of valley that it is.

(Source: Interview with Jenny Alexander, age nineteen, of Jacksonville, Oregon. *Conducted by Leslie D. Clason of Medford, Oregon. Randall V. Mills Archives, University of Oregon.)*

The Story of The Green Lady

JACKSONVILLE, OREGON

Here is another Jacksonville legend from Jenny Alexander's grandmother:

One of my favorite ones that I can remember my grandmother telling me ... she called it "The Story of the Green Lady" and it happened right here, in Jacksonville. My grandmother claimed that this story happened when my grandpa and her were first married. They rented this little cottage out behind this big estate, you know. It's on this little hill. And it was named The Old Hall. This is what they called it. It was owned by a family who made their fortune during the great gold rush, you know, when everyone came out West to make their fortune. And the lady who owned the house was the sole, the sole remainder.

The story goes that the lady of the house, The Old Hall, the owner of it, she was giving a large party, a large birthday party. And she invited a lot of people there, all the neighbors—the Johnsons, the Blacks, the Stevens—she invited them all. And they were all dancing, drinking and talking, having a great time you know. And the hostess, the lady of the house ... was older and she got really tired of all the ... festivities and stuff. So she decided to go up to her room to rest for a while, but she didn't want to spoil the fun for all the guests, so she said go ahead, keep dancing, enjoy yourselves, and she went up to her room to rest.

And my grandmother, who was invited to the party and she was there at the time ... she heard a scream. Well there was a big commotion and everyone ran upstairs. There was a lot of bustling around and they ran up to see what had happened. And outside the lady's bedroom, the maid had fainted.

They ... didn't know what had caused this so they were running around getting the smelling salts, getting her cold water, you know, trying to revive her. And they finally got her to wake up. She had, she claimed to see you know, that a green lady had passed through the door where her boss was sleeping, the lady of the house was sleeping .... Immediately everyone tried to hush her up, make her quiet, you know. They didn't want to spoil the fun for the rest of the guests. They didn't want anyone else to hear. So the party went on and there was no more mention of what had happened .... Everything went on as if nothing had happened.

But my grandmother, being the curious person that she is ... she wanted to know just what this maid had seen to make her, you know, make it such a big secret. So the next day she went out to the garden and kind of cornered the maid and kept asking her questions and, you know, just bugging her until she got the maid to tell her what had happened.

The maid informed her ... that the Green Lady was a family ghost who had haunted The Old Hall for many, many years, as long as the house had been there. And she would appear to family members to warn them that their death was coming. And two weeks later that person would be found dead. They would die after this warning.

Well, of course the maid was very, very concerned for ... the welfare of her mistress. And true to legend, the old woman fell ill and died exactly two weeks after the night the Green Lady had appeared. Which is pretty eerie. And the thing of it is, which kinda gives me the chills when I think about it is—the old house is still standing there today—you can see it right over there on the hill.

(Source: Interview with Jenny Alexander, age nineteen, of Jacksonville, Oregon. *Conducted by Leslie D. Clason of Medford, Oregon. Randall V.*

Mills Archives, University of Oregon.)

The Story of The Creaking Mantel

ROGUE RIVER, OREGON

Yet another Oregon tale from Jenny Alexander:

The story of the Creaking Mantel, one of my grandmother's famous ones. This occurred on an old dairy ... along the Rogue. If I remember right, my grandparents were invited to a housewarming party that was held by some friends of theirs that had just built one of those modern-style large ranch houses. And [these friends] had just moved out to this old country farm. And since, you know, this was a pretty big occurrence, this building of this new house ... they had invited most of the people of the valley to come and see their house .... Since it was pretty chilly outside all the guests gathered around the large fireplace in the middle of the room. And everyone was talking and having a good time, but as it neared midnight and the clock began to chime, the room fell silent. Because they were hearing strange creaking and groaning and, you know, that was coming from within the room. And they, you know, couldn't figure out where it was coming from. But they finally kind of located it. It seemed to be coming from the wooden mantel on the fireplace they were around. And between all this creaking and groaning they heard stomping and whinnying of horses. All this commotion! And everyone was just amazed. They couldn't believe what was happening right before their eyes .... My grandmother, a few weeks later, she called them ... and wanted to know if they had found out anything about this .... The hostess told her that she had went back and did some investigating of the property and had found out that the mantelpiece that they had put on their fireplace had once been a part of a central beam of an old barn that had stood on the property that had been torn down before they built the house.

But anyway, apparently many years ago on that same date of the house-warming party, a man had been hanged. And this occurred at midnight. From the barn's central beam. And this was done by a gang of outlaws who then fled. And the ghost of the man could still be heard ... on the anniversary of his death just creaking and groaning as he swung from the beams, the rafters.

(Source: Interview with Jenny Alexander, age nineteen, of Jacksonville, Oregon. *Collection by Leslie D. Clason of Medford, Oregon. Randall V. Mills Archives, University of Oregon.)*

Major, the Ghost-Biting Watchdog

ROCK CREEK, BRITISH COLUMBIA

In 1975-76 artist Frank Western Smith was living in a cottage at Rock Creek, British Columbia. The former park warden discovered that his cottage housed some unusual wildlife.

Smith was still unpacking when he heard a knock on the front door. He ran to open it, thinking he had his first friendly visitors. No one was there. Then he heard a knocking at the back door. "They've gone around to the back." So he hurried through the house to open the back door. No one there either. Puzzled, he went back to his unpacking.

This was just the beginning of weeks of door knockings. It got to the point where he would jump with surprise if he opened a door and actually found a living human on the step.

One evening the spirit came a bit closer. Smith was just dropping off to sleep when the sound of footsteps was heard in the kitchen. They came toward the bedroom door. Smith grabbed his rifle and got ready for the intruder.

"The footsteps had stopped, but an icy wind blew across my face. The windows were closed. Suddenly, the room was filled with the strong, pungent smell of pipe tobacco. I stood there with the rifle in my hands, wondering what the hell to do, while the wind grew colder and the pipe smoke seemed to be puffing right under my nose by some unseen presence. Then I heard footsteps retrace their route, away from my bedroom and across the kitchen floor. The wind stopped; the smoke disappeared."

Smith searched the house but found nothing.

Soon after this Smith adopted a Belgian shepherd. Major turned out to be a good companion and a fine guard dog. He would lay under Smith's table while he worked at his art. With Major at his side, Smith's sense of "spirit" visitations were verified because the dog would growl and crouch ready to spring at the approach of the phantom footsteps. Then one night the ghost sneaked up on Smith and the dog had had too much.

"I was busy at my art table, with Major lying beneath, without a moment's warning, the dog sprang up in a single bound. Whambo! The table flew up, throwing art supplies in all directions.

"Snarling, Major lept five feet in the air, opened his jaws, and closed his fangs on something I couldn't see. When he landed on the slippery tile floor, it took him a few seconds to get traction, then he shot through the kitchen to the back door, which he tried, frantically, to gnaw through."

Major's attack apparently made a strong impression on the ghostly visitor. It never came back.

Smith concludes: "I'll never know for sure what caused these disturbances, but if it was a ghost, Major saw to it that it is now haunting around with a big chunk removed from its transparent rear end!"

(Source: "The Ghost of Rock Creek" by Frank Western Smith in Extraordinary Experiences: Personal Accounts of the Paranormal in Canada *by John Robert Colombo.)*

Gentle Resident Spirit for Sale

SHAW ISLAND, WASHINGTON

When Shaw Island residents Al and Lotte Wilding put their property up for sale their ad included the note that the house came with a "gentle resident spirit." The ghost is believed to be the home's earlier owner, Fritz Lee, who died at the age of twenty-one during the 1921 flu epidemic. His grave is less than a block from their waterfront home on Blind Bay. The Wildings, who have occupied this home for twenty-eight years, first discovered that they were sharing the house with a former resident when an uncle came to visit.

"My uncle was sleeping there (in Fritz Lee's former room) and awoke twice with a feeling that someone was standing by his bed and looking down at him," Al Wilding said. "After spending two more nights there, he never slept in that room again."

The Wildings had found Fritz Lee's schoolbooks and letters to his mother in this upstairs bedroom. After the uncle's experience in the room, it was turned into a storage room rather than a guest room. But the ghost continued to disturb house guests.

Wilding is a retired Seattle policeman and once invited two fellow officers and their wives to use his house for the weekend. The two couples were awakened in the night by the sound of footsteps upstairs. The footsteps came down the stairs and the door into the room opened. One of the officers drew his gun and snapped on the lights. No one was there.

More recently a friend of the Wildings' daughter spent the night at the place. She awoke suddenly from a sound sleep sure that someone was standing at the foot of her bed.

The ghost also seemed to have its musical preferences. Once when Wilding and his children were listening to a rock station on the radio the program suddenly switched to a softer music station. One of the children turned the dial back to its original station, but the program switched again. They moved the radio to the kitchen table and all sat around it watching to see what was happening. No one saw the dial move, but the radio switched again to the soft music station, which was several bands away on the dial from the rock station the family preferred.

The ghost seemed fond of his house's inhabitants, reserving his haunting pranks for guests. Only once did he exhibit aggression. The Wildings used the house primarily as a summer home and weekend retreat, but there was a time when their daughter Juliana Barnes and her family lived in the house for about two years. On the day she was moving out of the house the ghost became very upset.

Wilding reports, "Juliana and I were alone in the house and I was helping her move. As I was walking down from the upstairs—with Juliana in front of me—I was hit on the back of the head with a pillow.

"It seemed like the ghost didn't want her to leave. I even turned and said, 'It's not my fault she's leaving.'

"Juliana asked me at the time why I looked so strange, but I didn't tell her what happened until later."

On the same day Barnes recalls seeing pots and pans hanging on hooks in the kitchen begin to sway slightly and knock together. "I thought that was strange," she said. "Maybe it's true that he didn't want me to leave."

Barnes said she "often felt a presence" while living there. "I once felt something tap me on the shoulder while vacuuming," she said. "But I never felt it was a harmful ghost. Rather than being afraid, I always felt protected by it. It wasn't a mean spirit. But it didn't seem to like strangers there."

(Source: Seattle Post-Intelligencer *reporter Don Tewkesbury.)*

The Snoring Ghost

VANCOUVER ISLAND, BRITISH COLUMBIA

Margery Wighton submitted this article to the Vancouver Sun *in 1952:*

It was the early summer of 1912. I was fifteen and living in British Columbia with my parents. Quite unexpectedly, my father had a very good offer for our fruit farm in the Okanagan Valley, and we moved to Vancouver Island where he intended to start a poultry farm. We bought twelve acres of cleared bush, and arranged for the delivery of a sectional bungalow.

The problem was to find somewhere to live for about eight weeks while the bungalow was under construction. This matter was soon solved by the offer of a shack belonging to a farmer, standing at the other side of a deep ravine filled with giant fir trees and thick under-growth.

For the first few days things were normal enough and, tired from helping my father unravel the plans of our bungalow, we came home each evening and after supper were only too ready to go to bed.

The third night, I went upstairs about 9 o'clock and while undressing, my mother sat on my bed talking to me. We had left my father reading in the little sitting-room.

In the middle of her conversation my mother stopped abruptly and laughed. My father was snoring downstairs!

"Daddy must be tired," she said.

We both listened to a comfortable, monotonous snore, so distinct one would have imagined the sleeper to be in the room. My mother rose and walked downstairs and I followed in my dressing gown.

"We thought you were asleep," Mother said. "We heard you snoring."

We found my father reading—very much awake. He adamantly denied having been asleep. So we returned to the upstairs bedroom. But in only a moment the snoring began again.

We took off our shoes and crept downstairs again, thinking to find my father pretending to snore. To our astonishment we found him as before, busy reading.

He looked annoyed and took off his glasses.

"If you two think this is awfully amusing, I don't," he said.

The laughter died from our lips, we told him about the snoring. He said we were still crazy and reluctantly followed us upstairs. And there it was again! Just a quiet, peaceful human snore.

"There's someone in here!" my father exclaimed, getting up impatiently. "But where?" he asked, looking round the bare walls, where there wasn't even a cupboard.

We banged about, thumping the walls, hitting the wooden

ceiling. We moved the bed and table around but the snoring continued.

We ransacked the second bedroom, but as we passed through the doorway we could not hear it any more.

My father went to the little kitchen, at the foot of the stairs, while my mother and I stood at the top. We said, "There," each time the snore came. He could not hear anything downstairs at all.

We then decided it must be something outside. But as we stood together outside the little shack there was not a sound to be heard but the faraway cry of a night bird in the bush.

My father then stood under my low bedroom window, while my mother and I went back to my room. The snoring went on unabated but my father could hear nothing whatsoever.

Completely nonplussed, my mother and I went to bed in the second bedroom. My father determined not to sleep till he had "laid the ghost."

The moon shone through the windows and I found myself unable to sleep. At 2 A.M. my father came into the room.

"I'm damned if I can stand it," he said. "I've tried everything to stop that snore. I thought I'd found one of you two snoring now."

The next day he and the owner raked the roof from end to end. That was really all they could do, since there was no loft and the place had no foundations. We could see under the flooring boards and there was absolutely nothing.

When evening came the owner returned to see if he could hear the snoring, and sure enough it started again most punctually.

Night after night our "snorer" enjoyed his slumbers while we had little rest.

People suggested owls, deer, chipmunks, spiders, and Indian tom-toms. But outside suggestions were disposed of, since once you left my bedroom, you could hear nothing.

My father couldn't stand it and slept downstairs, while mother and I nervously occupied the second bedroom.

And we stood this for six weeks, with no hope of solving the mystery. Then our architect friend, Clem Webb, arrived. We told him all about our snoring ghost.

We congregated in the little bedroom once more, as we had done so often—9 o'clock came, 9:30, 10. Nothing happened, for the first time for six weeks!

Clem Webb never heard it. He completely laid the ghost, and we never heard it again. We moved into our own bungalow about three weeks after his arrival and almost forgot about it.

But a year later, the owner of the shack wrote to a Vancouver firm for a new car. When it arrived, driven by a man from the garage, he decided he must have a few driving lessons before allowing the man to return to Vancouver. Having no room for him in the house, he put the driver to sleep in the haunted shack.

At midnight there was a wild knocking on his door and there stood the driver, trembling from head to foot.

"The place is haunted," the man kept repeating. "I heard someone come in, although I locked the door, walk upstairs and throw his boots off. Then the next thing I knew he was snoring loudly. Yet there's not a soul there. I went all round with a lamp." He refused to return and left the next morning.

The shack was still standing in its lonely setting among the tall dark pines when I visited the place in 1937. It was empty and had been for some years, people said.

I wandered once more through the deep gully, along the trail over the dried pine needles. The maple leaves had turned a burnished gold, and no one standing in that quiet spot would ever dream that such a disturbing mystery haunted the little shack.

Perhaps the Indians are nearest the truth. They say it's built over an old Indian burial ground. Who knows?

(Source: Vancouver Sun writer Margery Wighton.)

HAUNTED MANSIONS

The huge old buildings we think of as mansions seem fair game for ghostly lore. We drive by and glance up at their dark frames. Perhaps one sole light is gleaming from an upstairs window. It seems that such a place must be haunted. And of course the wealthy who once lived in those mansions are good subjects for a bit of folklore of their own. In addition to the five haunted mansions in this chapter you will find several haunted mansions in the section on Hotel Ghosts.

Sarah of Georgetown Castle

SEATTLE, WASHINGTON

When Rick McWade and Peter Peterson purchased the decrepit old Georgetown house known as the "Castle," they didn't realize they were taking on more than just a massive repair job. The huge old house had been known for years as "the Castle" because of its turret. Built in 1889, the fourteen-room mansion had at one time been a showplace. But by the time McWade and Peterson moved in windows were missing, handrails were gone from stairs, and entire walls had been ripped out. Over the years the house had attracted rumors of Depression era gambling and prostitution. A cache of illegally earned cash was thought to be hidden in its walls. One owner had even ripped out the walls and removed the floor of one room after a Ouija board suggested that gold was hidden there. Nothing was found.

McWade and Peterson believed none of these rumors. They purchased the home as an investment. It was near their catering and deli establishment in Georgetown and would be a convenient place to live. The once handsome building was sure to increase in value once it was renovated.

But strange things did begin to happen. One day they returned home to hear the sound of glass being broken. They feared kids were breaking out their newly installed windows and rushed inside. McWade checked out the kitchen, while Peterson ran upstairs. "I went up to the second floor bathroom and immediately it hit me," Peterson told reporter Paul Andrews. "I got cold all over. Chills went up my spine and the hair was standing up on the back of my neck. I told myself, this is silly, you're a grown man. There's nothing to be scared of."

Later McWade went up to the second floor to see what had terrified Peterson. He returned "white as a sheet of paper" and told Peterson he had felt as if someone were trying to strangle him. In his terror he had almost lost his balance and fallen down the rampless stairway. They never did find any broken glass, the cause of their search.

McWade and Peterson had only been living in the house for a few weeks when they had their first meeting with "Sarah." They were watching television in a back room when they both noticed moving shadows by a closet door. "Just out of the corner of my eye I saw something," recalled Peterson. "It was this old lady looking totally insane! My God! I tell you—one hand was around her throat like this," said Peterson, clutching his throat as though he were being strangled. "And with her other hand she started hitting Ray, like this," he said jabbing out with his fist. Peterson then described this apparition as a tall, slender, severe looking woman with eyes like burning coals. She wore her hair pinned atop her head in Victorian style with a white blouse and a floor length dress. Behind her floated a portrait of a swarthy-looking Sicilian whose appearance "gave an unavoidable suggestion of malevolence," said Peterson. "I was thinking, wait a minute! I'm not crazy! This can't be happening! Then, while she's flailing away at him, Ray all of a sudden says, 'Oh, you must be Sarah.' And just like that—she disappears."

Peterson sat in stunned silence staring at McWade. "How did you know her name?" He asked. McWade was confused.

"I guess she told me," he said, though Peterson hadn't heard her say her name.

By 1983, when *Seattle Times* writer Paul Andrews interviewed Peterson and McWade, the couple had been living in their "Castle" for over ten years. Sarah had grown accustomed to them, and they to her. Once a friend from Los Angeles was staying with them and awoke in the middle of the night to find Sarah rumaging through her suitcases. "Who was that old lady going through my belongings?" she asked the next morning.

Another time a visitor from Norway awakened in the middle of the night. Suffering from jet lag, he could not sleep. He went downstairs to make some tea and began looking around for some bread to toast. Suddenly a loaf came rolling down the counter at him.

Over three dozen friends and visitors have encountered Sarah over the years. Eventually Sarah convinced McWade, who was an artist, to paint her portrait. They hung this over the stairwell and Sarah seemed to calm down.

A short time later the mystery of Sarah was solved. An elderly woman arrived at their door one day. She just walked right in and said she was the granddaughter of the man who had built the house and wanted to see what we were doing to it. Then she noticed the picture of Sarah and exclaimed, "That's my dead great aunt!"

This lady then proceeded to relate a tale which put Sarah's case in perspective. The house had been a dance hall, house of prostitution, and gambling den during the 1920s and '30s. Sarah's brother-in-law had run the operation along with a partner. This partner had fallen in love with Sarah and given her an illegitimate child. Later the man murdered the child and hid the body under the porch. Sarah went insane with the anguish and later died a violent death, as did her lover. The man was rumored to have killed his business partner and hidden thousands of dollars in gold in the house. His description matched the picture of the man they had labeled the Sicilian which had appeared in their first meeting with Sarah. However the man had been of Spanish origin, not Sicilian. More than this they did not learn, but it was enough to give McWade and Peterson a deep sympathy for Sarah. She still hangs around the place, but by 1983 she had become less active. Still, "Every time we tell somebody she's gone, something happens," said Peterson.

(Source: Seattle Times/Post-Intelligencer *writer Paul Andrews.)*

The Gentlemanly Ghost of the Rhodes Mansion

TACOMA, WASHINGTON

When Lou Anne Sterbick-Nelson saw the real estate ad reading "6,000 square foot Rhodes Mansion, what would you do with it?" she was immediately hooked. She bought the old place and brought in crews of family and friends to repair, paint, and refurbish. The architect Dusty Trail who lived in the mansion before her had seen no ghosts, but Sterbick-Nelson found she had a gentle spirit in residence. She figured that it might have been a residue of the merchant Henry Rhodes, who had the house designed and built in 1901. In 1918 Rhodes moved on to an even grander mansion and car dealer Audsley Fraser bought the house. Later, from 1932 to 1966, Dr. Leo J. Hunt lived there and opened his offices on the first floor of the huge building.

Whoever the ghost was, he seemed polite; he opened and closed doors quietly, unlike the slamming inhabitants of some homes. He brushed gently past people in the halls, rather than pushing or shoving. And when seen, he just faded away into the woodwork. The family wasn't sure just who he was, but he seemed to be a balding, slim fellow of medium height. "The kind of man you wouldn't notice," said Sterbick-Nelson. "The kind of man who fades into the woodwork."

The friendly ghost was first noticed by a young child. The three-year-old daughter of Sterbick-Nelson's assistant was with the two women in the kitchen when she suddenly asked, "Mom, who's that man sitting in the corner?" The two women could see no one, but the child described a pleasant looking man, sitting in the corner watching them. Then he faded away.

Sterbick-Nelson's fourteen-year-old daughter Luciana has never seen the man in the kitchen but she told reporter Kathleen Merryman, "I know there have been little kids who have come and said, 'who's that man in the corner?' They are always little girls and they always point to the same corner. It's the one in the kitchen."

Luciana is not happy sharing her living space with a ghost. "I don't think he wants us in this house. He won't show us, but he will show everybody else. It's like he wants them to turn away from us because he wants us out of the house."

She has a particular beef with the ghost because he freaked out her friends during a slumber party. "At my birthday party a whole bunch of friends and I spent the night in the attic. The radio would turn on and turn off right in front of our face. It was really scary. Nobody was around."

Her cousin absolutely refuses to go into the storage room off the attic. Something happened there and he refuses to discuss it or go near the place again.

Still, Mrs. Sterbick-Nelson loves the house. She even goes up to the haunted attic to meditate and feels that a peaceful spirit welcomes her there.

*   *   *

—And a Ghost Next Door—

Right next door to the Rhodes Mansion at 705 North J Street lives yet another ghost. Bill Johnston says his "Mr. Hoffman" has always been there. "I don't recall a time when we were not aware of his presence." Once when Johnston was in the basement alone early in the morning, he heard someone walking up the cellar stairs. He went to see who it was. No one was there.

Another day he was on a ladder in the kitchen fixing a light fixture when he heard the door open and close and footsteps going upstairs. He thought his wife must have come home early from work and called to her. It wasn't her. And the front door was still locked.

The ghost likes best to hang out in the upstairs hall. It often can be heard climbing the stairs to that hall. And now and then it can be heard softly opening and closing doors.

Johnston says the ghost could be that of George Delprat, the insurance company owner who built the home in 1905. But he prefers to think it is that of Mr. Hoffman, who bought the house later and lived there for over thirty years before he died.

(Source: Tacoma News-Tribune *reporter Kathleen Merryman.)*

Haunted Governor's Mansion

SALEM, OREGON

In 1987 the State of Oregon acquired a new home for their governor. It seems they purchased a haunted house. The 10,000 square foot mansion in South Salem was built in 1925 by Thomas A. Livesly, a former mayor of Salem and millionaire hop broker. W. Gordon Allen, who lived in the house from 1961-1965, says Livesly still hangs out in his old home.

During the years Allen lived in the mansion Livesly's ghost would visit him often. "The old guy would sit on the foot of my bed regularly, every third or fourth day, the entire time I lived in the house. Conversation with the ghost was telepathic. He wore a black robe and seemed very sad. There was a real weight to him when he sat upon the bed." Allen's wife, who slept in a nearby bed, never saw the ghost. Allen, then owner of a Salem radio station, is now retired and lives in Woodburn.

Ben Colbath, a Salem real estate agent, lived in the house from 1958 to 1961. He never saw the ghost itself but he and his wife slept in the same bedroom where Allen's encounters occurred. Frequently they would be awakened in the night by something shaking the foot of their bed. They would snap on the light and it would stop. Colbath also heard strange, fluttering sounds in the kitchen of that house and in the house intercom system when he was in his bedroom. They thought it might be birds in an old chimney and had it sealed up. "But we still heard the fluttering noises once in awhile. They could really creep you if you were alone in the house. We called the police once, but they found nothing."

When Governor Neil Goldschmidt was told that his new home was already inhabited he just laughed. "My reaction was, 'the house is so big we could use some more help,'" said the Governor.

(Source: Article in Tacoma News Tribune.*)*

SECTION TWO:

PUBLIC GHOSTS

A great many Northwest ghosts hang out in public places. Hotels, restaurants, theaters, parks ... even hospitals and churches have their ghosts. You will find the staff in our haunted spots are often eager to relate their own experiences with the resident spirit. If you are planning a ghostly vacation in the Northwest here are a few spots you won't want to miss.

HOTEL GHOSTS

Interested in doing a little ghost hunting for yourself? Why not spend a night or two in one of the Northwest's haunted hotels? Several lovely old restored buildings in the Northwest which house bed and breakfast inns have permanent guests who don't bother checking in. And some of our heritage resorts and hotels come complete with inhabiting ghosts also.

The Pianist of Hot Lake Resort

LA GRANDE, OREGON

In its heyday the Hot Lake Resort near La Grande, Oregon was a prized vacation destination. Visitors arrived by train from distant cities, ready to enjoy the elegance and fine food of this spa. The first hotel was built on the spot in 1851, then in the 1880s a truly elegant resort and sanatorium was constructed. The spa, with its 205 degree mineral waters, was known as the "Mayo Clinic of the West." But in 1934 half of the building was destroyed in a fire and the resort's decline began. In 1977 a reporter for the *La Grande Observer* visited the former Hot Lake Resort, now reduced to a first floor hotel and restaurant, to investigate reports of ghosts roaming the halls. He heard some strange stories.

Richard Owens, a twenty-seven-year-old caretaker who had lived for over a year on the second floor of the hotel, was convinced that he shared the building with non-human inhabitants. "My room was directly under the old surgery room and you'd hear it real plain. There's a woman who screams up there. It sounds like somebody's got her tied up .... There could be a logical explanation. The wind blows a lot out there. Maybe the wind could make it sound like a woman's screams. But I've heard that when there was no wind. There's definitely something up on the third floor as far as I'm concerned. I was never the adventurous type, so I never investigated to see what it was.

"And then there was the piano on the third floor. Sometimes it would just play for five minutes. Sometimes it would play for a while. After you lived out there as long as I did, you didn't pay any attention to it. You don't want to pay any attention to it ...

"When I'd go up to the third floor, I would always push the piano chair under the piano. But when I'd get back, the piano chair would be out in the middle of the room, and it's a big room. Inside the piano chair was some sheet music, and once in a while that music would be out on the piano. There's just no way that prowlers or anything are going to do that. Besides they just couldn't get in. That third floor is locked up real tight ...

"Things would get out of locked rooms. I had some wheelchairs get out of a locked room once, and the room was still locked.

"And there were often footsteps on the wheelchair ramp between the first and second floors. You can hear the footfalls coming right up the ramp. You can jerk the door open and there won't be a soul there."

Donna Pattee and her husband had been operating a first floor hotel and restaurant in the building when a reporter from the *La Grand Observer* interviewed them in 1977. Though Mrs. Pattee said she didn't believe in ghosts, she could find no explanation for the three rocking chairs on the third floor. The seats of them never got dusty. It was as if someone rocked in them regularly. And it seemed to her that they had been moved around from time to time.

She decided to move them herself and see what happened. "I placed them in a certain way out of curiosity and I went back later and they were moved."

The Pattees' son David and his friends verify the self-playing piano story. They decided to move it down into the restaurant's dining room to lend atmosphere to the place. "The night we moved it down, there was a kind of restlessness on the third floor. You just heard a lot of creaking and groaning," reported Owens. And then one night David Pattee and his friends were talking just a few feet from the dining room after the restaurant was closed, when the piano began to play. Owens was there at the time. "We just let it play," he remembers, "It sounded like maybe how a kid would play, or like an older person in agony."

Though Owens was not a believer in ghosts before living at Hot Lake, he is now. "I'd say if a person lived in there for a month, they would come out believing in spirits."

(Source: La Grande Oregon Observer.)

The Femme Fatale of Rosario Resort

Orcas Island, Washington

Rosario Resort on Orcas Island occupies the former mansion of Robert Moran. In 1938 the mansion changed owners and a flamboyant lady by the name of Alice Rheem took residence. Rumor has it that her husband bought the remote property as a useful place to ensconce Alice and her drinking habit. She became a familiar figure on the island, riding around on a motor scooter, often after one drink too many, sometimes dressed only in her red nightgown. And she was known to have a proclivity for handsome young soldiers, bringing them back to the mansion whenever her husband was away. Alice eventually died in the mansion, supposedly a victim of too much drink. But she seems not to have left quite yet.

As recently as 1986 Alice was causing havoc. A tired housekeeping employee bedded down in an empty room in the mansion one night rather than drive home. Just as she was dropping off to sleep, she noticed a shadow pass across the wall. Turning on the light, she saw nothing. But the shadow moved again and something touched her hand. She waited and seeing nothing was about to turn off the light and go back to bed when she felt fingers caressing her hand. The girl bolted from the hotel, tossing the key to the desk clerk. "There's something in that room!" He shrugged, put the key back on the hook, and noticed that it was midnight.

As it happened, a trio of entertainers had been staying in the room next to hers that night. They complained as they dropped off their key in the morning. "How long will that woman be staying next to us?" The desk clerk assured them that she had already left at midnight the night before. But the entertainers had been kept awake all night, they said, by her carousing. Just before midnight they'd seen the light under the door go on and off three times. Then the bed began to creak and the moans of passionate lovemaking started up. They were kept awake all night. The key to the room still hung on its hook and the desk clerk hadn't given it to anyone else. The hotel staff suspect that Alice was at work.

(Source: Seattle Weekly *writer Kathryn Robinson.)*

The Tower Room of Manresa Castle

PORT TOWNSEND, WASHINGTON

The massive edifice standing atop a hill in Port Townsend, Washington was built in 1892 by Prussian baker Charles Eisenbeis for his young wife, Kate. Eisenbeis had made his fortune supplying bread and crackers to ships taking on provisions in Port Townsend. In 1925 the building was sold to the Society of Jesus, which added a wing to the original building and named the place Manresa Castle after the village in Spain where Saint Ignatius founded the Jesuit Order in 1522. Manresa Castle served as a Jesuit retreat and tertian school for many years.

In 1968 the building passed into private hands again when Dolly and Josh Norris bought the building and turned it into a hotel. Since that time stories of hauntings have multiplied among staff and guests.

Two legends have sprung up to explain the ghostly goings-on at the castle. A young English girl, named after Kate Eisenbeis, is supposed to have committed suicide by throwing herself from an upstairs window. She had learned that the young man she loved was lost at sea while coming from England to be with her. Mark Welch, a great-grandson of Charles Eisenbeis, says no such history exists in his family. A second legend tells of a Jesuit who hung himself in the attic.

Maids tell of quiet voices speaking their names as they clean on the third floor. Room 306, the tower room, is the site of most hauntings. Some say young Kate threw herself from the window in this room.

Former maid Tammi Headley told reporter Eleanor Nelson, "Once as I was walking down to the breakfast room, a regular drinking glass that I was carrying flew out of my hand and shattered into a bunch of different pieces. It was all over the place, everywhere. Another time the heater fans that work when you turn on the lights flipped on without being touched by me. Another time I smelled the worst odor of my life while I was cleaning. It came from the end of the third floor hall. It only lasted for so long and then went away. It would come and go. Another time I was vacuuming in Room 306 during the daytime, but the shades were pulled down. Two bright flashes of light came from the door. I just went away to the other end of the hallway. I got a feeling like the hair was standing on the back of my neck. It scared me because there was no one there, but the fact that it exists doesn't scare me."

A desk clerk also tells of smelling something unusual ... strong perfume late at night when no one is around.

Nick Gale, another Manresa Castle employee, tells of his experience: "While tending bar one night, a customer's glass shattered in his hand. I thought it interesting, but didn't pay it particular heed until the same thing happened to me—I was the one holding the glass that shattered into shards."

Owner Dolly Norris was skeptical about the hauntings. "I remember one night when my sister-in-law slept in the third floor turret room. She woke up one night soaking wet and found the water pitcher tilted on the table. She didn't know how it happened; but that doesn't mean anything. For anybody to think it was a ghost is ridiculous."

The presence of a spirit in the tower room seems to make that room the most popular in the castle! One local family books it on Halloween nights for special séances and has left warning notes in the hotel register. "Once again, Katie made her appearance—sitting at our table when we were all in bed, and then walking around the room. She wears a long whitish gown and has long grayish-white hair. She won't hurt you, but the priest is evil. Don't try to reach him—he wants to rest in peace! A chair was moved out of place in the morning when we got up. Charles was seen floating by the back bedroom door. We heard the priest walking above—restless—but not wanting to communicate. Be careful here …"

Through the years the sightings continued. One October two Canadian women were terrified by an apparition. Innkeeper Jill Tomasai told reporter Don Tewkesbury, "At 2:30 A.M., one of them said something woke her and she saw an apparition at the foot of the bed. It was outlined in light and she could see through it—like cellophane. She focused on it only for three seconds before she gasped and it disappeared. Both women said there then was the stench of decay in the room for about twenty minutes, followed by the smell of coffee."

Tomasai was skeptical. The guest was not wearing her contacts at the time of the sighting and admitted that she was pretty blind without them. And Tomasai notes that the nearby pulp mill sends forth a considerable stench many evenings.

(Source: The Port Townsend, Jefferson County Leader, writer Eleanor Nelson; Seattle Post-Intelligencer reporter Don Tewkesbury; Port Townsend, Jefferson County Leader reporter Patrick J. Sullivan; Manresa Castle guest register.)

transient quarters. In 1985 owners Cliff and Shirley Steelman began to dream of turning the place into a bed and breakfast for tourists visiting the Yakima Valley wineries. They hired Mike and Koni Wallace to do the renovating and manage the bed and breakfast. The couple and their five children moved into the huge old building and slowly began work on the thirty-three plus rooms. They soon learned that they had at least one permanent visitor. The spirit seemed fairly benevolent; it opened and closed doors, could be heard moving furniture around, and hid objects only to return them later. They guessed this was the ghost of a former manager of the Strand Hotel. His name was Carl and he lived in the hotel year round. "When he passed away he didn't have any family, so everything he had is still here," Koni Wallace told reporter Gale Metcalf. "In my kitchen that used to be his kitchen, things will be missing."

Mike Wallace doesn't believe in ghosts but admits there is something going on. "I believe it to be something I can't explain," Mike said. He has heard furniture being moved about in a room, opened the door and found no one there. Once he put his ear to the floor and could feel the vibrations from the movement of steps coming toward him. "I could feel the floor vibrate like somebody was walking right past me." He has thoroughly investigated every possible source of the disturbances—wind, animals in the crawlspace, movement in the tavern downstairs—and has come to the conclusion that the sounds and vibrations can't be explained away as normal phenomena.

The Wallaces seem comfortable living with the spirit. "Sometimes he scares me and sometimes he doesn't," said Koni, and Mike added, "I think he's pretty benevolent from what I can tell."

(Tri-City Herald *reporter Gale Metcalf.*)

The Governess of Roche Harbor Resort

ROCHE HARBOR, SAN JUAN ISLAND, WASHINGTON

When Neil Tarte took over management of the Roche Harbor Resort on San Juan Island, he had no idea he was also acquiring a permanent resident named Mrs. Beanning. Atta Beanning had been governess for the children of John S. MacMillan, former owner of the property and a company official for the Roche Harbor Lime and Cement Company. Tarte remembers the day in 1956 when MacMillan's son Paul called to ask him to come take Mrs. Beanning up to the mausoleum. "I had no idea Mrs. Beanning was in the mason jar on the mantle in Paul's old office. Ever since that day we put her ashes into the copper urn in the family crypt, she's refused to leave us alone at the resort. Lights go on and off. Doors open and close. The blender turns itself on. The usual ghostly pranks."

Restaurant manager David Gibbs has lived with Mrs. Beanning's "friendly spirit" for fifteen years. "Late at night after I've closed up the restaurant and I'm on my way out, I'll look back and a candle will have reignited. I'll go back to blow out the candle and she'll turn all the hood fans on."

(Source: Seattle Weekly *writer Kathryn Robinson.)*

HAUNTED RESTAURANTS

Haunted restaurants abound in the Northwest and fortunately many offer excellent cuisine. An evening's dining in these haunted spots will be well worth your while. And don't forget to ask the waiter for a ghost story when he or she brings the check. Chances are the waiter will have a more recent antic of the resident spirit to share.

E.R. Rogers Restaurant,
A Haunted Spot to Dine in Style
STEILACOOM, WASHINGTON

The E.R. Rogers Restaurant in Steilacoom is well known as a fine place to dine and a good place to spot a ghost. The nightly hauntings tend to hold off until all of the customers have left and the staff is at work cleaning up, but customers too have had unusual experiences. One visitor from England was drinking with friends in the bar when he suddenly turned pale. He had just seen a woman's stockinged foot stepping through thin air and disappearing upward into the attic overhead.

Hostess Jennifer Laughlin steers clear of that same attic. She was sent up for extra chairs one night and found herself enveloped in a cheap and heady perfume. She could see no person in the attic ... but her sense told her that someone or something was sharing that space with her.

There have been so many disturbing happenings associated with the attic that staff are forbidden to go up there alone during the day, and no one is allowed up there at all after dark.

The most annoying effect of the spirit's presence is the havoc it plays with the gadgets in the bar. Televisions, blenders, sound systems, lights—all switch on and off by themselves and change channels or gears when no one is around.

One evening after the bartender had locked up and was going to his car he turned to see the lights flare back on in the building and he thought he saw someone moving around in the restaurant. He called the sheriff's department. A deputy arrived with a K-9 dog and the dog was sent in to case out the building. The dog found nothing on the first two floors. When the deputy ordered the dog to check the attic the dog refused. The dog had never refused to obey a command before. But into that attic the dog would not go. The deputy finished the search himself but found no one there.

On another occasion a rug cleaning company arrived to clean the carpets during the restaurant's closed hours late at night. When co-owner Gordon Robertson arrived the next morning he found only one room had been finished. When he called the company they told him there would be no charge for the work done, but that they would not return. They said the place was haunted and they didn't want to talk about it.

The handsome old frame house was built in 1891 by seaman and merchant E.R. Rogers. Rogers, his wife, Catherine, and his grown stepdaughter Kate lived there only three years. In 1893 the family fortune was lost in a financial crash and the house was sold. Some think it is Kate who still hangs around the house that should have been her inheritance.

Another legend tells of a Native American who was hanged in the honey locust on the southwest corner of the yard. A face is seen from time to time hanging in the illuminated tree at night.

After the Rogers family lost the house, they moved back to their older home next door and Charles Herman turned the house with its seventeen rooms and South Sound view into a guest house. In 1928 Hattie Bair, who with W.L. Bair ran the drugstore and post office up the street, turned the place into a boarding house. Some think it is Hattie who still roams the building, worrying about cooking for her many boarders. However someone seems to be busy haunting the Bair Drugstore just down the block and that could be Hattie too.

(Source: Article by Tacoma Morning News Tribune *reporter Kathleen Merryman.)*

The Drugstore Ghost Who Hates Yuppie Sauces

STEILACOOM, WASHINGTON

The old Bair Drugstore, built in 1895, has been restored by the Steilacoom Historical Museum Association and turned into a museum and restaurant. Rosa Kreger, who runs the place, has constant problems with some resident spirit. Appliances just won't function properly here. Cinnamon buns are put into the oven at 350 degrees. Twenty minutes later the smoke alarm goes off and the buns are burnt to a crisp. Somehow the thermostat has been turned up to 500. The new dishwasher breaks down in bizarre ways, with insulation wire frayed from the inside out and other problems puzzling to repairmen. And the new hand mixer just won't stay put. It vanishes repeatedly only to be found somewhere else in the building.

Then there is the ice cream sundae-making ghost. One day an employee left a half gallon container of ice cream sitting out alongside a container of whipped cream—ready to make a sundae. He was called to the back of the store for a moment and when he returned, the whipped cream had been dumped on top of the ice cream! Surprising ... because there were no other living beings in the front of the store at the time.

Most peculiar is the behavior of a new product Kreger hopes to sell, a "Secret Salmon Sauce." At $3 a bottle they weren't flying off the shelves into customers' hands—but they were flying off the shelf. One patron swears she saw a bottle of this sauce leap from the top rear shelf of a display, fly five feet sideways through the air, and crash to the plank flooring. "That bottle didn't fall," said the patron, staring at the smashed glass. A waitress who had seen it happen agreed. "That salmon sauce flew off. It flew!" Two more bottles were found smashed on the floor later, but these flew when no one was looking.

Kreger and her partner Michael Mason call the bothersome spirit Cub Bair, the nickname of the store's founder W.L. Bair. "He worked here the longest, and is very finicky about changes," says Kreger. "He doesn't like all the changes we are making."

Mason agrees. "It's nothing bad. It just doesn't like the new stuff. Any type of new machine, it just goes wild." And it seems like that goes for trendy "Secret Salmon Sauce" too.

(Source: Article by Tacoma Morning News Tribune *reporter Kathleen Merryman. Comments by Bair Drug employee.)*

The College Inn Pub

SEATTLE, WASHINGTON

Tim Pfeiffer, who worked at the underground College Inn Pub from 1980 to 1983, recalls the first time he met the resident ghost.

"I had just started working at the pub, and I'd never heard any of the stories. I used to clean up, really early in the morning or late at night. I was by myself. One night I was cleaning in the Snug Room in the back, when all of a sudden I had a feeling there was somebody else in the room with me. I looked around and there standing behind me was this man, probably in his 70s, with white hair and wearing a khaki trench coat. He was just looking at me. I kind of turned my head to get a better look, and he was gone." Pfeiffer told his manager about the encounter the next day. "I couldn't believe it when he told me I hadn't been the first to see him. He said he'd seen it, along with a few others."

Employees call the resident spirit "Howard." Ron Bozarth, the owner of the building in which College Inn Pub is located, has heard of sightings of the ghost as early as the 1920s. In those days the building was a run-down apartment house and hotel. Earlier the building had been used as a hotel for the Alaska Yukon Exposition. Bozarth credits Howard with maintaining a comfortable temperature, good spirits, and a prevailing sense of humor in the pub.

(Source: Seattle Weekly *writer Kathryn Robinson.)*

The Dingle House Restaurant Ghost

VICTORIA (GORGE INLET), B.C.

The Dingle House Restaurant offers fine food, welcoming service ... and a friendly ghost. Owner Junine Oberg says guests often stop in mid-step upon entering the reception hall and tell her in a hushed tone: "My dear, did you know that this house has a ghost?" But they always reassure her, "It's a friendly ghost, though, I know; don't worry."

The Dingle House occupies a mansion built around 1880 by entrepreneur Charles Ringler-Thompson. Ringler-Thompson had arrived in Victoria in 1850 and worked hard at making his fortune ever since. He imported mules from Honolulu for a road building project in the Cariboo. He towed barges full of cattle around to North Saanich. He imported pheasants from Japan. And eventually he raised enough money to buy the Douglas Lake Cattle Company in the Nicola Valley. By 1882 he owned the city gas works and the Victoria waterworks. Yet he and his wife, a widow four years older than Charles, did not have running gas in Dingle House. He said he was in the business of selling gas, not using it up for free. Charles retired in 1905, and he and his wife lived a more and more reclusive life at Dingle House.

Late one evening in January of 1916 Mrs. Ringler-Thompson died. Within two hours Charles himself had passed away. A sparsely attended double funeral was held. They had had no children and Ringler-Thompson's only relatives lived in England.

The house was left to Charles's sister Janet, herself a spinster, and passed slowly through a series of Ringler-Thompson nieces and nephews. One of the last Ringler-Thompson descendants, Colonel J. Godreau abandoned, the house and used the downstairs as a greenhouse, storing sawdust in the master bedroom. In 1956 the building was condemned.

Rescue came in the form of Joe and Jessie Nordal who purchased the decrepit building as an adjunct to their motel next door. They worked hard at restoring the old building and began to serve meals to their hotel guests there. Later Helen and Bill Armson turned the Dingle House into a full restaurant, remodeling again and furnishing the building with fine old antiques. The current owner continues that tradition of fine food served in heritage surroundings.

As for the spirit ... no one knows for sure who he is, but the conjecture is that he must be Charles Ringler-Thompson himself. At any rate they refer to him as "Charlie." Though many sense his presence, Italian waitress Egle Debei is one of the few employees who has met Charlie personally. Every evening before opening time, Egle goes to the upstairs bedroom to plug in the intercom and stereo system. It is built into a stereo cabinet and rather than unlock the cabinet to fiddle with the stereo knobs, the staff just pulls the plug out of the wall. One evening Egle put the plug in as usual and started back down stairs. Halfway down she heard the music stop playing. She hurried back up and entered the bedroom. The plug was lying on the floor. She moved to put it back again, but when she turned she got the fright of her life. "Charlie" was standing right behind her! She saw him distinctly but was too frightened to pay much attention to his appearance. In fact in her terror she ran right through him! "I just run away, I am so scared!" she told reporter Alice Tomlinson in her Italian accent. She ran down the stairs and into the kitchen, white as a sheet. "Well, what's the matter with you, Egle?" asked the cook. "You look like you have just seen a ghost!"

"As a matter of fact," Egle told her. "I have just seen Charlie!"

It was months before Egle would take on the task of attending to the stereo alone again. Now she's settled herself back into the routine. At midnight she unplugs the stereo, slips downstairs, and leaves the building with the other waitresses. But she always calls over her shoulder a cheerful "Goodbye, Charlie!" as she leaves. "I do that for good luck," says Egle. "After all, if one is going to work alongside a ghost one had better keep on good terms with him."

(Source: Western Living *writer Alice Tomlinson.)*

GHOSTLY MUSEUMS

Visiting a ghost can be as simple as visiting one of the Northwest's museums. Here are art galleries and historical museums. In addition, many historic homes are open to the public as museums.

The Burnaby Art Gallery Hauntings

BURNABY, BRITISH COLUMBIA

At the Burnaby Art Gallery in Burnaby, British Columbia, a ghost or perhaps ghosts share the space with curators and paintings. The wispy shape of a woman has been seen by staff floating along on the top gallery or moving silently down the corridor of the unused third floor. Mysterious sounds, footsteps in unused rooms, and unexplicably moved objects all suggest a spirit at work. Though a bizarre procession of individuals have inhabited this mansion, tradition has settled on Grace Ceperley, the house's first mistress, as the ghost.

The old mansion, which has been restored to house the Burnaby Art Gallery, was built near Deer Lake in 1909 by Henry Ceperley as a place to retire with his second wife, Grace. Ceperley had made a fortune in real estate and insurance and the Ceperleys lived in luxury, throwing lavish parties for high society. Grace is reported to have been a quiet woman, who loved working in her garden and feeding the birds that visited it. The house had been registered in her name, and in her will she stipulated that the money from the property's sale, should her husband move or die, would be used to construct a children's playground in Stanley Park. However, after her death, her husband moved away and sold the home, ignoring her request. Many believe that this is reason enough for her haunting. Museum employees report that the spirit they encounter is a woman wearing a long evening gown. Some report seeing a figure in a long, flowing, white gown. Others say she wears blue or gray. So this seems to be a ghostess with an extensive wardrobe!

Here is what gallery employees report:

Around 6:30 one evening Carol Defina, the gallery program officer, was working late in her office. She was waiting for other employees to return for an evening meeting.

"It was very quiet," she said. "I was sitting at the front desk, doing some reading. I heard a noise. It sounded as if someone was standing there, wearing clothes that were rustling, like satin or crinoline. I had an eerie feeling." Delfina tried at first to ignore the sensation. "Then it was louder. I felt it was trying to communicate. It felt as if something was trying to fill up the space with a feeling, a chill. I knew it was something supernatural. I didn't feel I could deal with it."

Delfina ran outside the building and locked herself in her car. When the gallery director, Roger Boulet, arrived for their meeting, he found her trembling there.

Another gallery employee, thirty-four-year-old Roger Lagasse, also encountered something unpleasant during his work. "I was working late, removing prints from frames, using a little hammer and a screwdriver," he said. "I had done quite a few and felt I should move them out of the way. I turned around and, when I turned back, my tools weren't there. They were back on the tool rack. I thought at first that maybe I had put them away."

When Lagasse took some frames to the old wine cellar where he stored such things, "I fumbled for my keys and saw the padlock on the door was swinging back and forth very slowly. I stood and watched it swinging for two or three minutes." Lagasse waited until the swinging stopped and then unlocked the cellar and put away the frames.

"I went back to my table and my tools were gone again. They were back in the tool rack. Then I got this icy cold feeling on the back of my neck ... I knew something was definitely different, the atmosphere had changed."

Though the ghost is believed to be that of the home's first resident, Grace Ceperly, the history of the mansion has been anything but tranquil. Through its years it has served as a tuberculosis annex for Vancouver General Hospital, as a home for monks of the Order of St. Benedict, and as a fraternity house. The most unusual of the mansion's inhabitants, however, was "Archbishop" John Wolsey and his sect, The Canadian Temple of the Universal Foundation of More Abundant Life. This group disbanded in the mid-1960s and Wolsey fled to the U.S. The court froze the church's holdings, valued at two million dollars, according to Wolsey.

The sect instruction was harsh, especially for the children. At the Temple school, children were taught that they would die if they didn't believe what they were taught in classes. Following Archbishop John's orders, Carol Kjelson kept her baby Laurie Lynn in a dark room for a month. A six-year-old boy with a speech impediment was ridiculed from the pulpit when he couldn't recite as quickly as the others. Traumatized, he reverted to baby talk.

Psychic Joan Fontaine visited the house during a CBC filming but some of her readings were so disturbing that they were censored from the film. Gallery director Roger Boulet reported, "The medium expressed some comments [concerning child molestation] which were deemed not to be in the best interests of the gallery's public image. These episodes seem to relate to the occupancy of the building by the Society of the Foundation for a More Abundant Life."

Mark Stevens, who accompanied Fontaine and her associate John Morrison, says: "She found a number of spots that were heavily occupied." Two of them were in the basement. One was the wine cellar, where Lagasse saw the padlock swinging. She had the impression of children crying for help. "This is a very unhappy place," she said.

The part the press has played in developing this ghost scenario is interesting. The *Magazine* section of the December 15, 1985 *Province* held an intriguing account of the Burnaby goings on, much like that I have just provided. Reporter Damian Inwood and friend Les Bazso spent the night at the mansion in search of terror and had this to report:

"That snowy night saw Les Bazso and myself trudging up the stairs of the Ceperley Mansion, equipped with food and drink to keep body and soul together. We had cameras and a voice-activated tape recorder to capture any spirits for posterity.

"We spent an uneventful early evening, camped in the oak-paneled billiard room. Only once, when Les went out to scout the grounds, did I feel a sense of unease, but it soon vanished.

"We roamed the house, exploring the nooks and crannies. Then we decided to call it a night and unrolled our sleeping bags, set up the tripod and tape recorder, and lay in the flickering light of the gas fire.

"We must have fallen asleep, for the next thing I knew was the terror of that overwhelming Presence.

"I didn't sleep a wink after that, and anxiously played back the tape at daylight.

"I fully expected to hear myself crying out in my sleep. Instead, sandwiched between our conversations, was a weird, wailing warble followed only by a hissing silence.

"In the clear light of a beautiful Burnaby morning, I told myself the ordeal was nothing more than a nightmare, fueled by nerves and a fertile imagination. Or was it? I'm still not sure, but I don't plan on going back to find out."

*   *   *

On October 31, 1986 the *Vancouver Sun* had a go at the ghost too. Kim Bolan reported on an employee, Maria Guerrero, who heard footsteps and windows opening and closing upstairs at the gallery, later to learn that no one lived or worked up there. Visiting the top floor, she found a room full of junk and a life-size paper cutting of a woman's head and torso with eyes cut out, fastened against the window. When the newspaper ran the article, it featured a photo of Maria moving forward in terror along the wall, while the ghostly silhouette stared at her from the window. The photo seemed to suggest some supernatural origin for this paper silhouette, rather than an art student's prank.

*   *   *

Sunday, October 31, 1987, *The Vancouver Sun* took a closer look at the ghosts. Reporter John Armstrong and his wife spent the night at the gallery along with then Gallery Director Ted Lindberg. *The Sun* headlined one of its sections with a full page report about the house. The photo of the house's upper story shows an enhanced figure similar to the paper cutout featured in the 1986 article, only this time it is shown from the outside with hair and a dress drawn on. Here is Armstrong's account of a night in the haunted gallery:

"Ted Lindberg, director of the Burnaby Art Gallery, had decided to spend the night alone in the building and see if anyone/thing manifested itself.

"Having spent a week researching the gallery and its history, I finagled my way into joining him in hopes of meeting the shade of Mrs. Grace Ceperley, or possibly Mrs. Alexander Munro—front-runners in the 'Who's That Apparition' sweepstakes. Both women lived in the Fairacres estate and the woman-in-white who has been seen by gallery staff over the years is figured to be one of the two.

"Maybe we went about it wrong, but we tried. My wife, Mary (who had a poltergeist experience in her teens) insisted on coming, and we arrived at 9:30 P.M. armed with tape deck, camera and a half-bottle of VSOP in case of snakebite.

"She felt that if there was something there, her presence might make it appear more readily. I felt that if there was something there and it did show up, a little cognac might make it go away.

"The witching hour came and went. We went down to the basement, lights off, and sat in a circle. The basement has been the setting for some of the stranger occurrences in the house and we opened the door to the wine cellar (where medium Joan Fontaine had received strong emanations) and conjured mightily.

"We held hands and asked for anyone who inhabited the house to appear. They declined. I played Karnak and asked first Gracie, then Mrs. Munro to shake a leg. Ted tried some automatic writing. We discovered that while he doodles well, he is a better curator than cartoonist.

"Mary disliked the cellar intensely and we went to bed. Ted in the main room on the first floor and Mary and I on the second.

"I slept like a dead man. The most frightening moment occurred at 6:30 A.M. when Mary rammed two fingers Bruce Lee-style, into the small of my back and said 'Are you awake?' She had heard a scratching at the office door, and when it scratched again I heard it too. They have no cats or pets at the gallery and I don't know what it was ... well, yes, I do.

"It was a scratching noise. It wasn't an Amityville pig with glowing red eyes, it wasn't Linda Blair break-dancing from the neck up. It was just a scratching noise at a door an arm's length away and for a place with Fairacres' history, it was pretty small beer.

"Which doesn't prove that Fairacres isn't haunted. It only proves that unlike pizza, calling for ghosts does not carry a guarantee of twenty minute delivery."

It seems that with or without a ghost, sending a reporter to spend the night in a purportedly haunted spot each Halloween is a good way to keep the haunting traditions going.

(Source: Vancouver Sun *and* Vancouver Province.*)*

Fort George Wright Historical Museum

FORT WRIGHT COLLEGE, WASHINGTON

The Fort George Wright Historical Museum occupies one of the oldest buildings on the grounds of Fort Wright College. The old red brick building was the commandant's home back in the days when Fort Wright was a military outpost. Restored to its turn-of-the-century state, the old edifice now houses antique army uniforms, old guns, dolls, and antique furniture. The museum may also be home to one or more ghosts.

"I say 'Hello' every time I come in the house, just as a safety precaution, to let them know I'm there," said one museum official.

The hauntings are the usual: unexplained footsteps are heard when the building is empty; doors and windows open and close; lights are turned on when no one is in the building. Singing has been heard echoing through the house when no one was there.

One student worker had her own singing censored. When she began singing an old folk song about the Royal Canadian Mounted Police, doors in the house slammed. She stopped singing.

Many believe a female ghost roams the halls. She is drawn to the third floor where a former servant's quarters have been turned into a storage area and a doll display room. More than three hundred antique dolls crowd the space.

A museum official told reporter Christopher Bogan, "We turned it into a joke the minute we heard about it. We've had a lot of fun with it. But there's also this truthful aspect, which you can't get away from, which you can't overlook."

(Source: Spokane Spokesman-Review *reporter Christopher Bogan.)*

Uneasy Spirits at the Wing Luke Museum

SEATTLE, WASHINGTON

The Wing Luke Museum occupies an old building in the heart of Seattle's International District. The museum sponsors exhibits of Asian art and culture and provides educational services to the Seattle area. The Chinese culture holds a much closer relationship with the spirits of departed ancestors than do western cultures. Ancestors are revered, offered food at specified times, and treated with respect, not fear. Still each person has two spirits, both a good spirit, Shin, and an evil spirit, Kuei. If the body does not receive proper burial, the Kuei can be left to wander. These spirits are to be avoided. Such Kuei are said to hang about the basement of the Tai Tung restaurant and to haunt the alley behind the Wah Mee Club where thirteen men were murdered in 1983. Their pitiful howls are heard night after night.

The Wing Luke Museum attempts to put these events in cultural context, but since the museum provides exhibits from many Asian cultures its staff finds themselves dealing with a multicultural array of supernatural guests. In 1986 a group of Yiu Mien, a Southeast Asian hill people, asked to perform an exorcism in the museum. "There was just one ghost," said museum director Kit Fruedenberg, "but he was very small."

In 1987 Fruedenberg told reporter Kathryn Robinson of her growing realization that spirits were a factor to be dealt with in the administration of this museum. She hadn't been paying attention to this when she mounted an exhibit on Tibet a few years earlier. She said, "There is a religion in Tibet that predates and was actually the shamanistic predecessor of Tibetan Buddhism, called Bon. For the exhibit we managed to borrow several of these Bon shamanistic objects from a private collector, along with ritual objects of Tibetan Buddhism. The collector told me that there was a lot of tension between the gods and spirits of the two religions. I wasn't paying too close attention to it, and I put the two sets of objects together in the same case. Within five minutes the case shattered."

(Article by Seattle Weekly *reporter Kathryn Robinson.)*

The Lady Mayor in Seattle's Smith Tower

SEATTLE, WASHINGTON

Smith Tower, once the tallest building west of the Mississippi, is a favorite landmark of Seattle residents. Its slender white spire is now dwarfed by the mega-buildings of Seattle's recent construction madness. But Seattle residents still manage to pick the Smith Tower out of the city skyline and point it out proudly to visitors. In 1987 an historical museum was opened in the tower. The Smith Tower Museum displays photographs, maps, and paraphernalia of early Seattle. Included is a picture of Bertha Knight Landes, Seattle's only woman mayor, who had died in 1943 at the age of seventy-five.

Maybe the picture of Mayor Landes isn't needed. It seems that Bertha herself may be about the premises. A workman who was putting up the exhibits saw her several times. Museum curator Cathy Tuttle told reporter Judi Hunt, "He's seen her several times, very clearly. He describes her as a heavy-set woman who wanders into the room and comes up right behind him while he's putting up pictures and maps. But every time he's turned around to get a closer look at her, she's disappeared—gone too fast to just have walked out of the room." When he was shown a picture of Bertha Knight Landes, he was startled at the resemblance between his visitor, who usually appears in the early evening, and the former mayor. "If it's Bertha, as we think, maybe she's set up offices here."

(Source: Seattle Post-Intelligencer *reporter Judi Hunt.)*

GHOSTS IN MUSEUM HOUSES

For those of you who want to seek out ghosts, you are in luck here in the Pacific Northwest. Several haunted homes have been turned into museums open to the public. Here are a few of the historic homes you may wish to visit.

Oregon City's Historical Ghosts

OREGON CITY, OREGON

Oregon City boasts two restored old homes which sit side by side at 713 and 719 Center Street. Both are haunted not by just one ghost, but by a whole family.

Let's start with the McLoughlin House. This was the home of Dr. John McLoughlin, the founder of Oregon City, who laid out the town in 1840 and built his home in 1846. McLoughlin, a doctor trained in Paris, had practiced medicine in Montreal. But the fur trade lured him to the west. He arrived in the territory in the 1820s and held the post of chief factor for the Hudson Bay Company. The flamboyant McLoughlin ruled with an iron fist and is said to have taken his gold-headed cane to the head of a minister who preached that McLoughlin's marriage to a Cree wife was improper.

Since his death in 1857, his body and that of his wife have been moved three times. Their remains now reside on the property of the McLoughlin house and McLoughlin is thought to roam the building. A tall shadow is seen ducking through doorways. Doors slam shut. Objects fall to the floor. Footsteps are heard. And Dr. McLoughlin's rocking chair rocks back and forth all by itself.

"People claim they can see an actual figure," says museum curator

Nancy Wilson, "but what I have seen is a shadow that is so tall that when he moves away from you he has to duck in the doorways, as Dr. McLoughlin had to. One time I got tapped on the shoulder and I turned, but no one was there."

An oil portrait of McLoughlin hangs in the parlor of the house. At 9:35 in the morning each September 3, the day on which McLoughlin died, his face in the portrait is briefly lit by a bright oval of sunlight. McLoughlin is known to have died in the morning, but the exact hour of his death is unknown.

McLoughlin's ghost was particularly active a few years ago when curator Wilson brought in some mannequins and dressed them in clothing from pioneer Oregon City women. One was gowned in the wedding dress of one of McLoughlin's neighbors. This seemed to stir the haunting spirit up quite a bit. "Because those were dresses that belonged to women he knew," says Wilson.

Two men who jog by the house swear they have each seen a lady standing at the upstairs window. So perhaps Mrs. McLoughlin accompanies her husband in his hauntings.

More inexplicable is the ghost of a small black and white dog which is seen running through the house at times. Museum curator Nancy Wilson has even seen small paw prints on the rug of a room on the first floor which is not accessible to the public.

Next door live more ghosts. This was the home of Dr. Forbes Barclay who came to Oregon in 1840, also as an employee of the Hudson Bay Company. Barclay himself seems to rest in peace, but his brother lingers on. "Uncle Sandy" was a seaman who used to stay in Oregon City with his brother during shore leave. His furniture was left in his old room after his death. If someone slept in his bed, Uncle Sandy would walk through the wall, sit down in a chair, and stare at the sleeper. After a while he would get up and disappear back through the wall. Mildred Mendes, who knew the owners of the Barclay House before it was moved to this site to serve as a museum, remembers seeing Uncle Sandy twice when she was visiting.

But most delightful of the Barclay House ghosts is a small red-headed boy who runs through the downstairs hall. He was seen in the building back when it was used as offices and kept locked all day, so he could not have been a neighborhood child who wandered in. Visitors have seen him as well as staff. As recently as 1989 a five-year-old boy who was trailing along up the stairs after his parents during a tour asked the guide whether that little boy was supposed to be downstairs by himself. The tour guide saw no child below. Curious, the guide asked what color hair the little boy had. "Red," said the child.

(Source: Oregonian reporter Rod Patterson; Oregonian reporter Dennis McCarthy; and Haunted Houses, U.S.A. *by Dolores Riccio & Joan Bingham.)*

The Ghostly Guide of Point Ellice House

Victoria, British Columbia

Built between 1865 and 1867, the Point Ellice House was once one of the grandest homes in Victoria. Peter O'Reilly came to Canada from County Meath, Ireland in 1859. He was appointed stipendiary magistrate for Fort Langley and later made magistrate and gold commissioner for the Cariboo district. Though O'Reilly spent much of his time away in the country's interior, he built a handsome house in the most fashionable part of Victoria for his wife.

The house, on the banks of the narrow inlet known as the Gorge, was the scene of many parties and social events during the late 1880s and 1890s. The O'Reillys raised two sons and a daughter there. Kathleen O'Reilly, the daughter, did not marry and lived out her years in the house. She died in 1945. The property remained in the family, but with time the surroundings changed. The other fine houses were torn down to make way for industrial sites.

In 1965 Inez and John O'Reilly, the last O'Reillys to own the house, were offered a large sum of money for the property. The buyer planned to demolish the old building. But the O'Reillys could not bear to see their family heritage fall to the wrecking ball. They felt also that they were not alone in this old house. They were certain that a few O'Reilly spirits remained at hand. They made the bold decision to keep the property and somehow find the money to repair the old building. In 1967 they opened the newly refurbished Point Ellice House as a private museum. The ghosts must have been delighted because they went to work at once … showing visitors around!

Not long after the house was opened to the public, a woman upbraided Mrs. O'Reilly for bringing the public into a house full of ghosts. It seems they had frightened her small granddaughter. "You should warn people that the house is haunted! We should sue you. It's very dangerous."

One visiting family was shown around the house by a woman in an old-fashioned blue dress. But there was no one in the house at that time who fit such a description. Except that the dress was exactly like one once worn by Kathleen O'Reilly.

On another occasion, two men saw a woman fitting Kathleen's description waiting for them as they arrived. And she followed them down the road a piece as they left.

It is speculated that the ghost of Peter O'Reilly's wife, Caroline, haunts the house as well. She was very attached to her home, and an American psychic, Suzie Smith, claimed she sensed more than one spirit in the home.

The house was sold to the provincial government in 1974 and is now administered as a museum by the Ministry of Municipal Affairs, Recreation and Culture. The ghosts seem to be leaving the guided tours to the professional staff these days.

(Source: Ghosts: True Stories from British Columbia *by Robert C. Belyk;* Victoria Colonist *reporter Isabel Young;* A Gathering of Ghosts *by Robin Skelton and Jean Kozocari.)*

Tod House Ghost Laid

OAK BAY AREA, VICTORIA, BRITISH COLUMBIA

The pleasant little frame bungalow at 2564 Heron Street in the Oak Bay suburb of Victoria has stood on that spot since 1851. Said to be the oldest surviving home in British Columbia, this house was built by Hudson Bay Company chief trader John Tod. The house was a showplace in those early days ... one of the first buildings in the area to be built of milled lumber. A water-powered sawmill had recently opened.

Tod was a colorful man. He arrived from Scotland in 1813 to make his future in the new colony, then known as New Caledonia. His path to fame was a bumpy one. He soon incurred the wrath of the Hudson Bay Company's governor and was banished to remote Fort McLeod. During his nine years there he became fluent in Native American dialects. And he was not lacking in courage either. In 1847, while he was chief trader at Fort Kamloops, he held off Chief Nicola and his men by threatening to blow up himself and the entire fort with a keg of gunpowder if the Kamloop tribe did not leave the fort in peace. His bluff worked.

Tod married at least seven times, four times to native women. His house was constructed with defense of his current wife and his ten children in mind. The front door was thick ... a bullet hole in the door is attributed to an attack by some Cadboro Bay men. A tunnel ran from the cellar to a spot distant from the house, enabling the trapped family to escape if under siege.

When Tod died in 1882 the house passed to his heirs. It is not certain just when stories of hauntings began to arise, but by the time the house was purchased by Colonel and Mrs. T. C. Evans in 1944, the building had acquired a reputation as a haunted house.

Colonel Evans, a pragmatic man, did not believe in ghosts. Still, strange things did occur. The door to the dank cellar absolutely refused to stay closed. No matter how securely it was fastened they would soon find it ajar again. Colonel Evans' adjustments to the lock failed to keep the door shut.

Mrs. Evans' antique rocker in the living room would often take up rocking by itself. The ghost seemed quite fond of this rocker. The ghost also liked to amuse itself by tossing about the hats from the hall hat stand. They were found repeatedly strewn about the hall floor. And when Christmas came around, the ghost became particularly active. One morning they awoke to find that the Christmas decorations had been taken from the walls and tree and the cards swept from the mantel. All were in a pile in the middle of the floor.

None of these pranks seemed to particularly bother the family, but there was one aspect of their "haunted" house which did disturb them. The large upstairs room which seemed most suitable for their master bedroom proved uninhabitable. The Evans couple moved into it ... then moved out again after only a couple of nights. There was no real reason for this but the room left them with such a strange sensation that they could not bear spending another night there. One evening they heard a crash and discovered that the large window from that bedroom had fallen out onto the lawn. There was nothing wrong with the frame or the nails holding it in place ... no logical reason why it should have fallen.

Though Colonel and Mrs. Evans chose not to sleep in that room, they did put guests up there one weekend. It was during World War II and they had invited two airmen to their home for the weekend. The room had been completely refurbished and seemed a pleasant enough guest room.

The next morning Mrs. Evans found the room empty, with signs that it had been vacated in a rush. Later in the day the two airmen returned to explain their hasty departure. One of them told a Victoria paper:

"We had been asleep for several hours when I suddenly awoke. I can't really describe what woke me, although it sounded like the rattling of chains. Over in the corner stood an Indian woman, her hands held out toward me in such a manner that she seemed to be pleading with me to help her.

"On her arms and legs were what looked like fetters. She kept looking at me, her hands outstretched and saying something that I couldn't catch. As suddenly as she appeared she was gone. I'll never forget the sight."[1]

Colonel Evans had been doing some research on Tod and the history of the house. He had unearthed a rumor that one of the native women to whom Tod had been married had gone mad. According to the rumor, she had been kept in chains in an upstairs bedroom. Could this be the ghost?

An earlier owner of the home, Mrs. E. C. Turner, had lived at Tod House with her daughter from 1929-1944. She concurred with the Evans' about the strange sensations from that one bedroom. Neither she nor her daughter would ever sleep in that room. She disliked the feeling of living with unseen spirits. "Sometimes I would awake at night feeling a presence in my room. The door would slowly open although I couldn't see anything. I am still fully convinced that there was someone there …. Sometimes as I walked along the passageway, I felt that someone was walking behind me. It got very tiresome …. At night the cat would suddenly growl and arch her back and her fur would stand up. I feel sure she saw something that I could not see."

It seems that Colonel and Mrs. Evans did not really mind the ghost. Mrs. Evans told a reporter: "There's one thing about it. You're never lonely with these invisible personages around. I don't ever feel I am alone."[2]

However the haunting was soon to bring them unpleasantries of another sort. During a New Year's Eve party the ghost decided to act up in front of a roomful of guests. Mrs. Evans had hung an attractive porcelain cookie jar from a hook by the fireplace. Suddenly the porcelain jar started to swing. Back and forth it swung itself … for nearly thirty minutes … in full view of the New Year's guests.

After this notorious event the Tod House was famous. Reporters besieged the place and gawkers drove by slowly or tiptoed up to peer in the windows at the "haunted house." Fortunately relief was in sight. Just as the publicity flurry reached its peak in early 1947, Colonel Evans began work on installation of a new oil furnace. Workmen dug a deep hole beside the front porch to hold the oil storage tank. About seven feet down they found themselves digging into a human skeleton. No way would they continue to dig at haunted Tod House.

The Colonel was unwilling to pay the exorbitant fee they demanded to set shovel to skeleton. So he had to unearth the bones himself. The skull was in reasonable shape but the bones seemed to have been buried in quicklime as they were decomposed. A forensic specialist found them to be the bones of a female, either Asian or Native American, buried more than fifty years earlier. Were these in fact the bones of one of Tod's wives? One can only speculate.

However it is said that after these bones were unearthed the hauntings stopped.

Fred and Maveney Massie, who moved into Tod House after the Evanses, found no ghosts left behind. The ghost hunters still proved quite a nuisance, however. "They would stand on the lawn and take photographs and generally ignore the fact that the house is not a museum but a private residence," said Mrs. Massie.

The newspapers had published information about the ghost's demise after the unearthing of the bones, and eventually the public's interest waned. Mrs. Massie recounted one amusing conversation which she overheard while working in her garden one day. Two girls were telling a little boy about the house. "That house is haunted you know," one of the girls told him. "I don't think it's haunted now," replied the boy. "The ghost died."[3]

In 1974 Tod House was declared a heritage landmark. It is now owned by the municipality of Oak Bay and the provincial government. The house no longer seems haunted by spirits ... just by the past.

(Sources: 1. Vancouver Sun; Vancouver News-Herald *reporter Ron Baird;* Victoria Colonist *reporter Alice Tomlinson; 2.* Victoria News-Herald *reporter J.K.Nesbitt;* Victoria Times-Colonist *reporter Ed Goul; 3.* Victoria Province *reporter B. A.McKelvie.)*

SEATTLE'S HAUNTED MOVIE HOUSES

Going to the movies in Seattle can be a hair-raising experience ... even if the movie is not a horror flick. Three of Seattle's movie houses are haunted. Visitors to these theaters can easily believe the stories.

Take the Harvard Exit Theater. Tucked away on a narrow side street on Capitol Hill, the old building looms above the sidewalk. Light from its sitting room windows glows down onto the street. The forms of chatting movie goers pass to and fro inside. The building could easily be taken for a private home or for a clubhouse, which it once was.

Climbing steep stairs, we enter a narrow hallway to pay for our tickets, then pass into a large, handsomely apportioned living room where we join the other guests for hot cider or tea. All about are warm overstuffed chairs and couches and darkly polished wooden tables. Everything speaks of age and much living. One could easily imagine this place to have a resident ghost.

The Neptune Theater seems more what a movie goer expects. But its classic black tiled theater entrance evokes an earlier generation of movie houses. The bizzarely aquamarine walls of the theater itself are decorated with undersea motifs. Neptune and mermaid forms bulge from the walls overhead. The whole is obviously meant to echo the theater's name, but the effect is eerie ... and a bit bilious.

Our third haunted movie house, the Moore-Egyptian Theater, has spent much of its life hosting stage productions. But the particular sightings recorded here took place during a period when the theater was a movie house. Built in an era when regal trappings spelled theater success, every inch of this cavernous building is decorated with

Egyptian motifs. One enters through an echoing foyer, climbs steps, more foyer, and enters a high ceilinged ornate theater designed to take your breath away. And should one desire the restrooms, one travels down and down over winding stairs to a virtual catacomb of echoing rooms beneath the theater.

Given their decor and general ambience, it is no wonder that these Seattle movie houses come equipped with ghosts ... or the legends of ghosts.

The Harvard Exit Theater

SEATTLE, WASHINGTON

The Harvard Exit theater has been home to the Women's Century Club since the 1920s. Former manager Janet Wainwright thinks the ghosts wandering about may be part of that group. "I have no doubt that those early suffragettes who had such an attachment to the ideals set forth in that building are the ones who are still here. I've seen the ghosts of at least three different women there."

Wainwright managed the theater from 1969 to 1979 and encountered ghostly phenomena on many occasions. "The first time I saw anything, I had gotten to the theater early to unlock the doors. The procedure was to open the doors to the main lobby and light the fire. I looked toward the fireplace. A woman was sitting on a chair in front of the fireplace, sort of half-facing me. She didn't look at me, but I looked at her, long enough to watch her fade."

Sometimes on entering the building, Wainwright saw a tall woman who would turn off the light and walk toward the auditorium. "Several times I'd arrive and unlock the doors, only to find a fire already started in the fireplace and the chairs grouped around it in a semicircle. We were all paranoid about fire in that building, so this was a big no-no. But it kept happening."

The third floor of the building seemed to be the center of activity. "Several times I'd see walking forms out of the corner of my eye, always on the third floor," says Wainwright.

Alan Blangy, the manager in 1987, reported only one paranormal experience since his arrival. He said that one night as he was closing the theater, he thought he heard someone in the auditorium. "As I walked in, the fire escape exit door was closing. That made me suspicious. I went over to the fire escape door, which was ajar, and tried to pull it shut. Someone on the other side was pulling it too. We had this little struggle, and finally I pulled real hard and got it shut. I called for my assistant, who was there in a matter of seconds, and we both opened the door. No one was there." A long metal staircase lies outside the door and if anyone had jumped down those stairs, Blangy is sure he would have heard their steps. He is certain it was an entity. After that experience, the theater, which had felt hostile to him from the beginning, began to feel comfortable, as if he were finally accepted.

Paula Nechak co-managed the Harvard Exit from 1982-1983. One evening as she was closing up, an employee, an Asian woman whom Paula described as particularly prescient, came running down the stairs in tears. She kept saying, "Don't go to the second floor." She said she had opened a door and a woman was hanging there, crying.

The third floor has been the scene of other paranormal occurrences. Said Nechak, "I went up on the third floor one night to close the theater down and turn off the lights. As I was walking out, there were these people behind me, watching me. I just turned around and said, 'OK, OK, look at me. I'm not going to hurt you. Just look at me and get it over with.' Then I got out of there." Nechak has also heard of photographers who take photos of the third floor lobby when it is empty and later discover images of people sitting in the chairs.

Janet Wainwright, who left her job as manager of the Harvard Exit and later became president of the Seattle Foundation for Motion Picture Arts, feels strongly about the paranormal affinities of that theater. She feels that the sale of the property to the Landmark Theater Corporation has deeply affronted the resident ghosts. "I feel like I've betrayed the building. That building has a personality and something is awry now. I know that the ghosts are not happy and I feel guilty. That place has a really powerful, powerful energy. It scares me to the point where I've never been able to go back and see a movie since I left in 1979."

(Source: Article by Seattle Weekly *reporter Kathryn Robinson; article in* Pacific Northwest Magazine.*)*

The Neptune Theater

SEATTLE, WASHINGTON

The staff of Seattle Neptune Theater has quite a job on its hands. Not only does it have to deal with the crowds at its late night "Rocky Horror Picture Show" but after the live horrors go home, they have to clean up amid more ghostly horrors. For example, one janitor saw a screaming blue face emerge from the turquoise walls of the theater, another saw a woman in a flowing black gown floating five inches off the floor.

Pam Sprowl, a former manager of the Neptune, told reporter Jim Emerson of *Pacific Northwest* magazine that she had once seen something in the theater's organ loft that "was definitely not human." The huge Kimball Orchestral Pipe Organ featured in the 1921 opening of the theater had been the largest pipe organ on the West Coast. In 1985 the Puget Sound Theater Organ Society installed a Morton Pipe Organ in the loft to replace the long abandoned Kimball. The figure Sprowl saw prowling the organ loft was "a lady with dark hair and she was swathed in white and surrounded by light—only there's no way for light to get into that organ loft. I made sure that I was never in that theater alone again. You can have it happen and you think you're crazy, but the way to make sure you're not crazy is to see that it doesn't happen again!"

Janitor Sean Markland tells of using a gray lady ghost as an air conditioner. "We used to sort of summon her up and she would follow us around while we cleaned. We would get very hot when we cleaned, and she would keep us cool."

Markland tells also of a sinister entity in the theater. "It likes to hang out in the men's restroom and the balcony. You suddenly get this immense fear—it's so indescribable—and then you just have to leave."

Reporter Kathryn Robinson of the *Seattle Weekly* interviewed the Neptune Theater's manager, Dan Long. "I guess the infamous story is that I came in one weekend and found the top of the candy counter cracked," said Long. "On weekends we have *The Rocky Horror Picture Show* and janitors clean all night. I asked them what happened, and they're all hemming and hawing, and they said, 'Well, we dropped something,' but they were real elusive. Finally it came out that one janitor was pouring himself a Coke from the concessions counter at about 4 A.M. When he looked up he saw a young girl in a gray flowing dress moving through the lobby. 'Hey, we're closed,' he told her, and that's when he saw that she was transparent. She dissolved, and he dropped his Coke and cracked the counter."

Jeff Kurtti, a painter and odd hand at the theater told Robinson, "My friend Sean had quite a few experiences with the woman in gray, especially as a cold spot. She came in handy when you were cleaning and sweating like a pig, and she'd follow you around."

Late one night Kurtti had an unnerving experience. "It was about 2 A.M. I was just painting along when all of a sudden I felt the impact of another person rushing to get by me. I felt all the contact, pressure, and warmth I'd have felt if a person had pushed me out of the way. There was nobody there. When I regained balance, I looked over to see the swinging doors at the head of the aisle fly open."

And in the backstage area of the theater an odor of tobacco smoke often lingers, attributed by theater workers to a "smoking ghost."

Kurtti is philosophical about the hauntings: "These old quirky theaters are absolutely steeped in history. When you think of a three hundred seat theater that consistently sold out for years and years, of all the emotional energy that has gone through these spaces, you begin to wonder if those sounds you hear really are from the heating duct, or if it's a troop of ghost usherettes. I wouldn't be surprised at all to find out that the smoking ghost at the Neptune was actually some grizzled old theater manager that just couldn't let go of the space."

(Source: University of Washington Daily *reporter Shannon Gimble;* Pacific Northwest *writer Jim Emerson;* Seattle Weekly *reporter Kathryn Robinson.)*

The Moore-Egyptian Theater

SEATTLE, WASHINGTON

The ornate Moore Theater was built in 1907 as Seattle's first vaudeville theater. For a period during the late 1970s, it was run as a movie theater. The theater is heavily decorated in gilt Egyptian motifs so Dan Ireland and Darryl MacDonald called their enterprise the Moore-Egyptian. For a while they lived in the dressing room catacombs underneath the building. One night, returning home around 2 A.M., Ireland went up to the projection booth to turn off an amplifier. "I didn't turn on the lights because I'd never been afraid of the dark, especially not in that theater. I got to the top of the stairs and all of a sudden I just stopped. I heard this sound, this sighing, breathing sound, and there was a bad smell, like urine. I thought a rummie had gotten into the theater.

" 'Who's there?' I said, but there was nothing. I freaked and decided to run. I don't know what it was I ran through, but it was the most ... cold, tingling sensation I've ever felt. I locked myself in the booth and sat there for forty-five minutes screaming for Darryl. I was hysterical and wouldn't leave the booth until Darryl came up. When he did I was all white and shaking. I'd never had a supernatural experience until then."

When Ireland told their house manager about his experience she just looked at him. "Oh, did you meet him? We have a ghost."

Another employee who met the ghost was terrified. He felt like someone was following him ... and then the ghost ran through him!

When Ireland discovered several employees holding a seance in the theater lobby one night he fired the lot. "They had talked to three or four spirits in the theater. I just didn't think they should be playing around with stuff like that. I know this sounds really strange, but I believe the spirits in that theater liked us. We were the only people in thirty years who made a go of it there."

(Source: Pacific Northwest *writer Jim Emerson.)*

Haunted Theaters

Are theaters really the most haunted spots in the Northwest, or do theater folks just like to tell a good story. It seems that most theaters have a ghost of one kind or another. In addition to those detailed here, we hear of ghosts in Victoria in The McPherson Theater, Langely Court Theater, and Victoria's Royal Theater. And there are reports of ghosts at South Eugene High School theater, at Olympia's old State Theater, and at the Temple Theater of the Masonic Temple Building in Tacoma.

(

Shakespearean Ghosts at Ashland

Ashland, Oregon

There are reports of several Shakespearean ghosts on the prowl in the theaters of Ashland, Oregon. This small southern Oregon town's Shakespeare Festival has grown into an event lasting from April through November, with three theaters performing both Shakespeare and contemporary drama. It is said that the ghost of Charles Laughton haunts the Elizabethan Theater at Ashland. The story was told by actor Nathan Davis at a theater party one night:

I was talking to a lady, whose name unfortunately I have forgotten, but who is a receptionist in Ashland. She works in the office at the Shakespearean Festival, and we happened to get into a discussion about theater ghosts. And I suppose every theater has its own particular ghost, but anyway, among those supposedly haunting Ashland there's the spirit of Charles Laughton.

It wasn't very well known, but Laughton had always preferred legitimate theater over films, but being involved in films, he had many contracts to fill. He didn't have the opportunity to get as many stage performances as he'd like to do. And so in the summer of 1962 he was planning to be part of the summer festival at Ashland. He had sent in a resume and pictures just like everyone else, and of course he was immediately accepted. He was looking forward to it. It was the thing he most wanted to do, having finished umpteen films like *Spartacus* and *Advise and Consent* and so forth. And he was preparing to go to Ashland and he had to go to the hospital for a throat operation, and it turned out that he had cancer. And he died just a couple of months later, and he never made it to the Ashland Shakespearean Festival.

And as I understand it, in the summer of '62 they were doing *The Merry Wives of Windsor*, and Laughton was to play Sir John Falstaff. And so, of course, sadly, someone else had to be cast as Falstaff. But on the opening night in the outdoor theater during the midst of some of the funniest scenes a very distinct loud laugh was heard from the back of the stone wall which lines the back of the outdoor theater, and it was unmistakably Charles Laughton's. And his voice was heard several times during the course of the performance. And I thought it was a little amusing in a way, and was kind of joking about it with this lady, and she stopped me right there and said that it was taken very seriously in Ashland—that many people heard and experienced it.

And so later, she said, apparently someone saw Laughton wearing a costume of Falstaff. One of the people who was working backstage was walking down a corridor and this person was walking the other way. And she looked up and saw Laughton and recognized him, and he smiled at her and went on. It must have been pretty frightening.

But the whole thing is taken very seriously, and it's not talked about very much. You can't joke about it.

*   *   *

An Ashland worker, Dan Hayes, also remembered certain ghostly events that occurred while at Ashland:

The actor Charles Laughton was coming to Ashland to play King Lear, but died shortly before he was to come. Consequently whenever *King Lear* is performed in Ashland, his ghost haunts the

Theater. I was there when *King Lear* was first performed after Laughton's death. I was working backstage on sound. All of a sudden this eerie sound started moving through the audience and up onto the stage. Since I was working on sound, I had on my headphones and the eerie sound could be heard through them. The audience members were in complete amazement as were the actors. People who were there that evening will not talk about the event.

There is also a ghost that makes noises and moves around props during every performance of Shakespeare's *Twelfth Night* at Ashland. One night there was a very small crew and the stage manager heard the curtain track moving upstairs. He sent me up to check and I saw no one. After that he sent me up two more times and I finally realized that it was the ghost and came down to tell the stage manager that it was "only the ghost."

One more thing, there are four levels in the theater at the Shakespeare Festival in Ashland. On the third level there is an old abandoned Public Relations Office. There is a singing ghost outside the office. He sings madrigals every night and is a man and very tall and friendly. People would go and listen to him sing, and I, on one occasion, sat and listened to him.

(Source: Nathan Davis and Dan Hayes in Randall V. Mills Archives, University of Oregon.)

Showboat Theater Haunted by
Late Drama School Director

SEATTLE, WASHINGTON

For years the huge old Showboat Theater which stood at the water's edge just below the University of Washington was believed to be haunted. Chief candidate for the ghost was Glen Hughes, former head of the school of drama. An old, white-haired man was seen around the theater from time to time. He would vanish suddenly.

One evening as the ticket manager was counting receipts in his office, he heard the piano being played in the theater. The building was supposed to be empty so he checked. When he got to the stage, no one was at the piano.

Another evening a woman was rehearsing her lines alone on stage. Suddenly, she heard another actor behind her answering her cue lines. But when she turned ... no one was there.

Of course students are always eager to make the most of a good ghostly possibility. One student told *University of Washington Daily* reporter Jim Caple, "Have you ever been down to the waterfront by the Health Science building and seen that old showboat? It's an authentic showboat from the Mississippi River and then UW had it shipped out here and turned it into a theater. But the interesting thing about the Showboat Theater is the ghost that lives there. Seriously. I have a friend who's a drama major and he's heard all sorts of stories about the ghost. Curtains rising and closing by themselves, voices from empty rooms, a ghostly image of a white-haired man—crap like that. I don't believe a word of it myself of course, but my friends swear there's a ghost at the Showboat."

In fact the Showboat Theater is not a real showboat at all. It was built in the form of a showboat in 1938 and sits on pilings. Still it is an old, creaking wooden structure and appears to float mysteriously on the water. It has stood abandoned for years now, condemned to human inhabitants by building inspectors. It is not clear whether the ghost left with the over-imaginative students or whether it remains, waiting for renovations and a new batch of humans with whom to interact.

(Source: Article by University of Washington Daily *reporter Jim Caple.)*

Fifth Avenue Theater & Paramount Theater

SEATTLE, WASHINGTON

Sean Markland reports seeing a ghost in the balcony of the Fifth Avenue Theater back when it was a movie house, "but they cleaned it so thoroughly when they restored it that it's sterile now." The theater has been completely renovated and restored to its early grandeur. It is used for upscale touring stage productions.

Jeff Kurtti reports seeing a whole balcony full of ghosts one afternoon when he was working at the Paramount, but that was several years ago. Dan Long, manager of the Neptune movie theater, thinks ghosts don't reside so well in today's theaters. "They say at the Paramount that they've had so many rock concerts that it's driven them all away. It's like here at the Neptune. We've had *The Rocky Horror Picture Show* at midnight for eight years, so the spirits come out late at night and say, 'Oh damn! Not this again. Let's go someplace else!' "

(Source: Pacific Northwest writer Jim Emerson.)

Capitol Theater Ghost Saves Girl's Life

YAKIMA, WASHINGTON

The Capitol Theater in Yakima has lived comfortably with its ghost for over fifty years now. They call him "Shorty" and point to the inaccessible door twelve feet up a concrete block wall backstage. It stands just slightly ajar and leads to a space never entered by humans since there is no way to reach it without a ladder. They call it "Shorty's door."

What does Shorty do about the theater? Well, the usual theater ghost's tricks. He opens and closes doors, lowers the curtains when the crew wants them up, turns lights on and off for no reason. Except in this case, Capitol stage manager Roger Smith swears Shorty turned the lights on while Roger himself was actually sitting at the console. And lighting expert Moe Broom says Shorty turned on the work lights once when Moe himself was standing just three feet from the switch. Definitely not a human prankster in these cases.

Then there was the night Shorty made spotlights dance onstage during a ballet. Roger suspected a prankster in the catwalks and climbed up. He found footprints in the dust, but there was no way a person could have climbed up there and escaped without being seen.

Like his cousin ghosts in Seattle theaters, Shorty seems to hate rock and roll concerts. He hides tools and messes up the lights every time they try to present one at the Capitol.

However the stage girls try to woo Shorty's affection by leaving him cookies at night. They are always gone in the morning. And once he even saved a girl's life. A piece of light shutter broke loose overhead and was falling directly at her. Suddenly it moved sideways and stuck into the stage instead. Moe Broom saw it happen.

In 1988 theater director Steve Caffery allowed two ghost hunting experts to examine the theater. But he would hear no talk of exorcism. "I won't tolerate any interference with Shorty," Caffery ordered with a straight face. "I'm only permitting the study of his existence or non-existence."

The investigators, using a heat sensor, detected hot spots near "Shorty's Door" and at a spot in the beam lights high overhead. But the heat source was not strong enough to definitely say there was a presence there.

The staff, however, have no doubts about Shorty's existence. As *Yakima Herald Republic* writer Jim Gosney reported:

"In the front office ... when there is no one—repeat, no one—in the theater, there is occasionally heard the noise of a toilet flushing."

Have the office workers ever investigated? "No. Of course not. Even ghosts deserve their privacy."

(Source: Yakima Herald Republic *reporter Jim Gosney.)*

The Barkerville Theater:
A Chorus Line Ghost and an Actor in the Wings

BARKERVILLE, BRITISH COLUMBIA

The historic gold rush town of Barkerville has been restored in recent years to tourist attraction status. The Theater Royal on Main Street opened in May of 1868, but it was burned to the ground in the Barkerville fire only five months later. In 1869 the theater was rebuilt, but as the gold rush ran out, the theater's audiences dwindled, and by 1872 it closed its doors. The building served a number of uses after that. It even was the town morgue for a time. In 1937, the decrepit building was torn down. However, in the late 1950s, the Theater Royal was rebuilt on its original site as part of the town's historic reconstruction. This new building on the old site seems to be haunted.

Security officers who check the building's fire alarm system regularly report the sound of strange footsteps overhead when they are checking the alarm system under the stage. One day during rehearsals the sound of someone playing a hammer dulcimer came through the house sound system. Then it was joined by the sound of a woman's voice humming along. Neither of the house's two sound systems were turned on at the time.

On several occasions actors have glanced toward stage left during performances to see a nicely dressed gentleman standing in the wings. He wears a top hat and tails and sports a neatly trimmed moustache. When the performer glances back for a second look ... he is gone.

But most intriguing of the Barkerville theater ghosts is the mysterious dancer who appeared onstage in the chorus line a few years ago. No one knows who she was, but that evening, there was definitely an extra dancer onstage.

(Source: Ghosts: True Stories from British Columbia *by Robert C. Belyk.)*

The Blue Ghost of Everett High School

EVERETT, WASHINGTON

Several tales have been told around Everett High School about the "Blue Ghost" who haunts the auditorium. It is said that a workman renovating the civic auditorium ceiling stepped through the plasterboard and fell to his death on the seats below, breaking his neck. Student Bill Williamson told of his own experiences with the ghost.

"The first experience I had with the ghost was in 1969, the year that the high school put on *Carousel*. I was working the crew with Steve S., Laridon G., Darrel L. and Mark T., up on the pin, and Mr. Reber was the stage crew head at the time. He was head of construction, and we had all of our food and goodies in a place called the cave. The cave had a table with all of the food. We were watching the show and saw a helium balloon going up from the stage. It went up and we decided we would go up and retrieve it. So Mark started to go up the ladder and we didn't think anything of it because it was going to pop anyway. So Mark came back down the ladder and there was the intermission. There was a rope that was up on the grid, which is the highest area you can get to in the civic auditorium. The rope had come untied and was dangling down on the stage so we couldn't pull the curtain until it was tied back up. So Mark went back up the ladder to tie it up and as soon as he got up there he saw something. He didn't know what. He didn't even touch the ladder when coming down. He slid down with his hands and feet on the side of the ladder. We couldn't get anything coherent out of him for five or ten minutes, and he was white as a sheet.

According to Williamson, the next night "Mr. Reber was telling us that it was a bunch of malarky and he looked up and he saw a glow up on the grid, but all the power up there was off because of the show."

*   *   *

During 1968-1969, Mr. H., an Everett High teacher, had been working alone on stage one night when the follow spot from the lighting booth in the back of the auditorium suddenly came on and began to follow him around the stage. There was no one else in the building at the time. When his students made fun of his fear, Mr. H. dared one of them to spend the night in the auditorium. So Dennis and his girlfriend Lori set up camp on the stage one evening with their sleeping bags, flashlights, radio, and snacks. Suddenly around 1 A.M. the seats began coming down. The janitor always pushes the auditorium seats up before he leaves in the evening so he can sweep the theater. One after another they banged down. Dennis grabbed his flashlight and ran down into the auditorium thinking to catch Mr. H. trying to frighten him. He stood there and watched as row after row of seats came down all by themselves. He and his girlfriend fled.

Another night Bill Williamson encountered a ghost himself. He was working late developing photos for the school yearbook. The janitor left around 10:30. Williamson said goodbye to the janitor and retreated to his darkroom in a small room behind one of the classrooms. "I was in the back storeroom when I heard the front door to the classroom open and slam. I thought, 'The janitor's back. I won't worry about it.' Then I heard some laughter, and then I heard seats being moved around. I thought somebody was playing a trick on me, because I know that the ghost usually stays in his habitat. This wasn't in the auditorium, this was in the main building. So I opened up the door to the main classroom and it was incredibly cold. It wasn't that way before because I usually set the thermostat up because they never really had the room at the right temperature anyhow. They usually had them at seventy degrees and I always put them up to eighty degrees. I felt a cold blast of air. I didn't see anything and the door slammed shut.

"So I went back to the phone and told Mark to hang on, and I took a look out in the hall. Nobody was out there .... I didn't think anything of it then, you know, I just thought it was somebody trying to pull a prank on me. I went back to the room and I talked to Mark a little bit more, hung up, and went back into the darkroom to develop some more prints.

"Again I heard the door to the front classroom open and slam, laughter, and chairs being moved. I came out of the darkroom and I whirled around. I grabbed one of the photographic electric strobes and I decided that I was going to blind this guy for doing this to me."

Williamson followed footsteps up the stairs but found no one. He checked all classrooms and exit doors. All was locked. No one anywhere. "I decided, well, they're hiding somewhere and they're hiding quite well, so I'll just wait for them until the next time. So I went back down the stairs. I had left the door to the darkroom open and when I got back down there it was closed and locked. There was only one way to lock that door and that was from the inside. So I started towards the phone and just then the door just flew open. In fact, there's still a dent in the darkroom wall where the door flew open and banged the wall. I felt a blast of cold air and, somehow, as an automatic response, I flashed the strobe. All I saw was a shadow against the wall, but there was nothing to register the shadow. It was of a man and it looked as if it didn't have any clothes on other than maybe a faint outline of a shroud.

"I threw down the strobe and took off out of the building. I saw my friend's car at the south end of the building, but I ran completely around the block and beat him to the next corner. I jumped in the car and he was shouting, 'What's wrong? What's wrong!' I yelled, 'Shut up and drive!' And that's it."

(Source: Everett High School student Bill Williamson in Bananabread, Waterways.*)*

HAUNTED COLLEGES AND BOARDING SCHOOLS

Considering the proclivity of teens to create and expand horror tales, it would be surprising not to find ghosts on our college campuses. College and high school theater ghosts appeared in the chapter on Theater Ghosts. Here are a few more education-loving ghosts.

Ghost at the Burnley School of Professional Art

SEATTLE, WASHINGTON

Students working late at the Burnley School of Professional Art in downtown Seattle were never lonely. They usually had the company of a ghost. *Seattle Times* reporter Paul Andrews describes the ghost's approach: "He begins by walking slowly up the old wooden stairs, thock, thock, thock, like the ticking of a clock. He'll proceed down one of the narrow, high-ceilinged corridors, his feet making sandpapery sliding sounds on the worn plank floors—a sound that can make skin crawl and swallowing difficult.

"Then he'll turn into a room and maybe take a seat at a desk, maybe rearrange pens and papers or shift in his chair."

The school's owners believe "Burnley," as he is affectionately called, may be the ghost of an eighteen-year-old Broadway High School student who was killed in a fight playing pickup basketball in the Burnley School's tiny third floor gym. During the fight, the student fell down a back flight of stairs and died. Nan Cooper, daughter of the school's former owner, Jess Cauthorn, and a teacher at the school now, believes "he wants to play ball and doesn't like the fact it's an art school. That's why he keeps moving things around."

Robert B. Theriault, a graphics designer, remembers one night in 1966. He was working late at the school, around two or three in the morning.

"I was busy with a project and heard sounds like someone getting themselves a cup of coffee from the coffee room, which was a long room around the corner and about halfway down the hall from my studio.

"It sounded as though someone was moving around, adjusting their chair, that sort of thing. I figured I'd go say hello. I was literally walking right up into the room hearing more and more sounds. But when I got there, no one was around. The room was totally empty."

Marilyn Blume, daughter of Edwin and Elsie Burnley who opened the school in 1946, worked there as a receptionist. She often helped her father lock up at night and unlock in the morning. Time and again the doors, which had been carefully locked, were found open in the morning. "We never felt threatened or frightened," she said. "We were mostly baffled. We hoped that this ghost simply accepted us and could exist with us."

The ghost travels also to a bank on the main floor of the building in which the school is located. There a coffee machine switches itself on, dishes rattle in a back room kitchen, and strange cool pockets of air are experienced. Lights switch on and off by themselves, and security alarms are set off for no apparent reason. "Every time we have work done on the alarm system, it goes off by itself," says a bank representative. "We joke that maybe the ghost isn't aware we made a change and happened to walk the wrong way."

Source: Seattle Times/Post Intelligencer *reporter Paul Andrews.)*

* * *

Still more Burnley stories were reported to Kathryn Robinson of the *Seattle Weekly.* A morning janitor turning on the lights in the darkened building one morning heard a crash from one of the classrooms. Rushing to investigate, he found the middle row of desks all turned over on their sides. A student recalls standing in the hallway while footsteps approached and passed right by her ... without a body to make them. Nan Cooper tells of hearing something being dragged across the floor overhead one day. She hurried upstairs to see what was going on and found a heavy model stand had been moved from one end of the room to the other ... but no one was there who could have moved it.

The Burnley School of Professional Art moved from its haunted home at the corner of Broadway and Pine in 1983. Apparently the ghost stayed with the building. In 1987 employees of Seattle Community College, which was using the building as its south annex, reported continued contact with "Burnley." They concur with the suggestion that he is the ghost of a teenage boy. "Burnley" seems only to pester young women. "He never seems to bother the guys," complains Isabel Trejo-Conner, who manages the microcomputer lab on the building's second floor. One day as she was sitting in the middle of the storage room taking inventory, a shelf full of software hit her on the head. It came from a shelf in the corner ... too far away to naturally fall onto her head. A few days later the same thing happened again. "I told Burnley to cut it out, that I had work to do," says Trejo-Conner, "and he hasn't bothered me since. Not yet anyway."

(Source: Seattle Weekly *reporter Kathryn Robinson.)*

The Leg Pulling Old Woman
of Royal Roads Military College

VICTORIA, BRITISH COLUMBIA

The Dunsmuir family were at one time said to be one of the wealthiest families in the Pacific Northwest. Robert Dunsmuir arrived in British Columbia in 1851 from Kilmarnock, Scotland and began prospecting for coal on Vancouver Island. From his log cabin beginning he rose to become a wealthy coal baron with a magnificent home, Craigdarroch Castle, built in Victoria. His eldest son, James, wanting to equal his father's estate, built his own stone castle at Hatley Park in 1908 at a cost of $4,000,000.

Days of glorious entertaining at Hatley Park followed. But in

1929 most of the family fortune was lost in the stock market crash. James had already died by this time and his wife, Laura, lived on almost destitute in the now empty castle. After her death the property stood empty for four years and then in 1940 the defense department purchased it for $75,000—less than the original cost of just the stone fence which surrounds the property.

Shortly after Laura Dunsmuir's death one of the maids caring for the building reported an uncomfortable feeling in the mansion—as if someone unseen was watching her. She refused to enter some of the rooms alone.

In time the building was turned into a naval academy, and over the years many students have had strange encounters within its walls. A strange sensation, like that of walking into a mass of freezing cobwebs, is reported to occur on the second and third floors of the building from time to time. Students have awakened to see a little old woman standing by their beds.

One student reported that the little old woman did more than just stare at him. Sometime in the early hours of the morning he had been awakened by someone pulling his leg. He opened his eyes to see an old woman standing before him. He tried to shake his leg free but she held on with such strength that he could not break loose. Eventually he did manage to wrench his leg free, at which she vanished.

It is conjectured that the spirit is that of Laura Dunsmuir, still making the rounds of her home. Perhaps she is incensed to find so many young men camped in her rooms and is attempting to drive them out.

(Source: Ghost: True Stories from British Columbia *by Robert C. Belyk;* Alex Dunsmuir's Dilemma *by James Audain.)*

A Musical Ghost at
Gonzaga University's Monaghan Hall

SPOKANE, WASHINGTON

Gonzaga University's Monaghan Hall was the scene of some bizarre musical goings-on a few years ago. Reports that an exorcism had to take place to rid the hall of its organ-playing ghost were denied by university administrators. Later they explained to *National Observer* reporter Dan Morris that rites were performed, but that a complete exorcism was not carried out.

The mansion that became Monaghan Hall was built in 1898 by James Monaghan. In 1939 Gonzaga began using the structure. But the haunting troubles seem to have begun in the 1970s. One Friday evening in November a housekeeper stopped by the hall to pick up an item she had forgotten to take home. She was surprised to find the hall's front door unlocked. A one-finger exercise was being practiced on the organ upstairs. No students should have been in the building at this hour, so the housekeeper went upstairs to see who was practicing. The door to the organ room was locked and no light seemed to be on inside. She went for the key and unlocked the door. The organ continued to play its strange notes. But the room was empty. The windows were locked.

In January, Jesuit Walter F. Leedale heard flute music outside his Monaghan Hall studio. He searched and found no musician. In mid-February Leedale, sitting at the piano in his studio, began playing the eight note fragment he had heard from the phantom flute. The housekeeper overheard his playing and told him this was the same tune she had heard on the organ that November night.

"I was totally skeptical about the whole issue," said Leedale. "But I gradually began to investigate on my own what I considered pure imagination or the power of suggestion. Students reported different types of things, but mostly the footsteps sort of thing." Leedale began sleeping on a roll-out couch in his office in the music building to check out the strange reports. Soon he had enough experiences to convince him there were unseen forces about. One day he found "an absolutely locked door just opening in front of me as I went to put my key in the lock. The handle turned, and it opened. I went in, and the room was empty."

In February two security guards and two Gonzaga faculty members checked out the building. A student caretaker-guard was with them. As they stood outside the building talking on the grounds, one of the guards thought he saw something at a third floor window. Both guards then saw something at the second floor window. The men quickly inspected both the first and second floor, finding nothing. However, on the third floor, in a narrow hall which connected a practice room with a fire escape, they encountered what they called an "unseen force." A faculty priest and a guard both felt tingling in their skin. One of the guards felt a "strangling sensation" and the student was nearly overcome "with this oppressive presence." But they saw nothing.

On February 24 the Jesuit priest made the rounds of the building offering prayers of exorcism. Though this is not the same thing as a formal church exorcism, the use of these prayers seems to have excited the spirits. While reading the ritual prayers for exorcism the crucifix around the priest's neck began to swing. He steadied the crucifix, but it began to swing again. Music Department Chairman Daniel Josef Brenner described the swinging cross as about eight inches long, weighing at least half a pound. "It simply wouldn't stay the right way. I was assisting Father Leedale with the prayers, holding the holy water so that he could hold the prayer book and keep the cross still at the same time."

The priest went patiently from floor to floor for four days, reciting the entire ritual six times. By February 28 the mysterious presence seemed to have been laid to rest.

(Source: National Observer *reporter Dan Morris;* Western Gothic *by Carol J. Lind.)*

A Singing Ghost at Pacific University

FOREST GROVE, OREGON

In the autumn of 1971 a student working as night watchman at Pacific University had an unusual encounter. As he approached the school's music building to make his nightly check and lock the building, he was surprised to hear a woman still practicing in the third floor library. The music school was located in a stately old Victorian home known as Knight Hall.

The watchman entered to tell the singer it was time to leave, but as he climbed the stairs to the second and then the third floor he began to feel uneasy, for no apparent reason. When he reached the third floor landing the singing suddenly stopped. He pushed open the library door. No one was inside. At first the hair rose on his neck. But then he realized it must be a practical joke and began to search the room for a hidden tape recorder. He found none.

Assuming someone had been been singing in the room and then slipped out somehow, he began to search the house for the prankster. He checked the second floor and started to descend to the first. Then suddenly he saw her. She was standing in front of a professor's office. Just a woman's shape. Filmy and bluish white. Then she drifted away … and was gone.

The student continued to carry out his duties, making the rounds of the school's buildings each night. But after that experience, he bought a large German shepherd and kept the dog by his side … especially when locking up Knight Hall. One night as they approached Knight Hall the dog growled. The hair rose on its back. It whined and jumped up to the window, but refused to enter the building. Knight Hall did not get checked that night and the student-watchman did not encounter the "blue lady" again.

* * *

In the early 1980s Dr. Donald Schwejda, a retired music professor, came to the building on Christmas Day. He planned to record some music away from the noisy festivities at home. In the middle of the recording Dr. Schwejda heard footsteps coming down the hall. He worried that the person would come into his office and speak, ruining the tape. So he tiptoed to the door to warn the person to keep quiet. But no one was there.

Another professor, who had a similar experience during that same Christmas vacation, refused to ever go back ever into the building when it was empty.

* * *

In 1979 two reporters from the student paper spent a night in

Knight Hall and found plenty to be frightened by. Footsteps were heard, lights went out, an alto voice sang, and long, rustling skirts were heard brushing past. When one of the reporters began to play the piano, a female voice whispered in his ear twice, "Oh, please stop!" The reporters returned with some friends on the next night. When one of the friends began to play the piano a heavy sigh was heard. Apparently the ghost did not care for their performances.

Students have given the ghost a name. A Ouija board séance in the building drew the name "Vera" and a search of old records uncovered a music student named Vera who had died. Perhaps in this very building. Perhaps a suicide.

(Sources: Western Gothic *by Carol J. Lind;* The Ghostly Register: A Guide to Haunted America *by Arthur Meyers.)*

GHOSTLY SHOPS

Even shopping in the Northwest can be a ghostly experience. Here are a few haunted shopping sites, including Seattle's famous Pike Place Market, where ghost hunting tours are held at times!

The Boiler Room Ghost of
Mother's World Clothing Store

KENNEWICK, WASHINGTON

When Sue Schoonover moved her business, Mother's World, into an old downtown Kennewick building, it didn't take long for her to realize that something was amiss in her new shop. She would come into the store in the morning to find that large clothing racks had been shifted during the night. Lights she had turned off carefully before leaving the night before would be on again. "Things were where they shouldn't be. Doors were opened. At first we blamed each other," said Schoonover. After a while, they began to refer to the strange behavior as the work of a ghost. She thinks the source of the haunting may come from the building's dusty old boiler room. An old cot covered with a moth-eaten Army blanket and an old quilt were found there. The first time she set foot in this room the boiler began a horrendous clanking the moment she stepped out of the room. "It was really eerie," she recalled.

Schoonover and her staff began to refer to the ghost as "Freddy." When she removed an old oak desk that is now in her office, the spirit acted up and moved her for-sale clothing around in the store. "I think that (moving the desk) made him cranky," she smiled.

No one knows for sure who the ghost is. An old twelve by twelve inch safe was found perched on the edge of the boiler room cot one day. In it were the papers of a man named H.C. DeHaven dating from the 1950s. "Maybe Freddy is trying to tell us who he is," conjectured Schoonover. Or the safe may just have fallen from a nearby bookcase.

After an article about Freddy appeared in the *Tri-City Herald,* a reader wrote to suggest that the ghost might be that of former Kennewick mayor George Sherk who operated a mercantile store in that building from 1913 until 1924. He died when his car plunged off a thirty-foot embankment near La Grande, and she thought he might have returned to keep an eye on the business. Others suggest even more nefarious prospects. A secret staircase leads from a first floor trap door through the boiler room, and legend says that an adjoining room was a card room during Prohibition. The building was at one time home of the Commercial Club, and over the years was home to a series of businesses: a TV repair shop, flooring sales, music store, J.C. Penney's, and others.

Whoever Freddy is, Schoonover is content sharing the building with him. She went ahead and purchased the property despite his presence. "He's not a good Halloween ghost," she said. "He's more of a nuisance ghost. He never gives you the feeling of being afraid. I think he knows we are all right now, that we're going to take care of the building. Sometimes, when I'm working here alone, it's almost comforting to know he's here."

(Source: Tri-City Herald *reporter Kathleen Knutson.)*

Pike Place Market Hauntings

SEATTLE, WASHINGTON

During the daytime Seattle's Pike Place Market is a bustling, joyful place alive with bright colors and the sounds of shouting vendors, street musicians, groups of exploring tourists, and locals going about their shopping. However the market's vendors pack up and go home at 5 P.M. and the five stories of shops and vendor stalls turn into a cavernous, empty cement and wooden shell. Even during the day, the market's creaking wooden floors and darkly catacombed lower levels can give a moment of chill. No wonder that a ghost, or ghosts are expected to wander here.

Best known of the Pike Place ghosts is an Indian woman who wears her hair in braids. One rumor has it that she is Princess Angeline, daughter of Chief Seattle. Another suggests that she is a woman who visited the market in its earliest days to sell woven baskets. Lynn Hancock, who bought the Craft Emporium in 1982, has encountered the woman in her store on several occasions. "One day an Indian woman came into the store—I could draw you a picture, I remember her so clearly. She walked back to look at the seed beads on the back wall. After a while I went back and said, 'May I help you?' and she disappeared right in front of me. I closed the store. I went across to the restroom and just stood there." Eight months later the Indian woman came back in and went to stare at the wall of beads again. Hancock didn't recognize her until she disappeared. Since then the woman has come into the store "about four or five times." Hancock just lets her look at the beads. "I don't bother her, she doesn't bother me."

(Source: Seattle Weekly *writer Kathryn Robinson.)*

*   *   *

Seattle Times columnist Rick Anderson reported on another sighting of the Indian woman. A fellow named Leon told him about the figure.

"When I first saw it," he said, "I was standing with a couple other people outside our shops on the market's lower level one evening in 1964. I had a little gift shop down there then.

"The spectre came down the walk near the Needle Nook and turned as if to go toward the Goodwill store.

"All four of us saw it, and while it looked like a normal person to me, I was told by the other three that it was a ghost, so I tried to catch up with it as it walked past my stall and it simply vanished into thin air."

Leon's friends told him this was the ghost of an Indian woman who used to bring woven baskets to the market to sell in the early 1900s.

"I'd seen the Indian woman walk by my shop before," said Leon. "And although she seemed somewhat odd, moving slowly as if her feet barely touched the floor, and never turning her head, always looking straight ahead, I had thought she was human.

"That night we stood there. Someone said, 'There's the ghost.' I watched her go by, kind of a large woman, with grayish black hair. Her long dress seemed to be lavender and then pink, as if it changed color. I was stunned. The woman—you could, well, it seemed you could see right through her. A translucent thing.

"She walked up towards Goodwill and I went after her. I tried to catch up with her. She was just gone. I searched everywhere. One of the women even looked in a restroom nearby. She was just gone."

Though he never saw the woman again, Leon now worried about having seen the figure: "The other three people, Bill, Marie and Ruth, who saw it that day; they're all dead. Bill had a heart attack. Marie committed suicide. And Ruth was murdered. I think Ruth was affected by the sight most of all. I remember her trembling when we all first saw it.

"I've asked others if they've seen the ghost. If they have, they're not saying. Maybe they're afraid to talk about it."

This was reported in Rick Anderson's column July 23, 1983. Anderson probably succeeded in implanting the legend about a curse being attached to the sighting of the Indian woman ghost. He concludes the column by saying that since then his informant, Leon, has disappeared ... implying that foul play or death may have befallen Leon.

*   *   *

In October of 1983 Rick Mann, then a fifteen year veteran of the market and owner of Old Friends Antiquities, told writer Paul Andrews that the ghost had inhabited Goodwill on the Market's lower level until that space was closed for remodeling. "What I heard all along is that she would come out of Goodwill and walk up and down the ramps," he said. "She really doesn't bother anybody. She just kind of walks around. There is a white light that surrounds her so she glows as she moves along." Andrews reported that the Indian woman, stocky and crinkle-skinned, with a serene expression on her face, wore a quilted shawl, faded with age, and carried woven baskets.

(*Source:* Seattle Times *writer Paul Andrews.*)

* * *

Though the Market retains much of its earlier flavor, it has undergone renovation in recent years and its future seems constantly in turmoil as urban pioneers envision more lucrative uses for its spaces. For a brief period, the market was even sold to investors from New York, which horrified Seattle's residents.

By 1990, the Indian Woman ghost seems to have disappeared from the market. When Anderson interviewed Rick Mann, who he calls "the official keeper of the legend," Mann told him, "Indian woman, glowing white, she walked through walls. Everyone who saw her has since died an unusual death." Mann's shop worker, Dave Sweeny, had a theory about why the ghost had vanished. "She moved out just about the time The Urban Group moved in," said Sweeny. "She must have got scared."

However, no need for alarm. Anderson reports that another ghost is alive and well in the market. A lively male spirit haunts the mezzanine level, according to a Market security officer and a business woman there. Lynn Roberts of the Market Bead Shop described it as a mischievous presence. "The first time I knew he was there is when he came up and did this" (tugged on her sleeve). "There was no one there when I turned around." On another day he kept turning on her shop radio. "I turned it off. He turned it on again. I unplugged it. It has no batteries. And it still played. The ghost hangs around all the time," says Roberts. "It's just something you have to accept."

And then of course there's the Fat Lady Ghost. "That's got something to do with a three hundred pound woman who fell through a false ceiling and landed on a table." says Rick Mann. "But I can't be sure about her."

(*Source:* Seattle Times *columnist Rick Anderson.*)

* * *

By 1992 an entrepreneurial market merchant, Michael Yaeger, had begun leading guided tours of the market's haunts. The tours left from the Zamboanga Gallery and included:

+ The Ghost of Arthur Goodwin, a former market director, who has been seen gazing through the windows of the Goodwin Library to the left of the market clock.

+ The Swing Shift Dancer, a man who appears on the floor above the Goodwin Library where Boeing workers used to attend dances during World War II. The dancer is a dapper dresser, very light on his feet.

+ The Fat Woman Ghost, who haunts the lower level near the puppet shop. She is said to be the spirit of a woman barber who used to lull her clients to sleep so she could steal change from their pockets. She fell through this floor to her death below, according to the legend.

+ The Indian Woman Ghost described in detail above, who by 1992 had finally been exorcised by the Bead Shop owners.

+ The Little Boy Ghost who also haunts the lower levels of the market and likes to play with the marionettes in the puppet shop.

If Yaeger's tours are a success, one would expect ghosts to flock to the place for a piece of the action. So check out the Market again in a few years.

(Source: Seattle Times *reporter Jean Godden.)*

Is Pier 70 Haunted?

SEATTLE, WASHINGTON

Seattle's 550 foot long Pier 70 was built in 1889. In those days the pier was busy with ships from the British Blue Funnel Line and the German owned Hamburg America Line. A huge warehouse just up the hill from the pier is now home of the Old Spaghetti Factory restaurant. And Pier 70 itself has been remodeled to hold a plethora of tiny shops and restaurants.

Brad Aylward, manager of the Pier 1 Imports store (on Pier 70) hasn't seen anything, but others have. They believe the ghost to be a dark-haired, bearded sailor in a peacoat. Maybe he was done in and tossed into the sound during the rougher days of Seattle's youth, they speculate. At any rate, "They've all said that they felt a presence somewhere in the shop, usually while they were closing up or cleaning up. They would turn around, and there he'd be," says Brad. Employees have dubbed the ghost "Paddy" and he has been seen as well "in the mirror of a private rest room up near the front of the store."

Aylward tells also of his wife's experiences working in the store. "My wife, Amy, who was a management trainee at this location several years ago, said there were some strange, unexplained things. She said that at night, when the place was closed and the power was turned off, something or someone would turn on the electric cash registers and the tapes would run and run out onto the floor. Nothing was missing; nothing was damaged. Just a sort of mischief."

At the Astro-Bio shop near the end of the pier, Norman Foster told reporter John Hahn that he thought the spirit "is trying to communicate with us." He had seen "a pillar of smoke, swirling above a chair, as though someone or something was trying to manifest itself."

Kevin Callow, of the Earth Plants/Earth Lines shop on the Pier, also has "what I can only explain as a presence" in his shop. Callow also says some have seen a ghost ship lying off Pier 70.

(Source: Seattle Post-Intelligencer.*)*

Funeral Parlor Leaves Haunts Behind

SEATTLE, WASHINGTON

In 1903 E.R. Butterworth constructed a home for his mortuary business on First Avenue in downtown Seattle. He had been in the funeral parlor business in Seattle since 1892 and business was booming. The four story brick building which he constructed was a showplace among funeral parlors. The bottom floor held stables, a garage for hearses, a cremation oven, and a vault for ashes. On the first floor were viewing rooms, sitting rooms, and a chapel with choir loft. Business offices occupied the second floor, and Seattle's first hydraulic elevator carried the grieving to the top floor to shop for caskets. The embalming was also done on that floor. E.R. Butterworth is said to have coined the terms "mortician" and "mortuary." For twenty years The Butterworth Building saw the city's deceased pass through its doors. Then in 1923 the Butterworth family moved their firm to a Capitol Hill location, but they seem to have left a few of their customers behind.

The restaurant and shop owners who currently inhabit the Butterworth building experience regular visitors who are not of this world. Bill Perkins, a manager at Cafe Sophie on the building's first floor, tells of the night the electrician attempted to rewire one of the cafe's chandeliers. It was after midnight when the electrician began his work in the empty cafe. After a while he realized that two shadowy men were sitting at one of the tables talking. The two got up and came over to help hold his ladder when he began to work on a particularly tricky part of the wiring. They continued their conversation, but he was so absorbed in his work that he didn't pay much attention. Then a women in an "unearthly white linen dress" entered the dining room. The men stared at her and began to shout insults as she walked past. Then they began to shout insults at each other. The electrician suddenly realized that his "helpers" were not of this world. He raced from the cafe, leaving the work unfinished. He was reportedly found by the cooks early in the morning, sitting on the curb muttering that he couldn't take it anymore.

Cafe Sophie's pastry chef, Valerie Mudry, also had a run-in with supernatural inhabitants. She has tales to tell about silverware which slides off tables, and footsteps in the women's rest room when no one is in there. That she can put up with. But for one two-week period she had to struggle with a pastry cream thief every night! She would be stirring some lemon custard on the stove, turn away, and turn back to find it missing. Later she would find it sitting on a table. Finally she'd had enough. "I'd just found a pot of pastry cream I'd been looking for back on one of the tables with a spoon and fork beside it," she said. "I was getting really tired of all this. So I stood in the middle of the room and said, 'Hey, folks. Don't mess with me. I'm here too late, and I don't need assistance from you. If you want to help, stir something on the stove or carry something up to the front case, but otherwise leave me alone.' That did the trick. She was left to cook in peace after that."

* * *

Kells restaurant and pub on the bottom floor of the same building also has its ghosts. Cocktail straws mysteriously appear on patron's heads, locked doors blow open in the night, candles light themselves. And, well, a plumber discovered "wee little piles of ashes" beneath some of the floorboards. Remember there had been a crematorium on this lower floor. Owner Joe and Edna McAleese have their stories to tell.

"I've never seen nothing, to tell you the God's truth," Edna told reporter Johnny Dodd in 1990, "except for my Garrard telling me he saw a shadow on the floor." Her oldest son, Garrard, was putting fixtures into one of the restaurant's bathrooms one evening. The empty room slowly filled with the sound of mumbling voices. As time passed it grew louder until it disturbed him. He turned on his radio to drown it out so he could concentrate. Then he saw the shadow. "He got the chisel to whack it, only there was nothing there. Just that noise going 'gabbling, gabbling, gabbling.' " At that he abandoned his task and ran upstairs, begging someone to sit with him for the rest of the night.

Joe McAleese tells of a whiskey bottle rolling off a shelf into a stack of glasses without shattering. And relates how a customer who had recently died came back to visit the pub one evening. However, things are too quiet at Kells nowadays. It seems a priest came down and blessed the place.

* * *

Laura Delassandro ran an antique clothing shop, Isadora's, on the first floor for five years. She lived behind the shop with her two teenage children. She felt the space was already inhabited. "It definitely did seem to have more than its fair share of spiritual energy." She believed that the entities hovered near the ceiling during the day. After work she would sometimes lie on the shop floor and try to coax them down. One night she bumped into a spirit. "He was bad, very bad ... negative, dark, and heavy. He startled me and I startled him."

Other times passersby would call to say they had seen the dresses in her shop window dancing. Though Delassandro feels the space is obviously inhabited, she says, "If you don't believe, you probably won't feel it; and even if you do feel it, you probably won't believe it."

(Source: Johnny Dodd, Seattle Weekly.)

MORE GHOSTS
IN PUBLIC BUILDINGS

Ghosts seem apt to appear in just about any setting here in the Pacific Northwest. The following accounts tell of ghosts found in firehouses, churches, libraries, hospitals, and city halls.

The Firehouse Ghost

ASTORIA, OREGON

The Uppertown Fire Station in Astoria, Oregon has been turned into a museum now, the Uppertown Firefighter's Museum. But at least one former firefighter has refused to move out. A ghost resides on the third floor of the museum. He doesn't really bother anyone though, just makes noises and moves things around. It is assumed that he must be the ghost of an old firefighter who just can't bear to leave the place.

Around Halloween in 1993, *Oregonian* writer Erin Riley asked Astoria Fire Department assistant chief Leonard Hansen about the ghost. Local firefighters had apparently put together a $200 kitty for any fireman willing to spend the night in the old Uppertown Fire station. But as yet no one had collected on that bet. Riley asked Hansen, whose bravery has been demonstrated in fire fighting over the years, if he would ever spend the night alone in the museum. "I've heard too many stories from the guys who worked here when it was a fire station," Hansen told her. "And I've heard a few unexplained noises myself."

(Source: Oregonian *reporter Erin Riley.)*

The Ghostly Librarian

PENDLETON, OREGON

They say that Ruth, a former librarian at the Umatilla County Library, has never left the building. Many years ago Ruth committed suicide in the basement of the old Carnegie building by eating lye, a common but agonizing way out in those days.

Nowadays Ruth's more happy spirit wanders the library, knocking books from shelves, opening and closing windows, and walking gently around with soft footsteps that can be heard in the quiet hours.

(Oregon's Ghosts & Monsters *by Mike Helm.*)

A Ghostly Minister and His Wife

SEATTLE, WASHINGTON

Seattle's first Methodist minister, Rev. Daniel Bagley, and his wife refused to abandon their congregation, even after death. Though Rev. Bagley never actually served as minister of the Capitol Hill United Methodist Church founded over eighty years ago, he did lead its congregation in earlier days. In 1986 Douglas Jensen, a deacon and sexton for the church, encountered the white bearded Rev. Bagley. Jensen was locking up the chapel, a few steps from the main sanctuary.

"I opened the door—I was doing my nightly rounds—and there he was. He was looking past me. He didn't seem to see me. I've never seen anything like it. He was translucent, sort of like those holograms," Jensen told reporter Julie Schuster.

Rev. Eduard Perry, acting pastor for the Metropolitan Community Church, which shares the sanctuary with the Methodists, has also encountered the Reverend. He saw him in the balcony one day. "He was up there, just leaning on the railing, watching me." Next door in the parsonage, Mrs. Bagley holds forth. Patrick Shapard, who rented the parsonage, didn't understand at first what was going on: "When I first moved in, things would happen, like I'd put my coat down and then it'd disappear for a while and end up upstairs." Then one evening as he was laying down to meditate in his attic studio he saw her.

"I saw a form of a woman. I saw her very clearly ... she was diaphanous, dressed in a flowing gown, enveloped in bluish light." She asked, 'How do I get out?' "

Shapard pointed toward the door. But she ignored his indication and drifted in the opposite direction, passing out through a third story window.

"Then my roommate told me he'd seen an old woman walking down the hallway one night, and he described her. Our descriptions matched."

Browsing through a Capitol Hill bookstore later, Shapard was leafing through Archie Satterfield's *Seattle,* a collection of historical photographs. "I came across a picture of this old woman, and I got this really eerie feeling. I turned to my roommate and said, 'That's her.' He said 'Yeah. That's her.' " The woman in the photograph was Mrs. Daniel Bagley and is shown seated with her husband, the Rev. Daniel Bagley. Though they were founders of the Methodist church in Seattle, they never lived in this parsonage, so why they should haunt it is unclear.

A psychic, John Jennings, was called in to investigate. He feels there are several entities in the church. He suspects that Dr. Bagley and his wife are concerned about the decrepit state of the aging structure and its dwindling flock. "I sense that the group—and there's several entities moving through this sanctuary—are unhappy because they feel the conflicts within the church. They see this wonderfully grand old building literally decaying in front of them."

In 1991 the spirits had their worst nightmare come true. The Capitol Hill Methodist Church was torn down.

(Source: Seattle Times *reporter Julie Schuster.)*

The Bell-Ringing Ghost of Tacoma's Old City Hall

TACOMA, WASHINGTON

In the tower of Tacoma's Old City Hall hang four huge bells. They were donated in 1904 by former Ambassador Hugh C. Wallace and his wife in memory of their twelve-year-old daughter. The sixty pound bell clappers are connected by rods to the clock mechanism below them, but the striking mechanism has been disengaged for some time. Still, the clocks continue to strike in the night. City Hall Manager Jim Brewster thought pranksters must be causing the alarming bell ringing. He decided to sleep in the tower one night to catch them at their tricks. He came away convinced that the ringer of the bells was not human. "I can tell you in all honesty, there is a spirit up here," Brewster insisted. "Have you ever been alone somewhere and you knew somebody was standing near you?"

Police have been called repeatedly to the Old City Hall building. Lights go on and off. Fire alarms are set off. Guards pursue shadows. No intruders are ever found.

(Source: Tacoma News Tribune *reporter Bob Lane.)*

Duwamish Bend Housing Project's Singing Ghost

DUWAMISH RIVER, WASHINGTON

Beginning in 1949 the Duwamish Bend Housing Project near Seattle was treated to nightly serenades by a ghost which residents dubbed "The Voice." "The Voice" would not only wail but would often break into popular tunes such as "Blue Moon," "Fools Rush In," and one of its favorites—"Ghost Riders in the Sky." A journalist who stayed up to hear the ghostly singing described "The Voice" as having a "deep, rich, captivating voice ... as sweet as the note of a bell on a frosty morning." The serenades continued for years and no one ever found an explanation for "The Voice."

(Source: Seattle Post-Intelligencer *reporter William Arnold.)*

The Attendant Ghost of Vancouver General Hospital

VANCOUVER, BRITISH COLUMBIA

On October 3, 1975 a disaster occurred at the Burrard Terminals in North Vancouver. A horrific explosion in a grain elevator killed one worker and left sixteen others severely burned. The Burn Unit of Vancouver General Hospital treated the victims.

One of the most severely burned was a twenty-eight-year-old young man. He clung to life tenaciously and survived against the odds for one week … two … then a month … then another. After three months of intense suffering the young man gave up. He told a nurse he was going to die. "I'm very tired, and I've had so much pain." The next day his heart stopped.

But he did not leave. Not long after his death a night nurse from another ward was assigned to work in Room 415, his old room. She saw the covers of his bed shift as if a body had turned over and heard the sounds of a sleeper breathing.

Nurses began to report the feeling that someone was with them when they entered Room 415. One saw a distinct shape move slowly around the end of the bed and out the door.

Nurse Denny Conrad and another nurse entered Room 415 with a load of laundry bags one night to make up the bed. Conrad, busy making the bed, was aware of his companion standing by holding a dressing tray. But when he turned to speak to her the tray crashed to the floor. No person was there. It had been the ghost trying to help by holding the tray of dressings.

Soon the young man's ghost found better ways to be helpful. He began to visit the other burn patients at night to comfort them. A woman in an adjoining room told a nurse about the strange young man who had visited her. No one had heard or seen a young man around. A badly burned young man told his nurse one morning, "I'd like to thank that young doctor who took the time last night to come in and help me with the pain." Puzzled, the nurse checked and found that no doctor had been on the ward the previous night. She asked the patient to describe the doctor who had visited him. He described the young man who had died there. The nurses didn't tell their patient that the "doctor" who had helped him through the night in his pain was really a ghost.

The ghost remained in residence until the building housing the burn unit was torn down and the unit moved to a new facility. He kept his presence known by constant small acts ... suddenly turning up the radio to full blast, flushing the toilet, pushing the call button on Room 415 when it was unoccupied. One nurse told of a friend who confronted the ghost. When she was hanging an intravenous solution bottle in Room 415 one night, "suddenly she felt strange, and then very cold, like she was covered in ice." Displaying remarkable courage, she said in an even voice, "Look, I know you're here, but I'm really busy tonight, so please don't interrupt me." Then suddenly the coldness lifted and she was able to go on about her work.

Clearly this is one ghost who just wanted to be helpful.

(Source: Ghosts: True Stories from British Columbia *by Robert C. Belyk.)*

SECTION THREE:

HAUNTED GREENS, ROADS, SHORES, AND SEAS

It is not surprising that the storm swept wintry shores of the Pacific Northwest are plied by phantom ships and guarded by haunted lighthouses. Nor is it amazing that ghostly hitchhikers step from the fog or that phantom trains wind through our mountain passes. But the proclivity of Northwest ghosts to hang out in parks and golf courses *does* seem a bit unusual.

THE NORTHWEST'S HAUNTED PARKS AND GOLF COURSES

Though studies of apparitions suggest that most ghosts appear indoors, here in the Northwest we have several who, like their living Northwestern neighbors, prefer the out-of-doors. A few even frequent public parks and golf courses!

The Chatauqua Hunchback

ASHLAND, OREGON

The legendary hunchback who prowls Lithia Park is well known in Ashland. Here is a fairly detailed account by University of Oregon student Dan Hayes:

Now some legends, especially the ghost story type, can get started at any time. For instance, in Ashland around about the early 1920s, there was a hunchback who lived in this town. No one exactly knew his history, his name was apparently Vannetti. His father was a woodchopper, pulled a cart around and sold wood to schools and such. And around about 1926 (I can't give you an exact date, but somewhere in that general area) the hunchback disappeared and there was speculation at the time that he had been murdered. Some people thought he just went away. He was a "little bit wrong in the head" as they said in those days, and the biggest thing in town at the time was the Chatauqua, which was a traveling entertainment organization, and he occasionally was known to go through people's wagons and cars while the Chatauqua was in progress and carry things off in a gunnysack. The police always knew where to find him, and they got the things back, and he was considered harmless but a nuisance. And, as I say, he disappeared.

I first encountered the story of him maybe not disappearing completely about 1967, when I talked to a person who claimed to have seen a hunchback in the park. As a matter of fact, what she said [was that] when when she was walking through the park and saw this hunchback man kind of furtively running among the cars, she didn't think much about it until she saw he was looking into windows and occasionally reaching in.

So she went and told the police about it. The police station is only a block away from the entrance to the park, and she was right at the entrance when she saw him. They did come and look, found nothing, and they told her at the time that they occasionally had complaints about this same sort of thing. They would go no further— [wouldn't] say anything more about it than that.

Well, she told me about it and about talking to a few people who lived in the town for quite some time. Eventually my father recalled that soon after the disappearance of the actual hunchback, who had lived in Ashland, people claimed to have seen him in the park. And it is apparently still going on now, forty years later. It appears as a solid figure, not as a transparent figure. But it's something that occasionally comes up in town and the older people in town will talk about it, and for a little while in '68 and '69 it was a big topic of conversation among the college students. "The ghost in the park" type of story, which was new to them. But it had been around the town since the 1920s.

The last I heard of it was about six months ago, while I was in Ashland. Someone mentioned it to me, asked me if I'd ever heard the story. So it's still living as a kind of repeated, constant story and people still claim to see him. As to whether or not this is generated by the fact that recently there has been more talk about him than in the past, I don't know, but it's constantly been there for at least forty years.

It becomes embellished, yes, considerably embellished. He chases people, they claim, leaps out from trees scaring people. But the original story stays pretty much solid. That he's seen around the Chatauqua area, which is now the Oregon Shakespeare Festival Theater, and that he goes through cars with a gunnysack over his back, the way the real hunchback did, back in those days.

It's caused a little bit of a problem for an old man who lives in the town who is a hunchback. People occasionally turn and run when they see him coming. Whether or not because of this I don't know. He enjoys walking in the park. He does not go in there at night, probably because he figures he might frighten people too much. I have never spoken to him ... I imagine he knows the story. Whether or not the fact that this man lives in town contributes to the story, I don't know, except that he is considerably taller than the figure people claim to see. The one that they claim is the "ghost"—quote unquote—is consistently described as about five feet eight inches. This man who lives in Ashland is over six feet tall.

My father said that at the time the hunchback was alive (assuming that he did die when he disappeared) they called him the "dog-faced boy" because apparently—I don't know the name of the disease—but apparently, along with the humpback, he had an overgrowth of hair over most of the body. They used to tease him a lot. He also sold pencils on the corner, but the only place after his disappearance that he has been seen is in the park itself, especially around the parking area. The old Chatauqua parking area is still a parking area for the present park.

(Source: Dan Hayes, collected by University of Oregon student Stephanie Barrett.)

The Glenacres Golf Course Dancer

SEATTLE, WASHINGTON

Sightings of a gaunt, naked figure performing an Indian dance on the trail to the Glenacres golf course were reported off and on over a period of twenty or so years. Seattle police tried repeatedly to catch the phantom dancer without luck. Hundreds of people reportedly witnessed the dancing figure in the areas around South 10th and South 110th Streets. One explanation for the apparition was that the Glenacres golf course was believed to be built on the site of an Indian burial ground.

(Source: Seattle Post-Intellingencer *columnist William Arnold.)*

The White Lady of the Seventh Tee

VICTORIA, BRITISH COLUMBIA

The "white lady" of the Victoria Golf Course has become quite famous among Victoria's teens. Numerous young couples have visited the lonely golf course after dark in search of the wisping form of this spirit. Some say that couples who see her will never wed.

In early April of 1964, sixteen-year-old Anthony Gregson and his girlfriend went ghost hunting along the shore by the golf course. They were joking about ghosts but they didn't really expect to see one. They later said, "We could feel a definite change in the atmosphere. Then we saw her. She was about a thousand yards away and appeared to be running over the stones on the beach without touching them. She was a luminous gray, with an aura about her. When she reached the furthermost point of land, she stopped and looked out to sea as if she were expecting someone." The couple watched for about five minutes and then left. The ghost was still standing on the point. Gregson returned to the spot the next day to make certain of what he had seen. But he did not return again by night. "I believe in leaving ghosts to their own lives. I am not going back again. It was an unnerving experience."

But other teens did seek out the ghost. In April of 1968, sixteen-year-old Ann Smith was walking through the golf course with some friends around 9 P.M. Like Gregson, she suddenly noticed a change in the atmosphere. "There was no noise, but although it was a warm night, it began to get windy and cold near the sand pit. It was a clammy coldness." Then the misty form of a woman emerged from the darkness. The next night the group returned to the golf course again.

Again the ghost appeared. "It was about five feet tall and moved in an upright position, but I couldn't distinguish many of its features, although it looked like a woman," said sixteen-year-old Dennis Andrews. A young seaman with the group insisted, "It definitely was not swamp gas. I know what that looks like."

"At first I thought I could see right through it," said one observer, "But after a while I realized it was opaque." The group stared at this apparition for nearly five minutes. Ann Smith tried to approach for a closer look. "I started to walk toward her and she disappeared. But then we turned around and she was behind us, about twenty feet away."

* * *

These ghostly sightings, which began in the 1940s, are believed to be the phantom of Doris Gravlin, a woman in her thirties who was apparently strangled by her estranged husband, Victor. Her body was found by a golfer on the morning of September 23, 1936. He was looking for a lost ball near the seventh tee when he noticed a woman's sweater lying on the beach. He went to pick it up and discovered Mrs. Gravlin's body in a patch of tall grass and bush.

Police found that she had been murdered in a patch of wild broom near the seventh hole and then dragged down to the beach. She had been beaten and then strangled. Mrs. Gravlin had been seen leaving her apartment on Beach Drive in Oak Bay to go for a walk about 8 o'clock the previous evening. At the time she was wearing white kid leather shoes. The shoes were missing and a search of the golf course and beach failed to turn them up.

Four weeks later, on October 25, the case of the missing shoes was solved. Her husband's body was found entangled in a kelp bed offshore near the golk links. In the inside pocket of his coat were Doris Gravlin's white kid shoes.

It was imagined that Victor Gravlin and his wife had met on the evening of September 22, perhaps to try to arrange a reconciliation of their stormy marriage. Victor was known to have a drinking problem and the two had been separated for a time. Perhaps a fight ensued. At any rate Victor must have murdered Doris and then thrown himself into the ocean to drown. Perhaps the unhappy ghost staring out to sea is searching for her lost husband.

*　*　*

The white lady continues to haunt the green golf course and is especially active in April, it is said. Hence one of her names ... the April Ghost. In June of 1978 two *Times* reporters set out to photograph the phantom. They didn't get a picture but they did get a fright. Reporter Al Forrest tells the tale of his ghostly stakeout with photographer John McKay:

"We reached the spot and it was forlorn and scary. Not a sound except the swish of the waves against the shore. To the southwest, both the land and water were in total darkness—nothing visible except the lights of Port Angeles across the strait. To the northeast, where the ghost is supposedly seen, there was a bit of light, including one that sent reflections across the water.

"When the ghost was sighted on previous occasions, the viewers felt a cold, clammy chill that seemed to come up suddenly and change their mood, and then they claimed they saw the ghost as a swiftly drifting vaporous creature, moving along the beach.

"Twice I felt the cold, clammy chill. The first time I looked around excitedly—but nothing. Just the light playing off the water.

"It was about five minutes later that I saw something. It was a white shape, swirling in the tall grass about fifteen meters from the beach. I grabbed my binoculars but couldn't find it. When I put down the glasses and looked it had definitely vanished. 'I saw something,' I told McKay. 'But I don't know what it was.' He suggested that we should be satisfied with that and go home ....

"But we waited half an hour longer, giving the ghost every effort to show up. Suddenly it got very cold; there was a chill that cut right through me. 'Let's go,' I said.

"We began picking our way carefully through the dark when again I saw something. It was very quick, like a falling star, but moving just above the grass. By the time I wheeled around and got my glasses on the spot it had vanished. On both occasions I had felt cold and clammy and exactly five minutes later there was a glimpse of something—and both times in the tall grass near the beach. We have no pictures of anything. Just a chill that won't go away."

Most terrified of those sighting the pale lady may have been George Drysdale, a Toronto cab driver who was in Victoria with his sister and some friends. They drove out to the golf course on a lark to see if they could spot the ghost. They did. It was a brightly moonlit night. The ghost appeared and refused to disappear. "She was young and looked quite human," Drysdale told reporters. "Except for the fact that the whole outline of her body was shadowy at the edges—a very creepy effect. She looked sad—my God, how sad she looked!" Drysdale retreated from the apparition, but it followed him. He turned to flee—the apparition appeared in front of him. Wherever he turned, there it was. His friends watched in horror as the ghost tormented their terrified friend. Then suddenly it vanished. Drysdale has no doubt that this was indeed a ghost. "A human being cannot appear in different places in the twinkling of an eye and vanish the same way. I know I saw the ghost of the murdered girl."

(Source: Vancouver Province *reporter Fred Curtin;* Vancouver Colonist *reporters Arthur Mayse and Diane Janowski;* Victoria Times *reporter Al Forrest.)*

VANISHING HITCHHIKERS

One of the best known of our urban legends is the tale of the Vanishing Hitchhiker. Jan Brunvand recounts many variants of this story in his book *The Vanishing Hitchhiker*. The legend is told both here and abroad, and of course the Northwest has its own inimitable variants. Whether you believe these tales or not, I suggest you be careful who you pick up on our dark rainy nights.

The Vanishing Lady by the Road

SOOKE, BRITISH COLUMBIA

A ghostly lady appears from time to time on the East Sooke Road near Victoria. Here are some of the accounts.

Marion and Michel Desrochers were driving toward Victoria on East Sooke road just west of Park Heights Drive near Anderson Cove on November 7, 1989:

It was dark and raining about 11:30 pm. We were rounding the corner. You have to keep to the right. Suddenly we came across this figure at the yellow line on the left side. She was dressed in Edwardian clothing; a long dress and wide hat. I had the impression she had button-up boots on.

She didn't move at all when the car came past. If I had opened the window, I could have touched her. She had a very pale, gray face. She was not looking at us, it was like she was looking through us. She had a very sad expression.

As we passed, I put on my brake lights and she was still there in silhouette. What was also strange was it was raining and she wasn't wet.

* * *

Calvin Reichaelt saw the apparition in 1986. He was driving on East Sooke Road near the old oyster factory at noon on a wet and misty day. Reichelt said his ghost was wearing a long white dress:

There she was. I stopped, like a fool, to give her a ride and she just walked through the car and into the mist. She was different altogether from the other descriptions. She was about 25 and good looking. I know because I saw her as close as I can see my hand as she walked through the motor compartment. It must be she has aged since she came down or she can change her appearance for different people. I know it was a ghost.

* * *

Evelyn Beaulac saw a figure on Gillespier Road just off East Sooke Road on October 11, 1989. She was driving to work in the rain around 5:30 A.M:

I was coming around the corner. It was foggy, but not enough that you couldn't see the road. I saw her. She scared me. She had such a white, white face. She had dark clothing. It was raining and cold and this lady was very wet, but she didn't move."

There is a tradition in Sooke that the ghost is that of teacher, Louisa Mary Stiff, who died in Victoria in the late 1920s. She had taught in the East Sooke area and once had an accident when thrown from a buggy on a curve on East Sooke Road. However, the accident was not fatal and she died years later in a hospital in Victoria. It is not clear how the ghostly apparition came to be associated with her. Her niece objects that her Aunt Lulie would be the last person to want to become the subject of a romanticized myth. "Louisa Mary Stiff was a gentlewoman in the full sense of the word."

(Source: Victoria Times-Colonist *reporter Patrick Murphy.)*

The Klamath Lady

Siletz, Oregon

The legend of the Klamath Lady seems well known around Siletz, Oregon. Donna R., a University of Oregon student from Siletz, has heard several versions:

There's a legend connected with a certain piece of road which is right across from my house. In one version of the story I heard there was an Indian woman who threw herself and her baby off the grade after her husband jumped from it and drowned in the river. And now on stormy nights you might just see her walking along carrying a bundle. The Klamath Lady's all gray and has a covering over her head. If you don't pick her up she'll make you crash, but if you do pick her up she'll ride in back. If you look at her you won't see a face. After a while she disappears.

My brother Mansel told me this version of the legend. Living so near to the grade and after having driven over it several times at night, I find myself looking for her. Many people around Siletz believe in her.

Donna has a second version of the tale:

This was the first version of the Klamath Lady's tale that I ever came across. I can't remember who told it to me but it was one of my schoolmates in my junior year of high school. An Indian woman and her husband were crossing the Klamath Grade late one stormy night when the woman's husband pushed her and her baby off the grade. She fell into the river and drowned. Nobody ever found her or her baby's body. But they say that if there's a stormy night and you're driving over the grade and you see a woman carrying a bundle you'd better pick her up or she'll make you crash. But if you do she'll get in the back seat and as soon as you're past the grade she disappears. They say she's looking for her husband.

Donna reports that some think the Klamath Lady is buried in a cemetery on their property. Mary Teague, who owned the farm before Donna's family bought it, had passed on much of this legend and reported that Native American children in the area would not cross the grade at night on foot.

(Source: University of Oregon student Donna Roeser, Randall V. Mills Archives. University of Oregon.)

The White Lady Hitchhiker

MT. ST. HELENS, WASHINGTON

Since the 1980 eruption of Mt. St. Helens, reports of a ghostly hitchhiker, a lady in white, have grown in the areas around the mountain. Elizabeth Simpson of the University of Washington reports an early encounter with the legend. She heard it from "my husband's niece, who spent the night with us in Chehalis on her way from the Olympic peninsula to California in early September of 1980, four months after the two major eruptions in May. This is my rephrasing of Judy's story: "I stopped at a gas station in Centralia, and one of the attendants told me not to pick up any hitchhikers on my way south. I told him I wasn't in the habit of doing that, and he said, 'Well, especially a woman in white. There's been a woman in a white dress hitchhiking her way up and down I-5. She gets into the back seat, predicts that the volcano is going to erupt again between October 12 and 14, and then she disappears.' "

*   *   *

The September 23, 1980 edition of the *Seattle Post-Intelligencer* gave several variants of this story. According to that article the woman was picked up on back roads around the volcano. She predicted an eruption between October 12 and 14 which would devastate an area within a one hundred mile radius of the mountain. A Forks man thought she looked like the Hawaiian volcano goddess Pele.

*   *   *

Reports of the ghostly hitchhiker seemed to center in the Morton-Randle-Packwood area. Morton police chief Jim Enrud reported: "We picked up a rumor that some people picked up a lady with a white gown on. She gave her warning and when they looked in the back seat she was gone. And they were going sixty miles an hour down the road. But I don't know what they were smokin' or drinkin'."

(Source: Northwest Folklore; Seattle Post-Intelligencer.*)*

GHOSTLY TRAVEL

Even travel in the Northwest can be beset by ghostly experiences, as shown by two accounts of Spokane trains. And remember that sometimes the train or coach itself may be the phantom!

The Spokane Flyer and the Ghost Train

MEDICINE HAT, ALBERTA

The Spokane Flyer was a Canadian Pacific Railway train which crossed the border to end its run in Spokane, Washington. On July 8, 1908 a terrible train disaster occurred on this line. It was 8:30 on a sunny morning and the engine for the Spokane Flyer was racing from Medicine Hat to Swift Current to pick up its passenger cars and haul them to Moose Jaw. Engineer Jim Nicholson had to take the engine up the series of curves in a high embankment to reach the flatlands above. A farmer working at the top of the embankment saw something the engineer could not see—a passenger train whizzing down the same track from the opposite direction. Nicholson had failed to check with the CPR dispatcher to find out if the Lethbridge train had left on time. It hadn't, and was now barreling down on him. The farmer waved frantically but Nicholson and his fireman just waved happily back. The Lethbridge locomotive was thrown from the tracks in the crash and the baggage car smashed to bits. Seven men were killed, including engineer Nicholson and the Lethbridge train's engineer, Bob Twohey.

A fireman who often worked with Twohey connected the accident to a most mysterious happening which had occurred just two months earlier. Gus Day told of traveling with Twohey through those same cutbacks about eleven at night. They were taking the engine up to pick up some passenger cars at Dunmore junction for the Spokane run. Suddenly a huge, blinding light appeared in front of them. Twohey yelled for his fireman to jump, but it was too late. Then the approaching train veered to the right and flashed past the engine with its whistle blowing. But there was only one track there. Day and Twohey both saw the train barrel past. The coach windows were lit and passengers looked out as it sped past.

The two men were shaken beyond belief. They told no one of their bizarre experience, but agreed that neither had been drinking that night. Later Twohey confided in Day that a fortune teller had told him he would die within a month. Twohey had decided to stay off the trains for a while now, just in case.

Twohey avoided taking the next run up to Dunmore junction, calling in sick. So engineer Nicholson was sent instead, with Day as fireman again. In almost the same spot on the switchbacks the two men met that Ghost Train again. The blinding light appeared, the train flashed past, whistle blowing, and the passengers stared out of their ghostly windows.

Though several railroaders knew about the ghost train, it was not mentioned at the train wreck inquest. Years later, in the 1930s, Day revealed his story to a Vancouver reporter and other railroad men came forward to verify Day's story.

(Source: Ted Ferguson in Sentimental Journey: An Oral History of Train Travel in Canada.*)*

Saved by a Ghost

LEAVENWORTH, WASHINGTON

In December of 1960, Rufus Porter, later to become a noted Colorado journalist, was riding the rails on a train from Spokane to Seattle. He was huddled in an open car and nearly froze to death when the train began crossing the Cascade Mountains where the temperature had fallen below zero. Near Leavenworth he saw a work camp and jumped train to seek shelter. Seeing a light in a watchman's cabin he pounded on the door. A bearded man with kind eyes let him in and cared for him. The man seemed to know all about Porter without being told. He fed him and treated his frostbite. But there was only one phrase he would utter: "I am your brother."

The next day Porter made his way into Leavenworth and told his story of rescue in the watchman's cabin. His tale was treated with incredulity. That work camp had been abandoned for years and the watchman he described had long been dead. He returned to the camp by daylight and found the cabin where he had just spent the night abandoned, without a trace of life.

(Source: Seattle Post-Intelligencer *reporter William Arnold.)*

Phantom Trolley

EVERETT, WASHINGTON

An Everett high school student contributed this to a collection of local lore. Unlike others in the high school collection, this piece is unsigned and is written in short story format:

It was a cold snowy night in January, 1952. He was turning from 19th onto Colby. He had heard stories from his neighbors that on snowy nights you could look out and see a shadow similar in shape to the old Everett trolleys going down the road, but he did not believe it—and probably never would have if it had not been for his experience that night.

As he turned onto Colby, he noticed an odd, single light coming towards him down the center of the road. It grew brighter, and he turned farther off to the edge of the road, but it was shining at him— blinding him. He heard sounds like a railroad car makes and several shrill toots as wheels hit some ice. He slid out of control across the road and into the snow bank. The thing passed him. As he glanced back, he swore that what he saw fading into the snow looked like an old trolley.

(Source: Bananabread Waterway and Friends.*)*

Ghostly Stagecoach Stops at the Galesville Hotel

DOUGLAS COUNTY, OREGON

The old Galesville Hotel is gone now, it burned to the ground in 1931. But the northbound stage that stopped there at eleven each morning back in the 1800s still rolls in. The hotel was built in 1882. Its livery barn handled over ninety horses in those days and it served as an important stop on the stagecoach route. After the building burned, a home was built on its foundations. When newspaper reporter Lavola Bakken visited the home in 1973 the owners, Peggy and Charlie Van Vlake, admitted that the place seemed haunted. Peggy gave this account:

"The first time I noticed anything was when I came up here in '66. My daughter from Georgia came out and we were getting ready to paint the living room. We were taking the venetian blinds down, and all at once we heard two women talking. Both of us heard it, but we couldn't tell what they were saying. 'Charlotte,' I says, 'someone's here.'

"It was August and the doors were open. I looked out and she looked out the other end of the room, but neither of us saw a soul. Just two women talking like they were visiting, but there wasn't a body on the place 'sides us.

"Then we had trouble with a stairway window that wouldn't stay locked. The boys or me'd lock that window at night on the way to bed and in the morning it'd be plum open. Finally I had Darren jam the lock to keep it shut.

"Lots of times I'm sitting down here and hear things going on up those stairs. Hasn't been over two-three weeks ago we were all sitting here and I says, 'Van, what's upstairs?' and he says, 'I'm not goin' to go see!' Sounded like somebody leafing through magazines or turning pages in books. It wasn't the cats, because they were laying on top of the television. Finally I went up there, but nothing."

The most unusual incident of all was the hopping wine bottle:

"Van, Kelly, Darren and my daughter were all here. We finished drinking some wine and she put the bottle in that wastebasket sitting right there in the corner. Pretty soon, it jumped out and rolled across the floor. You know, that's kind of hard for a square bottle to do."

And then there is the stage they hear roll in some mornings. The first time it happened Peggy thought it was her grandchildren arriving in their car. They heard a door slam and the laughing voices of children. Her two Siamese cats jumped from their sunny kitchen napping spot and ran to hide in the stairwell. The cats, Omar and Simon, don't care for the noisy children. Peggy dried her hands at the sink and went out to greet them. But there was no one there. The house sits back at the end of a long lane. "A car couldn't come in our yard, turn around and disappear that quickly," Peggy explained. "Charlie said I just imagined the whole thing the first time this happened, but since then he hasn't been so sure, especially as the cats hear it too." Later they discovered that the northbound stage used to stop at the old Galesville Hotel every day at just about the same time Peggy and the cats hear their invisible guests arrive.

(Source: Roseburg, Oregon reporter Lavola J. Bakken.)

PHANTOMS
OF THE LIGHTHOUSES

Always windswept, often glimpsed through fog, lighthouses evoke a sense of mystery. They rise out of reach offshore, or stand alone on isolated points of land. It is no wonder that Northwesterners tell tales of the spirits who climb those lonely towers.

Tales of Tillamook Rock

TILLAMOOK ROCK LIGHTHOUSE, OREGON

Tillamook Rock Lighthouse stands atop a pinnacle of rock off the northern Oregon Coast. The only entry to this light station was by derrick. Visitors had to swing ashore suspended on a large boom which dangled them perilously seventy-five feet over the boiling waters at the rock's base.

That a human habitation should be built at all on such a spot is an amazing feat. A member of the surveying party who first visited the rock was swept to his death when his foot slipped and he fell into a whirlpool of icy water. Nevertheless the rock was surveyed and a party of construction workers were set ashore sometime later to begin the project. They soon found themselves abandoned on the rocktop, attacked by angry sea lions and swept by icy waves during winter storms. For weeks on end no ship could approach the rock because of the angry seas. But the work persisted. A building site was leveled by blasting more than twenty feet from the top of the rock and the lighthouse was built ... a building of such durability that it withstood years of winter storms, even when they swept over the rock, filling the lighthouse with water. When the winds blew heavy seas against the rock from the south, a crevice in the rocks caused storm waters to be thrown over 160 feet into the air at times, crashing over the one-hundred-foot-high rock and splashing into the top of the lighthouse itself. Construction began in 1879 and the lighthouse turned on its light for the first time in 1881. In 1957 the light station was closed for good and replaced with a radar system. During its entire life no more than three hundred individuals set foot on the rock, including the light station's keepers and repairmen.

*　*　*

Tillamook Rock holds an important place in the hearts of the Oregonians who glimpse its picturesque form offshore. Ghostlore about such a spot is bound to arise. Here are two stories collected by University of Oregon student Ann Zielony in 1975:

"There was this one lighthouse keeper who loved the Tillamook Lighthouse so much that he said he would kill the next man who tried to come and take his place. I think he went insane from being alone in that old lighthouse. So one day the man finally came who was supposed to replace him and he had a peg leg and when the madman started chasing him up the stairs—they were these long spiral stairs—old peg leg really had a hard time, but when they got to the top, he pushed the crazy guy down the stairs, and they had to take him away in a straitjacket.

"There was this really old keeper of the lighthouse and he said that when he died he wanted to be buried in the lighthouse. So when he died they of course took him away, but they say that that old man loved the lighthouse so much that his ghost returned. But he is a peaceful ghost and there have been people who have seen him or heard him."

Her informant told her the lighthouse was referred to as the "Terrible Tillamook" because of the cost in keeping it running and because the winter storms would flood through the top windows, slowly filling it with water.

*　*　*

A more accurate account of the lighthouse is given in West Coast

Lighthouses by Jim Gibbs, who once was stationed as a keeper at Tillamook Rock. He tells of lighthouse keepers working up to their necks in water to keep the light going during winter storms.

Gibb says that Indian legends told of an underwater tunnel running from the mainland to a hollow room inside the rock where spirits resided. He tells of numerous lighthouse keepers who heard a ghostly cry as they climbed the circular staircase to the tower. And to this day mainlanders claim to see at times a ghostly glow from the lamp room of the deserted lighthouse.

(Source: University of Oregon student Ann Zielony; West Coast Lighthouses: A Pictorial History of the Guiding Lights of the Sea *by Jim Gibbs.)*

The Ghost of Heceta Head Light

HECETA HEAD, OREGON

Legend has it that the Heceta Head Lighthouse is haunted. University of Oregon student Cheryl Lynn Phillips wrote down this version of the tale:

"Another story about a lighthouse is about the Heceta Head Lighthouse, which is pretty close to Florence. The story comes partly from the newspapers, but I'd heard it before, and afterwards I heard other stories about it too. That it's—that the house, the lighthouse itself and the caretaker's house—was haunted. And in this article and in the stories I'd heard, the person who was haunting the lighthouse was an old lady, in all the stories that I've heard, and in this one story the people who had been working on rebuilding the lighthouse ... one of the men had been working in the attic, and that's where it was supposedly where this lady was haunting it, and none of the workers liked to go up there. But one worker went up there, and he was putting in a window and ... he turned around and saw an apparition of this old lady floating across the floor and he got really frightened and he jumped down through the hole where they, where they climbed up the ladder and stuff. And the next day, he said he wouldn't go back up in the attic because of this lady up there and so he fixed the window from the outside. He knocked all the glass inside of the room and put in a window and no one else had gone up in the attic during that time, because they were all afraid of this ghost too. And that night, after he fixed the window, they'd heard scratching sounds in the attic, and none of 'em wanted to go up there that night. But the next day they went up there, and they found a pile of glass that had been swept up neatly in the middle of the room, and they knew it had to have been by this old lady. That's how the story goes."

* * *

Cheryl has another story about the Heceta Head:

"Another story about this same lighthouse was told to me after I told this story to someone else who hadn't heard it before. He was saying that one time he was in some group that had to stay up in the lighthouse ... or in the caretaker's house, I'm not sure which, and they all had their sleeping bags out and they had all gone someplace and did something. And when they came back, their sleeping bags had all been rearranged, and at the time, they thought it was a practical joke, but nobody confessed to it, so they think that it's possible that this old lady came and moved all the sleeping bags around."

* * *

Legends of haunted lighthouses are popular along the rocky, often stormy Oregon coastline. However, according to newspaper reporter Clay Eals, the spirit at Heceta Head lives not in the lighthouse, but in the caretaker's house. This four story, seventeen room house was formerly used as living quarters for the Heceta Head Light crews. It sits near the entrance to Devil's Elbow State Park and is now owned by the U. S. Forest Service. The building is over ninety years old so it has had plenty of time to age a bit and to acquire a ghost or two.

When Eals interviewed Harry and Anne Tammen, the current caretakers, the Tammens left no doubt that a spirit was indeed in residence there. Just a few of the signs: the loud, metallic "click" of a light switch being turned on; the thud-thud-thud of unseen feet coming up the cellar steps; the house's uncanny habit of becoming hot and stuffy every night from 2 to 4 A.M. no matter what the weather outside. "Honestly. You wake up and sweat and you throw the covers down and you look outside and it's cold and windy."

One night all of the dishes in the cupboards began rattling as if there was an earthquake. Harry Tammen ran for the cupboard. The minute he reached it the rattling stopped and all was silent again.

On another occasion two kitchen cupboard doors which had strong spring latches were found open at ninety degree angles every night for four nights in a row. Even though they had been securely checked before going to bed.

And one evening when the Tammens and two friends were playing cards in the kitchen a loud "Ahhhhhh!" came out of nowhere. It was so obvious that two cats on the floor jumped up and looked in the direction of the sound. No one was there.

Others encountered the ghost as well. Students staying in the house one weekend claimed they saw a long, gray "puff of smoke" go up a stairway.

A contractor who was repairing a broken upstairs window one day saw a "very old, wrinkled-face woman" in a gray, floor-length hoop skirt who "seemed to float toward him." The figure disappeared when she reached him. The contractor left and refused to return. That night the sound of sweeping was heard coming from the attic. In the morning the broken glass had all been swept into a neat pile.

Shortly before the Eals interview in 1977, Tammen himself had seen something he took to be the ghost. Running upstairs to get his car keys, he had been startled to see a long black skirt slowly disappearing through a closed bedroom door.

The identity of the ghost remains a mystery. A seventy-seven-year-old woman who visited the house in 1974 said that she had been born there and lived the first fifteen years of her life at the lighthouse. She told the Tammens of a long-forgotten baby's grave on the property. She hoped someone was putting flowers on the grave of the little girl, who was born shortly before herself. The Tammens wonder if the spirit is the baby's mother, or perhaps the baby herself ... now grown.

Whoever the ghost is, the Tammen's seemed content living with it. "The first question people ask us is, 'How can you live there?' But we've never been afraid. We never were at any point. Never. I'm not a believer in ghosts. I don't disbelieve that this is possible, but I'm skeptical," said Tammen.

"There is a presence in this house," he continued. "Maybe there are some other beings that we don't know about who are living adjacent to us. What we in humanity call ghosts may be some short circuit in the time zone. I'm not superstitious or anything else, but I think we're awfully eager to think we're the only thing on this world."

(Source: Oregonian *reporter Clay Eals; University of Oregon student Cheryl Lynn Phillips.)*

Yaquina Bay Lighthouse

NEWPORT, OREGON

Newport, Oregon is home to two lighthouses. When the Yaquina Head Lighthouse was built in 1873, it literally outshone the Yaquina Bay light. So the Yaquina Bay Lighthouse was closed in 1874 after only three years of service. The wood frame building remained on the site, growing more and more decrepit until it was finally rescued by the Lincoln County Historical Society.

James A. Gibbs, Jr. in his *Sentries of the North Pacific,* tells us, "Shortly after the abandonment, rumors were circulated that it was haunted. On certain nights, weird sounds were heard echoing from its chambers. The wind whistled about its gallery and balustrade and some claimed to have seen spirits of dead keepers drifting about in the fog where once the light had shown. The superstitious refused to go near the old tower."

Bruce Roberts and Ray Jones add in *Western Lighthouses,* "Some believe the building is haunted. Rumor has it that during the 1930s, a visitor disappeared without a trace."

* * *

The Yaquina Bay lighthouse is restored now and sits in the middle of a state park, but it still provides excellent fodder for local teens' fright stories. Here are two collected by University of Oregon student Cheryl Lynn Phillips. Cheryl's home was in Florence, Oregon. Cheryl refers to the lighthouse in her story simply as "The Newport Lighthouse." It is assumed she means "Yaquina Bay" rather than "Yaquina Head:"

We were driving to a football game and a friend and her mom started telling this story when we went past the lighthouse .... This is a lighthouse that's closed and it was closed then, but they said earlier it'd been open and they were letting people go in and walk through it and stuff. And this girl's mom took her and her brother to this lighthouse when they were really little, and they were walking through it, and her mom all the sudden had this really strange feeling. She said she couldn't explain it, but she just had this feeling and she just wanted to get out of there. She wanted to run away really bad. And this girl and her brother, they didn't want to leave though. They wanted to go upstairs and walk around and that's when her mother got this really, REALLY weird feeling and she said she just had to get out of there and she just took the kids and walked out as quickly as she could without making a scene.

And I guess they said that the next day that they had been reading in the paper and this story in the paper was about the unsolved murders that took place in Oregon in the last fifty years or something like that, and one of the murders that had not been solved was one that took place in the attic at this lighthouse. Which is where her mom got this really weird feeling and she said that she had to get out of there.

(Self-collected by Cheryl Lynn Phillips, Florence, Oregon.)

*   *   *

Another teen, Jill Whisler, age eighteen, told of a murder at the lighthouse:

Down in Newport is an old unused lighthouse that is still kept in pretty good condition. The caretakers will take groups of students from the high school on a tour of it starting with the top and going into the basement.

One time a group from high school came for the tour, and a girl and boy went down to the basement instead of up to the light part. One of their friends suddenly noticed that they were not there, so everyone began to search for them. Soon they heard a scream, and they all ran to the basement where they found the girl's blood-covered clothes. They never found the boy or the girl, and they have never been seen since.

(Collected by University of Oregon student Joan Anderson of Depoe Bay, Oregon from Jill Whisler, eighteen, a store clerk in Lincoln Beach, Oregon.)

Living with Ghosts at Point Wilson Lighthouse

PORT TOWNSEND, WASHINGTON

Coast Guard wives are finding that a posting at the Point Wilson Lighthouse is definitely creepy. Jennifer Rice and her husband live in one half of the old Point Wilson Lighthouse home located on the grounds of Fort Worden State Park. Working alone in her kitchen one day, Jennifer caught a motion out of the corner of her eye. She turned quickly ... but nothing was there. Then she heard footsteps and rummaging noises on the second floor. "At first it was just a bunch of sounds. Then I heard footsteps upstairs and I yelled, 'I have a gun!' But there was no one there."

Another night she heard something rummaging through her bathroom cupboard, taking out items and setting them down. "I was totally freaked out," she told reporter Randi Rice.

A friend, Steve Betts, slept on the couch one night and awoke from a dream that someone was smothering him. He sat up, clutching his throat, and gasping for breath. In the kitchen he saw a woman's figure. But when he got up and moved to the kitchen, no one was there.

Gerald Blaiff, a night security officer for Fort Worden State Park for twenty years, told of a Coast Guard watchman who had seen a glowing apparition of a woman in a long gown who would wander around the grounds and go up into the lighthouse. Legend has it that the apparition is a woman looking for her daughter who drowned on a steamship that went down in Puget Sound.

The Point Wilson Lighthouse home was built in 1879 but is kept in excellent condition and houses two Coast Guard families. Neither of the Coast Guardsmen, Dave Rice and Larry Buck, have experienced anything strange. But Buck's wife, Carol, who lives next door to Jennifer Rice, has also heard rummaging on her second floor. "It sounded like someone was on the second story walking around and moving things or doing something with an object. I investigated. There was a feeling of a presence—not scary or oppressive. Then I got a phone call from Jenny wondering if I heard any noises."

And Rice's mother, Elaine, witnessed a strange thing during a visit she made to the house. A mantle full of birthday cards in her room was dumped out onto the floor, though no windows or doors were open in the room at the time.

(Source: Peninsula Daily News *reporter Randi F. Rice.)*

HAUNTED SHIPS AND PHANTOM SHIPS

The Pacific Northwest leans tentatively into the powerful Pacific Ocean. The overwhelming roar of the ocean, the terrible roiling of its waters strike awe into those who set foot on our coastal beaches. Equally mysterious are the calmer waters flowing darkly around our many isles and inlets. Sheer black rocks drop into dark waters. Brown kelp beckons with lengthy tentacles reaching up from the ocean's floor. And overhead tortured pines cling to crumbling bits of dirt, fighting to evade the inevitable grasp of the sea for just one more winter.

Many of the sightings in this book take place along beaches or within sight of the mysterious sea. Here are a few phantoms from the ocean itself.

A Phantom Ship Escapes the Rocks

TILLAMOOK ROCK LIGHTHOUSE, OREGON

The four lighthouse keepers of Tillamook Rock witnessed an amazing sight one stormy day. A derelict ship drifted perilously close to the rock. Lighthouse crew member Jim Gibbs tells of how his early morning sleep was broken by shouts from a fellow crewman:

"Leaping out of bed and into my pants, I was outside in a flash and Swede was waiting for me, all wrought up as if his blood was boiling in his veins. He pointed to the dim outline of a vessel parting the strands of mist less than a quarter of a mile away—its dull gray silhouette blending with the sky and sea and hinting of mystery.

"Through the glasses one could tell that she was an old steamer that boasted a chronicle of long and hectic years—her seams had opened and the oakum had baked out through a series of summers. Badly hogged, her decks had grown sodden from rain and sea water, and the rigging hung limp from her fore and main mast, like a broken spider web, against the dismal sky. The dingy paint was peeling from her sides, and streaks of rust from iron fittings had left tell tale marks. The davits swung empty, the pilot house was partly stove in, and the cabin portholes creaked open and shut with the pulse of the ocean."

Gibbs told of how the derelict drifted closer and closer to the rocks. A Coast Guard cutter was radioed, but it was clear the cutter would not reach the vessel before she broke herself to pieces on Tillamook Rock. The ship showed no signs of life and bore no traces of name or registry on her hull. Just as the inevitable clash of ship with rock was about to occur ... In the clutches of destruction, a stone's throw away, she became almost motionless in a vicious tide rip that knifed about her hull. She then spun about as though some skillful navigator had taken the helm, but her stern stuck momentarily, dislodging a bulky wooden rudder, which drifted free as she squeezed by the perilous southwest corner by a gnat's eyebrow. We could have spit on her decks as she passed below us in her death agonies. It was almost supernatural. Spared from disaster, that sinister derelict pursued her ghostly course until she had vanished in the northwesterly mists, on her capricious voyage to nowhere.

A thorough sweep of the area by sea and air was conducted by the coast guard, but no ship or ship's wreckage was ever found. Except for one thing. One stormy evening when the sea was doing her worst, a huge wave crashed against Tillamook Rock, depositing a load of flotsam and jetsam in its wake. Among the debris was the ancient wooden rudder which had been torn from the ship. It lay there in full sight, tangled in seaweed, on the lighthouse's lower platform. But to descend and secure it in this storm was a frightening prospect.

Still the crew wanted badly to have this bit of evidence from the derelict experience. So young Jim Gibbs was rigged with a life line and lowered from the top of the east wall to the platform. He had only descended about twenty feet however when a shout from above came: "Look out below!" Looking up he saw a roaring mass of white water catapulting toward him. A huge wave had struck the opposite end of the rock and was sweeping everything before it. He clung desperately to the life line and took a deep breath as the sea swept over him. When he could breathe again he saw the ancient ship's rudder being drawn away to sea with the wake of the massive wave. Had there in fact been a derelict ship which simply foundered and was never found? The crew couldn't help recalling legends of the Flying Dutchman, a phantom ship said to sail the seven seas forever. Certainly the ship they witnessed had all the markings of a phantom sighting.

(*Source:* Tillamook Light *by James A. Gibbs, Jr.*)

The Ghost Ship Valencia

BRITISH COLUMBIA COAST

In January 1906 the passenger ship *Valencia* left San Francisco bound for Seattle via Victoria. She carried ninety-four passengers and sixty crew members. Just before midnight on January 22 the *Valencia* struck a submerged reef at Pachena Bay. The ship hung up on the reef and slowly began to fill with water. Because the ship was wedged among rocks close to shore, rescue ships could not approach her. High seas made rescue efforts almost impossible. The foundering ship slowly was beaten apart by the sea. Rescuers could only watch from shore as the terrible tragedy played out before their eyes. Survivors climbed into the rigging and clung there for two days until the last vestiges of the ship were dragged underwater and they too were washed away. Of the 154 aboard only thirty-seven were rescued. The *City of Topeka* carried some of the survivors toward Seattle. En route she met another ship and stopped to relay the tragic news of the *Valencia's* demise. The thick black smoke from the *City of Topeka* stack settled over the windless waters as she hove to to speak to the approaching ship. Suddenly a shape formed in the black smoke cloud. It was the ghostly shape of the *Valencia*.

For years after the wreck the form of the phantom ship would appear to seamen sailing the western coast of Vancouver Island. They would see waves washing over the foundering ship while passengers and crew clung for their lives, the death throes of the *Valencia* replayed over and over.

Fishermen along the coast reported sighting lifeboats moving among the open waters, manned by skeletons—doomed survivors of the *Valencia* wreck. Six months after the *Valencia* tragedy several Indians exploring caves in Pachena Bay not far from where the wreck had occurred discovered a lifeboat floating in one of the caves. Peering into the abandoned boat, they were shocked to see eight skeletons. The cave was large, around two hundred feet deep, with its entrance blocked by a large rock. The lifeboat would have had to be lifted over that rock to enter the cave. How it came to be there was a mystery. Perhaps a very high tide had enabled the boat to wash into the cave. Once there it was trapped, never to escape. Because of the dangerous waters at the cave's opening, the lifeboat and its grisly passengers were never recovered.

(Source: Breakers Away: A History of Shipwrecks in the Graveyard of the Pacific *by R. Bruce Scott.)*

The Haunted Sea King

SEATTLE, WASHINGTON

The *Sea King* plied the waters of the Pacific Northwest for years, visiting ports in Oregon, Washington, and British Columbia. She happened to be in San Francisco just after the 1906 earthquake, and since she was in need of ballast, she was loaded with twisted debris from earthquake damaged buildings. When the ballast was unloaded in Seattle, however, the crew received a shock. Smashed among the twisted girders and broken beams were the bodies of earthquake victims, crushed to death and buried in the earthquake debris.

The ship was henceforth believed to be cursed. Crew members heard nightly groans coming from the hold ... the death groans of the earthquake victims.

(Source: Ghosts: True Stories From British Columbia *by Robert C. Belyk.)*

How To Tell When You've Got a Boat Ghost

SEATTLE, WASHINGTON

William Rudolph, of Seattle, gives this advice:

I met a guy in Alaska once who told me how to tell when a spirit was aboard your boat. He ran too close to some haunted point and picked up one. You could tell when you walked right through it—it was like musty cobwebs. And your dog will jump straight up in the air for no reason. He said it was about driving him crazy so finally he went back to that same place, opened all the pilothouse windows and door and stopped the boat, went out on the back deck and waited. Evidently it did the trick.

(Source: Seattle Times *reporter William Rudolph.)*

SECTION FOUR:

PERSISTENT RELATIONS AND GHOSTLY PETS

Here are a few cases of persistent spouses and some examples of point-of-death apparitions, those spirits who appear briefly after death to reassure relatives or to take care of unfinished business. And as if our houses aren't full enough of ghostly people ... here are a few ghostly animals as well!

WIVES, HUSBANDS, AND LOVERS

Ghostlore and romance seem strange bedfellows, but in these tales the course of love runs up against some ghostly persuasion.

A Valentine's Day Visit from a Dead Wife Disturbs Lovers

SPOKANE, WASHINGTON

Spokane bandleader Russ Andrew misses his deceased wife Betty, yes. But still he'd just as soon she didn't come calling when he is entertaining another woman. That's just what happened on Valentine's Day in 1989, according to Doug Clark's account in the *Spokesman-Review.*

Betty was a strong-willed woman who had once managed the Davenport Hotel coffee shop. She never went anywhere without dabbing on her favorite scent: White Shoulders.

Valentine's Day 1989 was the tenth anniversary of Betty's death, but Russ may not have been thinking of that fact when he climbed into bed for the night with a lady friend. "I had just retired for the night when I felt something brush by my bed," Andrew told Clark. "In the darkness I heard something drop." Andrew turned on the light and looked around. A statue of Cupid hung on the wall of his room. The statue had fallen to the floor. Yet the nail was still firmly fixed in the wall. And the air reeked of White Shoulders perfume.

"I had a friend over that night," admits Andrew. "She had difficulty going back to sleep. In the words of Shakespeare, 'I am thy wife's spirit, doomed for a certain time to walk the night.' "

(Source: Spokane Spokesman-Review *columnist Doug Clark.)*

Haunts Drive Bride from New Husband's Home

MEDFORD, OREGON

When Ruth married Dale Flowers in September of 1969, she was delighted to move into his pleasant home. The couple redecorated to please Ruth's tastes and refurnished the home with many of her own things. Ruth, an avid grower of roses, tackled the garden eagerly, trimming back hedges and planting beds of bright flowers.

But almost immediately, the couple realized they had begun to lose things. When Christmas arrived, the box of Christmas decorations had vanished. They searched high and low and were at a loss to imagine what could have become of them. Then one day, the box appeared in the middle of the living room floor. Except for one large ornament, which was found shining in the doorway of the garage!

When Ruth spoke with reporter Marjorie O'Harra in November of 1970 she was still losing things. "My personal things are always getting lost," said Ruth. "I'll lose them and maybe find them several days later in the cutlery drawer in the kitchen or in some other odd place. A box of my favorite books on roses is gone. We can't find it anywhere. It has just disappeared."

At night the hall light switch turns itself on. The bedroom doorknob turns by itself. Footsteps are heard in the hall. "This has happened repeatedly," says Ruth. One evening as Dale and Ruth sat in the living room a terrible uproar of banging pots, pans and dishes came from the kitchen. But when the Flowers investigated, everything was in place. Nothing was broken or moved. Later that same evening an icy wind suddenly swept through the room, although all doors and windows were closed.

And then there is the lock on the front door. The Flowers make a point of both checking the locks when they leave. But they often return to find the door unlocked. One day they found the door standing open, just as far as the chain would let it swing. Inside on the living room floor was a package of books delivered by mail. Yet the chain would not have allowed a package of that size to be pushed through. Who had unlocked the door and then relocked the chain? And who had knocked over the umbrella stand behind the door?

"I'm not frightened, I'm furious. And anything that is not logical frustrates me," Ruth told Marjorie O'Harra. "Everyone who ever lived in this house before us is dead and I guess the vibrations, or whatever, are just unfriendly to me. I often get a cold, clammy feeling, or I'll sense someone and think Dale is home, but he's not. At first I said, 'Darn you house, you're not going to run me out,' but it has. We've purchased another home and we're moving. After we made the decision there were fewer disturbances."

(Source: Portland Oregonian *reporter Marjorie O'Harra).*

Point-of-Death Apparitions

The appearance of a relative at or near his or her moment of death is not uncommon and seems a quite different phenomena than that of the recurring ghost which attaches itself to a place and appears to total strangers. The point-of-death apparition usually appears only once, communicates briefly, and is not seen again. Here are a few such experiences.

Don't Forget Your Operation!

Victoria, British Columbia

In 1899 Alex Dunsmuir, son of Victoria's coal baron Robert Dunsmuir, married his longtime companion Josephine and took her off to New York City for a honeymoon. The couple had lived together for over twenty years and put off marriage only because of the objections of Dunsmuir's mother. Their marriage, however, came too late. Dunsmuir died in a New York hotel and Josephine herself was seriously ill with cancer. After returning the body to California for burial, Josephine went to Victoria to be with Alex's brother, James, and his family. But while there at James' home, her husband's ghost appeared to her and warned her. "Josephine, pet, you'd better not stay too long or you will be late for your operation."

She took him seriously, packed at once, and left by train for New York and an operation. However, the cancer was only temporarily halted and she died a year later.

(Source: Alex Dunsmuir's Dilemma *by James Audain.)*

A Son's Last Visit

PORT MELLON, BRITISH COLUMBIA

In May of 1985 Kathleen Belanger's son, Roger, was working as a logger up the Elaho Valley near Mile 47. Roger, along with his wife and small children, had just spent Mother's Day with Kathleen.

Kathleen recalled waking up on the morning of May 16 with an overwhelming feeling of dread which she was unable to shake as the day wore on:

"My feeling of dread persists. As a matter of fact, it is getting stronger and stronger ... what is going to happen? We go for coffee with friends. It doesn't help. I am unable to concentrate on shopping. I don't even feel like looking at things. It is two o'clock now and we may as well go home. As we turn into the driveway, I notice that the garage door is wide open. I enter the basement and every door there is wide open. As I turn, there stands Roger, with a big grin on his face. I'm about to ask him what happened, when all of a sudden he is no longer there!"

She decides it must have been her imagination. She and her husband go out to dinner and sit watching boats come into the bay, but her feeling of dread continues. That night the police came to her home.

"As soon as I see them I know that Roger is gone. Roger was hit by a tree 165 feet high and died instantly. I do feel that he came to tell me that he is happy and has not suffered. I am sure that one day we will meet again and that he will most likely still be opening doors for me—maybe this time to let me in."

(Source: Kathleen Belanger in Extraordinary Experiences *by John Robert Colombo.)*

A Ghost Child's Doll

TACOMA, WASHINGTON

Jack L. Sundquist told reporter Kathleen Merryman about a strange incident that happened to his father when Sundquist was a boy in the late 1920s. Sundquist's father worked for the St. Paul and Tacoma Lumber Company mill on the tide flats:

We lived in a company house on St. Paul Avenue …. Papa was into spiritualism and went to séances. Just down the street lived another company worker with his wife and young daughter. The man made fun of Papa's beliefs. Then the daughter died.

A month or so later, one morning Papa was sitting on the edge of the bed, dressing. Mama was in the kitchen making breakfast. Papa saw a light grow in the corner, and suddenly the little girl appeared. Papa said, "Can I help you?" The girl said, "Tell my mother and father to fix my doll in the closet," and she disappeared just as my mother came in.

Sundquist's mother had not seen the little girl, but his father was convinced her visit was real:

When Papa got to work, he went up to the young man, "I know you don't believe in this, but your daughter came to me this morning. She told me to tell you that she wanted you to fix the arm of her doll in the closet." The young man turned white, turned, and ran.

Several hours later, he came back and told my father that he and his wife had found the doll on the floor of the closet under some clothes. One arm was torn almost off. The young man added, "I'll never make fun of your beliefs again."

(Source: Tacoma News Tribune reporter Kathleen Merryman.)

GHOSTLY CRITTERS

A ghost dog, a phantom horse, a levitating pooch, and a ghostly snake! Supernatural visitors in the Pacific Northwest are not always human!

Skipper, the Phantom Dog

KAMLOOPS, BRITISH COLUMBIA

In 1945 a young Vancouver boy moved with his parents to a cattle ranch near Kamloops. The boy and his German shepheard, Skipper, were inseparable as they roamed the hillsides. Back in the hills, in a little log cabin, they discovered an old man. White-bearded Sandy was a friendly sort and soon became a good friend to this boy-dog couple. They often made the trek to his cabin.

Their pleasant life on the ranch continued for five years, but when the boy was fifteen his father decided to send him to the city to summer with his grandmother. Of course, Skipper went along to Vancouver too. But by now Skipper was wiser in the ways of the wild than in the ways of the city. One day the boy was sent on an errand to the corner store by his grandmother. He told Skipper to wait outside. He would just be a minute. But inside the store he heard the sickening squeal of brakes. It was Skipper. He had run into the street and been hit by a car.

The boy couldn't get over the loss of his dog. He imagined that Skipper was still with him, lying right beside his bed as he slept. He was sure he would see Skipper if he looked down.

But he never looked at the phantom dog, just imagined him lying there.

That fall when the boy went walking in the hills he was certain

Skipper followed him. Out of the corner of his eye he would catch a glimpse of the dog. But when he looked there was nothing.

When winter arrived the first snowfall came unexpectedly early and the boy's father sent him on horseback up to Sandy's cabin, to make sure the old man was prepared for the winter. As he rode his horse along the narrow, winding road that crossed the valley to Sandy's cabin he watched the smoke from the chimney and wondered if the old man had noticed him coming. Sure enough, as he drew near Sandy came outside waving. "Where's your dog?" asked the old man. "What?" Sandy knew about Skipper's death so why did he say such a thing?

"I was watching you and your new dog ride up the road. He looks just like your old one. But where'd he go?"

The old man insisted he had seen a dog just like Skipper running along behind the boy's horse. As the boy rode home he looked carefully at his horse's hoof prints in the snow. Sure enough, there was a set of paw prints … exactly like those Skipper used to make. They followed along behind the horse until they came within a hundred yards of the cabin … then suddenly stopped.

The boy received a new puppy the next spring and after that his ghostly companion seems to have faded away. But the boy, now grown, is convinced his ghostly dog was there for a time.

(Source: Ghosts: True Stories from British Columbia *by Robert C. Belyk.)*

A Phantom Horse

Rural Oregon

Mrs. Howard E. Bell recalls unnerving experiences at a former home:

This was a strange unexplained noise at a house we used to live in. And at the time we heard this noise, we had two horses. And the first time I ever heard it I was all alone in the house and I was lying down on the davenport. And this noise came right past the window where I was lying on the davenport. And it was a horse, not trotting, but on the dead gallop. And you could hear it real distinct, just right alongside the house. It scared me to death. Well, my first thought was that one of the horses got out. So I went and looked out the window and there wasn't a thing in sight. In a few minutes the noise came back, same way, on the dead gallop past the window. So I went out in the back and I looked, and both horses were in the pasture.

So I just missed it you know and thought there must be some reason or other for it. And then I got talking to Berniece, and she said she heard that noise in broad daylight—looked out the window and not seen a thing. But the noise was there.

And then one time when I wasn't home, one of my girlfriends came through—crawled through a window and got in my house and she was in the bedroom there, waiting for me to come home, and she heard it. And they looked out—ran and looked out the window. There was nothing there, and it scared 'em so bad they got out of the house; they didn't even wait for me to come home. But it—to be definite about it—it was just a noise of a horse on a dead gallop, thundering past real fast. And then in a few seconds time it would go back past the window. And you could look out in broad daylight and there would be nothing at all there.

(Source: Mrs. Howard E. Bell of Portland, Oregon, *collected by Gary Bell.)*

The Levitating Dachshund

WALLA WALLA, WASHINGTON

Marsha Moore of Walla Walla first knew her house was haunted when she saw her dachshund, Gretchen, run up the stairs and take to the air. "She just started floating and then it was like something threw her back down the stairs," said Marsha.

(Source: Spokesman-Review *columnist Doug Clark.)*

A Ghostly Snake?

TURNBULL NATIONAL WILDLIFE REFUGE
NEAR CHENEY, WASHINGTON

Doug Clark, of the Spokane Spokesman-Review, *solicited ghost stories from his readers. This one is most unusual:*

K atherine Healy ... wrote to tell of Slinky, the snake her husband, Jack, caught during an outing at the Turnbull National Wildlife Refuge. Her two boys wanted to take Slinky home, but Katherine said a photograph would have to do.

She aimed the camera carefully and said she snapped a clear shot as Slinky dangled from Jack's hands. But when they got the film developed, "We just stared, not believing our own eyes. There in perfect focus, was a flawless photograph of Jack's empty hands."

(Source: Spokesman-Review *columnist Doug Clark.)*

NATIVE AMERICAN DEAD DISTURBED

Northwesterners are aware that others have gone before them on this land. Several sightings of Native American specters have been recorded. The reports of Seattle's golf course dancer and Oregon's Klamath Lady show legendry typical of that composed by non-Native Americans.

The concern in the Northwest is not so much with hauntings as with uneasy spirits aroused by grave disturbances. When this problem is identified, a tribal shaman can often calm the disturbed spirits. Reports from the Vancouver, Washington army barracks and the museum in Bellingham relate such instances.

Since the communication with spirits traditional to Northwestern native cultures involves much more than the passing encounters with apparitions indexed here, I have included no Native American legendry in this collection.

One Is Missing

BELLINGHAM, WASHINGTON

This haunting true story serves well to point out Native American concern over the disturbance of their ancestors' skeletal remains:

Jewell James of Bellingham went into the mountains and bathed in freezing water four times to cleanse his spirit before reburying the ancient remains of his Lummi ancestors that bulldozers and archaeologists had unearthed.

Traditionalists told him to purify his mind and body and listen for any message his ancestors' spirits—imprisoned in the boxes with their bones—might tell him.

An archaeologist led James and other Lummi elders to the basement at Western Washington University, where the Lummi remains had been stored.

"As I walked in, I was shocked and overwhelmed," James said. "There were our people stacked in little boxes like cordwood."

As he stared at the pile of about eighty small boxes in front of him, he felt something on his right side—like a child softly climbing up his arm and sitting on his shoulder.

Another elder marked a box—the remains of a young woman. The box shook when he first walked in and in the ancient Lummi language told him, "One is missing."

The elder didn't fully understand the message then, but would soon. James turned and saw a second pile of boxes. "What's in those boxes?" he asked. "Nothing," scientists answered.

He went over and began to shake each box—nothing. But when he picked up about the 21st box, something rattled, he opened it and found rocks and elk antlers. "See," James remembers scientists telling him. "We told you there was nothing there."

James went quietly through about 15 more empty boxes. He got to the last box and opened it. Inside was a baby's skeleton.

"That was my first confirmation of the spirituality of death," said James, after he realized that the spirit of a young mother had implored him not to forget her baby. "Anyone else would have thought the wind was blowing across their shoulder. But I didn't ignore it. And I found the baby. ..."

"I wonder," James said, "how many people that keep these bones in boxes, drawers, and museums walk by and think all they heard or felt was the wind."

James added that he and other Lummi tribal members will not rest until the Smithsonian and other universities and museums have returned all Lummi remains from their collections.

(Source: Seattle Times *reporter Brigid Schule.)*

Uneasy Spirits at the Vancouver Army Barracks

VANCOUVER, WASHINGTON

In June 1993 the *Seattle Times* reported that a number of Cowlitz spirits had been laid to rest in Vancouver. The remains of these tribal members were discovered in 1982 when workers were looking for a water pipe in the basement of the auditorium near Fort Vancouver. The graves were in land formerly part of a Roman Catholic cemetery. In 1860 the marked graves from the cemetery had been moved to the Vancouver Barracks Post Cemetery, but these unmarked graves had been left behind. Many of them contained Indian remains. Later the barracks auditorium was built right over this site.

Cowlitz holy man, Roy Wilson, used smoke from burning sage and an eagle feather in his cleansing ceremony aimed at easing the troubled spirits, who had been restless since their graves were disturbed in 1982. The ceremony freed the spirits from the remnants of their earthly lives, Wilson said. "The old tradition is that spirits would stay in a disturbed area unless released from the earth. We don't think of it as haunting, but they were present here before the ceremony. We believe that after what happened today they will be happy. The remains will now be re-interred."

However, these seem not to have been the only restless spirits at the Vancouver Army Barracks. At least four employees have heard ghostly soldiers at work upstairs in the barracks at night. "If you work late at night you can hear footsteps upstairs, people talking, and doors opening and closing," said Lt. Col. Ward Jones, the post's commanding officer. "I don't think they're haunting us. I just figure it's a coexistence: we work during the day and they work during the night."

(Source: Seattle Times.*)*

Chief Seattle on the Invisible Dead

Perhaps it is fitting that we end this collection of ghost-lore of the Pacific Northwest with words from the prophetic speech given by Chief Seattle in 1854. His speech was recreated by Dr. Henry A. Smith who heard the Chief's oration:

And when the last Red Man shall have perished, and the memory of my tribe shall have become a myth among the white men, these shores will swarm with the invisible dead of my tribe, and when your children's children think themselves alone in the field, the store, the shop, upon the highway, or in the silence of the pathless woods, they will not be alone. In all the earth there is no place dedicated to solitude. At night when the streets of your cities and villages are silent and you think them deserted, they will throng with the returning hosts that once filled and still love this beautiful land. The White Man will never be alone. Let him be just and deal kindly with my people, for the dead are not powerless. Dead I say? There is no death. Only a change of worlds.

(Source: History of Seattle, Washington *by Frederick James Grant.)*

Afterword

So what do we make of all this? Clearly many indviduals in the Northwest have had experiences they believe were encounters with "ghosts." Parapsychologists have spent much effort trying to prove that apparitions and poltergeists are either (1) hallucinations (individual or group), (2) examples of psychokinesis, (3) examples of extrasensory perception (crises apparitions in which a living person appears in time of danger and point-of-death apparitions are considered in this theory), or (4) survivals of formerly living humans (though survival as an apparition does not necessarily imply a life after death).There is little agreement among parapsychologists on these matters. Some favor one theory, some another. For a review of parapsychological research to 1989 see *An Introduction to Parapsychology* by H.J. Irwin (Jefferson, N.C.: McFarland, 1989).

From the medical field comes another theory which may explain some supernatural experiences. A sleep disorder known as hypnogogic hallucination can cause terrifying experiences in the sleeper. In this disorder the body falls asleep before the brain with the result that the individual feels paralyzed and hears normal sounds magnified terrifyingly. This phenomena is discussed at length in the book by David Hufford, *The Terror That Comes in the Night* (Philadelphia: University of Pennsylvania, 1982).

Another fascinating explanation of ghostlore is the historical study of ghosts through the ages written by University of Puget Sound visiting professor R.C. Finucane. He suggests that ghosts have been toned down in terror and appearance for the last two hundred years. In his book *Appearances of the Dead* Finucane cites ghostly appearances from earlier ages: Roman, Greek, early-Christian, Medieval, Reformation, Baroque, Enlightened, and Contemporary. He shows that the grizzly, chain shaking, expounding ghosts of earlier ages have given way to gray, non-substantial forms which can only moan and stare. According to Finucane, beginning in the mid-eighteenth century, ghosts lost their ability to communicate and interfere with human affairs. He suggests that with the loss of identification with community and extended family, the ancestral ghost no longer had a function. Gradually ghosts became simply symbols of immortality. Then needed only to appear occasionally as proof of "something" on the other side of the grave. To Finucane this transformation of the ghostly form proves that the ghost is the product, not of another dimension, but of an inner dimension ... the mind of man.

On the other hand Northwest ghost hunters such as Robin Skelton and Jean Kozocari write convincingly of their personal encounters with ghosts in Victoria, British Columbia. They use the tools of witchcraft to exorcise these wandering spirits and explain it all quite sensibly in *A Gathering of Ghosts: Hauntings and Exorcisms from the Personal Casebook of Robin Skelton and Jean Kozocari* (Buffalo, N.Y.: Prometheus, 1992).

Or for a totally skeptical look at poltergeist activity you might want to read the writings of magician Joe Nickell. He has made it his business to investigate and debunk several noted hauntings. In books such as *Mysterious Realms: Probing Paranormal, Historical, and Forensic Enigmas* (Buffalo, N.Y.: Prometheus, 1992) Nickell uses his considerable skills as a magician to replicate exactly some of the more mysterious events reported in haunted houses and concludes that the hauntees are publicity seeking frauds.

However you explain the ghostly phenomena reported in this book, it is obvious that *something* strange is going on. You will have to decide for yourself just what that something is.

Here are some books to help you explore Northwestern folklore further.

A Ghostly BIBLIOGRAPHY
More Ghostlore of the Pacific Northwest:

Belyk, Robert C. *Ghosts: True Stories from British Columbia* (Ganges, British Columbia: Horsdale & Schubart 1990).

Columbo, John Robert. *Extraordinary Experiences: Personal Accounts of the Paranormal in Canada* (Willowdale, Ontario: Hounslow Press, 1989).

Columbo, John Robert. *Mysterious Canada: Strange Sights, Extraordinary Events, and Peculiar Places* (Toronto: Doubleday Canada, 1988).

Helm, Mike. *Oregon's Ghosts & Monsters* (Eugene, Oregon: Rainy Day Press, 1983).

Hervey, Sheila. *Some Canadian Ghosts* (Richmond Hill, Ontario: Simon and Schuster of Canada, 1973).

Lind, C.J. *Western Gothic* (Self-published by Carol Lind, 1983).

Salmonson, Jessica Amanda. *The Mysterious Doom and Other Ghostly Tales of the Pacific Northwest* (Seattle, Wa.: Sasquatch Books, 1992).

Skelton, Robin and Jean Kozocari. *A Gathering of Ghosts: Hauntings and Exorcisms from the Personal Casebook of Robin Skelton and Jean Kozocari* (Saskatoon, Saskatchewan: Western Producer Prairie Books, 1989)

Notes

These notes give complete citations for the sources used in preparing accounts. In addition, motif numbers are provided for those incidents occuring in each episode. By refering to these motif numbers in the Ghostly Index you will discover whether or not there are other instances of these occurrences in the Northwest.

Section 1: At Home with Ghosts

A House Like Yours and Mine—Only Haunted

PORTRAIT OF A GHOST: Chilliwack, B.C. "That's the Spirit: She's the Hostess With the Ghostess" by Michael Cobb, *The Vancouver Sun*, (Vancouver, B.C.) 30 May 1966. Based on interview with Mrs. Hetty Frederickson, owner of the house on Williams Street in Chilliwack, B.C.; "Hundreds Haunt Ghost," *The Province* (Vancouver, B.C.) 6 June 1966. Reporters spent the night with Mrs. Hetty Frederickson in her home; and "Portrait of a Ghost," *The Province* (Vancouver, B.C.) 30 May 1966.

    Motifs: E402.1.2 Footsteps of invisible ghost heard; E451.8.(c). Ghost laid when home it haunts burns; *F473.1.(g)(a). Spirit moves things around; E402.1.1(12). Sound of ghost breathing; E588.(1). Ghost leaves perfume odor; E421.(7). Ghost disappears as one watches; E334.2.1.(o). Ghost of murdered person haunts room where he was murdered; E334.4. Ghost of suicide seen at death spot or nearby; E402.1.7. Ghost slams door; E421.1.3. Ghost visible to dog alone; *F473.2.(6). Heat turned up, house stifling; *E532.(1). Other attributes of ghostly portrait; *E451.(0.1). Attempt to calm ghost by painting its portrait; E422.4.4.(k). Female revenant in red dress.

WATCH THE HANKY-PANKY, GRANDPA'S IN THE BEDROOM: Ellensburg, Wa. Doug Clark's column, *The Spokesman-Review* (Spokane, Wa.) 30 Oct. 1990: p. B1. Clark had asked for readers to send in their ghost stories.

    Motif: E378. Ghost continues to remain in usual surroundings after death; E422.4.5. Ghost in male dress.

A GHOSTLY WASHERMAN, A TV WATCHING GHOST, AND OTHER NEW WESTMINSTER HAUNTS: New Westminster, B.C. Source: "A Ghost That Stayed Away" by Shelly Fralic, *The Vancouver Sun*, (Vancouver, B.C.) 1 Nov. 1982: pp. A1-2. Based on interview with Jim and Lou Dodds, owners of home in New Westminster.

Motifs: E421.1.3. Ghost visible only to dog; E422.4.5.(b) Male revenant in old-fashioned garb; E422.4.4.(h). Female revenant in old-fashioned garb; *E542.(6). Ghost's nearness to person felt as chill; *F473.3.(2). Spirit sits close to person on bed or couch; F473.3.1. Spirit places cold hand on person; F473.2.3. Spirit puts out lights (or puts them on); *E440.(0).(1). Ghost investigated by medium but not laid; E425.(7). Revenant as other specific person; E421.6. Ghost visible only out of corner of eye.

SAVED FROM A BURNING HOUSE: Port Townsend, Wa. "Manressa Castle Ghost Rarely Materializes: No Historical Facts Back Halloween Story" by Eleanor Nelson, *Port Townsend/Jefferson County Leader*, 27 Oct. 1993.

Motifs: E363.1.(h). Ghost warns of fire.

THE MAN IN THE COWBOY HAT TEACHES MATH: Richland, Wa. "When the Spirits Move Them" by Kathleen Knutson, *Tri-City Herald* (Pasco, Wa.) 29 Oct. 1990: C1. Based on interview with Barbara Sponholtz, Richland resident.

Motifs: E402.1.5. Ghost knocks on furniture; E422.4.5. Revenant in male dress; *E421.(6). Ghost visible only out of corner of eye: E451.4.(0).(2). Ghost does not calm down when spoken to; E451.4. Ghost laid when living man speaks to it; E402.1.1.(9). Ghost speaks; *F473.2.(8). Spirit causes toilet to act contrary to nature; E338.1.(c). Ghost opens doors and windows repeatedly; *E440.(0.2). Ghost investigated by priest but no attempt to lay.

THE GLASS BREAKING GHOST: Spokane, Wa. Doug Clark's column, *The Spokesman-Review* (Spokane, Wa.) 21 Oct. 1990: p. B1. From letter sent to Clark by Bob Lund of Spokane, Wa.

Motifs: F473.1.(g). Spirit throws furniture and crockery around house, often destructively.

THE ROCKING GHOST: Spokane, Wa. Doug Clark's column, *The Spokesman-Review* (Spokane, Wa.) 21 Oct. 1990: p. B1. From letter sent to Clark by Irma Breesnee, owner of house on East 20th St. in Spokane, Wa.

Motifs: E338.1.(c). Ghost opens doors and windows repeatedly; E338.1.(hg). Ghost causes rocking chair to rock; E338.1(hb). Ghost cleans house; F473.2.1. Empty chair is rocked by invisible spirit who sits in it and rocks; E378. Ghost continues to remain in usual surroundings after death.

A SAD LITTLE GIRL: Spokane, Wa. Column by Doug Clark in Spokane, *The Spokesman-Review* (Spokane, Wa.) 21 Oct. 1990: p. B1.

Motif: E425.3. Revenant as child; *E338.14.2. Ghost haunts crisis nursery.

"COME OUT AND HELP ME!": Tacoma, Wa. Article "Come out and help me" by Dwight Jarrell, *Morning News Tribune* (Tacoma, Wa.), Sunday, 14 June 1970: A1. From interview with Mrs. Francine Pacinda of 4314 S. 8th St., Tacoma.

Motifs: *E402.1.1.1.1(1). Ghost cries "Help"; E 402. Mysterious ghost-like noises heard; E402.1.7. Ghost slams door; E402.1.1.2. Ghost moans; E402.1.2. Footsteps of invisible ghost heard; *E470.(2). Living flee building inhabited by ghostly presence; *F473.2.(5). Ghost causes objects to swing back and forth; F473.2.3. Spirit puts out lights; F473.1(g). Spirit throws furniture or crockery about, often destructively; E279.2.(a). Ghost disturbs sleeping child.

PINE PANEL VOICES: Tacoma, Wa. "Dark Shadows Lurk in Tacoma Homes: Readers Share Their Ghost Stories" by Kathleen Merryman. *Morning News Tribune* (Tacoma, Wa.) 31 Oct. 1985: B9-B11. Information from letter written to Merryman by Pat Stromberg of Tacoma.

Motifs: E451.4.(0.1). Ghost calms down when spoken to; E402.1.1.2. Ghost moans.

THE OBEDIENT GHOST: Vancouver, B.C. "Oscar's Tricks" by Robert C. Belyk in *Ghosts: True Stories from B.C.* (Ganges, B.C.: Horsdal & Schubart, 1990), pp. 49-51. Belyk interviewed Anne Houseman of East Second Avenue in Vancouver on March 25, 1989.

Motifs: E470.(1). Living content to live with ghostly presence; *F473.2.(5). Ghost causes objects to swing back and forth; *E402.1.5.(a).1. Ghost drags furniture around; *F473.1.(g).(a). Spirit moves things around; E402.1.2. Footsteps of invisible ghost heard; E281.3(b). Ghost lays hand on girl awake in bed; *E451.4.(0.1). Ghost calms down when spoken to; F473.2.3.(6). Appliances turned on and off or machinery runs unattended; F473.2.3. Spirit puts out lights (or puts them on).

THE ROSEWOOD BED: Vancouver, B.C. Article by Greg McIntyre in *The Province* (Vancouver, B.C.) 25 Oct. 1987; *Some Canadian Ghosts* by Sheila Hervey. (Richmond Hill, Ontario: Simon & Schuster of Canada, 1973), pp. 18-21.

Motifs: E337(a). Re-enactment of activities just before violent death; *E421.2.1.(1). Ghost leaves footprints; E539. Other ghostly objects.

A CARING HOSTESS: Vancouver, B.C. "The Woman Appeared to Me with Perfect Clarity" by Sylvia Taylor in *Extraordinary Experiences: Personal Accounts of the Paranormal in Canada* by John Robert Colombo (Willodale, Ontario; Hounslow Press, 1989), pp. 110-113. This account is from letters written by Sylvia Taylor June 4 and July 15, 1987.

Motifs: E378. Ghost continues to remain in usual surroundings after death; E422.4.4.(h). Female revenant in old-fashioned garb; E334.4. Ghost of suicide seen in death spot or nearby.

THE WASHING MACHINE GHOST: Victoria, B.C. From "More Houses" in *Ghosts: True Stories from B.C.* by Robert C. Belyk (Ganges, B.C.: Hordsdal & Schubart, 1990), p. 58. Belyk interviewed Rick Johnson, March 11, 1989.

Motifs: E338.1.(c). Ghost opens doors and windows repeatedly; *F473.2.3.(6). Appliances turned on and off or machinery runs unattended; *F473.2.(6). Heat turned up. House stifling; *E470.(2). Living flee building inhabited by ghost; E458.1.8.(e). Ghost laid when house it haunts is torn down; *F473.1.(g)(b). Objects sail across room in plain view.

Rental Ghosts

The Burglar Proof Apartment: Capitol Hill area, Seattle, Wa.: "Haunted Apartment Had Built-in Security System" by Leon A. Espinoza, *Seattle Times*, 11 Sept. 1991: p. H1. Appeared in Espinoza's column "Apartment Life." Taken from a letter written to Espinoza by Leon Thompson, and a follow-up interview with Thompson and his roommate Ray Tweedy.

Motifs: *F473.1.(g)(b). Objects sail across room in plain view; *E279.2.(1). Ghost sits on legs of person in bed; E293.1. Ghost scares thief, prevents theft; F473.3.(i). Spirit lifts person to ceiling, lets her down again; *E470.(1). Living are content to live with ghostly presence.

Children's Gravestones Pave the Path to a Haunted Fourplex: Coquitlam, B.C. Article by Salim Jiwa, *The Vancouver Sun*, (Vancouver, B.C.), 9 Dec. 1983: p. 3. From interview with Mrs. Lucille Schneider and her next-door neighbor Mrs. Hutton; "Wild About Harry" by Walter Melynek ,*The Province* (Vancouver, B.C.), 21 Feb. 1986: p. 4. Based on interview with residents of Coquitlam fourplex; "Is 'Harry' For Real?" by Walter Menyk, *The Province* (Vancouver, B.C.), 2 March 1986. Based on interview with psychic Ralph Hurst.

Motifs: E386.5. Offhand remark about what person would do if ghost appeared causes ghost to appear; *F473.2.3.(6). Appliances turned on and off or machinery runs unattended; *F473.2.(5). Ghost causes objects to swing back and forth; *E273.(1). Ghost haunts spot to which tombstones are removed; E425.3. Revenant as child; E425.2.3. Ghost of priest or parson; E338.1.(b). Ghost looks in at window; E279.2.(b). Ghost shakes bed of sleeper.

A Ghostly Tenant: Tacoma, Wa.: "Dark Shadows Lurk in Tacoma Homes: Readers Share Their Ghost Stories," *The Morning News Tribune* (Tacoma, Wa.), 31 Oct. 1985: p. B11. Based on interview with Phyllis Wire, owner of rental home in Tacoma.

Motifs: F473.3.(4). Spirit taps person on shoulder; E421.1.3. Ghost visible only to dog; F473.2.2. Spirit hides articles in strange places; *E470.(1). Living are content to live with ghostly presence.

A Neighborhood of Ghosts

Three Haunted Houses on One Dead End Road: Duvall, Wa. Article by Patricia Wren in *Journal-American* (Bellevue, Wa.), Tuesday, 31 Oct. 1978: p. 1. Based on interviews with Gil Hackenbruch, Einor Ryan, and Bob Cronin, residents of Bruett Road near Duvall, Wa.

Motifs: E422.4.4.(b). Female revenant in gray clothing; E402.1.2. Footsteps of invisible ghost heard; E338.1.(c). Ghost opens and closes doors repeatedly; E402.1.5. Invisible ghost makes rapping or knocking noises; E530.1.6.(d). Building seen to light up in mysterious manner before death occurs; E539. Other ghostly objects.

Three Haunted Houses on Lombard Loop Road: Sawyer, Wa. Yakima

County, Wa. "The Friendly Ghost of Lombard Loop" by Patricia Wren *Seattle Post-Intelligencer,* (Seattle, Wa.), Wednesday, 12 Oct. 1977: p. A-5. Reprinted from the *Yakima Herald Republic* (Yakima, Wa.). Based on interview with Helen Mahre, Mrs. Johnnie Finley, Mrs. James Young, and one other unnamed woman, all residents of homes on Lombard Loop near Sawyer, Wa.

Motifs: E338.1.(c). Ghost opens or closes door repeatedly; E402.1.2. Footsteps of invisible ghost heard; *E402.1.1.(1). Ghost cries "Help"; *E470.(2). Living flee building inhabited by ghostly presence; *F473.2.3.(5). Radio turned on or off, stations changed; *F473.2.3.(6). Appliances turned on and off or machinery runs unattended; *E451.8.(e). Ghost laid when house it haunts is torn down; E334.2.1. Ghost of murdered person haunts burial spot; *E470.(1.1). Person feels responsibility to ghosts.

A NEIGHBORHOOD RAPPING GHOST: Wells, B.C. "The Rapping Ghost" in *Ghosts: True Stories from B.C.* by Robert C. Belyk (Ganges, B.C.: Horsdal & Schubart, 1990), pp. 62-63. Based on interview with John Candy, December 6, 1989. Candy resided on a cul-de-sac in Wells, B.C.

Motifs: E422.4.4. Revenant in female dress; F473.5(a). Knocking or rappings that cannot be traced; E588.(1). Ghost leaves perfume odor.

RURAL GHOSTS

THE OLD APPLEGATE PLACE: Applegate River, near Yoncalla, Ore."Vibrations: Quavering Echoes of the Dead Still Live on, Some Say, in Creaky Old Applegate House" by Dean Baker, *The Register-Guard* (Eugene, Ore.), Friday, 31 Oct. 1975: pp. A1-A3; *Skookum: An Oregon Pioneer Family's History and Lore* by Shannon Applegate (New York: Beech Tree Books/William Morrow, 1988, p. 417).

Motifs: *E470.(1). Living content to live with ghostly presence; *E470.(1.1). Living feel responsibility to ghosts; E402.1.2. Footsteps of invisible ghost heard; E422.4.4.(h). Female revenant in old-fashioned garb; E338.1.(h)(g). Ghost causes rocking chair to rock; E555. Dead man smokes pipe; *E402.1.1.9.1. Sounds of ghosts talking, not intelligible; *E451.4.(0.1). Ghost calms down when spoken to; F473.5.(a). Knockings and rapping that cannot be traced; *E539.(6). Ghostly clock strikes without mechanism; E402.1.3.(a). Ghost plays violin; E402.3.(6). Clock without mechanism strikes.

THE ROCKING CRADLE: Preserving a Ghost For History's Sake: Applegate River, Ore. Interview from Jenny Alexander, age 19. Collected over coffee at kitchen table in her home in Jacksonville, Ore., April 21, 1984. Collected by Leslie D. Clason, age 19, Medford, Ore. University of Oregon student. Randall V. Mills Archives, University of Oregon.

Motifs: F473.2.1.(1). Cradle rocked by invisible spirit; E334.2.2. Ghost of person killed in accident seen at death or burial spot.

THE STORY OF THE GREEN LADY: Jacksonville, Ore. Interview with Jenny

Alexander, age 19. Collected at kitchen table over coffee in her home, Jacksonville, Ore., April 21, 1984. Collected by University of Oregon student Leslie D. Clason, age 19, Medford, Ore. Randall V. Mills Archives, University of Oregon.

Motifs: E422.4.4.(c). Female revenant in green dress; E574. Ghost as death omen.

THE STORY OF THE CREAKING MANTEL: Rogue River, Ore. Interview with Jenny Alexander, age 19. Collected at kitchen table in her Jacksonville, Ore. home, April 21, 1984. Collected by Leslie D. Clason, age 19, Medford, Ore. Randall V. Mills Archives, University of Oregon.

Motifs: E402.2.3. Hoofbeats of ghost horse; E334.2.1.(o). Ghost of murdered person haunts room where he was murdered; E539. Other ghostly objects.

MAJOR, THE GHOST BITING WATCHDOG: Rock Creek, B.C."The Ghost of Rock Creek" by Frank Western Smith in *Extraordinary Experiences: Personal Accounts of the Paranormal in Canada* by John Robert Colombo (Willodale, Ontario: Hounslow, 1989), pp. 131-133.

Motifs: *E462.(1). Dog bites ghost; E338.1.(a.a). Ghosts knock on door; E402.1.2. Footsteps of invisible ghost heard; *E542.6.(1). Ghost's nearness to person felt as chill; E555. Dead man smokes pipe; E421.1.3. Ghost visible only to dog.

GENTLE RESIDENT SPIRIT FOR SALE—THE PILLOW FIGHTING GHOST: Shaw Island, Wa. "Gentle Resident Spirit for Sale" by Don Tewkesbury, *Seattle Post-Intelligencer*, (Seattle, Wa.) 19 Jan. 1987: D1.

Motifs: E421.1 Invisible ghost; E402.1.2. Footsteps of invisible ghost heard; E338.1.(c). Ghost opens doors and windows repeatedly; *F473.3.(e.2). Spirit pushes man violently from behind; F473.2.(5). Ghost causes objects to swing back and forth; F473.3.(l). Spirit places cold hand on person; E470.(1) Living are content to live with ghostly presence; *F473.2.3.(5). Radio turned on or off, station changed; *F473.3.(4). Spirit taps person on shoulder or taps at sleeve; *F433.2.3.(6). Appliances turned on and off or machinery runs unattended; F461. Fight of revenant with living person.

THE SNORING GHOST: VANCOUVER ISLAND. Source: "The Snoring Ghost" by Margery Wighton, *Vancouver Sun,* (Vancouver, B.C.) 27 Dec. 1952.

Motifs: E402.1.1.5. Ghost snores; E334.2. Ghost haunts burial spot; E402.1.2. Footsteps of invisible ghost heard.

HAUNTED MANSIONS

SARAH OF GEORGETOWN CASTLE: Seattle, Wa. "Ghost Stories" by Paul Andrews, *Seattle Times/Post-Intelligencer,* (Seattle, Wa.) 30 Oct. 1983: *Pacific Magazine* pp. 6-7. Based on the reporter's interview with Rick Peterson of Seattle.

Motifs: E542.(5). Ghost's nearness to person felt as chill; E402.1.6.

Crash of breaking glass, though no glass is found; E422.4.4(h). Female revenant in old-fashioned garb; E461. Fight of revenant with living person; *E470.(1). Living are content to live with ghostly presence; *F473.1(g)(b). Objects sail across room in plain view; E337.(a). Re-enactment of activities just before violent death; *E451.(0.1). Attempt to calm ghost by painting its portrait.

THE GENTLEMANLY GHOST OF THE RHODES MANSION: Tacoma, Wa. "Hosts For Ghost: Homeowners Say Polite Spirits Pose No Special Problems" by Kathleen Merryman, *The Morning News-Tribune* (Tacoma, Wa.), 31 Oct. 1993: pp. 3-4. Based on interview by reporter Merryman with Tacoma resident Lou Anne Sterbick-Nelson.

Motifs: E338.1(c). Ghost opens and closes doors and windows repeatedly; *E542.(7). Ghost brushes past person; *E421.(7). Ghost disappears as one watches; E422.4.5.(6). Revenant in male dress; *E421.1.1.(2). Ghost visible to child alone; *E470.(2.1). Living uneasy with ghostly presence; *F473.2.3.(6). Appliances turned on and off or machinery runs unattended; *E470.(1). Living are content to live with ghostly presence; E402.1.2. Footsteps of invisible ghost heard; *E338.1.(j). Ghost haunts hall.

HAUNTED GOVERNOR'S MANSION: Salem, Ore. "Oregon Governor Prepares To Move into New Haunts" in *The Morning News Tribune* (Tacoma, Wa.) 18 November, 1987, B5. From interviews with W. Gordon Allen, Ben Colbath, and Governor Neil Goldschmidt.

Motifs: E279.2.(b). Ghost shakes bed of sleeper; *E279.2.(1). Ghost sits on legs of person in bed; E402.1.8. Miscellaneous sounds made by ghost of human being; E422.4.5.(b). Male revenant in old-fashioned garb.

Section 2: Public Ghosts

HOTEL GHOSTS

THE PIANIST OF HOT LAKE RESORT: La Grande, Ore. "Are There Ghosts at Hot Lake?" *The Observer* (La Grande, Ore.), 27 Oct. 1977: p. 11.
Motifs: E402.1.1.3. Ghost cries and screams; *E402.1.3.(b).1. Ghost plays piano; *F473.1.(ga). Spirit moves things around; F473.2.1. Empty chair is rocked by invisible spirit who sits in it and rocks; E402.1.2. Footsteps of invisible ghost heard.

THE FEMME FATALE OF ROSARIO RESORT: Orcas Island, Wa. "Seattle Spirits" by Kathryn Robinson, *Seattle Weekly*, October 28-November 3, 1987: p. 36.
Motifs: E421.4. Ghost as shadow: *E338.6.(1). Ghost haunts resort; *F473.3.1. Spirit takes hand of person.

THE TOWER ROOM OF MANRESA CASTLE: Port Townsend, Wa. "Manresa Castle Ghost Rarely Materializes: No Historical Facts Back Halloween Story" by Eleanor Nelson, *Port Townsend/ Jefferson County Leader,* (Port

Townsend, Wa.) 27 Oct. 1993. "Ghosts of … Maresa Castle" by Eleanor Nelson, *Island Independent* (Langley, Wa.), 28 Oct. 1993: p. 11; "Eerie Apparition Drives Adults from Castle" by Don Tewkesbury, *Seattle Post-Intelligencer*, (Seattle, Wa.): C1-C2; "Ghost" Makes Pre-Halloween Appearance at Manresa Castle" by Patrick J. Sullivan, *Port Townsend/ Jefferson County Leader*. Page from Manresa Castle guest book, signed by Sam Johnston, Sue Johnston, Lee Bramlet, Spencer Freeman, and Rod Freeman. Dated October 31, 1992.

Motifs: E402.1.1.(9). Ghost speaks; E34.4. Ghost of suicide seen at death spot or nearby; *F473.1.(gd). Spirit causes glass to shatter; *F473.1.(ga). Spirit moves things around; E422.4.4.(a). Female revenant in white clothing; *E421.(0.1). Transparent ghosts; E421.3. Luminous ghosts; *E338.6. Ghost haunts hotel; E588. Ghost leaves stench behind; *E558.(1). Ghost leaves perfume odor; *E363.1.(h). Ghost warns of fire; E425.2.3. Ghost of priest or parson; F473.2.3. Spirit puts out light (or puts them on).

OLD STRAND HOTEL PROPRIETOR STAYS ON IN NEW HARVEST HOUSE BED & BREAKFAST: Prosser, Wa. "Is the Harvest House Haunted?" by Gale Metcalf, *Tri-City Herald*, (Pasco, Wa.) June 23, 1995: pp. B1-B2. Based on interview with Mike and Koni Wallace who manage the Harvest House Bed & Breakfast.

Motifs: *E470.(1). Living are content to live with ghostly presence; E338.1.(c). Ghost opens doors and windows repeatedly; F473.2.2. Spirit hides articles in strange places; F473.1.(ga). Spirit moves things around; E402.1.5.(a.1). Ghost drags furniture around; *E338.6. Ghost haunts hotel.

THE GOVERNESS OF ROCHE HARBOR: Roche Harbor, San Juan Island, Wa. "Seattle Spirits" by Kathyrn Robinson, *Seattle Weekly*, (Seattle, Wa.) October 28-November 3, 1987: p. 36.

Motifs: F473.2.3. Spirit puts out lights (or puts them on); *F473.2.3.(1.1). Spirit re-ignites candles; *F473.2.3.(6). Appliances turned on and off or machinery runs unattended; E338.1.(c). Ghost opens doors and windows repeatedly; *E338.6.(1). Ghost haunts resort.

HAUNTED RESTAURANTS

E.R. ROGERS RESTAURANT: A HAUNTED SPOT TO DINE IN STYLE: "The Spirit of Steilacoom" by Kathleen Merryman, *The Morning News Tribune* (Tacoma, Wa.), 31 Oct. 1991: pp. 3-4.

Motifs: *E338.(13). Ghost haunts restaurant; E422.4.4. Revenant in female dress; E588.(1). Ghost leaves perfume odor; F473.2.(6). Appliances turned on and off or machinery runs unattended; F473.2.3. Spirit puts out lights (or turns on); E421.1.3. Ghost seen only by dog; *E470.(2). Living flee building inhabited by ghostly presence; E425.2.4. Revenant as American Indian; E422.1.11.2. Revenant as face; E334.2.1. Ghost of murdered person haunts burial spot; *F473.1.(gb). Objects sail across room in plain view.

THE DRUGSTORE GHOST WHO HATES YUPPIE SAUCES: Steilacoom, Wa.

"The Spirit of Steilacoom" by Kathleen Merryman, *The Morning News Tribune* (Tacoma, Wa.) 31 Oct. 1991: pp. 3-4.

Motifs: *F473.2.3.(6). Appliance turned on and off or machinery runs unattended; *F473.2.(6). Heat turned up, house stifling; F473.2.2. Spirit hides articles in strange places; F473.1.(g). Spirits throw furniture and crockery about, often destructively; *E338.(13). Ghost haunts restaurant; *E338.(15). Ghost haunts store; E422.4.5.(b). Male revenant in old-fashioned garb.

THE COLLEGE INN PUB: Seattle, Wa. "Seattle Spirits" by Kathryn Robinson, *Seattle Weekly*, (Seattle, Wa.) Oct. 28-Nov. 2, 1987: p. 34.

Motifs: *E338.(13). Ghost haunts restaurant; E422.4.5. Revenant in male dress.

THE DINGLE HOUSE RESTAURANT GHOST: Victoria (Gorge Inlet), B.C.. "The Haunting of Dingle House" by Alice Tomlinson, *Western Living*, Oct. 1981: pp. 45-49.

Motifs: *E338.(13). Ghost haunts restaurant; *F473.2.3.(2). Spirit unplugs equipment; *E572.(1). Person walks through ghost; *E470.(1). Living are content to live with ghostly presence; E422.4.5. Revenant in male dress; *E470.(1.1). Person feels responsibility to ghost.

GHOSTLY MUSEUMS

BURNABY ART GALLERY HAUNTINGS: Burnaby, B.C. "Is Somebody There?" by Damian Inwood, *The Province* (Vancouver, B.C.), 15 Dec. 1985: Magazine pp. 3, 10; "Ghost Eludes Our Intrepid Reporter" by John Armstrong, *The Vancouver Sun*, (Vancouver, B.C.) 31 Oct. 1987: H1; "Ghost in Gallery" by Kim Bolen, *The Vancouver Sun*, 31 Oct. 1986: A3.

Motifs: *E440.(0.1). Ghost investigated by medium but no attempt to lay; *E422.4.4 (b). Female revenant in gray clothing; *E422.4.4(f). Female revenant in blue clothing; E422.4.4.(a). Female revenant in white clothing; E338.(ba). Female ghost in rustling silks seen and heard walking about in house; E542.(6). Ghost's nearness to person felt as chill; *F473.1.(ga). Spirit moves things around; *F473.2.(5). Ghost causes objects to swing back and forth; E425.3. Revenant as child; E402.1.5.(g). Ghost scratches at door; E422.4.4.(g). Female revenant often invisible in rustling silk dress.

FORT GEORGE WRIGHT HISTORICAL MUSEUM: Fort Wright, Wa. "Ghosts" by Christopher Bogan, *The Spokesman-Review* (Spokane, Wa.), 26 Oct. 1980: pp. D1-2.

Motifs: E422.4.4. Revenant in female dress; E402.1.2. Footsteps of invisible ghost heard; F473.2.3. Spirit puts out lights (or puts them on); E402.1.7. Ghost slams door; E338.1.(c). Ghost opens doors and windows repeatedly; F402.1.1.3. Ghost cries and screams; F402.1.1.4. Ghost sings.

UNEASY SPIRITS AT THE WING LUKE MUSEUM: Seattle, Wa. "Seattle Spirits" by Kathryn Robinson, *Seattle Weekly*, (Seattle, Wa.) Oct. 28-Nov. 3, 1987: p. 33.

Motifs: E338.1.(g). Ghost haunts cellar; *E338.(13). Ghost haunts restaurant; E334.2.1.(o). Ghost of murdered person haunts room where he was murdered; E443. Ghost exorcised and laid; E299.4.(1). Force shatters glass case. A paranormal force, not a ghost; E402.1.1.3. Ghost cries and screams.

The Lady Mayor in Seattle's Smith Tower: Seattle, Wa."Smith Tower Site Becomes a Historic Haunt" by Judi Hunt, *Seattle Post-Intelligencer,* (Seattle, Wa.) 5 Mar. 1987: p. C8.

   Motifs: *E379.(5.2). Ghost in museum which houses possessions; E421.(6). Ghost visible out of corner of eye; E422.4.4. Revenant in female dress.

GHOSTS IN MUSEUM HOUSES

Oregon City's Historical Ghosts: Oregon City, Ore. "Resident Ghosts Get Halloween off at Oregon City Historic Homes" by Rod Patterson, *Oregonian,* Thursday 26, Oct. 1989: p. 2; Article by Dennis McCarthy *Oregonian,* 30 Oct. 1987; "The McLoughlin House and the Barclay House" in *Haunted Houses,* U.S.A. by Dolores Riccio & Joan Bingham (New York: Pocket Books, 1989), pp. 29-34.

   Motifs: *E378.(g). Ghosts seen in museum which was home; E421.4 Ghost as shadow; E402.1.2. Footsteps of invisible ghost heard; F473.2.1. Empty chair is rocked by invisible spirit who sits in it and rocks; F473.3.(4). Spirit taps person on shoulder or tugs at sleeve; E402.1.7. Ghost slams door; E532.(1). Other attributes of ghostly presence; E521.2. Ghost dog; *E521.2.(2). Paw prints of ghost dog found; E338.1.(ca). Ghost opens door or window and looks out; E425.3. Revenant as child; E572. Ghost walks through solid substance.

The Ghostly Guide of Point Ellice House: Victoria, B.C. Article by Isabel Young, *Colonist* (Victoria, B.C.), 23 Aug. 1979. *Magazine Section* p. 16; *A Gathering of Ghosts* by Robin Skelton and Jean Kozocari (Regina: Western Producer Prairie Books, 1989), p. 106.

   Motifs: *E378.(5). Ghost seen in museum which was home; E470.1.1. Living feel responsibility to ghost; E422.4.4.(f). Female revenant in blue dress; E338.1.(ib). Ghost gives tour of museum houses; *E440. (01). Ghost investigated by medium but no attempt to lay; E425.1. Female revenant; *E378.(5.1). Ghost gives tours of museum which was home.

Todd House Ghost Laid: Oak Bay Area, Victoria, B.C. "Haunted Houses Ooze Eerie Vibes" by Ed Gould, *Times-Colonist* (Victoria, B.C.) 28 Oct. 1989: C3; "Oak Bay's Famous Tod House Spook is 'Gone Ghost' " by B. A. McKelvie, *The Province* (Vancouver, B.C.) 15 May 1952; Article by Alice Tomlinson, *Colonist* (Victoria, B.C.) 23 Sept. 1979: Magazine Section, pp. 14-15; "Haunted House Stirred by Spooks" by Ron Baird, *News-Herald* (Vancouver, B.C.) 13 Feb. 1950: p. 18; "Victoria 'Ghost House' Antics Excite Interest of Psychic Experts" by J.K. Nesbitt, *News-Herald* (Vancouver, B.C.), 25 Jan. 1947: p. 6; "Century-Old Ghost Haunts Ex-Tod House at

Oak Bay," *The Vancouver Sun* (Vancouver, B.C.) 13 Feb. 1950.

Motifs: E334.2.(f). Strange occurrences seen above spot where bones are later discovered; E334.2.1. Ghost of murdered person haunts burial spot; E337. Ghost re-enacts scene from own lifetime; E338.1.(h.c). Female ghost in chains cries and sobs; F473.1.(g.) Spirit throws furniture and crockery about, often destructively; E338.1.(c). Ghost opens doors and windows repeatedly; E421.5. Ghost seen by two or more persons; *E542.(7.1). Ghost walks behind person; *F473.2.(5). Ghost causes objects to swing back and forth; *F473.1.(g.a). Spirit moves things around; F473.2.1. Rocking chair is rocked by invisible spirit who sits in it and rocks; E425.2.4. Revenant as American Indian; E421.1.(7). Ghost visible only to cats; E299.4. Ghost breaks windows; *E378.(5). Ghost seen in museum which was home; *E470.(1). Living are content to live with ghostly presence.

SEATTLE'S HAUNTED MOVIE HOUSES

THE HARVARD EXIT THEATER: Seattle, Wa. "Seattle Spirits" by Kathryn Robinson, *Seattle Weekly* Oct. 18-Nov. 3, 1987: pp. 32-39. "Ghost Stories: Haunted Movie Houses," *Pacific Northwest Magazine,* Dec 1985: pp. 24-35.

Motifs: *E338.(11.1). Ghost haunts movie theater; E422.4.4. Revenant in female dress; E421.(7). Ghost disappears as one watches; E578. Dead persons build fires; *E421.(6). Ghost visible out of corner of eye; E338.1(cd). Ghost holds door shut so person cannot pull it open; E402.1.1.3. Ghost cries and screams; E334. Non-malevolent ghost haunts scene of former misfortune, crime or tragedy; E499. Meetings of the dead: miscellaneous; E532.(ca). Ghost does not appear in photograph; E470.1.1. Person feels responsibility to ghosts.

THE NEPTUNE THEATER: Seattle, Wa. Feature article by Shannon Gimble, *The Daily* (University of Washington) Apr. 27, 1987: pp. 1-3; "Ghost Stories: Haunted Movie Houses" by Jim Emerson, *Pacific Northwest Magazine,* Dec 1985: pp. 24-25; "Seattle Spirits" by Kathryn Robinson, *Seattle Weekly,* (Seattle, Wa.) Oct. 28-Nov. 3, 1987: pp. 32-39.

Motifs: *E338.(11.1). Ghost haunts movie theater; E334.2.1.(o). Ghost of murdered person haunts room where he was murdered; E402.1.1.3. Ghost cries or screams; F473.2.2. Spirit hides articles; E402.1.3(b). Ghost plays organ; E422.4.4.(d). Female revenant in black dress; E422.4.4.(b). Female revenant in gray dress; E422.4.4.(a). Female revenant in white clothing; E421.3. Luminous ghost; *E542.(6). Ghost's nearness to person felt as chill; *E421.7. Ghost disappears as one watches; E555. Dead man smokes pipe; *E421.2.(2). Ghost floats … feet don't touch ground; E440.(0.1). Ghost investigated by medium but no attempt to lay; *E338.(11.3). Ghost haunts rest room; *E338.(11.2). Ghost haunts theater balcony; F402 Evil spirit; *E542.7 Ghost brushes past person; E422.11.2. Revenant as face or head.

THE MOORE-EGYPTIAN THEATER: Seattle, Wa. "Ghost Stories: Haunted Movie Houses" by Jim Emerson, *Pacific Northwest Magazine,* Dec 1985: pp. 24-25.

Motifs: *E338.(11.1). Ghost haunts movie theater; *E572.(1). Person walks through ghost; *E572.(1.1). Ghost walks through person; E588. Ghost leaves stench behind; *E470.1. Living are content to live with ghostly presence; *E542.(6). Ghost's nearness to person felt as chill; E402.1.1.(10). Ghost sighs.

HAUNTED THEATERS

SHAKESPEAREAN GHOSTS AT ASHLAND: Ashland, Ore. Collected from Dan Hayes, age 27, a graduate student at the University of Oregon, May 13, 1973. Collected by Margaret Shuey, Eugene, Ore. Randall V. Mills Archives, University of Oregon

Motifs: *E338.(11). Ghost haunts theater; *E425.(5). Revenant as actor; E402.1.1.7. Ghost laughs; *F473.1.(ga). Spirit moves things around; E402.1.1.4 Ghost sings; E422.4.5. Revenant in male dress; E555. Dead man smokes pipe.

SHOWBOAT THEATER HAUNTED BY LATE DRAMA SCHOOL DIRECTOR: Seattle, Wa. "University of a Thousand Tales" by Jim Caple, *The Daily* (University of Washington) July 25, 1984: p. 1.

Motifs: *E402.1.3.(b.1). Ghost plays piano; E402.1.1.(9). Ghost speaks; *E425.(5). Revenant as actor.

FIFTH AVENUE THEATER & PARAMOUNT THEATER: Seattle, Wa. "Ghost Stories: Haunted Moviehouses" by Jim Emerson, *Pacific Northwest Magazine*, Dec 1985: pp. 24-25.

Motifs: E338.(11). Ghost haunts theater; E338.(11.2). Ghost haunts theater balcony; E499. Meetings of the dead; miscellaneous; *E338.(11). Ghost haunts theater.

CAPITAL THEATER GHOST SAVES GIRL'S LIFE: Yakima, Wa. "Watch out Shorty. They're on Your Trail." by Jim Gosney, *Yakima Herald-Republic*, (Yakima, Wa.) July 7, 1988: p. 2. "A Ghost in the Capitol?" by Jim Gosney; *Capital Theater Program*, Oct. 15, 1987: pp. 27-28.

Motifs: E338.1.(c). Ghost opens doors and windows repeatedly; *E338.(11). Ghost haunts theater; *E421.2.1.(1). Ghost leaves footprints; F473.2.3. Spirit puts out lights (or puts them on); E363.1. Ghost aids living in emergency; *E440.(0.1). Ghost investigated by medium but no attempt to lay; *F473.2.(8). Spirit causes toilet to act contrary to nature; *E470.(1). Living are content to live with ghostly presence; E402.1.8. Miscellaneous sounds made by ghost of human being; F473.2.2. Spirit hides articles in strange places.

THE BARKERVILLE THEATER—A CHORUS LINE GHOST AND AN ACT IN THE WINGS: Barkerville, B.C. *Ghosts: True Stories from B.C.* by Robert C. Belyk (Ganges, B.C.: Horsdal & Schubert, 1990), pp. 123-124.

Motifs: E338.(11). Ghost haunts theater; E402.1.2. Footsteps of invisible ghost heard; *E402.1.3.(b.2). Invisible ghost plays musical instrument; E402.1.1.4. Ghost sings; E425.(4) Revenant as dancer; *E425.(5). Revenant as actor.

THE BLUE GHOST OF EVERETT HIGH SCHOOL: Everett, Wa. *Bananabread Waterway & Friends: The Folklore of Everett* (Everett High School, Spring 1976). Copyright Joni Isaacson, 1976. This is a collection of local folklore collected by Everett High School students.

Motifs: E422.4.4.(f). Female revenant in blue dress; E339.(11). Ghost haunts theater: F473.2.3. Spirit puts out lights (or puts them on); *F473.2.1.(2). Theater seats slammed down by invisible spirit; E425.2. Revenant as man; E421.4. Ghost as shadow; E421.3. Luminous ghost; *F473.1.(ga). Spirit moves things around; E542.(b). Ghost's nearness to person felt as chill; E572. Ghost walks through solid substance.

COLLEGES AND BOARDING SCHOOL GHOSTS

BURNLEY SCHOOL OF PROFESSIONAL ART: The Burnley Ghost: Seattle, Wa. Source: "Seattle Spirits" by Kathryn Robinson, *Seattle Weekly*, (Seattle, Wa.) October 28-November 3, 1987, p. 35.

Motifs:*E338.7. Ghost haunts educational institution; E402.1.2. Footsteps of invisible ghost; *E338.1.(cc). Ghost unlocks door; F473.3.(6). Appliances turned off or on or machinery runs unattended; F473.1.(g). Spirits throw furniture and crockery about, often destructively; *E542.(6). Ghost's nearness to person felt as chill; F473.2.3. Spirit puts out lights; F473.2.3.(3). Spirit sets off alarms; *F473.1.(ab). Ghost throws shelf of software at person.

THE LEG PULLING OLD WOMAN OF ROYAL ROADS MILITARY COLLEGE: Victoria, B.C. Source: *Ghosts: True Stories from B.C.* by Robert C. Belyk (Ganges, B.C.: Horsdal & Schubart, 1990), pp. 76-79; *Alex Dunsmuir's Dilemma* by James Audain (Victoria, Canada: Sunnylane Publishing Company, 1964), p. 3.

Motifs: E279.2.(a). Ghost disturbs sleeping child; E422.4.4. Revenant in female dress; E338.7. Ghost haunts educational institution; *E542.(6). Ghost's nearness to person felt as chill.

A MUSICAL GHOST AT GONZAGA'S MONAGHAN HALL: Spokane, Wa. "Ghosts at Gonzaga? Jesuit Challenges 'Force' Haunting Old Mansion" by Dan Morris, *National Observer,* Mar. 3, 1975: p. 3; "The Gonzaga Exorcism in *Western Gothic* by C.J. Lind, (self-published, 1983), pp. 4-5.

Motifs: E402.1.3.(b). Ghost plays organ; *E402.1.3.(f). Ghost plays flute; E443.2.2.(e). Ghost laid by Roman Catholic priest (presumably by prayer); *F473.2.(3). Ghost causes objects to swing back and forth.

A SINGING GHOST AT PACIFIC UNIVERSITY: Forest Grove, Ore., "Nightwatchman" story from information in "The Haunting of Knight Hall" in *Western Gothic* by C.J. Lind (©1983 by Carol Lind), pp. 29-30. Lind collected the story from Peg Oslund, public information officer at Pacific University, Forest Grove, Ore. She cites also an article from the college newspaper *Pacific Index* but gives no date. Other information from: *Haunted America* by Arthur Myers (New York: Dorset Books, 1986), pp. 300-304.

Myers received information from Charlotte Filer, director of public information for Pacific University, Dr. Donald Schwejda, Kenneth Combs, Dr. Elliot Weiner, and the one-time student watchman who now holds a "responsible position in a conservative community" and declined to be identified. Myers also consulted uncited articles in *Pacific Index* and *Pacific Today*.

Motifs: E402.1.1.4. Ghost sings; E422.4.4.(f). Female revenant in blue dress; E421.1.3. Ghost visible only to dog; E402.1.1.(9). Ghost speaks; E402.1.1.(10). Ghost sighs; E338(c). Rustling of invisible ghost heard in room as ghost walks about in room.; E402.1.2. Footsteps of invisible ghost heard; F473.2.3. Spirit puts out lights; E334.4. Ghost of suicide seen at death spot or near by; E422.4.4.(g). Female revenant (often invisible) in rustling silk dress.

GHOSTLY SHOPS

THE BOILER ROOM GHOST OF MOTHER'S WORLD CLOTHING STORE: Kennewick, Wa. "When the Spirits Move Them" by Kathleen Knutson, *Tri-City Herald* (Pasco, Wa.) 28 Oct. 1990: C1; "Downtown Spirit Shades of an Ex-Mayor?" by Kathleen Knutson, *Tri-City Herald* (Pasco, Wa.) 31 Oct. 1990: A1.

Motifs: F473.2.3. Spirit puts out lights or puts them on; F473.1.(ga). Spirit moves things around; E338.1.(c). Ghost opens doors and windows repeatedly; *E470.(1). Living are content to live with ghostly presence; *E338.(15). Ghost haunts store.

PIKE PLACE MARKET HAUNTINGS: Seattle, Wa. "Seattle Spirits" by Kathryn Robinson, *Seattle Weekly*, (Seattle, Wa.) October 28-November 3, 1987: p. 33; "Goodwill Ghost?" Rick Anderson, *Seattle Times,* 12 July 1983: B1; "Ghost Stories" by Paul Andrews, *Seattle Times/Seattle Post-Intelligencer*, (Seattle, Wa.) 31 Oct. 1983: *Pacific Magazine*, p. 9; "It's Time to Conjure up Tales of Ghosts and Goblins," Rick Anderson, *Seattle Times*, (Seattle, Wa.) 29 Oct. 1990: B1; "Ghost Stories—Early Enough to Get Really Scared," Rick Anderson, *Seattle Times* 26 Oct. 1987: B1; Article by Jean Godden, *Seattle Times,* 26 Oct. 1992: B1.

Motifs: E421.(7). Ghost disappears as one watches; E425.2.4. Revenant as American Indian; *E422.4.4.(i). Female revenant in lavender dress; *E422.4.4.(j).; Female revenant in pink dress; E265.3. Meeting ghost causes death; E421.3. Luminous ghosts; *E338.(15). Ghost haunts store; E422.4.5.(b). Male revenant in old fashioned garb; *F473.3.(4). Spirit taps person on shoulder or tugs at sleeve; *F473.2.3.(6). Appliances turned on or off or machinery runs unattended; *E470.1. Living are content to live with ghostly presence; E334.2.2.(b). Ghost of person who died in fall or in act of falling; E425.(4). Revenant as dancer; E425.(7). Revenant as other specific person; E425.3. Revenant as child; E338.1.(b). Ghost looks in at window; E443. Ghost exorcised and laid; E571. Ghostly barber.

PIER 70 HAUNTED? Seattle, Wa. "Pier 70 Haunted by Rumors of a Ghost," *Seattle Post-Intelligencer,* (Seattle, Wa.) 2 May 1989: C2.

Motifs: *E338.(15). Ghost haunts store; *E338.(17). Ghost haunts wharf; E281.3.(e). Ghost looks over person's shoulder in mirror, frightens person; *F473.2.3.(6). Appliances turned on and off or machinery runs unattended; *E421.4.(1). Ghost as mist; E535.3. Ghost ship.

FUNERAL PARLOR LEAVES HAUNTS BEHIND: Seattle, Wa. "Seeking the Urban Ghost" by Johnny Dodd, *Seattle Weekly*, (Seattle, Wa.) 3 Oct. 1990: 45-51.

Motifs: E338.(13). Ghost haunts restaurant; E338.(15). Ghost haunts store; E422.4.5. Revenant in male dress; E363.(0.1). Ghost aids living. No sense of having returned for this purpose; E422.4.4.(a). Female revenant in white clothing; *E470.(2). Living flee building inhabited by ghostly presence; E337. Ghost re-enacts scene from own lifetime; F473.1(g). Spirit throws furniture and crockery about, often destructively; E402.1.2. Footsteps of invisible ghost; E470.(1). Living are content to live with ghostly presence; F473.2.2. Spirit hides articles in strange places; *E451.4.(0.1.). Ghost calms down when spoken to; F473.2.3.(1). Ghost puts out candles; F473.1.(gc). Spirit rattles objects; E421.4. Ghost as shadow; E378. Ghost continues to remain in usual surrounding after death; E338.1.(c). Ghost opens doors and windows repeatedly; *F473.1.(g.b.). Objects sail across room in plain view; E443.2.2.(e). Ghost exorcised or laid by Roman Catholic priest; *E402.1.1.(g.1). Sound of ghosts talking. Not intelligible; F402. Evil spirit.

MORE GHOSTS IN PUBLIC BUILDINGS

THE FIREHOUSE GHOST: Astoria, Ore. "Ghost of Firefighters Past" by Erin Riley, *The Oregonian* (Portland, Ore.), 28 Oct. 1993, p. C2.

Motifs: *E338.(18). Ghost haunts firehouse; *F473.1.(ga). Spirit moves things around; H1411. Fear test: Staying in haunted house.

THE GHOSTLY LIBRARIAN: Pendleton, Ore. *Oregon's Ghosts & Monsters* by Mike Helm (Eugene, Ore.: Rainy Day Press, 1983), pp. 73-74. Helm cites no source, but did extensive research in the collection of his material and thanks the Umatilla County Library in his acknowledgements.

Motifs: E378. Ghost continues to remain in usual surroundings after death; *E338.8. Ghost haunts library; E338.1.(c). Ghost opens door and windows repeatedly; F473.1.(g). Spirit throws furniture and crockery about, often destructively; E334.4. Ghost of suicide seen at death spot or nearby.

A GHOSTLY MINISTER AND HIS WIFE: Seattle, Wa. "Holy Terror: Psychic Wants to Relocate Spirits Haunting Church on Capitol Hill" by Julie Schuster, *Seattle Times,* (Seattle, Wa.) 29 Oct. 1986, G1, G5.

Motifs: *E421.(0.1). Transparent ghosts; F473.2.2. Spirit hides articles in strange places; E422.4.4. Revenant in female dress; E421.3. Luminous ghost; E402.1.1.(9). Ghost speaks; E572. Ghost walks through solid substances; E338.4*(a). Ghost of rector walks invisibly through the rectory; E425.2.3. Ghost of priest or parson.

THE BELL-RINGING GHOST OF TACOMA'S OLD CITY HALL: Tacoma, Wa. "Ghosts in Tacoma? It's No Laughing Matter" by Bob Lane, *Morning News*

Tribune (Tacoma, Wa.) 19 Feb. 1979, B1.

Motifs: *F473.2.3.(3). Spirit sets off alarms; F473.2.3. Spirit puts out lights; *E542.(7). Ghost brushes past person; E338.5.(1). Ghost haunts city hall; E402.3.(a). Sound of ghost bell; E402.3.(ab). Bells rung by ghost; E338.1.(ab). Ghost causes bells to ring.

DUWAMISH BEND HOUSING PROJECT'S SINGING GHOST: Duwamish River, Wa. "Horrors That Haunt the Northwest" by William Arnold, *The Seattle Post-Intelligencer*, (Seattle, Wa.) Sunday, 31 Oct. 1976, *Northwest Magazine,* pp. 4-5. E402.1.1.4. Ghost sings.

THE ATTENDANT GHOST OF VANCOUVER GENERAL HOSPITAL: Vancouver, B.C. "The Phantom of the Burn Unit" in *Ghosts: True Stories from B.C.* by Robert C. Belyk (Ganges, B.C.: Horsdal & Schubart, 1990, pp. 64-68). Belyk interviewed two nurses, Denny Conrad and an unnamed female nurse, on March 28, 1989.

Motifs: E338.(14). Haunted hospital. E402.1.1.(12). Sound of ghost breathing; F473.2.(8). Spirit causes toilet to act contrary to nature; *F473.2.3.(6). Appliances turned on and off or machinery runs unattended; E338.1.(ab). Ghosts cause bells to ring; *E542.(6). Ghost's nearness to person felt as chill; *E451.4.(0.1.). Ghost calms down when spoken to; E451.8.(d). Ghost laid when house it haunts is torn down; E338.1.(fb). Ghost sleeps in bed, leaving impression of body in bed; *E363.7.(d).1. Ghost soothes patients in burn ward; *F473.2.3.(5). Radio turned on or off, stations changed.

Section 3: Haunted Greens, Roads, Shores, and Seas

HAUNTED PARKS AND GOLF COURSES

THE CHATAQUA HUNCHBACK: Ashland, Ore. Collected by University of Oregon student Stephanie Barrett. Informant Dan Hayes, age 28, from Central Point, Ore., also a University of Oregon student. Collected March 3, 1973 in Eugene, Ore. Randall V. Mills Archives, University of Oregon

Motifs: E425.(6). Revenant as hunchback; *E338.(12). Ghost haunts park.

THE GLENACRES GOLF COURSE DANCER: Seattle, Wa. "Horrors That Haunt the Northwest" by William Arnold, *Seattle Post-Intelligencer*, (Seattle, Wa.) 31 Oct. 1976.

Motifs: *E493.(g). Ghosts of American Indians dance; E425.2.4. Revenant as American Indian; E334.2. Ghost haunts burial spot.

THE WHITE LADY OF THE SEVENTH TEE: Victoria, B.C. Article in *Province* (Victoria, B.C.) 25 Oct. 1987; "Clammy Chills, Strange Flashes in the

Darkness" by Al Forest, *Times* (Victoria, B.C.), 6 June 1978: p. 25; article by Arthur Mayse, *Colonist* (Victoria, B.C.), 31 Oct. 1964: p. 13; Article by Fred Curtin *The Province* (Vancouver, B.C.), 9 April 1964: p. 23; "She Has That Certain Glow: One Poltergeist Per Night Par For Course" by Diane Janowski, *Colonist* (Victoria, B.C.), 19 May 1968: p. 24.

Motifs: *E599.10.(2) Ghost teases man, appearing first in front then behind; E338.(12.1). Ghost haunts golf course; E422.4.4.(a). Female revenant in white clothing; E421.3. Luminous ghosts; E422.4.4.(b). Female revenant in gray clothing; *E421.2.(3). Ghost floats. Feet do not touch ground; *E421.4.(1). Ghost as mist; E334.2.1.(o). Ghost of murdered person haunts room where he was murdered; E542.(6). Ghost's nearness to person felt as chill.

VANISHING HITCHHIKERS

THE VANISHING LADY BY THE ROAD: Sooke, B.C. "Is Ghost of Sooke Spinster Prowling Midnight Road" by Patrick Murphy, *Times-Colonist* (Victoria, B.C.) Sunday, 26 Nov. 1989: A3.

Motifs: E332.2.(h). Ghost seen on road at night; E422.4.4.(h). Female revenant in old-fashioned garb; E572. Ghost walks through solid substance; E422.4.4.(a). Female revenant in white clothing; E334.2.2.(db). Auto accident victim seen every year at accident spot.

THE KLAMATH LADY: Siletz, Ore. Written down by Donna E. Roeser, age 20, white middle class University of Oregon student, from legends heard in Siletz, Ore. from adult Mary Teague and Donna's brothers Mansel (no age given) and Tommy, age 12. Collected Feb. 27, 1971. Randall V. Mills Archives, University of Oregon

Motifs: E422.4.4.(b). Female revenant in gray clothing; E425.2.4. Revenant as American Indian; E423.1.1. Revenant as dog; E332.3.3.1. The Vanishing Hitchhiker.

THE WHITE LADY HITCHHIKER: Mt. St. Helens, Wa. "Mount St. Helens and the Evolution of Folklore" by Elizabeth Simpson, *Northwest Folklore* (1985, v.5, no.1) pp. 43-47. " 'Goddess' warns of eruption—then vanishes," *Seattle Post-Intelligencer*, (Seattle, Wa.) 21 Sept. 1980.

Motifs: E332.3.3.(a). Ghostly rider is Hawaiian deity Pele, whose appearance foreshadows eruption of Mauna Loa; E332.2.1.(d). Woman or old woman given ride in automobile makes a prediction or prophecy. She disappears suddenly or gives other evidence of ghostly nature.

GHOSTLY TRAVEL

THE SPOKANE FLYER AND THE GHOST TRAIN: Medicine Hat, Alberta. Collected by Ted Ferguson and published in *Sentimental Journey: An Oral History of Train Travel in Canada* (Toronto: Ontario: Doubleday Canada, 1985), pp. 82-83. Ferguson does not cite his sources.

Motifs: E535.4. Phantom railway train; E375. Ghost as omen of impending calamity.

SAVED BY A GHOST: Leavenworth, Wa. Story given by William Arnold in "Horrors That Haunt the Northwest," *Seattle Post-Intelligencer*, (Seattle, Wa.) Sunday Oct. 31, 1976, *Northwest Magazine*, pp. 4-5. Arnold states that this story was reported in a "nationally syndicated column datelined Seattle" by Westbrook Pegler.

Motif: *E363.1.(g). Ghostly watchman takes freezing man into shelter by railroad and warms.

PHANTOM TROLLEY: Everett, Wa. *Bananabread Waterway and Friends. Volume II: The Folklore of Everett* (Spring 1977). Copyright Joni Isaacson, 1977.

Motif: *E535.(5). Phantom trolley.

A GHOSTLY STAGECOACH STOPS AT THE GALESVILLE HOTEL. Douglas County, Ore. "Pioneer Spirits Haunt Galesville Hotel Site" by Lavola J. Bakken, *The News Review Umpqua Edition* (Roseburg, Ore.), February 1973, p. 22C.

Motifs: E535.1.(b). Phantom coach and horses heard only; *E402.1.1.(9.1). Sound of ghosts talking. Not intelligible; E338.1.(c). Ghost opens doors and windows repeatedly; E402.1.2. Footsteps of invisible ghost heard; *E402.1.8.(1). Sounds of paging through books or magazines, papers; *E421.1.(7). Ghosts visible only to cats; *F473.1.(gb). Objects sail across room in plain view; E535.1.(b). Phantom coach and horse heard only.

PHANTOMS OF THE LIGHTHOUSES

TALES OF TILAMOOK ROCK: Tillamook Rock Lighthouse, Ore. Ghost stories are from interviews by University of Oregon student Ann Zielony of Vancouver, Wa. Her informant was Jim (anonymous), age 24, of Cannon Beach, Ore. The interview was conducted in May 1975 in Eugene, Ore. Information on the Tillmook Rock Lighthouse is from *West Coast Lighthouses: A Pictorial History of the Guiding Lights of the Sea* by Jim Gibbs (Seattle: Superior Publishing Company, 1974), pp.112-115.

Motifs: E378. Ghost continues to remain in usual surroundings after death; E402.1.1.3. Ghost cries and screams; E530.1. Ghostlike lights; F402.6.4.1. Spirits live in caves.

THE GHOST OF HECETA HEAD LIGHT: Heceta Head Lighthouse, Ore. Legends self-collected by Cheryl Lynn Phillips, March 14, 1978, University of Oregon student from Florence, Ore. Randall v. Mills Archives, University of Oregon; "Spirits Roam Real Haunted House" by Clay Eals, *The Oregonian* (Portland, Ore.), 31 Oct. 1977: A1.

Motifs: E402.1.2. Footsteps of invisible ghost heard; F473.2.3. Spirit puts out lights (or puts them on); E402.1.1.(10). Ghost sighs; *E421.1.(7). Ghosts visible only to cats; E338.1(c). Ghost opens doors and windows repeatedly; F473.2(6). Heat turned up. House stifling; F473.1(g). Spirits throw furniture and crockery about, often destructively. E422.4.4(b). Female revenant in gray clothing; E422.4.4.(h). Female revenant in old-fashioned garb; E422.4.4(e). Female revenant in black dress; E402.1.8. Miscellaneous sounds made by ghost of human being; E470.(1). Living are content to live with ghostly presence; E338.1.(hb). Ghost cleans house.

YAQUINA BAY LIGHTHOUSE: Newport, Ore. *Sentinels of the North Pacific* by James A. Gibbs, Jr. (Portland, Ore.: Binfords & Mort, 1955), p. 75; *Western Lighthouses: Olympic Peninsula to San Diego* by Bruce Roberts and Ray Jones (Old Saybrook, Connecticut: Globe Pequot Press, 1993), p. 49; "Frightened Mother" story self-collected by Cheryl Lynn Phillips, March 14, 1978, Florence, Ore. Randall V. Mills Archives, University of Oregon; "Murdered Students" story collected by University of Oregon student Joan Anderson of Depoe Bay, Ore. Collected from Jill Whisler, 18, a store clerk in Lincoln Beach, Ore., March 1973. Randall V. Mills Archives, University of Oregon.

   Motifs: E334.2.1.(0). Ghost of murdered person haunts room where he was murdered; F473.2.3. Spirit puts out lights (or puts them on).

LIVING WITH GHOSTS AT POINT WILSON LIGHTHOUSE: Port Townsend, Wa. "Ghost of Point Wilson: Spirits Spook Women" by Randi F. Rice, *Peninsula Daily News* (Port Angeles, Wa.), 20 April 1994: A1-A2.

   Motifs: *E421.(6). Ghost visible only out of corner of eye; E402.1.2. Footsteps of invisible ghost heard; E402.1.8. Miscellaneous sounds made by human being; F471.2.1. Succubus: female incubus; E422.4.4. Revenant in female dress; F473.1.(g). Spirit throws furniture and crockery about, often destructively; E334. Non-malevolent ghost haunts scene of former misfortune, crime, or tragedy.

HAUNTED SHIPS AND PHANTOM SHIPS

A PHANTOM SHIP ESCAPES THE ROCKS: Tillamook Rock Lighthouse, Ore. "Phantom Ships," *Tillamook Light* by James A. Gibbs, Jr. (Portland, Ore.: Binfords & Mort, 1953), pp. 122-125.

   Motifs: E511. The Flying Dutchman; E535.3. Ghost ships.

THE GHOST SHIP VALENCIA: B.C. Coast. *Breakers Ahead! A History of Shipwrecks in the Graveyard of the Pacific* by R. Bruce Scott (Sidney, B.C.: Review Publishing House, 1970), p. 111.

   Motifs: E337.2. Re-enactment of tragedy seen; E535.3.(g). Phantom ship in harbor re-enacts tragedy occurring to actual ship at sea; E535.3. Ghost ship.

THE HAUNTED SEA KING: Seattle, Wa. *Ghosts: True Stories from B.C.* by Robert C. Belyk (Ganges, B.C.: Horsdal & Schubart, 1990), pp. 140-141.

   Motifs: *E338.(16). Ghost haunts ship; E334.2.2. Ghost of person killed in accident seen at death or burial spot.

HOW TO TELL WHEN YOU'VE GOT A BOAT GHOST: Seattle, Wa. William Rudolph in *Seattle Times,* (Seattle, Wa.) Sunday 25 Oct. 1987, *Pacific Magazine*, p. 7.

Motifs: E421.1.3. Dog alone sees; *E338.(16). Ghost haunts ship; *E542.(6). Ghost nearness to person felt as chill.

Section 4: Persistent Relatives and Ghostly Pets

WIVES, HUSBANDS, AND LOVERS

A VALENTINE'S DAY VISIT FROM A DEAD WIFE DISTURBS LOVERS: Spokane, Wa. "The Spooks Are Special in Spokane" by Doug Clark, *The Spokesman-Review* (Spokane, Wa.), 30 Oct. 1990: B3.

> Motifs: E221.1. Dead wife haunts husband on second marriage; E421.1. Invisible ghosts; E588(1). Ghost leaves perfume odor; F473.1(g). Spirits throw furniture and crockery about, often destructively.

HAUNTS DRIVE BRIDE FROM NEW HUSBAND'S HOME: Medford, Ore. Source: "Ghost Drives Newly-Married Medford Couple from Hated Home" by Marjorie O'Harra, *The Oregonian,* (Portland, Ore.), 2 Nov. 1970: p. 14. Based on reporter's interview with Medford resident, Ruth Flowers.

> Motifs: F473.2.2. Spirit hides articles in strange places; F473.1.(g). Spirits throw furniture and crockery about, often destructively; E402.1.2. Footsteps of invisible ghost heard; *E338.1(cb). Ghost turns doorknob; *E338.1(cc). Ghost unlocks door; E421.1. Invisible ghosts; *E542.(6). Ghost's nearness to person felt as chill; *E470.(2). Living flee building inhabited by ghostly presence.

POINT-OF-DEATH APPARITIONS

DON'T FORGET YOUR OPERATION! Victoria, B.C. *Alex Dunsmuir's Dilemma* by James Audain (Victoria, B.C.: Sunnylane Publishing Company, 1964), p. 127.

> Motif: E723.7. Wraith speaks.

A SON'S LAST VISIT: Fort Mellon, B.C. "The Death of Roger" by Kathleen Belanger in *Extraordinary Experiences: Personal Accounts of the Paranormal in Canada* by John Robert Columbo (Willowdale, Ontario: Hounslow Press, 1989), pp. 88-89.

> Motif: E723.6.1*. Death announcing wraith appears in or near building.

A GHOST CHILD'S DOLL: Tacoma, Wa. "Dark Shadows Lurk in Tacoma Homes: Readers Share Their Ghost Stories" by Kathleen Merryman, *The Morning News Tribune* (Tacoma, Wa.), 31 Oct. 1995: B9. From information given to columnist Merryman by Tacoma resident Jack L. Sundquist.

> Motifs: E425.3. Revenant as child; E723.7. Wraith speaks.

GHOSTLY CRITTERS

SKIPPER THE PHANTOM DOG: Kamloops, B.C. From an account by Robert C. Belyk in *Ghosts: True Stories from B.C.* (Ganges, B.C.: Horsdal & Schubart, 1990), pp. 110-12. Belyk interviewed his informant on October 29, 1989 but does not give the name.
    Motif: E521.2. Ghost of dog; E521.1.(2). Paw prints of ghost dog found.

PHANTOM HORSE: Rural Oregon. Collected from Mrs. Howard E. Bell, housewife, at her home in Portland, Ore. on July 8, 1972. University of Oregon student Gary Bell, 34, of Eugene, Ore. collected the story. Randall V. Mills Archives, University of Oregon Incident took place in an unidentified rural Oregon community.
    Motif: E402.2.3. Hoofbeats of ghost horse.

A GHOSTLY SNAKE?: Turnbull National Wildlife Refuge near Cheney, Wa. Doug Clark's column, *The Spokesman-Review* (Spokane, Wa.), Tuesday, 30 Oct. 1990: B1. Based on a letter received from Katherine Healy.
    Motifs: *E526. Ghost of snake; E532.(ca). Ghost does not appear in photograph.

THE LEVITATING DACHSHUND: Walla Walla, Wa. Doug Clark's column, *The Spokesman-Review* (Spokane, Wa.), Tuesday, 30 Oct. 1990: B1. From letter sent to Clark by reader after he asked for true-life ghost stories.
    Motif: *E251.2.(1). Haunted dog.

NATIVE AMERICAN DEAD DISTURBED

ONE IS MISSING: Bellingham, Wa. "A Gentle Touch, and Then Words: 'One is Missing' " by Brigid Schule, *Seattle Times*, Monday, 9 Sept. 1991: p. B5.
    Motifs: E235.6. Return from dead to punish disturber of grave; *E402.1.1.(9). Ghost speaks; E419.4. Dead move when cemetery is moved; E421.3. Dead without proper funeral rites cannot rest; E425.2.4. Revenant as American Indian.

UNEASY SPIRITS AT THE VANCOUVER ARMY BARRACKS: Vancouver, Wa. "Cleansing Ritual in Vancouver Puts Roaming Spirits to Rest," *Seattle Times*, (Seattle, Wa.) 27 June 1993: p. B1.
    Motifs: E325.6. Return from dead to punish disturber of grave; E419.4. Dead move when cemetery is moved; E425.2.4. Revenant as American Indian; E402.1.2. Footsteps of invisible ghost heard; E338.1.(c). Ghost opens door and closes repeatedly; *E402.1.1.(9). Ghost speaks; E338.10*. Ghost haunts fort.

CHIEF SEATTLE SPEAKS OF THE INVISIBLE DEAD: From a speech given in 1854 by Chief Seattle. Dr. Henry A. Smith, who was conversant with the Chief's language, took notes on the speech. His English rendering of the speech was printed in the *Seattle Sunday Star*, October 29, 1887. This was reprinted in *History of Seattle, Wa.* by Frederick James Grant (New York: American

Brief Notes on
More Northwest Hauntings

One book cannot begin to describe the many ghostly experiences of the Pacific Northwest. To make the motif-index as complete as possible, here are brief notes and motif references for thirty-four more hauntings which were not discussed in this book.

BREMERTON, WASHINGTON. Steaming cup of coffee found in kitchen of policeman who had left for work hours earlier. Article by Seabury Blair Jr. in *Bremerton Sun* (Bremerton, Washington), Monday, 31 Oct. 1977: p.1.
Motif: *F473.2.(6).(1). Coffee heated.

BREMERTON, WASHINGTON. Ghost visits each October 10. Dog dies of heart attack. Article by Seabury Blair Jr. in *Bremerton Sun*, Monday, 31 Oct. 1977: p.1.
Motifs: E421.1.3. Ghost visible to dog alone; E542.(6). Ghost's nearness to person felt as chill; E425.3. Revenant as child; E402.1.1.3. Ghost cries and screams; E402.1.1.6. Ghost sobs.

CHENEY, WASHINGTON. Eastern Washington's Streeter Hall believed haunted by dead workman. Doug Clark's column, *The Spokesman-Review* (Spokane, Washington) 1 June 1989, B1.
Motifs:E402.1.2.Footsteps of invisible ghost; *E338.7. Ghost haunts educational institution; E402.1.3.1; *F473.2.(5). Ghost rattles objects; E402. Mysterious ghostlike noises heard; E588. Ghost leaves stench behind; E334.2.2. Ghost of person killed in accident seen at death or burial spot; E338.1.(c). Ghost opens door and windows repeatedly.

CHILLIWACK, BRITISH COLUMBIA. "Brooks Ave. Ghost Takes Holiday" *in Chilliwack Progress*, 5 Dec. 1951: p.1; Chilliwack Progress (Chilliwack, British Columbia), 21 Nov. 1951: p.1; and "Poltergeists" in *Ghosts: True Stories from British Columbia* by Robert C. Belyk, (Ganges, B.C.: Horsdal &

Schubart, 1990), p.100-102.

Motifs: E402.1.5. Invisible ghost makes rapping or knocking noise; E299.4. Ghost breaks window; *F473.0.1. Poltergeist in home with teen resident; *E440.(0.2). Ghost investigated by priest but no attempt to lay.

CLATKANIE, OREGON. Children see ghostly face looking out of window at them. Later a dead husband's ghost returns. Collected by University of Oregon student Jonn M. Gerritz from his mother, Joanne Gerritz, age 56, at his home in Troutdale, Oregon, November 24, 1976.

Motifs: E331. Dead husband's friendly return; E338.1.(a). Ghost opens door or window and looks out; E402.1.4. Invisible ghost jingles chains; E402.1.2. Footsteps of invisible ghost heard.

COLBERT, WASHINGTON. Home haunted, ghost laid. "Ghosts" by Christopher Bogan in *The Spokesman-Review*, (Spokane, Wa.), 26 Oct. 1980: p.D1. Based on an interview with Mr. Heston of Colbert, Washington.

Motifs: E338.1.(c). Ghost opens windows and doors repeatedly; F473.1.(ga). Spirit moves things around; E588. Ghost leaves stench behind; E421.1.3. Ghost visible only to dog; E279.2.(a). Ghost disturbs sleeping child; E402.1.5. Invisible ghost makes rapping or knocking noise; E338.1.(fab) Man walks through bedroom, carrying bloody knife; E443.2.2.(e) Ghost laid by Roman Catholic priest (presumably by prayer). E421.1.6.(1). No birds on haunted property.

EUGENE, OREGON. Ghost at South Eugene High School Theater. "Is somebody up there?" by Mike O'Brien, *The Register-Guard* (Eugene, Ore.) Sunday, 27 Oct. 1974: Section E, p.1.

Motifs: E572. Ghost walks through solid substance; F473.3. Poltergeist mistreats people; E402.1.2. Footsteps of invisible ghost seen; E421.3. Luminous ghosts; E422.4.4.(f). Female revenant in blue dress; *E338.(11.2). Ghost haunts theater lobby; *E338.(11). Ghost haunts theatre.

FORT ST. JOHN, BRITISH COLUMBIA. A grandmother visits trapper in remote cabin at time of her death. Some Canadian Ghosts by Sheila Hewey (Richmond Hill, Ontario: Simon and Shuster of Canada, 1973), pp. 149-51.

Motif: E723.4.4. Wraith of dying woman goes to see children for last time before death.

FOREST GROVE, OREGON: "The Legend of the Phantom Bugler." Murderous wildman attacks campers. University of Oregon student Jay Wells of Creswell, Ore. retells this based on his memory of the tale as told by Forest Fire Warden David Kuhns of Forest Grove, Ore. Self-collected May 7, 1977. Randall V. Mills Archives, University of Oregon.

Motifs: *E402.1.3.(A). Ghost plays bugle.

HOQUIAM, WASHINGTON. Lytle Mansion haunted. "Five Rather Scary

Tales" by Carol J. Lind, *Seattle Post-Intelligencer*, (Seattle, Wa.) Sunday, 31 Oct. 1976: *Northwest Magazine*, p. 6. Based on interview by author Carol Lind with Mr. and Mrs. Robert Watson of Hoquiam.

Motifs: E334.2.2. Ghost of person killed in accident seen at death or burial spot; *E338.1.(j). Ghost haunts hall; *E334.(6). Ghost of person who died a natural death at scene of death.

KENNEWICK, WASHINGTON. Ghosthunter's experiences. "Kennewick man chases ghosts from houses" by Dave Eshelman, *Tri-Cities Herald* (Pasco, Washington), Thursday, 30 Oct. 1975: p. 29. Based on interview with Brent Christiansen who lives on Okanagon Loop in Kennewick. Includes motifs: F473.1.(g). Spirits throw furniture and crockery about, often destructively; E338.1(c). Ghost opens door and windows repeatedly; E443. Ghost exorcised and laid; E421.1. Invisible ghosts; *E470.1. Living are content to live with ghostly presence. King County, Washington. Ghost of Mr. MacDougall shares family home. "With the ghost gone, family home is silent" by Gale B. Robinette, *The Morning News Tribune*, (Tacoma, Washington) Oct. 27-Nov.5 19 *Entertainment P.S.*, p.2. From interview with young woman who lived in South King County house.

Motifs: £473.1.(ga). Spirit moves things around; E588.(1). Ghost leaves perfume odor; E402.1.5. Invisible ghost makes rapping or knocking noises; *E402.1.1.(9). Ghost speaks; E443. Ghost exorcised and laid; *E421.4.(1). Ghost as mist; E421.1.3.1. Ghost visible only to dog.

KENT, WASHINGTON. Halloween haunted house is really haunted. Recorded tape of Beatles suddenly begins to play jazz, speeds up. "Haunted houses may really be" by Merry Nye. *Seattle Post-Intelligencer*, (Seattle, Wa.) 21 Oct. 1991 D9.

Motif: *F473.2.3.(5) Radio turned on and off or stations changed.

PUYALLUP, WASHINGTON. Community College instructor gives classes in the paranormal, has ghost in own home. "There may be ghostly explanation for strange events" by Christine Corbett, *The Morning News Tribune*, (Takoma, Wa.) Saturday, 23 April 1983: Sparetimer, p.2. Based on interview with Mycki Fulda, Puyallup resident.

Motifs: F473.2.2. Spirit hides articles in strange places; F473.1.(g). Spirits throw furniture and crockery about, often destructively; *E470.(1). Living are content to live with ghostly presence; E451.4.(0).(1). Ghost calms down when spoken to.

SAANICH, BRITISH COLUMBIA. Home of Hanging Judge haunted. Column of light hangs over spot in photo. "M" appears on mirror. "Saanich/ The Spirit of the Hanging Judge" in *Mysterious Canada: Strange Sights, Extraordinary Events, and Peculiar Places* by John Robert Colombo. (Toronto: Doubleday, 1988), p.370-371.

Motifs: *E440.(0).(1) Ghost investigated by medium but no attempt to lay; E532.(c) Ghost appears in photograph; *E557.(2) Mysterious letters appear; E557. Dead man writes.

SEATTLE, WASHINGTON. Ghost in Metro Bus Barn. Column by Jean Godden, *The Seattle Times* (Seattle, Wa.) 4 Aug. 1991, B1. Motifs: *E542.(6). Ghosts nearness to person felt as chill; F473.5.(a). Knocking and rappings that cannot be traced; *F473.1.(ga). Spirit moves things around; E334.2.2. Ghost of person killed in accident seen at death or burial spot.

SEATTLE, WASHINGTON. Foul odor in house on Queen Anne Hill. "If there's a ghost in the attic, don't call a witch doctor" by Judi Hunt. *Seattle Post-Intelligencer,* (Seattle, Wa.) Wednesday, 31 Oct. 1984: p. C7.

Motifs: E588.(T) Ghost leaves stench behind; E443 Ghost exorcised and laid.

SEATTLE, WASHINGTON. Native American ghost on horseback seen in park in West Seattle. *Bananabread Waterway and Friends* (Volume II). *The Folklore of Everett* (Spring 1977). Copyright Joni Isacson, 1977. Entry by student Teresa Espinosa.

Motifs: E425.2.4. Revenant as American Indian; E402.2.3. Hoofbeats of ghost horse; E334.2.4. Ghost of person haunts burial spot; E338.12. Ghost haunts park.

SIUSLAW RIVER, NEAR FLORENCE, OREGON. Family killed in landslide. Spot haunted. *Oregon's Ghosts and Monsters* by Mike Helm (Eugene, Oregon: Rainy Day Press, 1983) p. 17. Helm cites no sources for this story. He grew up in Oregon and heard many of his stories from fellow Oregonians.

Motifs: E425.3. Revenant as child; *F974.(2). Cows refuse to graze in certain spot; E402.1.1.2. Ghost moans; E334.2.2. Ghost of person killed in accident seen at death or burial spot.

SPOKANE, WASHINGTON. Mannequin takes off its head and holds it. Doug Clark's column, *The Spokesman-Review,* (Spokane, Wa.) 21 Oct. 1990: p. B1. From letter written to Clark by Doug Spence, owner of house at 603 W. 14th St. in Spokane.

Motifs: E436.3. Bats flying in house sign of ghosts; *F473.1.(ga). Spirit moves things around; *E402.1.5.(a).(1). Ghost drags furniture around in room overhead.

SPOKANE, WASHINGTON. Spokane Technical Institute ghosts. "Ghosts" by Christopher Bogan, *The Spokesman-Review* (Spokane, Washington), 26 Oct. 1980, D1.

Motifs: *E338.7. Ghost haunts educational institution; E338.1.(c). Ghost opens doors and windows repeatedly; F473.2.3. Spirit puts out lights; *F473.1.(g)(a). Spirit moves things around; E402.1.2. Footsteps of invisible ghost heard; *E402.1.1.(9)(1). Sounds of ghost talking not intelligible.

SPOKANE, WASHINGTON.   Informant lives with ghosts for thirteen years. "Ghosts" by Christopher Bogan, *The Spokesman-Review* (Spokane, Washington), Sunday, 26 Oct. 1980: D2. From interview with a Northeast Spokane woman.

Motifs: *E402.1.1.(9(.(1). Sounds of ghost talking. Not intelligible; E402.1.2 Footsteps of invisible ghost heard; F473.7.2 Spirit hides articles in strange places; E338.1. (aa) Ghosts knock on door; *E542.6.(1) Icy wind indication of ghost's presence.

TACOMA, WASHINGTON.   Two men hung in courthouse. Haunted upstairs room where hanging took place. "Courting History: Teacher discovers intrigue in Washington's County seats" by Jack Broom, *The Seattle Times*, (Seattle, Wa.) 13 April 1992, A1. Information from David Chapman's book, *Cathedrals for the Common Man: The Courthouse of Washington State*, which was in draft form at the time this article was written.

Motifs: E338.5. Ghost haunts courthouse; E338.2.1.(a). Ghost of murdered person haunts room where he was murdered.

TACOMA, WASHINGTON.   Masonic Temple Theatre. Spirits felt in theatre balcony, man fell to death in elevator. "The Temple Spirits?" by Jim Erickson, *The Morning News Tribune* (Tacoma, Wa.), 11 May 1983: Bl.

Motifs: E402.1.5.(a).(1). Ghost drags furniture around in room overhead; E422.4.5.(6). Revenant in male dress; *E338.(11.2). Ghost haunts theatre balcony; *E338.(11). Ghost haunts theatre; E338.1.(c) Ghost opens door and windows repeatedly; E421.3. Luminous ghosts; *E542.(6). Ghosts nearness to person felt as chill; *E334.2.2. Ghost of person killed in accident seen at death or burial spot.

TROUTDALE, OREGON.   Many strange happenings in Lloyd family home. Interview with Beth Lloyd, age 19, of Troutdale, Oregon. Collected by John Gerritz at the University of Oregon. Randall V. Mills Archives, University of Oregon.

Motifs: E402.1.2. Footsteps of invisible ghost heard; E402.1.5.(a).(1). Ghost drags furniture around in room overhead; E338.1.(c). Ghost opens doors and windows repeatedly; *F473.1.(gb). Objects sail across room in plain view; *F473.1.(ga). Spirit moves things around; *E402.1.1.(9.1). Sound of ghosts talking not intelligible; E451.8.(a). Ghost laid by remodeling house it haunts.

VALDEZ ISLAND, BRITISH COLUMBIA.   Reporter spends night on beach and wakes to see Native American dancing. "Jack Scott remembers: The night I began to believe in ghosts," *The Vancouver Sun*, (Vancouver, B.C.) Sunday, 28 Aug. 1971: p.5.

Motifs: E425.2.4. Revenant as American Indian; E493. Dead men dance.

VANCOUVER, BRITISH COLUMBIA. Mandarin Gardens nightclub haunted. Strange happenings frighten owner. Jack Wasserman, *The Vancouver Sun,* (Vancouver, B.C.) 6 Aug. 1952: p.10.

Motifs: *E338.13 Ghost haunts restaurant; *F473.2.3.(2) Spirit unplugs equipment; *F473.1.(g).(c). Spirits rattle objects; E422.1.11.3 Ghost as hand or hands; E402.1.1.7 Ghost laughs; E402.1.1.(9) Ghost speaks; E451.8.(e) Ghost laid when house it haunts is torn down.

VANCOUVER, BRITISH COLUMBIA. "Hub Clark, the Headless Brakeman." Brakeman's head cut off in train accident. Haunts railyard. Collected by Ted Ferguson and published in his *Sentimental Journey: An Oral History of Train Travel in Canada* (Toronto, Ontario: Doubleday Canada, 1985), p. 86. Ferguson does not cite his sources.

Motif: E422.1.1.(a). Headless man. Mention of appearance only.

VANCOUVER, BRITISH COLUMBIA. Boy talks to man in buckskins at night. "Mother, son share house with ghost" by Philip Mills, *The Province* (Victoria, British Columbia) 23 Dec. 1976: p.1, 8; " 'Johnny' the ghost debunked: Pychokinesis goes bump in the night," by Douglas Sage, *The Vancouver Sun* (Vancouver, B. C.), 23 Dec. 1976, p. 1-2.

Motifs: F473.1(g). Spirits throw furniture and crockery about, often destructively; *E402.1.1.(9)(1). Sound of ghosts talking, not intelligible. E425.2.4. Revenant as American Indian; *E421.1.1.(2). Ghost visible to child alone.

VICTORIA, BRITISH COLUMBIA. Husband stays until widow marries mutual friend, then leaves, "Ghost That Care and Guard" in *A Gathering of Ghosts: Hauntings and Exorcisms from the Personal Casebook of Robin Skelton and Jean Kozocari* by Robin Skelton and Jean Kozocari (Saskatoon, Sakatchewan: Western Producer Prairie Books, 1989), pp. 136-39.

Motifs: E321. Dead husband's friendly return; *E402.1.1.(11). Ghost coughs; *E421.5.(1). Ghost heard by two or more persons.

VICTORIA, BRITISH COLUMBIA. Barbary Banjo Restaurant haunted. Formerly was sight of Little Denmark. Psychic witnesses scene from past while dining. "Dancing and Dining with Ghosts" in *A Gathering of Ghosts: Hauntings and Exorcisms from the Personal Casebook of Robin Skelton and Jean Kozocari* by Robin Skelton and Jean Kozocari. (Saskatoon, Saskatchewan: Western Producer Prairie Books, 1989), p.123-24.

Motifs: *E338.(13) Ghost haunts restaurant; *F473.2.3.(3) Spirit sets off alarms; F473.1.(g) Spirits throw furniture and crockery about, often destructively; *F473.2.(7) Spirit turns on taps; E556.1 Ghost drinks alcoholic beverage; E337 Ghost re-enacts scene from own lifetime; F473.2.3. Spirit puts out lights (or puts them on).

VICTORIA, BRITISH COLUMBIA. Cryings heard in attic, and running feet of a child. "Was That a Child Crying?" in *A Gathering of Ghosts: Hauntings and*

Exorcisms from the Personal Casebook of Robin Skelton and Jean Kozocari by Robin Skelton and Jean Kozocari. (Saskatoon, Saskatchewan: Western Producer Prairie Books, 1989), pp.128-34. Based on investigations in Victoria by mediums Skelton and Kozocari and on information given to Kozocari by Victoria resident Barbara Andrews.

    Motifs: E402.1.2 Footsteps of invisible ghost heard; E425.3 Revenant as child; E443 Ghost exorcised and laid.

VICTORIA, BRITISH COLUMBIA. McPherson Theatre haunted, ropes swing, ghost heard. *A Gathering of Ghosts: Hauntings and Exorcisms from the Personal Casebook of Robin Skelton and Jean Kozocari* by Robin Skelton and Jean Kozocari (Saskatoon, Saskatchewan: Western Producer Prairie Books, 1989), p. 117-118.

    Motifs: *E338.(11) Ghost haunts theatre; E473.2.(5) Ghost causes objects to swing back and forth; E402.1.2 Footsteps of invisible ghost heard; E402.1.1.(9.1) Sound of many ghostly voices; *337.1.3.1. Sounds of ghostly party.

VICTORIA, BRITISH COLUMBIA. Child walks through wall and confronts sleeper. *A Gathering of Ghosts: Hauntings and Exorcisms from the Personal Casebook of Robin Skelton and Jean Kozocari* by Robin Skelton and Jean Kozocari (Saskatoon, Saskatchewan: Western Producer Prairier Books, 1989), pp.128-134.

    Motifs: E425.3. Revenant as child; E572. Ghost walks through solid substance.

WELCHES, OREGON. Haunted mountain retreat. Perhaps three ghosts, love triangle. Woman fell to death from cabin. Ghost breaks man's finger when he tries to light candle ghost had put out. "Did the Lady Fall, Jump, or Was She Pushed? A Psychic-Historical Investigation of a Cabin in Oregon at the Foot of Mt. Hood" in *The Ghostly Gazetteer* by Arthur Meyers (Chicago: Contemporary Books, 1990), p.239-147. Meyers solicited information from: Debbie Anderson, Aaron Anderson, Donna Kinlan, Roger Mead, Michael Jones, Suzanne Jauchius, Suzy Black, and Carol Crisler.

    Motifs: E422.4.4. Revenant in female dress; E279.2.(a). Ghost disturbs sleeping child; F473.3. Poltergeist mistreats people; F473.2.1. Empty chair is rocked by invisible spirit; E402.1.1.(9). Ghost speaks; F473.2.3. Spirit puts out lights; E402.1.2. Footsteps of invisible ghost heard; *E402.1.3.(g). Ghost plays music box; *E402.1.1.4.(1). Ghost hums; E338.1.(ca) Ghost opens door or window and looks out; E593. Ghost takes things from people; *F473.2.3.(5). Radio turned on and off or station changed; E422.4.4.(h). Female revenant in old-fashioned garb; E470.(1). Living content to live with ghostly presence; F402. Evil spirit; *F473.2.3.(1). Spirit puts out candles.

WALDO, B.C. Ghost of cottage's original owner rearranges books and other items. Some Canadian Ghosts by Sheila Hervey (Richmond Hill, Ontario: Simon & Schuster of Canada, 1973), pp. 15-18.

Motifs: E338.1.(c). Ghost opens doors and windows repeatedly; E470.(1). Living are content to live with ghostly presence; F473.1.(g). Spirits throw furniture or crockery about, often destructively; *E402.1.3.(b).1. Ghost plays piano; *E539.(6). Ghostly clock; E402.3.(ac). Clock without mechanism strikes.

Index of Ghostly Motifs

This is a folklore index to the motifs found in this collection. Each motif number is followed by a description of that motif, a listing of the northwestern locales where the motif occurred, and the page number in this book which describes the event. A subject index follows on page 247. By consulting the subject index, you can observe the frequency of occurrence of certain motifs.

These indexes use the folktale classification scheme developed by folklorist Stith Thompson and set out in his *Motif-Index of Folk-Literature* (Bloomington, Indiana: Indiana University, 1966, six volumes). Ernest W. Baugham extended the Thompson Index, applying it to folktales of England and North America. This "Index of Ghostly Motifs" is derived from Baughman's *Type and Motif Index of the Folktales of England and North America*. Indiana Folklore Series No. 20. (The Hague: Mouton, 1966). Most of the motifs appearing in our Northwestern citings are indexed in Baughman's book. An asterisk preceding the motif number indicates that I have extended Baughman's motifs.

Three other sources that index much ghostlore are cited here. They are: *Popular Beliefs and Superstitions: A Compendium of American Folklore: From the Ohio Collection of Newbell Niles Puckett* edited by Wayland D. Hand, Anna Cassetta, and Sondra B. Thiederman (Boston: G.K. Hall, 1981); *The Frank C. Brown Collection of North Carolina Folklore,* seven volumes (Durham, North Carolina: Duke University Press, 1952-1961); and *Popular Beliefs and Practices from Alabama* by Ray B. Browne (Berkley: University of California Press, 1958).By referring to these indexes, the reader can locate instances of ghostly occurrences similar to those in this Pacific Northwestern collection.

E. THE DEAD

E200-599. Ghosts and Other Revenants.

E221.1. Dead wife haunts husband on second marriage.

(Hand, Ohio 29782); Spokane, Wa.: husband with new lover. See also E322 Dead wife's return.

E235.6. Return from dead to punish disturber of grave.

Bellingham, Wa.: archeological ghosts; Seattle, Wa.: golf course; Vancouver, B.C.: army barracks.

E261.4. Ghost pursues man. Victoria, B.C.: golf course.

E265.3. Meeting ghost causes death. Seattle, Wa.: Pike Place Market. See also E574.

E272. Road ghosts. Ghosts which haunt roads. See E332.

E273. Churchyard ghosts. See also E334.2. Ghost haunts burial spot.

*E273.(1). Ghosts haunt spot to which tombstones are removed. Coquitlam, B.C.: used as paving stones for path.

E275. Ghost haunts place of great accident or misfortune. See E334, E337(a).

E279.2 Ghost disturbs sleeping person. See also E338.1(fab).

E279.2(a). Ghost disturbs sleeping child. Colbert, Wa.: bends over child brandishing knife; Tacoma, Wa.: sounds from ceiling keep awake; Victoria, B.C.: old woman pulls boy's leg; Welches, Ore.: pulls child from bed, glares at sleeper.

E279.2(b). Ghost shakes bed of sleeper. Coquitlam, B.C.; Salem, Ore.: Governor's Mansion.

*E279.2.(1). Ghost sits on legs of person in bed. See from E338.1.(Fae). Seattle, Wa.: Capitol Hill; Salem, Ore.: Governor's Mansion.

E279.3. Ghost pulls bedclothing from sleeper. (Hand, Ohio 29661). See E281.3.(6).

E279.4. Ghost haunts park, terrifies watchers. See *E338.(12).

E281.3. Ghost haunts particular room in house. See E338.1.(f); *E338.(11.3); E338.1.g.

E281.3(b). Ghost lays hand on girl awake in bed. Vancouver, B.C.: Tucks her in.

E281.3(d). Ghost paces room at night. See E402.1.2.

E281.3(e). Ghost looks over person's shoulder in mirror, frightening person. Seattle, Wa.: Pier 70.

E283. Ghost haunts church. See E338.2.

E293. Ghosts scare people (deliberately).

E293.1. Ghost scares thief, prevents theft. Seattle, Wa.: Capitol Hill.

E299.1. Ghost causes machinery to run unattended. See *F473.2.3.(6).

E299.4. Ghost breaks windows. Chilliwack, B.C.: shakes house so hard windows break; Oak Bay, B.C.: pushes window out of wall; See also E402.1.6; E338.1c+.

*E299.4.(1). Force shatters glass case. A paranormal force, not a ghost. Seattle, Wa.: Wing Luke Museum.

E300-399. Friendly return from the dead.

(Note: Ghostly actions which fit these motifs may be indexed here regardless of whether or not their intent was friendly.) For wraithes (moment of death appearances) see E723.

E321. Dead husband's friendly return. Victoria, B.C.: leaves when wife marries his friend; Clatkanie, Ore.: leaves when wife re-marries.

E332. Non-malevolent road ghosts. See from E332.

E332.2(h). Ghost seen on road at night. Sooke, B.C.: lady.

E332.3.3.1. The Vanishing Hitchhiker. Siletz, Ore.: Native American woman.

E332.3.3.1(d). Woman or old woman given ride in automobile, makes a prediction or prophecy; she disappears suddenly or gives other evidence of ghostly nature. Centralia, Wa.; Morton/Randall/Packwood,

E332.3.3.2(a). Ghostly rider is Hawaiian deity Pele, whose appearance foreshadows eruption of Mauna Loa. Forks, Wa.: Mt. St. Helens.

E334. Non-malevolent ghost haunts scene of former misfortune, crime, or tragedy. Seattle, Wa.: Georgetown Mansion, Wa.; Seattle, Wa.: Harvard Exit hanging victim; Hoquiam, Wa.; Port Townsend, Wa.: mother seeks daughter lost in storm.

E334.2. Ghost haunts burial spot. Vancouver Island, B.C.: Indian burial grounds; West Seattle, Wa

Indian burial site. See also *E273.(1).

E334.2.(f). Strange occurrences seen above spot where bones are later discovered. Victoria, B.C.: Tod House.

E334.2.1. Ghost of murdered person haunts burial spot. Seattle, Wa.: Neptune Theater; Sawyer, Wa.: Lombard Loop, grave found on property where ghost resides; Steilacoom, Wa.: Native American hung in tree; Victoria, B.C.: Tod House.

E334.2.1(o). Ghost of murdered person haunts room (or place) where he was murdered. See from E338.1(f). Chilliwick, B.C.; Newport, Ore.: Yaquina Bay Light; Rogue River, Ore.: beam from which man hung groans; Seattle, Wa.: alley behind Wah Mee Club; Seattle, Wa.: Neptune Theater; Tacoma, Wa.: courthouse where room where two men hung; Victoria, B.C.: golf course.

E334.2.2. Ghost of person killed in accident seen at death or burial spot. (Baughman); Applegate River, Ore.: Girl killed in mudslide protecting baby in cradle; Cheney, Wa.: Eastern Wa. University; Florence, Ore.: mudslide; Hoquiam, Wa.: fell to death or was stabbed or died stoking fire; Tacoma, Wa.: janitor killed in elevator; Seattle, Wa.: Metro Bus Barn; Seattle, Wa.: earthquake victims in ship's ballast; Siuslaw River, Ore.: family killed in mudslide.

E334.2.2(b). Ghost of person who died in fall or in act of jumping. Seattle, Wa.: Pike Place Market.

E334.2.2(db). Auto accident victim seen every year at accident spot. Sooke, B.C.:

but was not killed.

E334.4. Ghost of suicide seen at death spot or nearby. (Hand, Ohio 29788 89); Chilliwack, B.C.; Forest Grove, Ore.: Pacific University; Port Townsend, Wa.: Jesuit priest hung, woman leaped to death; Pendleton, Ore.: librarian; Vancouver, B.C.: teacher in home.

*E334.(6). Ghost of person who died natural death at scene of death. Hoquiam, Wa.: stoking furnace.

E337. Ghost re-enacts scene from own lifetime. Seattle, Wa.: Butterworth Building, two men insult woman ghost and each other; Vancouver, B.C.: old man washes clothes; Victoria, B.C.: Barbary Banjo Restaurant, psychic sees scene; Victoria, B.C.: wife in chains.

E337(a). Re-enactment of activities just before violent death.

Seattle, Wa.: Lady clutches throat and strikes out, perhaps only a struggle; Vancouver, B.C.: lady in bed.

*E337.1.3.1. Sounds of ghostly party. Victoria, B.C.: McPherson Theater. See also E499.

E337.2. Re-enactment of tragedy seen. B.C. Coast: Valencia sinking.

E338. Non-malevolent ghost haunts building.

E338(a). Male ghost seen. See E425.2.

E338(b). Female ghost seen in house. See also E422.4.4; E425.1.

E338(ba). Female ghost in rustling silks seen and heard walking in house. See also E422.4.4.(g). Burnaby, B.C.: Burnaby Art Gallery.

E338.1. Non-malevolent ghost haunts house or castle.

E338.1(aa). Ghosts knock on door. Rock Creek, B.C.: repeatedly; Spokane, Wa. See also E402.1.5.

E338.1(ab). Ghosts cause bells to ring. Portland, Ore.: Buttertoes Restaurant doorbell; Tacoma, Wa.: Old City Hall steeple bells; Vancouver, B.C.: hospital call button. See also E402.3(a) Sound of ghost bell.

E338.1(b). Ghost looks in at window. (Baughman); Coquitlam, B.C.: Seattle, Wa.: Pike Place Market.

E338.1(c). Ghost opens doors and windows repeatedly. (Brown, North Carolina 5717; Cannon, Utah 10609; Hand, Ohio 29602, 29809-11, 29656-7); Cheney, Wa; Colbert, Wa.; Douglas, Colorado, Ore.: stairway window; Duvall, Wa.; Fort Wright, Wa.; Heceta Head, Ore.: kitchen cupboard doors; Kennewick, Wa.: opens doors, rattles windows; Kennewick, Wa.: doors in store; Pendleton, Ore.: librarian is ghost; Prosser, Wa.: old hotel; Oak Bay, B.C.: cellar door; Richland, Wa.: china closet door; ; Seattle, Wa.: Butterworth Building; Shaw Island, Wa.: door opens; Spokane, Wa.: home on E. 28th St.; Sawyer, Wa.: Lombard Loop; Spokane, Wa.: Spokane Technical Institute; Tacoma, Wa.: Rhodes Mansion; Tacoma, Wa.: 705 N. J. St.; Tacoma, Wa.: theater trap door; Troutdale, Ore.: sliding glass door; Vancouver, B.C.: barracks; Victoria, B.C.: bedroom door; Waldo, B.C.; heavy door opens; Yakima, Wa.: Capitol Theater. See also E402.1.7. Ghost slams door; E299.4. Ghost breaks windows.

E338.1(ca). Ghost opens door or window and looks out. Clakkanie, Ore.:

Skeleton-like face at door's window; Oregon City, Ore.: Lady looks out window; Welches, Ore.: lady looks out second floor window at river. See also E402.1.7.

*E338.1(cb). Ghost turns doorknob. Medford, Ore.: bedroom door; Tacoma, Wa.: Mrs. Pacinda.

*E338.1(cc). Ghost unlocks door. Medford, Ore.: Front door, repeatedly unlocked; Seattle, Wa.: Burnley School of Art.

*E338.1(cd). Ghost holds door shut so person cannot pull it open. Seattle, Wa.: Harvard Exit Theater.

E338.1(f). Ghost haunts bedroom. See also E334.2.1(o); E279.2; E281.3.(b).

E338.1(fab). Man walks through bedroom, carrying bloody knife. Colbert, Wa.: bends over child's bed.

E338.1(fae). Ghost sits on foot of bed. See *E279.2.(1)

E338.1(fb). Ghost sleeps in bed, leaving impression of body in bed. Vancouver, B.C.: Burn Unit, ghost turns over under covers.

E338.1(g). Ghost haunts cellar. Seattle, Wa.: Tai Tung Restaurant.

E338.1.(h). Miscellaneous activities of ghosts in house.

E338.1(hb). Ghost cleans house. Heceta Head, Ore.: sweeps; Spokane, Wa.: folds and stacks laundry; New Westminster, BC: laundryman.

E338.1(hc). Female ghost in chains cries and sobs. Victoria, B.C.: Tod House.

E338.1(hg). Ghost causes rocking chair to rock. Brown, North Carolina 5718); Applegate, Ore.; Portland, Ore.: Buttertoes Restaurant; Spokane, Wa.: scratches piano. See also F473.2.1.

*E338.1.(ib.). Ghost gives tour of museum house. Victoria, B.C.: Point Ellice House.

*E338.1.(j). Ghost haunts hall. Hoquiam, Wa.: Lyttle Mansion; Tacoma, Wa.: 705 N. J.; Tacoma, Wa.: Rhodes Mansion.

E338.2. Non-malevolent ghost haunts church. See from E283.

(Brown, North Carolina p. 676).

E338.4*(a). Ghost of rector walks invisibly through the rectory. Seattle, Wa.: Methodist.

E338.5*. Ghost haunts courthouse. Tacoma, Wa.: Pierce County.

*E338.5.(1). Ghost haunts city hall. Tacoma, Wa.: rings bells in tower.

E338.6*. Ghost haunts hotel. Port Townsend, Wa.: Manresa Castle; Prosser, Wa.: Harvest House.

*E338.6.(1). Ghost haunts resort. Orcas Island, Wa.: Rosario Resort;: Roche Harbor Resort.

E338.7* Ghost haunts educational institution. Cheney, Wa.: Eastern Wa. University; Seattle, Wa.: Burnley School of Art; Spokane, Wa.: Spokane Technical Institute; Victoria, B.C.: Royal Roads Military College, old woman haunts dormitory.

E338.8*. Ghost haunts library. Pendleton, Ore.: librarian.

E338.10*. Ghost haunts fort. Fort Vancouver, Wa.: Barracks.

*E338.(11). Ghost haunts theater. Ashland, Ore.: Elizabethan Theater; Barkerville, B.C.: Barkerville Theater; Corvallis, Ore.: Eugene, Ore.: high school theater; Everett, Wa.: high school theater; Seattle, Wa.: 5th Avenue Theater; Seattle, Wa.: Paramount Theater; Seattle, Wa.: Showboat Theater; Tacoma, Wa.: Temple Theater; Victoria, B.C.: McPherson Theater; Yakima, Wa.: Capitol Theater.

*E338.(11.1). Ghost haunts movie theater. Seattle, Wa.: Harvard Exit; Seattle, Wa.: Moore-Egyptian; Seattle, Wa.: Neptune.

*E338.(11.2). Ghost haunts theater balcony. Eugene, Ore.: high school theater; Seattle, Wa.: 5th Avenue Theater; Seattle, Wa.: Neptune; Seattle, Wa.: Paramount; Tacoma, Wa.: Masonic Theater.

*E338.(11.3). Ghost haunts rest room. Seattle, Wa.: Neptune.

*E338.(12). Ghost haunts park. See from E279.4. Ashland, Ore.: Lithia Park, hunchback; West Seattle, Wa.: Hiawatha Park.

*E338.(12.1). Ghost haunts golf course. Seattle, Wa.: Native American dancer; Victoria, B.C.: white lady on 7th Tee.

*E338.(13). Ghost haunts restaurant. Portland, Ore.: Buttertoes Restaurant; Seattle, Wa.: Butterworth Building, two restaurants; Seattle, Wa.: College Inn Pub; Seattle, Wa.: Tai Tung; Steilacoom, Wa.: E. R. Rogers; Bair Drug Store; Vancouver, B.C.: Mandarin Gardens; Victoria, B.C.: Barbary Banjo; Victoria, B.C.: Dingle House.

*E338.(14). Ghost haunts hospital. Vancouver, B.C.: Vancouver General.

*E338.(14.2). Ghost haunts crisis nursery. Spokane, Wa.: child ghost.

*E338.(15). Ghost haunts store. Kennewick, Wa.: Mother's World clothing; Seattle, Wa.: Pike Place Market—bead shop, Goodwill, puppet shop; Seattle, Wa.: Pier 70; Seattle, Wa.: Butterworth Building; Steilacoom, Wa.: Bair Drug store.

*E338.(16). Ghost haunts ship. Seattle, Wa.: *Sea King* has dead bodies in ballast; Seattle: boat ghost.

*E338.(17). Ghost haunts wharf. Seattle, Wa.: Pier 70.

*E338.(18). Ghost haunts firehouse. Astoria, Ore.

*E363.(0.1). Ghost aids living. No sense of having returned for this purpose. Seattle, Wa.: two men hold ladder for workman.

E363.1. Ghost aids living in emergency. Yakima, Wa.: moves falling light shutter away from girl onstage.

*E363.1(g). Ghostly watchman takes freezing man into shack by railroad and warms. Leavenworth, Wa.: Train from Spokane, Wa.

*E363.1.(h). Ghost warns of fire. Port Townsend, Wa.,

*E363.6(d).1. Ghost soothes patients in burn ward. Vancouver, B.C.

E378. Ghost continues to remain in usual surroundings after death. (Note: This is assumed in many cases. Cited here are those in which the identity of the ghost is believed to be known.) Ellensburg, Wa.: grandfather in chair; Pendleton, Ore.: librarian; Seattle, Wa.: bar patrons at Butterworth Building; Spokane, Wa.: Mr. McCloud rocks; Tillamook Rock, Ore.: lighthouse keeper; Vancouver, B.C., B.C.: teacher in home; Victoria, B.C.: husband.

*E378.(5). Ghost seen in museum which was own home. Oregon City, Ore.: Dr. John MacLoughlin, Uncle Sandy Barclay; Victoria, B.C.: Point Ellis House, Caroline O'Reilly, Kathleen O'Reilly; Victoria, B.C.: Tod House.

*E378.(5.l). Ghost gives tours of museum which was own home. Victoria, B.C.: Point Ellis House.

E378.(5.2). Ghost in museum which houses possessions. Seattle, Wa.: Bertha Knight Landes.

E386.5. Offhand remark about what person would do if ghost appeared causes ghost to appear. Coquitlam, B.C.

E402. Mysterious ghostlike noises heard. (Song, animal cries, footsteps, etc.). See also E338.1+, E337.1.3. (Hand OHIO 29664); Cheney, Wa.; Seattle, Wa.: voices; Tacoma, Wa.: scurrying in attic.

E402.1.1. Vocal sounds of ghost of human being. See from E545.

*E402.1.1.1(1). Ghost cries "Help." Sawyer, Wa.: Lombard Loop; Tacoma, Wa.: Mrs. Pacinda.

E402.1.1.2. Ghost moans. Siuslaw River, Ore.: family buried by mudslide; Tacoma, Wa.: Mrs. Pacinda; Tacoma, Wa.: rambler walls.

E402.1.1.3. Ghost cries and screams. Fort Wright, Wa.; La Grande, Ore.: woman screams; Seattle, Wa.: Neptune Theater; Seattle, Wa.: Harvard Exit; Seattle, Wa.: Wah Mee Club; Tillamook Rock, Ore.

E402.1.1.4. Ghost sings. Ashland, Ore.; Barkersville, B.C.; Duwamish Bend, Wa.: Sings "Blue Moon"; Fort Wright, Wa.; Pacific Grove, Ore.: female alto in music building.

*E402.1.1.4.(1). Ghost hums. Welches, Ore.

E402.1.1.5. Ghost snores. (Hand, Ohio 29820); Vancouver Island, B.C.

E402.1.1.6. Ghost sobs. Bremerton, Wa.: Child ghost.

E402.1.1.7. Ghost laughs. (Baughman)Ashland, Ore.: Charles Laughton; Vancouver: Mandarin Gardens Restaurant.

*E402.1.1.(9). Ghost speaks. (Baughman) Bellingham, Wa.: voice in Lummi language says "One is missing"; Forest Grove, Ore.: Pacific University, ghost tells pianist to "Please stop"; King County, Wa.: "murder, murder, murder"; Port Townsend, Wa.: whispers names of maids; Richland, Wa.: "Mommy, mommy, mommy," taunting cry; Seattle, Wa.: "How do I get out?"; Seattle, Wa.: Showboat Theater, ghost answers cues of actress; Vancouver: Mandarin Gardens; Vancouver, B.C.: army barracks; Welches, Ore.: tells man to stop doing drugs.

*E402.1.1.(9.1). Sound of ghosts talking. Not intelligible. Applegate, Ore.: man and woman arguing; Douglas County, Ore.: two women talking; Spokane, Wa.: voices in empty classroom; Spokane, Wa.: in home; Troutdale, Ore.: man's voice; Seattle, Wa.: murmuring; Vancouver, B.C.: "Johnny"; Victoria, B.C.: McPherson Theater.

*E402.1.1.(10). Ghost sighs. Heceta Head, Ore.: during card game; Pacific Grove, Ore.: when piano played; Seattle, Wa.: Moore-Egyptian Theater.

*E402.1.1.(11). Ghost coughs. Victoria, B.C.: husband on wife's wedding day.

*E402.1.1.(12). Sound of ghost breathing. Chilliwack, B.C.; Vancouver, B.C.: Deceased patient still in bed.

E402.1.2. Footsteps of invisible ghost heard. Brown, North Carolina p. 673); Applegate, Ore.; Barkersville, B.C.: Barkersville Theater; Cheney, Wa., ; Chilliwack, B.C.; Clatkanie, Ore.; Corvallis, Ore.: Douglass County, Ore.: up stairs; Duvall, Wa.; Eugene, Ore.: high school auditorium ceiling; Forest Grove, Ore.: music building; Fort Wright, Wa.; Heceta Head, Ore.: Lighthouse; La Grande, Ore.; Medford, Ore.; Oregon City, Ore.; Port Townsend, Wa.: lighthouse; Rock Creek, B.C.; Seattle, Wa.: Burnley School of Art; Seattle, Wa.: Butterworth Building; Shaw Island, Wa.: Sawyer, Wa.: Lombard Loop, two houses; Spokane, Wa.; Spokane Technical Institute; Tacoma, Wa.: Rhodes Mansion; Tacoma, Wa.: Mrs. Pacinda; Tacoma, Wa.: 705.N. J. St.; Troutdale, Ore.; Vancouver: "Oscar"; Vancouver Island, B.C.: climbs stairs and throws off boots; Vancouver, Wa.: in barracks; Victoria, B.C.: child runs in attic; Victoria, B.C.: McPherson Theater; Welches, Ore.

E402.1.3.(a). Ghost plays violin. Applegate, Ore.: fiddle.

E402.1.3. Invisible ghost plays musical instrument. (Hand, Ohio 29815). See from E554.

E402.1.3(b). Ghost plays organ. (Brown, North Carolina p. 676); Seattle, Wa.: Neptune Theater; Spokane, Wa.: Gonzaga University.

*E402.1.3(b).l. Ghost plays piano. La Grande, Ore.; Seattle, Wa.: Showboat Theater; Waldo, B.C.: in cottage.

*E402.1.3(b).2. Ghost plays dulcimer. Barkersville, B.C.: Barkerville Theater.

*E402.1.3(f). Ghost plays flute. Spokane, Wa.: Gonzaga University.

*E402.1.3.(g). Ghost plays music box. Welches, Ore.

E402.1.4. Invisible ghost jingles chains. (Baughman); Clatkanie, Ore.: rattles chains in closet.

E402.1.5. Invisible ghost makes rapping or knocking noise. (Brown, North Carolina p. 673; Hand, Ohio 29807-8, 29815); Chilliwack, B.C.: banging on outside walls of house; Colbert, Wa.: hammer-like pounding on wall; Duvall, Wa.: bookshelf; King County, Wa.: noises in walls; Richland, Wa.: rattles dresser and mirror. See also F473.5.(a).

*E402.1.5(a)(1). Ghost drags furniture around in room overhead. Seattle, Wa.: Burnley School of Art; Seattle, Wa.: Capitol Hill; Spokane, Wa.: downstairs in living room; Tacoma, Wa. ; Masonic Temple; Troutdale, Ore.: shuffles boxes; Vancouver, B.C.: drags kettle across hearth. See also F473.1.(g.a.).

E*402.1.5.(g). Ghost scratches on door. Burnaby, B.C.: Burnaby Art Gallery.

E402.1.6. Crash as of breaking glass, though no glass is found. Seattle, Wa.: Georgetown. See also E209.4.

E402.1.7. Ghost slams door. Chilliwack, B.C.; Fort Wright, Wa.: slams door when girl sings; Oregon City, Ore.; Tacoma, Wa.: Mrs. Pacinda. See also E338.1(c)+.

E402.1.8. Miscellaneous sounds made by ghost of human being. Heceta Head,

Ore.: sweeping sounds; Port Townsend, Wa.: rummaging; Portland, Ore.: rummaging in bathroom cabinet; Salem, Ore.: fluttering; Yakima, Wa.: flushing toilet.

*E402.1.8.(1). Sounds of paging through books, magazines, or papers. Douglas County, Ore.; Portland, Ore.: Buttertoes Restaurant.

E402.2. Sounds made by invisible ghosts of animals.

E402.2.3. Hoofbeats of ghost horse. Rogue River, Ore.: stable noises, stomping and whinnying; Rural Ore.: gallops past house; West Seattle, Wa.: whinnying. See also E535.1.

E402.3. Sound made by ghostly object.

E402.3(a). Sound of ghost bell. See also E338.1.(ab). E402.3.(ab). Bell rung by ghost. Tacoma, Wa.: Old City Hall.

E402.3.(ac). Clock without mechanism strikes. Waldo, B.C.; Yoncalla, Ore.

E402.4. Sound of ethereal music. See also E402.1.3; E533.

E410. The unquiet grave. See E334.

E412.3. Dead without proper funeral rites cannot rest. Bellingham, Wa.: Native American dead.

E419.4. Dead move when cemetery is moved. Bellingham, Wa.: Native American bones moved.

*E421.(O.1). Transparent ghosts. Port Townsend, Wa.: like cellophane; Seattle, Wa.: Capital Hill Church; Spokane, Wa.: faint image.

E421.1. Invisible ghosts. Kennewick, Wa.: Peculiar feeling; Medford, Ore.: Senses someone there; Shaw Island, Wa.: At foot of bed; Spokane, Wa.: Dead wife brushes by bed; Spokane, Wa.: Gonzaga University.

E421.1.1. Ghost visible to one person alone.

*E421.1.1.(2). Ghost visible to child alone. Tacoma, Wa.: Rhodes Mansion; Vancouver, B.C.: "Johnny."

E421.1.3. Ghost visible only to dog. (Brown, North Carolina 5722, 5729, 5756-7; Browne, Alabama 3323; Cannon, Utah 10626; Hand, Ohio 29618); Bremerton, Wa.: Dog dies of heart attack; Chilliwack, B.C.; Colbert, Wa.; Forest Grove, Ore.: night watchman's dog; King County, Wa.: dog and girl see; New Westminister, B.C.: dog looks at something invisible while sitting on couch next to owner; Rock Creek, B.C.: dog bites ghost; Seattle, Wa.: dog on boat; Steilacoom, Wa.: police dog; Tacoma, Wa.

*E421.1.(7). Ghosts visible only to cats. Douglas County, Ore.: cats hear phantom stage; Heceta Head, Ore.; Oak Bay, B.C.: Tod House.

E421.1.6.(1). No birds on haunted property. See F989.16.3.

*E421.2.1.(1). Ghost leaves footprints. Vancouver, B.C.: prints of bed's legs; Yakima, Wa.: on theater catwalk. See also E521.2.(2).

*E421.2.(2). Ghost floats—feet do not touch ground. Seattle, Wa.: Neptune Theater; Victoria, B.C.: golf course.

E421.3. Luminous ghosts. Eugene, Ore.: High school theater, glow; Everett, Wa.: High school theater; Port Townsend, Wa.: Manresa Castle; Seattle, Wa.: Neptune Theater; Seattle, Wa.: Pike Place Market; Seattle, Wa.:

enveloped in bluish light; Tacoma, Wa.: Masonic Theater, yellow glow; Victoria, B.C.: golf course.

E421.4. Ghost as shadow. Everett, Wa.: High school theater; Orcas Island, Wa.; Oregon City, Ore.: tall shadow has to duck through doorways; Seattle, Wa.: Butterworth Building.

*E421.4.(1). Ghost as mist. King County, Wa.: green and white mist; Seattle, Wa.: Pier 70; Victoria, B.C.: golf course; Victoria, B.C.: husband as gray, whirling column.

E421.5. Ghost seen by two or more persons; they corroborate the appearance. Seattle, Wa.: Georgetown, by two men; Victoria, B.C.: two airmen in bedroom.

*E421.5.(1). Ghost heard by two or more persons. Victoria, B.C.: husband coughs and sighs in room full of women.

*E421.(6). Ghost visible only out of corner of eye. Duvall, Wa.; New Westminster, B.C.; Port Townsend, Wa.: lighthouse; Richland, Wa.; Seattle, Wa.: Harvard Exit Theater; Seattle, Wa.: Smith Tower workman, ghost looks over shoulder.

*E421.(7). Ghost disappears as one watches. Chilliwack, B.C.; Portland, Ore.: Buttertoes Restaurant; Seattle, Wa.: Harvard Exit Theater; Seattle, Wa.: Neptune Theater; Seattle, Wa.: Pike Place Market; Tacoma, Wa.: Rhodes Mansion.

E422.1.1.(a.) Headless man—appearance only. Vancouver, B.C.: headless brakeman.

E422.1.11.2. Revenant as face or head. Seattle, Wa.: Neptune Theater, blue face emerging from wall; Steilacoom: face in tree.

E422.1.11.3. Ghost as hand or hands. Vancouver, B.C.: Mandarin Gardens.

E422.4.4. Revenant in female dress. Fort Wright, Wa.; Port Townsend, Wa.: lighthouse; Seattle, Wa.: Smith Tower, heavy set woman resembling former Seattle mayor Bertha Knight Landes; Seattle, Wa.: Harvard Exit Theater, tall woman; Seattle, Wa.: minister's wife in flowing gown; Steilacoom, Wa.: stockinged feet; Victoria, B.C.: little old woman; Wells, B.C.; Welches, Ore. See also E338.(c); E425.1.

E422.4.4 (a). Female revenant in white clothing. "The white lady" etc. (Cannon, Utah 10667); Burnaby, B.C.: Burnaby Art Gallery; Port Townsend, Wa.: Manresa Castle; Portland, Ore.: Buttertoes Restaurant; Seattle, Wa.: Neptune Theater; Seattle, Wa.: Butterworth Building, white linen dress, presumably of modern style; Sooke, B.C.: roadside lady; Victoria, B.C.: golf course.

E422.4.4(b). Female revenant in gray clothing. Burnaby, B.C.: Burnaby Art Gallery; Duvall, Wa.: Bluett Road; Heceta Head, Ore.: old, wrinkled face, hoop skit; Seattle, Wa.: Neptune Theater; Siletz, Ore.: Klamath Lady; Victoria, B.C.: golf course.

E422.4.4.(c). Female revenant in green dress. Jacksonville, Ore.

E422.4.4.(e). Female revenant in black dress. Heceta Head, Ore.; Seattle, Wa.: Neptune Theater, flowing dress.

E422.4.4.(f). Female revenant in blue dress. Burnaby, B.C.: Burnaby Art Gallery; Eugene, Ore.: High school theater; Everett, Wa.: High school theater; Forest Grove, Ore.: Bluish-white gown, filmy; Victoria, B.C.: Point Ellice House.

E422.4.4.(g). Female revenant (often invisible) in rustling silk dress. See from E338(ba). Burnaby, B.C.: gallery; Forest Grove, Ore.: Pacific University.

E422.4.4.(h). Female revenant in old-fashioned garb. (Note: All of above female revenants are assumed to be in long gowns unless otherwise noted. Those cited here have specific features of the costume mentioned other than color and length). Applegate, Ore.; Heceta Head, Ore.: hoopskirt; New Westminster, B.C.: shadow of woman in long dress; Seattle, Wa.: hair up, white blouse, floor-length dress; Sooke, B.C.: roadside lady; Vancouver, B.C: long skirt, bib apron; Welches, Ore.: floor length, puff sleeves, low yoke, bonnet, hair up.

*E422.4.4.(i). Female revenant in lavender dress. Seattle, Wa.: Pike Place Market.

*E422.4.4.(j). Female revenant in pink dress. Seattle, Wa.: Pike Place Market.

*E422.4.4.(k). Female revenant in red dress. Chilliwack, B.C.: red flowered.

E422.4.5. Revenant in male dress. Ashland, Ore.; Ellensburg, Wa.: Old man in coveralls, girlfriend's grandfather; Richland, Wa.: western style clothing; Seattle, Wa.: Butterworth Building, two men taken for contemporaries; Seattle, Wa.: College Inn, older man, white hair, khaki trench coat; Victoria, B.C.: Dingle House.

E422.4.5.(b). Male revenant in old-fashioned garb. New Westminster, B.C.: middle-aged man in long coat and hat; Salem, Ore.: black robe; Seattle, Wa.: dark haired, bearded sailor in peacoat; Seattle, Wa.: College Inn, older man, white hair, khaki trench coat; Seattle, Wa.: Pike Place; Tacoma, Wa.: balding, slim, medium height; Tacoma, Wa.: long coat or masonic robe; Vancouver Island, B.C.: Dingle House.

E423. Revenant in animal form. See also E520+.

E423.1.1. Revenant as dog. Siletz, Ore.: white dog. See also E521.2.

E425.1. Female revenant. Victoria, B.C.: Point Ellice House, lady in blue dress gives guided tour, assumed to be living person. See also E422.4.4; E338 (b).

E425.2. Revenant as man. Everett, Wa.: Everett H.S. Theater; Vancouver,: Vancouver Hospital, young man soothes patients. See from E42.2; E338.(a).

E425.2.3. Ghost of priest or parson. Coquitlam B.C.: hooded faceless figure with red scribbling on robe believed to be monk; Port Townsend, Wa.: Jesuit; Seattle, Wa.: Methodist minister. See also E338.4.

E425.2.4. Revenant as American Indian. Bellingham, Wa.: disturbed skeletons, uneasy spirits; Oak Bay, B.C.: Tod house, woman in fetters; Seattle, Wa.: Pike Place Market, old woman; Seattle, Wa.: golf course, dancing man; Seattle, Wa.: horseback on golf course; Siletz, Ore.: woman; Steilacoom, Wa.: hung in tree; Valdez Island, B.C.: ghostly dancers; Vancouver, B.C.: disturbed graves, uneasy spirits; Vancouver: "Johnny"; Victoria, B.C.: woman in chains.

E425.3 Revenant as child. Bremerton, Wa.: sound of sobbing child; Coquitlam B.C.; Oregon City, Ore.: red haired boy; Seattle, Wa.: Pike Place Market; Sislaw River, Ore.: voices of children trapped in mudslide; Spokane, Wa.: crying child; Tacoma, Wa.: asks for doll to be mended; Vancouver, B.C.: Burnaby Art Gallery; Victoria, B.C.: child runs in attic; Victoria, B.C.: child at foot of bed.

*E425.(4). Revenant as dancer. Barkerville, B.C.: dancers; Seattle, Wa.: Pike Place Market, male tap dancer.

*E425.(5). Revenant as actor. Ashland, Ore.: Charles Laughton; Barkerville, B.C.: actor; Seattle, Wa.: Showboat Theater, actor answers cues.

*E425.(6). Revenant as hunchbacked person. Ashland, Ore.: hunchback with gunnysack in parking lot.

*E425.(7). Revenant as other specific person. New Westminster, B.C.: Chinese washerman; Seattle, Wa.: Pike Place Market, barber; Seattle, Wa.: Pike Place Market, market director.

E436.3 Bats flying in house sign of ghosts. Spokane, Wa.: Bat found on window blind when moved in.

E440. Walking ghost "laid."

*E440.(0.1.). Ghost investigated by medium but no attempt to lay. Burnaby, B.C.: art gallery; New Westminster, B.C.; Saanich, B.C.; Seattle, Wa.: Neptune Theater; Victoria, B.C.: Point Ellis; Yakima, Wa.: theater.

*E440.(0.2.). Ghost investigated by priest but no attempt to lay. Chilliwack, B.C.: priest orders teen to leave house; Richland, Wa.

E443. Ghost exorcised and laid. Kennewick, Wa.: ghost hunter feels with his "aura," tells to leave; King County, Wa.; Seattle, Wa.: Queen Anne Hill; Seattle, Wa.: Wing Luke Museum; Seattle, Wa.: Pike Place Market; Victoria, B.C.: child running in attic.

E443.2.2(e). Ghost laid by Roman Catholic priest (presumably by prayer). Colbert, Wa.: priest blesses house, has no effect; Seattle, Wa.: Butterworth Building; Spokane, Wa.: Gonzaga University.

E451. Ghost finds rest when certain thing happens.

*E451.(0.1.). Attempt to calm ghost by painting its portrait. Seattle, Wa. ; Chilliwack, B.C.

E451.4. Ghost laid when living man speaks to it. (Brown, North Carolina 5725; Hand, Ohio 29763-29772); Richland, Wa.: woman yells at ghost.

*E451.4.(0.1). Ghost calms down when spoken to. Applegate, Ore.; Puyallup, Wa.: woman scolds ghost; Tacoma, Wa.: teen tells ghost to go away; Seattle, Wa.: Butterworth Building; Vancouver, B.C.: burn unit; Vancouver, B.C.: "Oscar" obeys commands.

*E451. 4.(0.2.). Ghost does not calm down when spoken to. Richland, Wa.: becomes more obstreperous.

E451.8(a). Ghost laid by remodeling house it haunts. (Browne, Alabama 3320); Troutdale, Ore.

E451.8(c). Ghost laid when house it haunts is burned. Chilliwack, B.C.

E451.8(d). Ghost laid when house it haunts is torn down. Sawyer, Wa.: Lombard Loop; Vancouver, B.C.: Mandarin Gardens Restaurant; Vancouver, B.C.: Burn Unit; Victoria, B.C.: washing machine.

E460. Revenants in conflict.

E461. Fight of revenant with living person. Seattle, Wa.: Lady ghost hits man, Georgetown, Wa.; Shaw Island, Wa.: ghost hits man in back with pillow. See also F473.3.(e).

E462. Revenant overawed by living person.

*E462.(1). Man's dog bites ghost. Rock Creek, B.C.

E470. Intimate relations of dead and living.

*E470.(1) Living are content to live with ghostly presence. Applegate, Ore.; Duvall, Wa.; Heceta Head, Ore.: lighthouse keeper; Kennewick, Wa.: ghosthunter's own home haunted; Kennewick, Wa.: clothing store; Oak Bay, B.C.: Tod house; Prosser, Wa.: Old Strand Hotel; Puyallup, Wa.: teaches course on how to live with ghost; Roche Harbor, Wa.: restaurant; Seattle, Wa.: Capitol Hill; Seattle, Wa.: Moore-Egyptian Theater; Seattle, Wa.: Pike Place Market; Seattle, Wa.: Georgetown Mansion; Seattle, Wa.: Butterworth Building; Shaw Island, Wa.; Tacoma, Wa.: renters content with ghost; Tacoma, Wa.: Rhodes Mansion; Vancouver, B.C.: Oscar; Victoria, B.C.: Tod House; Victoria, B.C.: Dingle House; Waldo, B.C.: renters; Welches, Ore.: cabin; Yakima, Wa.: theater.

*E470.(1.1). Person feels responsibility to ghosts. Applegate, Ore.; Seattle, Wa.: Harvard Exit Theater; Spokane, Wa.: Lombard Loop; Victoria, B.C.: Point Ellice House; Victoria, B.C.: husband returned to home; Victoria, B.C.: Dingle House.

*E470.(2) Living flee building inhabited by ghostly presence. Duvall, Wa.; Medford, Ore.: couple buy another house and move; Sawyer, Wa.: Lombard Loop, family moves out; Seattle, Wa.: Butterworth Building; Steilacoom, Wa.: E.R. Rogers Restaurant, rug cleaners; Tacoma, Wa.: Mrs. Pacinda wants to flee; Victoria, B.C.: moves out, house torn down.

*E470.(2.1). Living uneasy with ghostly presence. Tacoma, Wa.: Rhodes Mansion.

*E493(g). Ghosts of American Indians dance. Seattle, Wa.: man on golf course; Valdez Island, B.C.: many dancers on beach.

E499. Meetings of the dead: miscellaneous. Seattle, Wa.: Paramount Theater; Seattle, Wa.: Harvard Exit. See also E337.1.3.1.

E500. Phantom hosts.

E511. The flying dutchman. (Cannon, Utah 10405). See E535.3.

E520. Animal ghosts.

E521.2 Ghost of dog. Kamloops, B.C.: boy's pet returns; Oregon City, Ore.: small black and white dog. See also E423.1.1.

*E521.2.(1). Haunted dog. Walla Walla, Wa.: levitating dog.

*E521.2.(2). Paw prints of ghost dog found. See from E421.2.1.(1) Kamloops, B.C.: in dirt; Oregon City, Ore.: in carpet.

*E526. Ghost of snake. Turnbull National Wildlife Refuge, Wa.

E530.1. Ghost-like lights. Tillamook Rock, Ore.: lighthouse

E530.1.6.(d). Building seen to light up in mysterious manner before death occurs. Duvall, Wa.: owner of home dies.

E532. Ghost-like picture.

E532(ca). Ghost does not appear in photograph. Seattle, Wa.: Harvard Exit, patrons in chairs; Turnbull National Wildlife Refuge: snake does not appear.

*E532.(cb) Other ghostly manifestations in photographs. Saanich, B.C.: white pillar covers house foundation.

*E532.(1) Other attributes of ghostly portrait. Oregon City, Ore.: face lights up at 9:35, Sept. 3 each year; Chilliwack, B.C.: ghost's portrait painted, gradually changes from woman to man.

E533. Ghostly bell. See E402.3.(a); E338.1.(ab).

E535.l. Phantom coach and horses. See also E402.2.3

E535.1.(b). Phantom coach and horse heard only. Douglas County, Ore.

E535.3. Ghost ship. See also E511, E338.(16). Tillamook Rock, Ore.; Seattle, Wa.: Alki Point; Seattle, Wa.: Pier 70; B.C. Coast.

E535.3.(g). Phantom ship in harbor re-enacts tragedy occurring to actual ship at sea. B.C. Coast: Ship Valencia

E535.4. Phantom railway train. Medicine Hat, Alberta.

*535.(5). Phantom trolley. Everett, Wa.

E539. Other ghostly objects. Duvall, Wa.: Bookcase raps; Rogue River, Ore.: Mantel creaks and groans; Vancouver, B.C.: Bed leaves prints in carpet.

E539.4. Ghostly chair. See F473.2.1

*E539.(6). Ghostly clock. Waldo, B.C.; Yoncalla, Ore. See also E402.3.(6).

E540. Miscellaneous actions of revenants.

E542. Dead man touches living. See also F473.3. Poltergeist mistreats people.

*E542.(6). Ghosts' nearness to person felt as chill. See also F473.3.(1). Brown (North Carolina) 5716; Browne (Alabama) 3312; Cannon (Utah) 10618; Hand (Ohio) 29649-20651; Bremerton, Wa.: Burnaby, B.C.: Burnaby Art Gallery; Everett, Wa.: High School Theater; Medford, Ore.: cold, clammy; New Westminster, B.C.; Seattle, Wa.: boat ghost feels like musty cobwebs; Seattle, Wa.: Burnley School of Art; Seattle, Wa.: Georgetown, Wa.; Seattle, Wa.: Moore Egyptian Theater; Seattle, Wa.: Neptune Theater; Seattle, Wa.: Metro Bus Barn; Spokane, Wa.; Tacoma, Wa.: Masonic Temple; Vancouver, B.C.: Vancouver General Hospital; Victoria, B.C.: Victoria Golf Course; Victoria, B.C.: Royal Roads Military College, like freezing cobwebs.

*E542.6.(1). Icy wind indication of ghost's presence. Rock Creek, B.C.: icy wind on face; Spokane, Wa.,

*E542.(7). Ghost brushes past person. Portland, Ore.: Buttertoes Restaurant; Seattle, Wa.: Neptune Theater; Tacoma, Wa.: Rhodes Mansion; Tacoma, Wa.: Old City Hall (felt near).

*E542.(7.1). Ghost walks behind person. See from E402.1.2.(a). Victoria, B.C.:

Tod House.

E545. The Dead speak. See E402.1.1.+.

E554. Ghost plays musical instruments. See E402.1.3

E555. Dead man smokes pipe. Applegate River; Ashland, Ore.; Rock Creek, B.C.; Seattle, Wa.: Neptune Theater.

E536.1. Ghost drinks alcoholic beverages. Victoria, B.C.: Barbary Banjo Restaurant.

*E557.(2). Mysterious letters appear. Saanich, B.C.: letter "M" on mirror.

E558. Ghosts forced to labor. New Westminster, B.C.: old Chinese man doing hand laundry.

E568.1. Revenant leaves impression of body in bed. See E338.1.(fb).

E571. Ghostly barber. Seattle, Wa.: Large lady barber.

E572. Ghost walks through solid substance. Eugene, Ore.: High school theater, walks through wall; Oregon City, Ore.: walks through wall; Seattle, Wa.: walks out third story window; Sooke, B.C.: walks through car; Victoria, B.C.: child ghost walks through wall.

*E572.(1). Person walks through ghost. Seattle, Wa.: Moore-Egyptian Theater; Victoria, B.C.: Dingle House Restaurant.

*E572.(1.1.). Ghost walks through person. Seattle, Wa.: Moore-Egyptian Theater.

E574. Ghost as death omen. See also E265.3. Jacksonville, Ore.: Green Lady.

E575. Ghost as omen of impending calamity. Medicine Hat, Alberta: Ghost train.

E578. Dead persons build fires. Seattle, Wa.: Harvard Exit Theater, ghost starts fire in lobby fireplace repeatedly

E588. Ghost leaves stench behind. Cheney, Wa., ; Colbert, Wa.: foul odor; Port Townsend, Wa.: Manressa Castle; Seattle, Wa.: Moore-Egyptian Theater, urine; Seattle, Wa.: Queen Anne Hill.

E588.(1). Ghost leaves perfume odor. Chilliwack, B.C.; King County, Wa.: scent of roses; Port Townsend, Wa.: Manressa Castle; Spokane, Wa.: White Shoulders perfume; Steilacoom, Wa.: E.R. Rogers Restaurant; Wells, B.C.: flower scent in winter.

E593. Ghost takes things from people. Welches, Ore.: orange blanket. See also F473.2.2.

E599.6. Ghosts move furniture and household articles. See F473.1.(g.a.); F473.2+.

E599.10. Playful revenant.

*E599.10.(1). Ghost plays peek-a-boo. Portland, Ore.: Buttertoes Restaurant.

*E599.10.(2). Ghost teases man, appearing first on one side, then another. See from F473.3. Victoria, B.C.: Victoria Golf Course.

*E599.10.(3). Ghost plays catch. Drops objects which others must catch. Portland, Ore.: Buttertoes Restaurant

E723. Wraiths of persons separate from body. (Wraith: An apparition of a living person in his exact likeness that is to be seen usually just before his death.) (Hand, Ohio 29525-29538, 29866). See from E300.

E723.4.4. Wraith of dying woman goes to see children for last time before death. Fort St. John, B.C.: grandmother visits grandson.

E723.6.1* Death announcing wraith appears in or near building. Port Mellon, B.C.: son appears to mother.

E723.7. Wraith speaks. Tacoma, Wa.: child asks for doll to be fixed; Vancouver, B.C.: warns wife to have cancer operation.

F: TESTS

F402. Evil spirit. Seattle, Wa.: Neptune Theater; Seattle, Wa.: Butterworth Building; Welches, Ore.

F402.6.4.1. Spirits live in caves. Tillamook Rock, Ore.: underground tunnel from mainland to cave in rock filled with spirits.

F471.2.1. Succubus: female incubus. Port Townsend, Wa.: man feels self smothered by female spirit.

F473.1. Poltergeist throws objects.

*F473.0.1. Poltergeist in home with teen resident. Chilliwack, B.C.: niece.

F473.1(a). Spirit throws stones (at individuals or houses).

*F473.1.(a.b) Ghost throws shelf of software at person. Seattle, Wa.: Burnley School of Art.

F473.1(g). Spirits throw furniture and crockery about, often destructively. Heceta Head, Ore.: dishes rattle; Kennewick, Wa.: breaks dishes; Medford, Ore.: pots bang; Oak Bay, B.C.: hats from hat stand repeatedly fly to floor; Pendleton, Ore.: books from bookshelves; Port Townsend, Wa.: birthday cards tossed from mantel; Puyallup, Wa.: pots on kitchen floor, teacups fall, books fall from bookshelves; Tacoma, Wa.: rattles dishes; Seattle, Wa.: Butterworth Building; Seattle, Wa.: turns desks over in classroom at Burnley Art School; Spokane, Wa.: drops cupid statues from wall; Spokane, Wa.: breaks dishes; Steilacoom, Wa.: bottles of salmon sauce; Vancouver, B.C.: Christmas cards tossed from mantel; Vancouver, B.C.: child sees ghost; Victoria, B.C.: causes window to fall out of house; Waldo, B.C.: rifles through books, spins fishing reel.

*F473.1(g)(a). Spirit moves things around. See also E402.1.5.(a.1). Ashland, Ore.: Shakespeare Festival; Astoria, Ore.: Firehouse; Burnaby, B.C.: tools; Chilliwack, B.C.: bed; Colbert, Wa.: picture flies from dresser; Everett, Wa.: seats in classroom; Kennewick, Wa.: clothing racks; safe perched on bed; King County, Wa.: porcelain dolls, bathroom mirror; La Grande, Ore.: rocking chairs moved; piano music taken out; Oak Bay, B.C.: hats tossed from hat rack, cards from mantel; Portland, Ore.: restaurant menus, pot lid, breadboard; Port Townsend, Wa.: Pitcher of water tipped over; Prosser, Wa.: hotel; Seattle, Wa.: Neptune Theater; Seattle, Wa.: Metro Bus Barn; Seattle, Wa.: model stand dragged across floor; Spokane, Wa.: mannequin takes off head; Spokane, Wa.: Spokane, Wa. Technical Institute; Troutdale,

Ore.: picture turned face down; Vancouver, B.C.: moves kettle across hearth; Vancouver, B.C.: Johnny the ghost; Victoria, B.C.: dishes broken, restaurant tables disturbed.

*F473.1.(g) (b). Objects sail across room in plain view. Douglas, B.C.: wine bottle leaps from wastebasket; Seattle, Wa.: Capitol Hill, kitchen towels, ashtray sails across coffee table; Seattle, Wa.: Butterworth Building, dresses in shop window dance; Seattle, Wa.: loaf of bread rolls down counter; Steilacoom, Wa.: salmon sauce bottle; Troutdale, Ore.: clock; Victoria, B.C.: ashtray sails across coffee table; Victoria, B.C.: Christmas cards put on floor, hats from hat rack.

*F473.1.(gc). Spirit rattles objects. Heceta Head, Ore.: dishes in cupboard; Medford, Ore.: pots and dishes; Tacoma, Wa.: Dishes in cupboard; Seattle, Wa.: Butterworth Building; Seattle, Wa.: Burnley School of Art; Vancouver, B.C.: dishes and utensils at Mandarin Gardens.

*F473.1.(gd). Spirit causes glass to shatter. Port Townsend, Wa.: Manresa Castle, goblet shatters in hand.

F473.2. Poltergeist causes objects to behave contrary to their nature.

F473.2.1. Empty chair is rocked by invisible spirit who sits in it and rocks. See from E539.4. See also E338.1.(hg). (Brown, North Carolina) 5718. La Grande, Ore.: Hot Springs Resort; Oak Bay, B.C.; Oregon City, Ore.; Spokane, Wa.: Mr. McLoud; Victoria, B.C.; Welches, Ore.: shadow of lady in chair.

*F473.2.1.(1.) Cradle rocked by invisible spirit. See also Applegate River, Ore.

*F473.2.1.(2). Theater seats slammed down by invisible spirit. Everett, Wa.: High school theater.

F473.2.2. Spirit hides articles in strange places. See also E593. Ghost takes things from people. Astoria, Ore.: firehouse; La Grande, Ore.: librarian; Medford, Ore.: Christmas decorations box; Prosser, Wa.: hotel; Puyallup, Wa.: earrings and car keys; Seattle, Wa.: Neptune Theater; Seattle, Wa.: Butterworth Building, pastry chef's pots moved; Seattle, Wa.: coat in parsonage; Spokane, Wa.: Steilacoom, Wa.: hand mixer in restaurant; Tacoma, Wa.: apartment; Yakima, Wa.: theater crew's tools.

F473.2.3. Spirit puts out lights (or puts them on). Everett, Wa.: follow-spot in theater; Forest Grove, Ore.: music building, off; Fort Wright, Wa.: turned on; Kennewick, Wa.: store lights turned on; Newport, Ore.: Yaquina Bay Lighthouse, click of switch heard; New Westminster, B.C.: flicks bathroom switch on & off; Port Townsend, Wa.: Manressa Castle; Roche Harbor, Wa.: restaurant lights; Seattle, Wa.: Burnley School of Art, turns on and off; Spokane, Wa.: Spokane Technical Institute; Steilacoom, Wa.: E.R. Rogers Restaurant, turns on; Tacoma, Wa.: on and off, Pacinda home; Tacoma, Wa.: Old city hall; Vancouver, B.C., B.C: Christmas tree lights turned off; Victoria, B.C.: Little Denmark Restaurant, turned on; Welches, Ore.: turned off; Yakima, Wa.: spotlights dance.

*F473.2.3.(1). Spirit puts out candles (Hand, Ohio 09605-29607); Seattle, Wa.: Butterworth Building restaurant; Welches, Ore.: breaks finger of candle lighter.

*F473.2.3.(1.1). Spirit re-ignites candles. Roche Harbor, Wa.:

*F473.2.3(2). Spirit unplugs equipment. Vancouver, B.C.: Mandarin Gardens;

Victoria, B.C.: Dingle House Restaurant.

*F473.2.3.(3). Spirit sets off alarms. Tacoma, Wa.: Old City Hall; Seattle, Wa.: Burnley School of Art; Victoria, B.C.: Little Denmark Restaurant electric eye.

*F473.2.3.(5). Radio turned on or off, stations changed. Kent, Wa.: tape changed to jazz; Sawyer, Wa.: stereo; Shaw Island, Wa.: stations changed; Spokane, Wa.: stereo turned on full blast; Tacoma, Wa.: radio on & off; Vancouver, B.C.: radio turned up, Burn Unit; Welches, Ore.: stereo turned down.

*F473.2.3.(6). Appliances turned on and off or machinery runs unattended. See from E299.1. ghost causes machinery to run unattended. Coquitlam, B.C.: toaster; Roche Harbor, Wa.: blender, hood fans in restaurant; Sawyer, Wa; Seattle, Wa.: cash register, Pier 70; Seattle, Wa.: Burnley School of Art, coffee machine; Seattle, Wa.: Pike Place Market; Shaw Island, Wa.; Steilacoom, Wa.: Bair Drugstore, oven turned up to 500; Steilacoom, Wa.: E.R. Rogers Restaurant, blenders, television, lights, sound systems; Tacoma, Wa.: Rhodes Mansion; Vancouver, B.C.: burn unit; Vancouver, B.C.: tea kettle whistles; Victoria, B.C.: ringer washing machine.

*F473.2.(5). Ghost causes objects to swing back and forth. Burnaby, B.C.: keys in key chain hanging from door; Cheney, Wa.: coat hangers in closet; Coquitlam B.C.: chain; Oak Bay, B.C.: porcelain cookie jar; Shaw Island, Wa.: pots and pans on kitchen hooks; Spokane, Wa.: Gonzaga University, crucifix of priest trying to exorcise building; Tacoma, Wa.: chandelier; Vancouver, B.C.: poker; Victoria, B.C.: ropes in theater; Victoria, B.C.: andiron, porcelain cookie jar; Victoria, B.C.: chandelier.

*F473.2.(6). Heat turned up. House stifling. Chilliwack, B.C.; Heceta Head, Ore.; Steilacoom, Wa.: Bair Drugstore; Victoria, B.C.: washing machine ghost.

*F473.2.(6).(1). Coffee heated. Bremerton, Wa.: steaming cup of coffee found.

*F473.2.(7). Spirit turns on taps. Portland, Ore.: Buttertoes Restaurant; Victoria, B.C.: Little Denmark Restaurant.

*F473.2.(8). Spirit causes toilet to act contrary to nature. Richland, Wa.: Explodes; Vancouver, B.C.: burn unit; Yakima, Wa.: flushes.

F473.3. Poltergeist mistreats people. See also E542; E599.10.(2). Eugene, Ore.: drops brick from ceiling; Welches, Ore.: breaks man's finger.

F473.3(e). Spirit pushes man violently from behind. See also E461.

*F473.3.(e).(2). Ghost hits man in back of head with pillow. Shaw Island, Wa.

*E473.(e).(3). Spirit knocks bowl out of hands. Portland, Ore.: Buttertoes Restaurant.

F473.3(i). Spirit lifts person up to ceiling, lets her down again. Seattle, Wa.: Capitol Hill.

F473.3.(l). Spirit places cold hand on person. See also E542.8+. Shaw Island, Wa.

*F473.3.1. Spirit takes hand of person. Orcas Island, Wa.: Rosario Resort, caresses hand; New Westminster, B.C.: holds man's hand as he climbs stairs.

*F473.3.(2) Spirit sits close to person on bed or couch. New Westminster, B.C.: watching TV.

*F473.3.(4). Spirit taps person on shoulder or tugs at sleeve. Oregon City, Ore.: tap on shoulder; Portland, Ore.: Buttertoes Restaurant; Tacoma, Wa.: while working on rental unit; Seattle, Wa.: Pike Place Market, tug at sleeve; Shaw Island, Wa.: tap on shoulder.

F473.5.(a). Knockings and rappings that cannot be traced. See also E402.1.5. Applegate River, Ore.; Seattle, Wa.: Metro Bus Barn; Wells, B.C.: knocking on roof.

F974. Grass refuses to grow in certain spot.

*F974.(2). Cows refuse to graze in certain spot. Siuslaw River, Ore.: family buried in mudslide there.

*F989.16.(3). No birds sing in haunted spot. Colbert, Wa.: haunted property.

H: MARVELS

H1411. Fear test: staying in haunted house. Astoria, Ore.: Firefighter's Museum.

Subject Index

This index will lead you to motifs listed in the Index of Ghostly Motifs beginning on page 228, which, in turn, will lead you to specific stories. To find ghostly encounters from specific locales, see the Location Index beginning on page 253.

Location Index

This index lists the page numbers of the ghostly encounters in this book by location.